The Wind is the Breath of God

A Novel

by Barbara Rogers

First Edition Title, *The Pearl of Great Price*. PublishAmerica, *2006*

Second Edition, *Revised,* The Wind is the Breath of God, *SpiritBooks, LLC, Newport, Oregon, 2013.*

ISBN: 978-0-9834956-7-3 *(previously 1-4241-3962-7)*
Library of Congress Catalog Number:2013932765
Cover Art: Serafina Andrews
Cover and Text Design: Tom Repasky
Printed in the United States of America by Lightning Source

Note to readers of all faiths and none

The word "God" is to be understood as an attempt to name what cannot be described or limited in any human way. Many cultures and individuals choose to give no name at all to the Holy One who is beyond any imagining, language or thought.

In the Judeo-Christian tradition, this Holy One is called Ha-Shem or The Name, Adonai or The Lord, Abba or Father. Many honoring the Source of Being use a more personal name—

Emmanuel, or God-With-Us, Jesus or, in the Hebrew, Yeshua.

Mystics are open-hearted enough to experience directly that Divinity Who is beyond all human concepts, beyond space, time, and culture yet present in them all. They feel the touch of this life-giving Spirit that blows through us like wind through the world. They know the essence of this Spirit is Love.

On the entanglement of all our lives:

"Two [once-connected] particles become so deeply linked that they share the same existence, even when they are separated by the width of the universe."
--MIT Technology Review, August 1, 2012

Dedicated to

The "Righteous Gentiles" who risked their lives to save their Jewish brothers and sisters during the Holocaust, knowing that we are all one Body, all children of God

Table of Contents

1

France *1940*

Although Claire Leclerq had often imagined her first trip to Paris, never in all her sixteen years had she imagined arriving there just ahead of an invading German army. Nor in all her fantasies had she imagined that she would have a small Jewish child under each arm. An uneasy suspicion was stirring in her that romantic imaginings, especially her mother's, were not to be trusted. Madame Leclerq had a long history of precipitous decisions based on whim, fear, or a combination of the two. She had a habit of regretting the past and dreading the future, missing any pleasure in the moment. However hard Madame Leclerq tried to impress her gloomy vision of life on her daughter, Claire insisted on being upbeat, saying she was too young to believe that this world was merely a vale of tears. Claire, who was also too young to share Madame Leclerq's memories of the German invasion in 1914, thought her mother was being a worrywart, as usual.

"What we should have done, Maman," Claire said, as her mother politely let a truckload of pigs cut in front of their laboring Citroën, "is to stay put in Rheims. Even though the house got bombed, at least people know us there. We could have stayed with friends." As soon as she heard herself, she wondered if she were beginning to turn into a fretful younger edition of her mother, arguing with what was.

"And let the Germans blow us up in our beds?" Her mother was seeing the scene through her usual veil of exaggeration, Claire thought, looking stubbornly out the window at what was undeniably real. Madame Leclerq glanced in the rearview mirror and ran her fingers through her frizzed pompadour. "When the Germans come, nobody but a fool stays. If you had lived through the Great War, as I did, you would know."

Madame Leclerq kept her eyes on the truck full of pigs, staying close, so the gap would be too small to admit an insistent Peugeot bouncing along the road shoulder beside them. Her hands clutched the wheel, which was wrapped in a jacket of velvet, presumably to disguise its utilitarian steel. "Our things may be old," Madame Leclerq always said to her friends, "but I make the most of them."

At home, cracks in the plaster walls had been masked by peacock-patterned wallpaper copied from a Loire chateau. A chintz drape and cushion had disguised their toilet, an appliance Madame Leclerq considered vulgar. Its gross character was redeemed in her eyes by purple flowers and a long skirt, reminiscent of Victorian piano legs made modest by being covered to the floor. Now the flowered toilet and the walls behind the peacocks were gone, blown up by the Nazis during their surge southward, behind the Messerschmidts flying low overhead, spitting bullets at the slow-moving tide of refugees flowing south to Paris from the Belgian border.

"If only there weren't so many cars on the road," Madame Leclerq muttered as another truck cut in front of her, grazing a bumper. "If only we had started sooner."

Claire rolled her eyes. *Not another "if only."* "I guess the Boches want the roads crowded," she said, shifting the weight of the sleeping children she held in either arm. She moved slowly, so as not to wake them. "That way none of the Allied troops can come up from the south."

She knew her mother hated forwardness, as she called Claire's recent habit of being upfront with her opinions. All her life she had heard her mother say that as long as you behaved properly and acted like everyone else, nothing could hurt you. Conformity was Madame Leclerq's religion and had been Claire's until her baptism in a small Huguenot church three years earlier. Suddenly, as the pastor raised her from immersion in a chilly pool, she had felt a shaking all through her, straight to the soul. For a moment she swayed so that she had to be held upright, and her eyes misted making it hard to see. Since then, she had come to believe that there was more to religion than what her parents or even the pastor had told her. Claire had grown up on that day and had come to realize that church doctrines needed to be reevaluated in the light of the grace that had touched her.

Now she had to let that grace transform her life and keep her from having such a smart mouth and so many opinions. "Lord Jesus, help me not to sass my mother," she prayed quickly, hoping to undo the hurt she had caused, but knowing that sharp words could not be recalled, any more than the bombs that had destroyed their home could be sucked back into the planes that had dropped them.

If her father and older brother hadn't been away at the front, trying to hold back the unstoppable Panzer tanks, Claire wouldn't have been so quick to answer her mother back. She was the youngest in the family and kept quiet when three adults outnumbered her. Now it was just herself and Maman. Claire had been practicing independence in her mind for the past two years, ever since she had grown taller than her mother. When Madame Leclerq wanted her daughter to wear her waist-long auburn hair in braids, Claire cut it to the shoulders and wore the ends turned under in a sleek pageboy. When her piano teacher at the conservatory wanted her to practice baroque pieces, Claire played dissonant Bartok études. Her baptism had taught her that being contrary was not the same as being grown-up, but it was a hard lesson that she had been slow to learn.

Now the piano was gone too, like the peacocks and chintz. Claire remembered seeing the keys lying around the Leclerq's little yard after the bomb fell, like teeth knocked from a broken jaw. She had tried to gather them up, but there was no time. Her mother was waiting in the loaded Citroën. Claire had only a dozen ivory keys in her bag to remind her of her piano.

Don't look back, she told herself, staring out the window at the Peugeot, which was bumping along inches from their car, its driver making rude gestures that her mother pretended not to see. *Don't ever look back.* It was a resolve she had made on her thirteenth birthday, when she had decided that all her mother's grief came from looking back on a dying world and obeying its last wishes.

Now, with her father gone, Claire felt her own power. These people around her, who had once stood so tall and been so sure, seemed only small, frightened children. The families spilling onto the road to Paris were all children, all helpless, like Dora and Maxi, whose heads lay heavily against Claire's shoulders. The fleeing refugees knew nothing except that they must copy their neighbors, as they had always done. At that very moment in Germany, ordinary people looked around them to see if their friends objected to the arrest of Jewish families, saw that no one dared, and shrugged their shoulders. It had taken a French nun to smuggle these two children into Rheims and deliver them to Pastor Vence, who had found a foster home for them with the Leclerqs.

Now there was no home for them or for the Leclerqs either. The Lebenthal children had brought them bad luck, Madame Leclerq had wept, standing in front of her ruined house and wringing her hands after the bomb had fallen. She had thought God would reward them for their charity in accepting the children and resented his ingratitude. Claire had glared at her, putting a finger to her lips, afraid that Dora and Maxi would hear. But the two children were running around the yard finding piano keys for Claire. Six-year-old Dora sang a little tune in a low voice as she picked through the rubble littering the tulip-edged lawn.

"Our house fell down, our house fell down," she repeated, putting piano keys carefully in the pockets of her pinafore. "God made a big frown and our house fell down."

Maxi, two years younger, followed her closely, hanging onto her skirt. He began to bawl, his eyes closed tightly so nothing real could get in. "It didn't fall down," he cried. "It didn't!" His round, red-cheeked face, framed by a crown of soft, black ringlets, crumpled in despair.

Dora saw he had found only one piano key and gave him another from her pocket. "Here. Give them to Claire. Never mind about the house falling down. It was an ugly old house anyway."

Claire let the children drop the piano keys into her shoulder bag and ran her fingers through the thick brown bangs cut just above the straight line of Dora's heavy eyebrows. Dora's face was square and firm at the jaw, not like a little girl's. The child had a habit of making up stories and telling them to anyone who would listen, waving her arms and preaching her urgent social messages. Once when Maxi had taken her toy tea set to use in the sandbox and would not give it back to her, Dora jumped up on a picnic table and with sweeping gestures made a short speech: "We should all share toys," she announced to the busy playground where Claire brought them every afternoon. "God will love you if you share your toys." Shamed, Maxi came over and gave her a teacup full of sand, wanting God to love him.

Having been the one to tell them about God their Father, Claire wondered when they would ask her why God had let the house fall down if he loved them so much. She had some questions of her own along the same lines, which she would have asked the pastor, if he had not stayed behind at the church, hoping like the Good Shepherd to set the right example for his frantic, scattering flock. He had told Claire to be sure that Maxi and Dora were taught lessons from the Old Testament, as their parents would want the children to be trained in their Jewish faith.

The children had left their home in Frankfurt over a year ago with letters from their parents pinned to their elegant fur-trimmed coats. They carried two teddy bears, all they had been able to bring with them. Pastor Vence had brought them to the Leclerqs, and Claire had taken their care on herself, loving the two children on sight, as they had loved her. She remembered that first day, when Dora and Maxi climbed onto her lap, holding up their bears to touch her face with soft, velvet noses. When the evacuation had begun, the bears were all that the children wanted to take with them, their only link with home and with their parents, who expected to be arrested at the time they gave their children to a nun traveling from Frankfurt to Rheims.

"What do you call your bears?" Claire had asked the children knowing how it felt when grown-ups didn't take toys seriously. The children called both bears Ben-Ari.

"It was my father's real name," Dora explained. "Lebenthal is only a silly old made up German name. Someday, when I'm big, I'll change my name back. Even now the child wrote "Dora Ben-Ari" on her school papers, putting Lebenthal in small letters and parentheses. Dora's school had been closed, since the principal was afraid the invasion would happen any minute. He had been right.

Because General Rommel had been told to take his Panzer divisions across Belgium and into northern France, the Lebenthal children were in flight again and Claire with them. Rommel had begun to move on May 9, 1940. By May 11, one hundred thirty-two thousand German troops, with their tanks, artillery, and air support, stretched in a line one hundred miles long, on their roll through Belgium into France. Ahead of them, the Leclerq family, like sheep chased by wolves, was fleeing south, followed by Mersserschmidts and Henkels that bombed British installations and French cities alike.

Madame Leclerq's Citroën pulled into Paris well ahead of the German army and even of the diabolically swift Luftwaffe. From a distance, the City of Light had looked grander than it did in the cramped streets leading to the Place de la Bastille, where they hoped to catch a bus going southwest to the coast. The Citroën, too old and tired for cross-country trips, had begun to groan when Madame Leclerq leaned on the accelerator. The car was left with a cousin who met them at the Square and was glad to have the use of it.

"Word is out that the Germans will make their headquarters here," the cousin warned them, lifting their bags out of the car. She glanced at the Lebenthal children and shrugged. "If you want my advice, you'll send these children south with someone else and wait the war out here. I have a room for you and Claire, but not for them. I value my life, *tu comprends.*"

Madame Leclerq wrung her hands. "Can we give the children to the nuns? Perhaps the nuns will take them away."

"Dora and Maxi were given to us," Claire said firmly, standing beside her mother. "We'll take them away ourselves." She knew her mother had accepted the children in the first place only because the pastor shamed her into it. To Claire's knowledge, Madame Leclerq had never in her life acted without the approval of someone she admired. Luckily for Maxi and Dora, she admired Pastor Vence.

"I don't think the pastor would like to hear that we'd sent the children away," Claire said, staring her mother down. "I don't think he'd like that at all."

She stood waiting, her blue-green eyes wide and cool, her slim arms hugging her chest, knowing she was able to command. A year before she had not yet known it. Since then Jacques, who was now off learning to fly fighter planes for the English, had told her he loved her because she was strong and beautiful besides. He had run his fingers over the smooth pink skin on her high cheek bones and down to her long, full lips, making her tingle until she thought she would either have to lean against him or fall down. Actually, she had hardly known Jacques, who had waltzed with her at the last school dance before the invasion and had come once to her home afterwards, bringing flowers. He was no more real in her daydreams now than the voices from the past that ruled her mother.

At the moment, Madame Leclerq was clearly in the midst of listening to a lifetime of contradictory voices, none of them helpful in this situation. Claire stood beside her in the station, the rain puddling in her shoes, while Dora and Maxi sat on the suitcases, hugging their bears and staring straight ahead. Their large brown eyes were wide and fixed, as if they were seeing into a faraway place, faraway and inside at the same time. Claire felt a rush of tenderness for them that made her daydreams about Jacques seem poor and cheap, just as her grand idea of Paris had shrunk to fit the shabby, winding streets near the square. *Only one part of me is grown up,* Claire realized. *And that's the part that loves Dora and Maxi enough that I would risk my life to keep them safe.*

Madame Leclerq muttered that God had abandoned them. If only they had been able to give the children away, they would be free to hide in this big, anonymous city. Claire was at the same time thanking God silently for keeping Maxi and Dora with her. *Perhaps,* she said to herself, *God answers only unselfish prayers.* She pondered this possibility all the way to the bus terminal and determined that in the future, she would pray only for others, never for herself.

A bus loaded with passengers pulled out of the station slowly. Among the waiting crowd were some who ran alongside and banged on the door to be let in, but the bus went on its way.

Madame Leclerq sighed. "I'd better see what other buses are leaving. Perhaps we will find nothing and stay here after all. Sit here with the children and I'll see what I can do."

An hour later, Madame Leclerq arrived with four tickets to Dunkirk. "The only tickets left," she explained. "A woman on the queue told me that the other roads are closed. The British are keeping Route 19 open so they can evacuate their troops across the channel."

"From Dunkirk we can take the children to England," Claire agreed. "They'll be safe there."

"Let's get to Dunkirk before we talk about being safe," her mother said, picking up a suitcase in each hand.

Though they had tickets, the Leclerqs began to doubt they would be able to get on the bus to Dunkirk. The crowd of people on the platform surged and shoved, cursing, stepping on each others' feet. All of them waved tickets when the bus appeared and called out to the driver, trying to make him stop closer to where they stood. The bus pulled up near the Leclerqs. A sudden push from a fat old man carrying a carpetbag under one arm and a chicken under the other sent Maxi tumbling over the edge of the platform, right in front of the bus.

Claire screamed and waved her hands at the approaching bus. She jumped down from the platform, grabbing the child just as the bus shrieked to a stop above them. When the bumper came to rest against her leg, Claire fell against a headlight, her heart pounding. Maxi clung to her with both arms and legs, like a monkey, his face buried in her shoulder, too frightened to cry.

The bus driver left his seat and cleared the crowd away from the door. "The child, is he hurt? Let this family through," he ordered. Two English soldiers, bigger than the short, slim driver, tried to force their way in the folding door, but the driver was stronger than he looked. He pushed the soldiers back down the steps and gestured to Claire, who had been hauled back up on the platform.

"I'll take the child, mamselle," the driver said.

Claire lifted Maxi into his arms, and climbed back up on the platform. "He has a sister." She heard her voice coming out high and thin, like someone else's. "They both have to get on. So does my mother."

"You and your family will get on first, mamselle," the bus driver promised, apparently determined to preserve what civility he could, despite the barbarism around him. He held the crowd back as the Leclerqs boarded, Madame Leclerq handing the suitcases up to her daughter.

After they had found their seats, the others piled on, knocking the driver into his steering compartment in their haste to get away from the Germans. From the talk of the other passengers as they settled into their seats or piled onto the laps of those who got on before them, Claire tried to piece together a picture of the invasion.

"The Boches are headed straight for Paris," said one tall, elegant lady. She was wearing what looked like all her family jewelry and sweating in her silver fox coat, which she couldn't bear to leave behind for one of the Nazi officers' girlfriends. "And they're driving the British into the sea."

"No, the British will stand at Dunkirk," an older, mustached gentleman said, tightening his tie as if he were settling himself at his office desk. "They will not retreat. I heard it from Churchill himself, on my shortwave."

"The English will run," said the lady in the silver fox, not bothering to look at him.

"Believe me, they will not." The gentleman leaned forward. "My son is an officer with De Gaulle. I know what is happening."

"And I hear the Boches are coming from the south and north at once, like pincers," the woman said, making appropriate motions. "Snip, and the British will be cut off." She snapped her fingers. "Just like that."

"I wish this bus were going anywhere but Dunkirk," whispered Madame Leclerq to Claire. "The Germans may be leaving the road open for a reason, herding us all to this one town, like lambs to the slaughter."

Claire looked down at her own two lambs, sure that God intended them for no such sacrifice. "Look, Dora, the sea!"

She pointed out the window and the little girl knelt in her lap. The May sunshine was burning through the morning haze, and they could see the waves sparkle, breaking on the beaches in the distance. Brown, newly plowed fields stretched almost to the wide sandy beach. Children stood outside of stone cottages to watch the parade of cars pass, and Dora waved to them, holding up her bear so he could enjoy the view.

"This land was once under the sea," Claire told the children.

Dora looked doubtful. "The sea is heavy," she objected. "No one would be strong enough to hold it back. Only God could, the way he held back the Red Sea so the Children of Israel could run away from the Germans."

"From the Egyptians," Claire corrected her absently, glancing up at the sky to see if the Messerschmidts were coming yet. Dora was right, in a way; the persecutor was always the same, and so were the victims. *But God did not always send fire or water against the enemies of the innocent,* Claire thought. *Sometimes, most times, the enemies won.* Up ahead, dull, throbbing explosions went off, shaking the road under the bus.

"Night is coming," Maxi called out, pointing at the black clouds billowing on the horizon ahead of them and rising darkly into the sky. "Time to sleep."

"The oil reservoir in Dunkirk. That's what the Germans want." Madame Leclerq said in a low voice. "Listen. You can hear the planes."

Over the columns of black smoke came the Dorniers and Messerschmidts straight at the refugees spilling over both sides of the road. Some of them dove from their cars and rolled into the fields, hoping to avoid the random strafing from the guns of low-flying planes. Claire pushed Dora and Maxi down under the seats and huddled above them as bullets spattered through the windows of the bus, richocheting against the walls. A woman seated behind them was hit and began to moan. At the rear of the bus glass, shattered over some of the passengers, sparkling like snow and falling onto their hair.

Maybe it is my time, Claire thought. *Lord Jesus, let it not be the time of Dora and Maxi. They are so young. Please Lord, help me save them.* Her prayer made her feel less helpless, and she put an arm around each child. It was time to make a decision.

"We'd be better off walking through the fields," Claire said, standing up and pushing her way into the aisle. "This bus is nothing but a coffin."

"The Panzers will come across the fields," said the woman in fur, who seemed to enjoy knowing so much bad news. "Rommel's right behind us with his tanks. I would not try the fields, if I were you."

A cry rose from the back of the bus, and heads turned. "The sea! The sea is rising!"

The land behind them was suddenly shining where the water rushed over it in shallow waves, turning the fields into ocean bed again, sowing them with salt.

"The British did it," asserted the knowledgeable man with a mustache. "They broke the dams so Rommel's tanks can't get across the fields."

"How can they be sure the road won't flood as well?" Claire gasped, her hand on her throat. "We could be drowned and their own soldiers too."

"They can't be sure of that," the man replied curtly. "They're risking it because no one can think what else to do. Like the rest of us."

Suddenly the bus dipped down a slight decline into which water was pouring from the surrounding fields. Cars ahead were stalling, and the bus itself began to cough, as water swirled above its wheels. Another wave of Messerschmidts bore down on them from the west, and Claire knew they would more easily hit their helpless targets.

While the bus was still moving, the driver tried to pull around the stalled cars in front of it, but succeeded only in miring its wheels in the mud. "Lie down," Claire ordered Dora and Maxi. "Here they come again."

She bent over them, praying with her eyes closed, until the drumming of the bullets on the roof receded with the motors of the planes, sweeping off to be rearmed with more bombs and bullets. She had heard for months that the Germans would never run out of ammunition. Now it seemed the rumor was true.

"This bus is going nowhere," muttered Madame Leclerq. "You're right, Claire. We'd best get off and start walking before those planes come back." She pulled a suitcase down from the overhead rack and hunted through it, letting clothes fall at her feet. "My jewelry," she said. "Here it is. Put it in your shoulder bag. Diamonds are better than money. Our papers, too. You may need them."

Between sentences Madame Leclerq pressed her lips so tightly together that the wrinkles above them made her look like an old woman. Claire knew how hard it was for her mother to leave things behind, so hard the leaving had aged her like a disease. At least there had been no choice about what to take from the house. *Almost everything was lost in the firebombing,* Claire remembered. *The strongbox in the cellar survived and a few suitcases full of clothes, but nothing else. Wherever we go next, we will go empty-handed, starting from scratch.* That was fine with Claire. She had always lived in the same cluttered house and looked forward to filling blank space with things she had never seen except in the movies, instead of with dark, heavy old armoires and fat velvet chairs. The Lord had said in the Gospels that possessions could not save anyone, and Claire believed it.

Madame Leclerq looked about her severely and clapped her hands, encouraging herself to take charge. The bus was now half-empty, others having decided it was a death-trap and left. "Come, Claire," she called out. "We will walk to Dunkirk."

Clutching their stuffed animals, the pale, silent children followed Claire down the crowded aisle. Already the bus had sunk so deep that water made the floor slick. The two women were up their calves in seawater and mud as soon as they stepped down from the bus. Claire held a child under each arm, high up enough that their shoes cleared the surface of the water.

"Over here, Maman," Claire called to her mother, splashing ahead. "On the shoulder of the road." Madame Leclerq came after her, falling once and soaking her neat navy blue skirt in mud. The only traffic moving past them now was powered by men, not machines. Bicycle riders balanced delicately on the road shoulders, whizzing along like racers. Some peasant horse-drawn carts lumbered by, half off the road, to pass the stalled cars, wheels sunk deep in muddy seawater.

"Two kilometers to Dunkirk," Claire read from a half-submerged sign at the crossroads. She put the children down on higher ground. "Not far, Dora. Hold my hand tight."

Soldiers, stray dogs, and lost children wandered through the lines of people, often in the wrong direction. Everyone was running into everyone else, like a panicked crowd in a burning building, and no one listened to the shouting of exasperated British and French officers trying to get their tanks through the tangle of vehicles, people, and animals. One woman struggled along the side of the road trying to keep her baby carriage from tipping into the mud. It had no baby in it, just a cuckoo clock and a fur coat. Farm men and women dressed in black, their heads down and feet shuffling, had the look of a funeral cortège. Beside them, heavy, big-footed horses strained and panted, pulling carts full of furniture. The flooded fields left them nowhere to run. Claire looked around her at the road, now so solidly packed with people and vehicles that no one could budge. She saw a horse cart stalled in mud by the roadside.

"Under it, quick," she ordered, pushing the two children between the wheels before ducking under the driver's seat. She and her mother hid their heads in their hands as the low-flying, cross-marked planes cleared the tops of the poplar trees. Claire could see only the feet of the people in the crowd. She knew when the shots struck home because the feet and legs disappeared as the impact of the bullets hurled the refugees off the highway into the rising seawater. Above the high-pitched whine of the airplane engines, Claire could hear women screaming and the groans of men who lay underfoot, trampled by the surging crowds. She reached out and pulled a small, wounded boy under the cart. He was lying beside them for a few minutes before she realized from the angle of his head against the ground that half his skull was gone. Claire felt dry heaves rise into her throat and leaned over the body, choking.

"So many dead children," she cried soundlessly. "God, why do you let them kill the children?" She remembered hearing Pastor Vence say that early death may mean being spared some terrible suffering in later life. *So only God knows what the fate of these children might otherwise have been. Faith in God means accepting mystery,,* Claire reminded herself. *He is Lord of the whole universe, after all, and can manage it without my input.*

Swallowing the sickness stuck in her throat, Claire pulled Dora and Maxi out from under the cart. "We'll carry you," she said, keeping her voice low and steady. "The only thing to do, Maman, is go along the sides of the road. We'll try to get to the shore ahead of this jam. We need to be wherever the British soldiers are and go wherever they're going."

With Maxi on her shoulders and Dora in her arms, Claire slogged half a kilometer through mud up to her ankles, climbing onto the shoulder of the road where she could. Once she was certain her mother was following behind, she kept her eyes fixed straight ahead. She wished she could remember the words of the Psalmist, how ten thousand fell to the right of him and ten thousand to the left, yet he was not harmed. One Psalm she remembered, and she sang it softly over and over. *Though I walk through the valley of the shadow of death, I shall fear no evil. . .* Dora took up the chant and sang it in a high, thin little voice, squeezing Claire's hand as if to encourage her friend.

Even the bicycles had been abandoned by now and left in the shallow water, their wheels spinning in the air. From over the low, nearby hill, clouds of black smoke from the burning oil reservoirs blew inland toward them in the sea breeze. Claire was afraid to look down at the city when they reached the crest of the low hill and instead looked outward toward the sea. Cars had been overturned in the streets and lay smoking amid glass shards. Holes gaped where houses had been and soldiers had to pick their way through the broken pavement to get outside the city and onto the road leading to the beach. While Claire stood resting for a moment in the fine drizzle that had begun to fall, a jeep roared up behind her and stopped.

"Like a lift?"An Englishman's voice, polite as if offering tea, spoke just behind her, and Claire turned around.

Two young officers sat in the front seat of a jeep. The Englishman was sandy-haired, with a gentle bucktoothed grin, and repeated his question. Claire knew only a little English and had thought lift meant elevator. *No elevators around her,* she thought. *What*'s *he talking about?* The other officer, a Frenchman with a southern accent, translated for her.

"There are four of us," Claire told him. My mother and these two children. We have to get them to the coast before the Nazis come."

"Jewish, I suppose they are," the southerner said, inspecting Dora and Maxi coolly, as if through an invisible monocle. Perhaps he was like the other aristocrats Claire had known, indifferent to the persecution of Jews and even sympathetic with the fascists.

"I see," the man said when she nodded an answer. "*Eh, bien.* Come along. We will do what we can for you."

Noticing how neat the officer was, with his white gloves and riding crop tucked absurdly under one elbow, Claire looked down at her muddy legs and school uniform, stained with the blood of the dead boy she had left under the cart. *This young officer must think me a peasant,* she felt, not liking him despite his offer of help. *It is indecent of him at such a time to look so untouched by blood and dirt.* Silently she lifted the children into the back seat of the jeep, wishing perversely that she dared put muddy little Maxi on the immaculate lap of the southern officer. When her mother was seated with Maxi on her sodden navy skirt, the jeep roared off down a crossroad, taking the highway that went around Dunkirk, directly to the sea.

The southern officer turned to look at Maxi who rubbed his eyes and sobbed, his head on Madame Leclerq's shoulder.

"No more crying," he said gently. "Save your tears, little fellow." He reached into his breast pocket and pulled out a candy bar. "Have some chocolate."

Maxi put his finger in his mouth, stared at the candy, then turned his head shyly away.

"Your bear looks hungry," the officer said, smiling."Will you take it for him?" Without turning his head, the child held out his hand and took the bar. Claire smiled back at the young man, changing her mind about people who wore white gloves and carried riding crops. The officer's face looked like a boy's now, long dimples framing his smile with its square, even white teeth.

"Can't leave the little girl out," said the Englishman, keeping his eyes on the road but handing another chocolate bar over his shoulder. "Give her this."

His voice broke suddenly. "Damnation, here come the planes again. Hang on. I'm going to drive off the road, onto the beach. They aren't likely to chase one lone car.

Bracing her knees against the front seat, Claire bent low over Dora, as bullets kicked up the sand around them. One struck the left front tire, and Claire heard the air begin to hiss out.

"They're turning for another run over the beach,"cried the Englishman. "Everybody out of the jeep. Head for that tank." He pointed twenty yards ahead to an overturned British tank, its treads still uselessly rolling. "Get under it if you can."

From under the tank, Claire looked out at the beach, her heart beating so hard it hurt her chest. "Our Father, she began, the words sticking in her throat, "who art in heaven..."She wanted God to be on earth, close to her, not far away in heaven, so she could not finish the prayer.

Lines of soldiers stood eight deep in the water, then broke ranks as the waves knocked them down. They staggered up again, hanging onto each others' shoulders. Those in the ocean waved their hands, shouting, trying to attract the attention of the little boats that bobbed just beyond the writhing human coastline.

All Claire's confidence fell away, like dreams in daylight. *How had I thought to fight grown, maddened men for the few places in these fragile boats?*

Oh God, she prayed, then stopped, unable to pray anymore. Just the name of God, she hoped would cry down the help she wanted for Dora and Maxi. They were beyond any help of hers.

The boats are here from England to take us away," the buck-toothed Englishman called out. "We'll have to get the children down there too, Paul. It's a hundred yards to the water, and even if we make it, there's no telling if we can get a place in the boats."

"The men are panicking," the southern officer observed in his soft voice that sounded as if the air were coming around something stuck in his throat. "Look, Henry, they have ripped off their regimental insignias so no one will hold them to order."

More than one boat had capsized, Claire saw, because too many men were clawing at its gunwales. As the boats moved out to sea, some were dragged under by the men who clung to them. The German planes had wheeled back and swooped in low over the beach, cutting swaths in the rows of struggling soldiers, turning the foam around them pink. A squadron of RAF Hurricanes roared in above the Messerschmidts and in a thunder of machine gun fire drove three of the German planes, now trailing black smoke, into the sea, then sped away, leaving the men on shore unprotected once again. A British destroyer, its anti-aircraft guns pulsing, worked its way through the smaller boats to a pier and began to take on passengers. Men jumped from beam to beam of the burning pier to reach the gangplank.

"Too big," Henry the Englishman muttered. "That baby's going to get it from the Huns, sure as the devil lives. Me, I'm going for one of those little jobs."

As he spoke, a Messerschmidt swept low over them, its guns crackling, and Claire saw the bullets hit a truck full of gasoline drums a dozen yards away from them, as they headed for the sea.

"Lie down," cried the French officer, throwing himself across Claire and the children, forcing their faces into the sand. At that moment, the truck exploded, flames and bits of metal flashing toward them. Claire saw one strike the southern officer on the shoulder, spreading blood across his neat tan uniform. Her mother screamed once, and then stopped short. Something hit Claire on the side of the head. *Maybe I'm going to die now,* she thought, wondering why she felt no fear, only the strong arms around her. She had no time to pray, but heard the wounded officer above her mutter, "*Mon Dieu.*" Whether it was a curse or a prayer, she could not tell. Then she sank down into a blackness deeper than sleep.

When she awoke, dark clouds rolling from the burning town were colliding with the sunset over the sea. A few boats were still taking men from the beach, but not many living men were left. The sand was dark with sprawling bodies and damaged tanks. Claire sat up quickly, feeling her stomach heave. Her head ached and swam, and her sight blurred. Beside her lay her mother, stiff and white, a jagged hole torn in her throat. Claire got to her knees. It was hard to stand up while she was retching and dizzy. She had not eaten in so long there was nothing in her to vomit up, but the heaves kept coming anyway.

Claire pulled her mother's body away from the bank to a clean patch of sand and began to dig with her bare hands. She felt nothing at all, but watched herself from far way, as people were said to watch themselves dying. Until she had covered her mother with a mound of sand and prayed a requiem over it, she did not stop to think of anything. At last she rested, letting her hands fall into her lap. *I have no mother now,* she said to herself slowly, letting the words sink in. *Never again will I be my mother's child.*

Suddenly she jumped to her feet and looked around her. Dora and Maxi were gone, and so were the young officers, both the wounded southern

Frenchman and Henry the Englishman. It was as if she had dreamed them all. Claire put her hands to her aching head and pressed her fingers against her temples, trying to clear her blurred vision, hoping to see the world as it had been before the explosion. She called out the children's names, but knew as she heard the sound of her own voice that there would be no answer. They were lost, as she was, in the crowd of bodies on the sand.

Claire picked up the young southerner's helmet, which was lying on the ground beside her feet, and began to walk slowly, carrying the helmet in front of her like a begging bowl. She felt her gesture was a sort of wordless prayer that God would give the children back to her so she could protect them, but the bowl remained empty. *God is giving nothing back that I can see.*

Until the moon was darkened by smoky clouds, Claire passed among the fallen soldiers on the beach, looking for two little bodies, not finding them. At last she gave up and headed back toward what was left of Dunkirk, still carrying the officer's helmet. *The jewels in my shoulder bag,* she thought. *They should get me back to Paris.* Whoever survived this massacre would wind up in Paris where there was safety in numbers. So might Dora and Maxi if they had lived and if someone had found them. So too might the young southern officer. Paul, the Englishman had called him.

Don't look back, she told herself, keeping her eyes on the dark cloud hanging over the ruined town. She had a sense of unfinished business about the helmet, perhaps because it was all she had left as proof that this day had not been just a bad dream. *The Germans, too, might have been a dream,* Claire thought, but to be on the safe side, she would stay off the main road. After all, the great mistake others had made was to think the Germans were not a real danger. *As for God, He does not always answer on cue,* Claire said to herself. *This is a lesson I have learned today that I could have done without.* Cutting across the fields, away from the deserted road, she swung the French officer's helmet by its strap and took in moist air from the sea with deep, steadying breaths.

2

Dora's Journal

London..............................1945

I'm writing this journal for Claire, though I don't know if she's even alive. I wanted to write it as a letter, but my teacher said she wanted a journal, so a journal it shall be. The teacher says I have had a vivid life, and should tell about it. To my mind, the only person in the class whose life has been vivid is the girl who sits next to me. Her big brother is in the movies and went to Hollywood last year, taking his sister along for a vacation. That's my idea of vivid. Other children have mothers and fathers or at least photographs to help them remember what happened to them when they were little, but my brother Maxi and I don't. So what I remember is in my head, not somebody's secondhand story. Because I have only bits and pieces of my first six years, I'll put what I remember down like a movie, the kind where the scenes change so fast you aren't sure where you are.

Scene I............................Frankfurt, Germany

A cloudy day, and cold. Mother and Father pushed us on swings so that we went higher than their heads, even though they were very tall. I could see the pointed roofs of the city. The buildings looked like gingerbread houses in my storybooks. On the closer houses I could see carved railings decorating the balconies. From my swing, Frankfurt looked like a city of dollhouses. Maxi just sat there in the swing, his legs stuck out, not helping, but I pumped back and forth, bending my head to the front and then sticking my legs out straight and hard, until pretty soon my parents could stop pushing me. Father clapped and said in his big voice that filled the whole synagogue where he was a cantor, "Dora can do it herself now, Mimi."

His cheeks were bright red from the wind and one end of his muffler was flying. He had little twinkling brown eyes, deep in his head, not like Mutti's wide open blue ones. That's all I remember about my mother's face, just the eyes. Sometimes at night she sat with me in the dark if I couldn't sleep, leaving the door open a crack so that light fell across just her eyes. She would sing, too. *"Shlofzhe, yidele, shlof,"* which was about a peddler and a white goat and ended with a command for the little Jewish child to sleep.

Each night, when she left me, she would kiss my forehead and say, "Next year, in Jerusalem." Because she said it so often, I thought maybe my parents were planning to move there. Now I know it's just something Jews say to remind each other that they could go home if they wanted to, that they have a homeland just like everybody else. Both my parents would say the words about Jerusalem when we lit the candles at Hanukkah. Maxi always got to ask the questions about the holiday because he was the youngest. It seemed to me that we should take turns each year, but Hanukkah was not done that way. No use arguing about it. Mutti said it had been done like this for two thousand years, ever since Judas Maccabeus won the fight against the Romans, and it will be done like this for the next two thousand years, whatever one little girl might have to say about it. Now, light your candle and open your present. That particular Hanukkah is the one I really remember because it was when we got our bears.

On our last day in Frankfurt, the nanny, Frau Oder, put on our new coats and leggings over our blue velvet party clothes and hustled us out into the snow, which stuck on the fur of our bears and on our fur collars. Maxi kept putting his tongue out to catch snowflakes on it, but Frau Oder told him to stop that and hurry along. She brought us to a big glass building with a sign outside that read "I. G. Farben Industries." It was many floors high, where our parents worked, though I never knew exactly what they did. Frau Oder pulled us along the hallways to their office. Mutti was writing at her desk, and father was talking to a little man with a headful of yellow curls. It looked like a wig. But he kept pulling on his hair as he talked to Father, so the hair must have been real. Mutti was writing two short letters, both almost the same. I still have mine, but Maxi's fell apart when his coat got wet in the English Channel.

Mine reads like this:

Dora, b. 1934, June 10th, daughter of Albert and Miriam Lebenthal, address 705 Friedenstrasse, Frankfurt. Reference, Herr Heinrich Schroeder, Head of the Chemical Division, I.G. Farben, Frankfurt. To be instructed in their Jewish faith. If manner of instruction is not clear, ask a local rabbi or Jewish family, if any. (This 'if any' was a reasonable doubt, for we never found another Jewish family in our neighborhood.) *Shots for childhood diseases all given in infancy, smallpox vaccination did not take, allergy to dust and sulfa, catches cold easily. Please take care.*

She pinned the notes into our coat pockets and held us very hard. Her eyes were wet, but she wasn't crying. Just smiling, telling us to smile. Mr. Schroeder took our hands and pulled us away, saying, "We don't have much time, Mimi. I've got to get them out of here." I looked back as we were going through the door, and Mutti's head was on my father's shoulder. She was saying, "Oh God, Oh God," over and over. That was the last I saw of my mother.

Scene II……………………………The Frankfurt Station

Herr Schroeder brought us to the train station, where we met his sister, Veronica. She was a real Catholic sister, as well as being Herr Schroeder's, with a black cape, like a witch. We had to run down the platform because the train was ready to go. The sister's veil stood straight out behind her because she ran so fast. Maxi had to be carried. His legs were too short to keep up. Steam was pouring out of the train and making us choke, it was so full of cinders. Maxi got one in his eye, but we had no time to take it out. He dropped his bear over Herr Schroeder's shoulder while he rubbed his eyes, and I ran back for it. Herr Schroeder yelled at me, but I went back anyway to get the other Ben-Ari. Just as the train started to move, the metal elbows in the middle of the wheels pumping back and forth and turning the wheels against the rails, Herr Schroeder grabbed me and put me on the steps of the coach, beside Sister Veronica and Maxi. She was holding onto us both too hard for me to wave good-by, but we saw him wave to us. He got smaller and smaller until he disappeared.

Scene III…………………………Rheims, France

Sister Veronica gave us to a pastor who promised to find a family to take us in. Claire's family was the one he chose, and I am glad he did. She was the best friend I ever had, except for Maxi. He and I used to sit on either side of Claire while she played the piano. Sometimes she would make up songs and write them out on the page in notes, so she could play them again. With one hand she would make little black dots very fast, hardly lifting the point of the pencil, and still she would keep playing the song. The best one was about the Ben-Ari bears and their travels. There was a verse for the bears in China and one for Africa. In the last verse, the bears went to Yellowstone Park in America, where people fed them popcorn and ice cream. They liked it so well that they stayed. Maxi and I still sing that song.

Claire got mad at her mother one day for making her wash her hair so often. She cut off her long braids and threw them on the floor. I cried because Madame Leclerq yelled so, and because I liked to brush Claire's hair and braid it for her.

"You look like a hussy with your hair bobbed," Madame Leclerq told Claire, stamping her foot. "No decent mademoiselle wears her hair short."

Since Claire's hair hung to her shoulders and was not bobbed at the ears like mine, I felt her mother was exaggerating. I thought of saying so, but decided against it.

Claire didn't answer her mother but just sat down with me on the couch. "Don't cry, Dora," she said. "Here. You can keep the braids."

After that, I pinned her braids to the back of my winter hat and wore it whenever I played outside. I pretended to be Claire and made the braids swing back and forth so they would swish against my back.

I brought that hat with me when we left Rheims, along with my bear. That day, while we were at the piano, the sirens blasted, and Maxi held his ears. Madame Leclerq came running with two big suitcases. She always kept them ready in case the bombs hit our house.

"The shelter," Claire called, running after Maxi and me because we were on our way to the playroom to get our bears. She had snatched up our warm, fur-collared coats and tucked them under her arms.

I managed to put on my braided cap before Claire hurried us out the door and down the street to the cellars under the wine store. Already the planes were coming and houses were puffing into smoke and fire, all in a row, falling like dominos. The whole neighborhood was crowding down the steps of M. Brie's wine cellar, and there was barely room to stand up, once we were down there between the big barrels. M. Brie got out glasses and gave everybody free wine, even the little children. Madame Leclerq was crying in the corner and wouldn't drink any, But Claire had a few glasses. She got us all singing songs like "*Joli Tambour*," about the minstrel who came back from the wars. One man belched noisily after each refrain, and everyone laughed when he did it.

The ceiling over us was shaking from the bombs so much that the bare, hanging bulb swayed and flickered. Maxi and I stood on either side of Claire and held onto her skirt, so people wouldn't crowd us away. I remember Claire standing with her glass up high, her face all pink, singing in a loud voice and telling me to clap my hands. Some people stamped and shuffled their feet, trying to dance, but there wasn't much room for dancing.

Later we went back to the place the house had been and found Claire's piano keys all over the yard. While Madame Leclerq got the car from the garage down the street, we collected the white keys. We even found pieces of the clay menorah Claire had bought for us so we could have a real Hanukkah that year, but we never got to use it. By the time Hanukkah came, the Jews in Rheims were in hiding or dead or gone. We, the Ben-Aris, were gone.

Scene IV……………………………Dunkirk, France

If Claire's mother had been looking for safety when we drove south toward Paris, she was looking in the wrong place. We nearly drowned, nearly got smashed by German bombs, and finally were nearly killed by an explosion on the beach. Everybody was running around on the bloody sand, trying to get away from the Nazi bombers. I just held onto Maxi and Claire, hoping for the best, but not expecting it.

I don't know what happened to Madame Leclerq and Claire after the explosion. The French officer who had given us a ride in his car was lying on top of them. He had a hole in his shoulder and the blood got all over my coat. Claire didn't wake up when we left, though I shook her arm. I wanted to stay there, but the British officer with the odd teeth made us go with him.

"Hold my hand tight and run like the devil's after you," he said to us.

We had just said good-by to a man with a red cross on his arm whose face was pressed against Claire's. Henry Harrison, for that was the name of our British officer, said Claire was being given artificial respiration and that the French captain with the white gloves would be given the same thing, if he weren't dead already.

As we ran, I tried to look back over my shoulder. "Will they come to England too? Or are they dead?"

"Dead, most likely." Henry didn't slow his pace. "And we will be too, if we can't find a boat to take us away from here. Quit blubbering, boy."

Maxi pulled back at the water's edge. "We'll drown," he shrieked as Henry dragged us into the waves. "You're drowning me!"

Henry set Maxi on his shoulders and kept hold of him with one hand. The other clutched my arm. I put my bear up on my shoulders too, so he wouldn't drown and tried to stay alongside Henry. The waves were up to my waist, and I could hardly move my feet through them. A little sailboat darted toward shore like a waterbug, veering close to us. Some soldiers were splashing toward it, knocking others out of the way.

"Hurry up, mates," the sailor said, grabbing Maxi off Henry's back. "Those nutter blokes will be on us in a minute and pitch us all out. Give me the little girl. That's right, Missy. Don't struggle. I've got you."

He put me down beside Maxi, under the deck, so we could barely see outside where the shells were hitting the water, the boats, and the other people, still flapping their arms as they tried to get to our boat or any boat.

"Now you, matie," he said, pulling Henry over the side by his belt. "Grab the rope and put your head down," he ordered. "We're coming about."

The little boat swung suddenly around, away from the soldiers who splashed and yelled as they struggled to reach us. They tried to grab the sides of the boat so they could pull it over, the way others were doing with even bigger boats, but Henry hit their hands with an oar. I sat holding Maxi, not wanting him to see the soldiers crying because their hands hurt. Up high, hanging in the gray sky, were white birds, their wings still as they rode the air. They were looking down at us with round black eyes. Maxi said they looked surprised.

Scene V………………………….Dover, England

Because our boat was so small, I heard later, it got across safely, just as Henry thought it would. One big troop carrier blew up near us, and men fell out all over the water, but we weren't hit. Maxi and I shut our eyes when the big ship blew, and said the prayers Claire had taught us. She said these were the prayers of the Hebrews when they crossed the Red Sea. We pretended the men who had tried to pull our boat over were Egyptians. Maxi thought they really were, but I knew they were just British soldiers who were trying to get home to England. We got there, even if they didn't, and it wasn't even our home. Somehow this didn't seem fair, but when I asked Henry about it, he said people who had good luck shouldn't complain. That was when I first began to think of myself as lucky.

We docked at Dover, where most of the other boats were coming in. People ran down the road onto the jetty, calling out names and waving. As our sailor threw out his curled rope, several hands reached for it and wound it around a post. If Henry hadn't held onto me as we got out, I would have been pushed into the water by the crowd. The tired-looking soldiers, lots of them without their helmets and guns, were trying to work their way down the Admiralty Pier, while the families of still-missing men pushed the other way, past wooden barriers set up to stop them.

Sometimes they would see their person and start yelling and jumping to get his attention. One man, with a bandage over his ear, shoved Henry aside and ran forward into the arms of an old lady. Then he turned and picked up a little boy beside her, hugging him too.

Maxi and I stood still, hanging onto Henry's hand. No one was going to be waiting for us. Not my father or mother, not Claire. For the first time I guessed that Maxi was all I had left of family, and ran around to Henry's other side so I could hold my brother's hand. If he had been pushed into the water, I would have jumped in after him, just the way Claire jumped in front of the bus when he fell. In fact, I almost wished it would happen, so I could save him as she had. All those people on the pier would look at me afterwards, thinking how lucky Maxi was to have a sister like me.

No one was waiting for Henry either, so when we could push by the people still crowding the pier, we started down the Folkestone Road. An army truck picked us up, and we got to sit with the soldiers all the way into town. They were feeling fine, after the escape from France, and passed a canvas-covered bottle around, singing a song that was sad-sounding, even though they had nothing to be sad about, not now. They closed their eyes and leaned their heads back against the canvas arching over the truck, singing, "There'll be bluebirds over the White Cliffs of Dover, tomorrow when the world is free." I didn't think the world would be free any time soon, certainly not tomorrow. Still, it didn't do any harm to hope.

But the Nazis weren't planning to give up right away. On the trip from Dover to London, where Henry was planning to leave us, we began to see German bombers coming across the Channel for their night raids. Even from miles away, the fire-bombing lit up the road in front of us. Maxi slept with his head in my lap. Whenever a plane passed low over us, shaking the air with noise, Maxi's face would turn against my tum, and his finger would go into his mouth, without his waking up. He said later that he was dreaming about bombs falling on our house back in Rheims, so in some ways he didn't exactly miss what was going on. I always say it's too bad to miss anything, even the bad times. If you don't know what's happening, it's being wasted on you. I'd rather know than not know what happened to our parents, for instance, though I guessed even then that what had happened was bad.

Scene VI……………………………London, England

None of us in London missed the Blitz that first year, except the children who were sent out to the country, away from the German bombardment. Later I heard that the ones who were sent away cried a lot and wet their beds, even the big ones like me. Maxi and I never once did that, but then we were used to doing without our parents and being in strange places. Maybe it's better to get all the worst things over with fast, right at the beginning of your life, so what happens later on doesn't seem so bad. You're likely to be glad of whatever you get, and are pretty sure things will be better tomorrow, "when the world is free," as the soldiers sang. Claire used to say, "You can't fall out of bed when you're already on the floor." I think she even said it at Dunkirk, our last day together. We were on the floor that day, for sure, and again during the Blitz, our first autumn in

London. But that's getting ahead of when we came to St. Hilary's and met Father Jonas Grey.

It was dark by the time we arrived at the boarding school where Henry left us at the gate with a quick hand to his cap, a big-toothed smile, and only the words, "Have to rejoin the old regiment, you know." A sister took us inside the tall stone school. Inside, the lights were kept low, well away from the windows, which were covered with heavy black drapes to fool the Nazi planes into thinking there was no St. Hilary's.

The sister put Maxi in a trundle bed, taking off his shoes, not waking him up, and gave me the bed next to his when I asked for it. With the bombs falling not very far away, I was afraid he would wake and not know where he was. I wasn't too sure myself, but could pretend better than he could. As it was, the bombs kept me awake most of the night. To me, the sirens were scarier than the bombs, sounding like screams. Just before we left Frankfurt, sirens in the streets meant that Jews were being picked up. Mutti used to drop her fork when the sirens came during dinner. She refused to eat anything more until they stopped. Sometimes she would fold her hands and say something in Yiddish. They would make my father frown, since he thought Yiddish barbaric. We were supposed to speak only proper German, for we *were* German, my father said, whatever Hitler thought we were.

St. Hilary's……………………………The War Years

Proper Germans though we may have been, we found it easy to turn from being Germans to being French and then to being English, like the prince in the fairy tale who was turned into a frog, then into a prince again. I always wondered if the Frog Prince looked a little froggy after the change. Maybe a few lumps on his wide, chinless face, not at all the sort a princess would want to kiss, I should think. We spoke English with a German growl at first, when we would speak at all, and looked quite unlike the bleached-face, light-haired children of St. Hilary's.

Maxi knew only a few words of English, but I had spoken some in school. Talking to Father Jonas, whom we were brought to see the next morning, was easy, since he knew German. I thought at first he was Catholic, since he was called Father, but he was an Anglican priest. Or Church of England, as he called it. To me, one church was the same as another, though I rather favored the Catholics. Catholic girls got to wear bridal veils at their first communions and carry white prayer books with gold-rimmed cards in them. I would have given anything except my Ben-Ari bear for some of those cards, which had pictures of gentle Jesus with his lambs or with his mother holding him when he was a baby. The figures on the cards were dainty as china paintings on my mother's plates. For the longest time, I thought Jesus and Mary were made of tissue paper or clouds, not quite real.

In Father Jonas's office, we were led to big chairs that looked like they had been made for ogres, not people, let alone children. They reminded me of the fairy tale picture books Claire used to read to us and made me wonder if what was happening to us was real or part of a long, bad dream. We had to climb the huge chairs as if they were jungle gyms, and when we finally got seated, our feet dangled high above the carpet. Father Jonas sat behind his carved oak desk with his fingers pointed together like a church steeple, staring at us seriously with his blue eyes. They were surrounded by dark hollows, as if he hadn't slept much the night before. He had a long, pale face with full lips, and when he smiled, which he finally did, his teeth were so big and yellow that Maxi turned to me in fright and whispered, *"Der Oger!"* It was true. The man's mouth looked just like the picture of an ogre in Claire's fairy tale book.

"Keine Oger, liebchen," Father Jonas laughed. *"Nur ein schlecter Priester."*

Only a poor priest, he thought he was. Even with us, he seemed to feel as if he didn't deserve God's love, often calling himself a sinner like everybody else. I don't remember my parents telling me any such thing and am sure they thought themselves quite as good as they needed to be. Father Jonas was better than he knew. At least we always thought so. That day he came around from his desk and knelt on the floor between our chairs, looking up at us, probably so that we wouldn't be bothered by how big he was. For a moment, he made me think of the picture of Jesus with his lambs that I had seen on the coveted holy card back in Frankfurt. It was not the only time Father Jonas made me think of Jesus.

"You can live here, if you wish," he said slowly, watching my eyes to see if I was getting his meaning. "If you're afraid of the bombing, I can have you sent to another family, in the country. Do you understand, Dora?"

"Yes." I swung my feet and listened carefully. His German sounded stiff, like he was reading aloud from a book. "We will stay with you. This is a good place. Thank you."

I reached out and poked Maxi, who bowed his head politely, as I did. Suddenly I looked over Father Jonas's shoulder and saw on his desk a thick, open book with Hebrew letters. Slipping down from my ogre's chair, I went to the desk to look at the book more closely.

"Excuse me," I said, trying not to be rude, for Claire and my mother had explained to me that people don't want you to jump right in with whatever you have to say. "Can you read Hebrew?"

"Fairly well, Dora," he said, coming over to stand beside me. "Can you?"

"No," I sighed, reaching up to touch the book and then pulling back my hand quickly. It wasn't my book after all. "I was going to learn. But then we left Germany, and I learned French instead."

"You would still like to learn Hebrew?" Father Jonas put his hand on my shoulder. "None of my other pupils does. I would enjoy teaching you and Maxi, if he would like to learn."

Maxi was sitting with Ben-Ari on his lap, his chin resting on the bear's head, and watching us. He seemed to know what was being asked and nodded when we looked at him.

"Then you'll both learn," Father Jonas said. "You can come to my wife and me here in the vicarage, after the school day, and when the air raids are on, we will study Hebrew together."

He shook my hand as if sealing a bargain. Since Maxi and I never found a rabbi in South Kensington, Father Jonas had to do. For us, he was a rabbi and later, a father. The others at St. Hilary's saw him as a priest for whom they had to pretend to be good. For the people who came to services at the church, he was the one they complained to about the air raids and sons-in-law and the price of flour. After services, there would be tea in the vicarage and after dinner, when it was time for our lesson, we would find Father Jonas sighing in the parlor, his head in his hands, having forgotten that he had asked us to come. I would get the book from his shelf and lay it on the table, then clap my hands near him and say *Shalom!* or *Sh'mai, Israel!* Then he would smile and begin the lessons.

Our lives at St. Hilary's School would have been easier if he had taught us more English than Hebrew, instead of the other way around. We had been there only two weeks when I heard the word Nazi. The biggest boy of the Third Form, Thomas Leighton, pointed his finger at Maxi and me. We were standing in the shadow of the stone arch near the playing field, watching the others play soccer during the lunch hour.

"They're Nazis," called Thomas Leighton to the other boys at our end of the field. "They talk Kraut with Father Jonas. I heard 'em."

"Nazis!" The boys echoed, coming closer, shuffling the soccer ball back and forth among them. Thomas Leighton was first, and the others had followed him. He pushed Maxi into the stone arch and held him up by the shoulders so that his feet were off the ground and his face, with its wide, serious dark eyes, was opposite Thomas's pale one.

"I am not a Nazi," Maxi objected calmly, his voice no different than usual."I am a German."

Thomas Leighton banged the back of Maxi's head against the wall so hard that my brother blinked, and his eyes filled with tears. The other boys pushed forward and one pulled hard on a lock of Maxi's hair.

"Nazi, Nazi," Thomas Leighton chanted and spat in Maxis' face. Maxi tried to wipe the slobber off his cheek, but another boy held his hands, bending them behind his back while Tom dragged my brother's head from side to side, holding him by the hair.

I put my books down, not wanting them involved in what I was going to do, figuring they would get bloody with my blood. Though I was almost as big as Thomas Leighton, I was a girl and had never fought before. Swinging my shoulder first against one boy, then another, I pushed my way to Thomas and shoved my hand hard into his chest.

"See that kid?" I was trying to copy their voices and the voices I remembered from American films. "He's my brother."

"So?" Thomas pushed me back, a little uncertainly, because I was a girl. "He's a Nazi."

"He's a German Jew, you stupid shmuck," I said spitting out the Yiddish word my father would never let me use. "Nazis kill Jews. Where have you been, anyway?"

Thomas let go of Maxi and looked at me sullenly. "I've been around," he said. "I know what Nazis do." His hand darted out and gave me another shove, harder this time.

My fist curled up, and I swung it smack into his nose. He groaned, then punched me in the mouth. I felt my lip split and a tooth shake loose. Then blood poured down over my chin. I kicked him hard in the knee with my steel-toed German shoes. When he yelled and fell down, I grabbed his cap and threw it high up, so it stuck on the limb of a tree.

"Get my hat down," he cried, broken-hearted as if I had shamed him forever. "Somebody get it down."

"You'll never get it," I said, dancing up and down, my fists waving. "Dummkopf, shmuck, you'll never get your hat!"

When Father Jonas came out to stop the fight, I was still shouting, punching the air, winning, while Thomas Leighton sobbed about his lost hat, and the other boys slunk away. Maxi stood quietly with his hands in his pockets.

"Your loose tooth is out, Dora," he said with pleasure. "All this time we tried to pull it and now it's gone."

Father Jonas cleaned me up, dabbing at the blood on my white collar. "Who hit you, Dora?" he asked, frowning. "What was the fight about?"

"It was that big boy," Maxi began helpfully, but I gave him a nudge to keep him quiet. If Thomas Leighton got in trouble because of us, I knew he'd give it to Maxi again, and a lot worse, too.

"Just a lot of bullies, that's all," I shrugged. "They won't try it again."

From that night on, instead of sleeping in the dormitory with the other boarding students, we slept in the vicarage. Father Jonas and his wife had no children and so had room for us in their home. The downstairs was full of furniture, and we never played there for fear of running into some skinny-legged little table wedged between the fat armchairs and sofas. Small china statues of shepherdesses sat on the mantelpiece. Mrs. Grey dusted them every week and sometimes would stand looking at them for a long while.

She was a thin, nervous lady who didn't talk much. One of the school children told me she had lately gone through a breakdown and become odd. Father Jonas's parishioners avoided her as she avoided them, except on Sundays after services, when she set out tea and cakes at the vicarage. Then she would smile a good deal, twist her fingers in the sides of her skirt and be glad when the occasion was over. I think she liked having Maxi and me there because we gave her an excuse not to spend time with the parishioners. When Father Jonas asked her to come with him to Vespers, she would shake her head and say she had to be sure Maxi and I had our baths or finished our homework or whatever it was we hadn't done.

The Reverend Mrs. Jonas Grey was a gardener and spent most of her day working in the vegetable garden or in the small greenhouse attached to the vicarage. When she saw that I respected her plants and didn't trample them, she let me work alongside her on weekends and even taught me to grow whole plants from tiny cuttings. This was the task I liked best. You cut a little pie-shaped wedge of leaf, put it into a tray of dirt with other little pieces, and two months later the whole new plant would appear. After three weeks more, you tug the plant gently, and if the roots hold, you put the new baby in its own pot or into the ground outside, if the weather is warm enough. The little cuttings, which were in a way orphans, growing not from seeds and in foreign soils, belonged especially to me, and Mrs. Grey let me tend them by myself. When I had finished my weeding, I would kneel for a while beside the new plants, looking at the tiny, pale green shoots pushing through the damp soil and out of the now invisible cutting which had served as its seed. A plant might seem to be coming out of nowhere, from nothing, but I knew that it had sprung from a secret other self that had dissolved into this new life, leaving no trace of what it had been before.

From time to time, especially in the garden, I would think of my parents, of our big house in Frankfurt, and of Claire, who gave me my second home. Out of these various soils, Maxi and I had been born and now the soils were gone, leaving no traces either. Whatever life they had once, Maxi and I have now, so we have become them, even while we are ourselves. Sometimes I have the strangest feelings while I work with the plants setting them into pots which in a few months will be carried into the greenhouse for the winter. My hands feel like they aren't mine. They seem to be other people's or maybe they are growing out of the ground, not out of me. When I told Mrs. Jonas how I felt, she looked serious.

"We will write to Frankfurt and see if we can find out about your parents," she said. "Perhaps some of your family is still there."

"Aunt Rachel lived near us," I said, putting down soil around a tray full of bean plant cuttings. "Her name was Lebenthal too. I think all the rest of the family was in Warsaw."

Mrs. Grey turned her head away and didn't answer. At that time I didn't know that thousands of Jews had been burned up in the Warsaw ghetto, but I know now. Except for my parents and aunt in Frankfurt, none of the family could be left.

"Yes," I told Mrs. Grey, wondering why she didn't want to look at me. "I would like to know about my parents. Please."

Summer went by without Father Jonas being able to find out anything. He worked through a parishioner of his in the War Ministry, who had contacts in neutral Switzerland. A network apparently existed between Zurich, London, and Berlin, maybe because of all the money that was being stashed away in Swiss banks. That's what Father Jonas thought, anyway.

When autumn came, no one was thinking of anything but bombs. From 7, September to 3, November, London was hit every night. First, we would hear the "alert" sirens which meant a Luftwaffe squadron had been spotted on its way toward us. Then the alarm went off, and we would begin to hear the drone of the planes. After that came the long, screaming whistle sounds and then explosions, wherever the bombs were going off. The whole sky would light up. Sometimes Maxi and I would sneak into a dark room and turn back a flap of black curtain, so we could see the flaming red sky.

New British anti-aircraft guns swung around like carousels, trying to hit the German planes before the German planes could hit our own aircraft. The guns must not have been effective, for you never heard of any German planes going down, and the bombs never stopped falling. Still, we all felt very proud of our gunners because of the great noise they made. We felt like we were finally fighting back, the same way I felt when I hit Thomas Leighton, not minding my knocked-out tooth.

Mostly we didn't watch the German air attacks. Father Jonas had fixed up a sleeping and study place in the cellar under the low stone arches that supported the vicarage. The same arches had held up other buildings for the past thousand years without falling. Our shelter was the safest in London, according to Father Jonas, except for the "Paddock," where Prime Minister Churchill sat in a tiny, steel-encased concrete room, giving the orders that kept London alive during these months. Actually, almost nowhere in London was really safe, even the tubes, where thousands of people would hide if the alarm caught them away from home. Somehow, even if you could get to the tubes, you would still rather hide in your own cellar, as long as you could get there in time.

One day, when Father Jonas had taken us to the dentist downtown, we saw a lot of soldiers in the street, wearing gas masks that made them look like giant crickets, and ordering people underground. We saw a U.X.P. man who defused unexploded bombs. He had been lowered into a pit to defuse a bomb down there. Even though the alarm was sounding, we stopped to watch. Suddenly we heard him shout. They pulled him up and ran with him across the street, then threw themselves down to escape the expected blast. We did too, but popped our heads up again when no blast came.

The soldier who had been pulled from the hole scratched his chin and looked embarrassed. When they asked him what happened down there, he shuffled a bit and then explained, "There was this bloody great rat!" We all laughed and ran down to the tubes, just as the first German airplanes roared overhead. We found it very funny that a man brave enough to take an unexploded bomb apart was afraid of a rat. In those days, Londoners didn't seem to be afraid of anything, and in that way, Maxi and I felt we fit in. We weren't afraid either. We had, after all, been through a few things ourselves. Besides, I had come to believe I was lucky. Father Jonas said no, that I was blessed, but I didn't understand what he meant.

Our Hebrew lessons mostly went on in the cozy little cellar room under St. Hilary's. Mrs. Grey had brought down all her Hummel figurines and set them on book shelves where she would sit reading her gardening books, making notes, while Father Jonas taught Maxi and me our Hebrew lessons. Since that time, memorizing foreign verbs has reminded me of those bombs.

Father Jonas had once hoped to be a scholar and seemed confused about how he had come to be a schoolmaster instead. He was a good teacher, though he preferred studying by himself. Rather than making us write out our lessons, he had us speak them in Hebrew until we could carry on conversations with him. Then he had us make up stories in Hebrew. Maxi's stories were about things like the Red Sea parting for the fleeing Hebrews and Judith driving a spike through the enemy general's head. I made up stories about the Ben-Ari bears and their trips to Frankfurt and Poland to look for their family. In all my stories, the bears, like Maxi and me, had been lost for a long time and were trying to find their way home.

When we all got home, somehow Claire was there, not our parents. The same thing happened in my dreams. It was her face I saw, not Mutti's.

On 29, December, the water mains were purposely broken by the German bombardiers during the incendiary bomb drops, so no one could fight the fires with hoses. At six o'clock in the morning, just as the dawn came up, Father Jonas took me out for a walk. We went to St. Paul's, his favorite church, and stood watching the fire fighters put out the last of the smoldering ashes. The columns were charred and the dome cracked. We peeked inside, though we were ordered to stay out. The walls were half-crumbled, so that the light came in and lit up the broken paintings on the stone. It seemed to me that the cathedral could be considered half-built, with the best to come, not half-destroyed. But Father Jonas stood in front of it, tears running down his face, whispering to himself.

"The Huns take everything," I heard him say. "Every good and blessed thing."

"It's not all gone," I said, holding his hand tightly and putting it against my cheek. "Maybe the church can be fixed. Wait and see. They'll make it better than new." As it turned out, I was right, for later, St. Paul's became a miracle of patchwork, mortared together by love and sweat.

On the way back home from St. Paul's, Father Jonas told me that my parents were no longer in Frankfurt. His contacts said they had been taken to one of the camps, probably Bergen-Belsen. At that time, no one understood what the camps were. I imagined them as holiday places or dormitories like the one at St. Hilary's. The song that the soldiers had sung on the way from Dover came suddenly to mind, and I said aloud, "tomorrow when the world is free," thinking that my parents would one day be let out of the camp, and we would be with them again. Not until a few years ago, after the war ended, did Maxi and I see pictures of prisoners at Bergen-Belsen and understand that we would not see our parents again. Maybe I knew this in some dark part of my mind, which is why I never dreamed about them, only about Claire.

Father Jonas seemed to know more than he was telling me that night of the big raid. He would start to say something, then yawn or mumble. At the time, I thought he was just tired, but later I figured out that he was not sure how much of the truth to tell us. He took me to breakfast and then stopped at a pawnshop, where the proprietor seemed to know him.

"I've been wanting to get something for you," Father Jonas said, holding up a small, bronze menorah that the pawnbroker brought out from the back. "I'm told it came from Germany."

The menorah was made of nine little hands, reaching up to hold the candles that would be put in for the Festival of Lights. The hands were of all kinds—baby hands, old wrinkled hands, workers' hands, all of them reaching for a handful of light.

"Thank you for this," I said to Father Jonas, holding the menorah up to the window, where it caught the morning sun and shone like gold. "I will take it with me wherever I go."

"I hope you won't go very far away," he said and bent down to hug me. I kissed him for the first time. Soon after that, I started calling him Papa, and Maxi did too. That year we held our first Hanukkah at St. Hilary's, and Father Jonas read the service in Hebrew, while the bombs fell over us. Claire would have said he was a good pastor, like her Pastor Vence, who had brought us to the Leclerq home in Rheims. More than Father Jonas's own parishioners, Maxi and I were his flock, his children.

3

Paris..............................1944

Avoiding the German guards near the river was not easy, even for native Parisians defying the Nazi curfew. For Paul de Montfort, a southern French officer now serving the Resistance, it was harder still. Every week he left the city, crossed the German lines into Allied territory, and at dawn came back with a message from de Gaulle to the few troops the general could be sure were loyal to him. *Slipping past the Germans was only half the battle,* Paul thought, as he stood with his back to the damp stone wall beside the Seine. He leaned out over the water, trying to spot the boat that was supposed to take him into the heart of Paris. *If the Nazis don't catch me,* he warned himself, *the communists will.* Paul tried to breathe deeply to calm himself, but the air caught in his throat.

Like everyone else in Paris, he was aware that the city's survival depended on de Gaulle's forestalling both a communist takeover and German plans to blow up the city center. Paul lifted his worker's cap and ran his fingers through his thick, wet dark hair. The humidity and temperature were getting to him. No cultivated Parisian ever stayed in the city during August, and the rank heat was why they left, in better days, for the Pyrenees, the Mediterranean, anywhere but home. These certainly were not the better days.

As he waited, Paul repeated the message to himself. *De Gaulle has flown to France against Roosevelt's orders. He says the communists must be stopped from taking advantage of the city's danger. Hitler has ordered Paris destroyed, and Eisenhower refuses to defend it. At this moment, France must save her capital without help. Attack the Communications Headquarters and hold it at all costs until we arrive.*

De Gaulle was right, Paul felt, to expect no help from the Americans in the great enterprise of saving Paris. Eisenhower, always the pragmatist, had no intention of wasting what little gasoline he had left on street-by-street fighting in the City of Light. Eisenhower's plan was to avoid Paris, let it starve or burn, and win the war somewhere in the open. *Americans prefer to fight in the open,* thought Paul, remembering in a flash of hard light and with a bitter taste in his mouth, how all his men had been cut down in the streets of Courtrai. They had expected American cover fire from the air, but none had come. His eyes stung, and he rubbed them with the back of his hand, wanting to erase what they had seen and still saw.

All the lost men, my fault, my fault. Mea culpa. Paul swallowed the bile that rose in his throat and tried to think of anything but the way he had lost his men. Better to think of taking that shrapnel in his shoulder at Dunkirk, better to remember the smooth, heart-shaped face of the girl who had been trying to get two Jewish children to England, and who had, for all he knew, died trying. Claire, the children had called her. His last memory before the explosion was throwing himself down over Claire and the children, trying to shelter them from the blast. *To no purpose, probably.* Everyone was trying, but no one could change anything. He would not call upon God, for God had abandoned him at Courtrai. In Belgium, he had said his last prayer, a futile one, as events proved. Since then, Paul de Montfort had wandered, a lost soul, depression settling around him like a shroud.

Paul wondered what good it would do if he delivered his message from General de Gaulle to General Leclerq. The generals were all so sure they were right. Tanguy, the communist commander, had said, "Paris is worth two hundred thousand dead!" On its ruins he would no doubt build a worker's paradise, raising barracks and soup kitchens over the ashes of the Sainte Chapelle and Notre Dame. *Well,* Paul said to himself, *perhaps the churches might better be soup kitchens than vast, rich theaters for religious charades. Still, the Sainte Chapelle is beautiful.* Paul remembered painting copies of the stained glass windows in the chapel when he was an art student. *What little beauty is left in the world should be saved,* he felt, *and it is the work of artists to save it*. An English poet had said, *"Beauty is all ye know on earth and all ye need to know,"* Paul recalled, but somehow Beauty as a religion left him feeling as cold and dead inside as before. He had hoped to be an artist, but the dark shroud covering him now blocked form and color. He felt like a house smothered with black curtains so that bombs could not find it, nor, it seemed to Paul, could God.

Freezing suddenly, his palms tight against the wall behind him, Paul heard the mechanical sound of German boots tramping across the bridge overhead. Perhaps they were going to the torpedo depot of the Kriegsmarine, which had enough TNT to blow up all of Paris. One mortar shell, he knew, could destroy a city block. The KARL siege mortar, ordered to Paris by Hitler on 14, August, had been used at Stalingrad and could hurl a two-an-a-half ton shell four miles. Hitler wanted Paris destroyed, Eisenhower didn't seem to care, and everyone knew what the communist colonel Tanguy wanted. All of them had other fish to fry. Who cared about a few hundred thousand starving Parisians and a city that was a wonder of the world, beautiful enough to make a savage weep. It was especially beautiful at night, Paul thought, when the lights danced in the air over the fountains of Montparnasse and lovers held hands in the shadows of the Bois de Boulogne. He was risking his life not for de Gaulle, not for an idea or a cause, but for the right of Paris to exist. Since he had lost his men and his faith in God, Paris and its beauty were all he had left to believe in.

He saw the lightless rowboat drift, its oars unmoving. It came close and hardly tipped as he stepped in, carefully placing himself in the middle, between the two pea-jacketed figures who rowed like ferrymen of the underworld, dark, silent, on business of their own. They dropped him at the Pont Neuf, not speaking, and Paul climbed up the stone steps to the street, his body tense and ready to run. He had not said goodnight to the men because he knew that they, like him, wanted nothing between them that might be recognizable later. Nazi torture might break any one of them to inform on the others. The Paris underground was a conspiracy of strangers, a family in which brothers did not own each other, but lived side by side, silent as shadows.

At the street corner where he had been told to look for number 44 was a stack of empty wooden cases marked *Achtung Ecrasit*, with a skull and crossbones. Paul knew they contained TNT that was now ready to be blown up as soon as the Nazi commandant gave the orders. All over Paris, German demolition experts sat ready to push the plungers that would blow Paris off the map of human memory.

Paul stepped around a homemade barricade made of carts and train grills. *Someone has fought and died here today,* he thought, seeing the stain of blood. *Tomorrow others will fight and die, the way my men did when they lined the frontier between Belgium and France with the living membrane of their own bodies. No,* Paul said to himself, taking a breath so deep it hurt his chest, *not that memory, not that one.* .He lit a match beside a wooden door, two houses down from the Hôtel de Ville and knocked at number 44. He expected to find General Leclerq there, but also had to expect a room swept clean of resistance fighters by the Gestapo, or filled with SS troops looking for spies like him.

A woman opened the door, sticking her nose outside, but keeping the crack small. When she heard that Paul was carrying a message to Leclerq, she let him in, rubbing her hands and staring into his face as if she did not trust him to bring good news. What news he brought didn't change the expression on Leclerq's lined, spare face when the general heard it. Lighting a cigarette, he gestured with the match as he shook it out.

"Sit down, young man. Who'd you say you were? Paul de Montfort? I knew your father." He paced up and down the small, sparely furnished room, his hands twisting behind his back, ashes dropping to the floor. "So, the German Commandant has been ordered to blow up Paris. What does de Gaulle have to say about that?"

"I have no idea," Paul said. "I am only his messenger, not his confidant." His words came out more coldly than he meant them to. He did not want the other man to know how weak, useless, and depressed he felt.

For a moment he seemed to be back in Belgium with his troops around him. They were in a foreign country, wondering why they were not back home defending the south of France. His second-in-command, eyes filming over in death, had asked him then, "What have you to say about our dying here?" And he had had nothing to say, which was why Paul no longer prayed the mechanical prayers of his childhood. He knew no other prayers and consequently did not pray at all.

"De Gaulle says to hold Paris against the Nazis and the communists," he told Leclerq, his voice hollow and low, as if amplified by machinery. "That's all I know."

"You sound like you don't think that's a good idea," the general said, blowing smoke in Paul's face. "Not much for fighting, are you? Spying is more to your taste, *n'est-ce pas*?"

When Paul looked straight ahead, not answering, Leclerq shrugged.

"Barricades are springing up like mushrooms all over the city," Leclerq said, holding his cigarette with all five fingers, so that it couldn't be seen, a habit no doubt learned in night combat. "They are being raided by the communists, often as not. Everything is in the hands of the communists. De Gaulle knows this?"

"Yes." Paul felt like a tube through which one voice was being blown at another. These men believed that what they did made a difference, that God was on their side. They believed what it was in their best interests to believe. Leclerq might become a cabinet minister if de Gaulle won. If Tanguy won, Leclerq would be shot as a traitor. Naturally, he would rather be a cabinet minister.

"Then how does he expect me to do as he wishes?" Leclerq threw up his hands.

"He wants you to bring up troops from the southeast, by the gate of Orleans," Paul went on, still standing at attention. "Tomorrow he will be here in person to lead them into the city."

General Leclerq poured himself a glass of cognac, not offering Paul any.

"Don't let the Americans know." He kept his eye on Paul as he drank. "The Americans don't understand why we would die for Paris."

"What can we do but die?" Paul asked, half to Leclerq, half to himself, "I don't know what else to do now. It's been a long time since I knew what to do."

"Dying won't get you anywhere, young man. Snap out of it. Try fighting. And pray." Leclerq finished his cognac. "Yes, I think one must pray, too."

So Paul went with one-fourth of Paris the next day, the thirteenth of August, to pray at the feet of the Virgin, or as close to her feet as he could get. He joined the crowd in the square of Notre Dame, hurting his knees as he fell to the pavement, wishing he believed his words were heard. "Holy Mary, Mother of God," he said out loud, "Pray for us. Don't let them burn this city down. Don't let those devils take Paris away from the world." He looked up at the spires of the cathedral, listened to the bells burst in his ears, and waited for God to tell him that nothing was lost, that something was won. His eyes were wet, and he saw nothing but blurred shapes surging across the plaza, stepping between the kneeling figures. Someone stopped in front of him, and Paul looked up.

"Aren't you the officer from Dunkirk? The one who saved me?"The girl's light, high voice said as she leaned forward, her hand on his shoulder. "I'm Claire Leclerq. I've kept your helmet for you. But of course you don't need it anymore, now that the Germans are leaving."

Paul felt as if she had precipitated out of his imagination, where he had carried her since he saw her last. He reached up and laid his hand over hers. "We're supposed to be praying," he said. "And I can't seem to. Help me."

She knelt beside him, swaying as thousands of bodies pressed against each other like cattle before a storm. "Dear God, save us, save this lovely city." Claire said softly. "In the name of our Lord Jesus Christ. Amen."

The damp wind rose with twilight and whirled around them as they knelt, crying like lost children, wondering where they had left themselves that they could not be found, not even by God.

Behind the square, on the right bank, the Panzers rolled down the Champs Elysées, shaking the pavement under heavy treads. After the tanks came trucks and wagons loaded with furniture—tall carved clocks, rolled up carpets, even bidets. The Germans were taking with them whatever they could of Paris.

"They've been ordered north," Claire whispered to him, her lips close to his ear. "My father's a general. He told me just an hour ago that Paris isn't German anymore."

Paul bent his head, considering whether or not to thank God, especially since Claire's father might well be the General Leclerq whom he had offended the day before. "I want very much to be thankful," he said. "But it is hard to know whom to thank. Just now, I want to thank you."

The bells of the cathedral shook and rang, resonating through Paul, until his hand trembled as it held Claire's.

"Don't thank me," Claire answered, her damp, pale face turned up to the sky. "It's God who won't let the Nazis blow up the city. He's sending them away." She folded her palms together, tears running from the corners of her eyes. "Lord Jesus, thank you for saving Paris."

The bells kept ringing. Paul's head began to hurt, and he put it so close to Claire's that their temples touched. Though he was numb, unable to cry or smile, it was enough that Claire was crying and smiling for them both. *If I can stay close to Claire*, Paul thought, *I can feel through her, let her be my heart, for I need one. Since Courtrai, I have needed one.* Long ago Paul had hoped to be a priest, and join himself to the love of God so that he could love without wanting anything back. Now, as he looked at Claire, he remembered wanting to love in that way, and once again, such love seemed possible.

As Claire prayed, her eyes closed, lashes wet with tears, Paul looked at her as if at his own child-self, long lost and nearly forgotten. Forgetting everything had become natural to Paul, ever since the war started. Memory was a curse, like the one that banished Adam from Eden. Paul wanted to remember nothing.

If Claire had lost anything in the war, it didn't show on her face, which was smooth, except for the little lines at the corners of her smile. She had evidently smiled a great deal in her short life. Underneath the delicate skin, almost transparent to the blood beneath it, one pale blue vein pulsed near her temple. Paul found himself wondering at the infinity of cells and tissue, nerve and bone that held together this particular human being, this Claire. An invisible universe of small worlds spun inside her, as in himself, run by the same divine laws that ruled the stars, woven on the warp of electrical energy which would always live, even when the matter it had briefly shaped dropped away into dust. That much of immortality Paul believed in, though he no longer connected it with God. *I am glad I can believe that some part of Claire will always live, but cannot help sadness that this look of hers, this moment of child-face and girl-form will not.* Like Faust, he wished he could violate the laws of God and nature, holding this moment forever. Knowing he could not, he sank again into depression as he realized that he could not keep anyone from drowning in the flood of time.

"You aren't supposed to look so sad," Claire reproached him, having turned to stare at his face as he stood up. "You aren't one of those soldiers who wants a war going on, are you? My father's like that. He enjoys ordering people around. If not his men, then us, the family. My brother and me. Actually, just me, now. My brother was killed a month ago. In battle."

"I am sorry to hear it." Paul felt the rush of sadness that always choked him when he heard another soldier had been killed. He tried to answer her, not knowing what to say. "No, I am not the kind of soldier who likes war."

As he stood up, Paul looked down at his uniform and brushed off his dirty knees, "I hate killing. Until the Germans invaded, I thought being an officer meant merely wearing a uniform to balls and riding horseback in parades."

"What were you? Claire asked standing up beside him, the crowd pushing them close together. "Before the war, I mean. Not an officer?"

"Only an officer on ceremonial occasions," he said, taking her hand and pushing ahead of her through the crowd that milled in the square, kissing, cheering, and waving scarves as the bells rang. "In civilian life, I painted pictures. Sometimes I made statues of clay and bronze, but mostly, I painted."

He dropped her hand when they reached the other side of the square and started walking, not wanting her to think him too bold. They had not been introduced, and Paul had never before been seen with a girl to whom he had not been formally introduced. Only the war could have made it possible for him, the son of Count Henri de Montfort, to be walking down the Champs Elysées beside a stranger with whom he was perhaps falling in love and whose family he did not know. His mother would be scandalized if she heard of it. *I will have to make up a story about how I met Claire, perhaps at a military ball,* Paul thought, *or a dinner party given in honor of her father, who is, after all, a general. That should count for something, at least with my father.* The thought struck him that he did not know Claire's place in society. His mother would insist on finding out.

As they walked, Claire took his arm easily, without a blush, just looking directly into his eyes as if she and he had always been close.

"Did you live in a garret? I've wished to be an artist living in a garret, looking out over the whole city. Only I could never imagine how the movers would get my piano up those high winding staircases. You know, like the ones in the films."

Paul thought of his parents' fifty-room chateau just outside Carcassonne, its broad lawns and gardens misted with the spray of fountains. Or at least that was how he remembered it. By now, Champs-de-lys might be only a heap of rubble, its statues and eighteenth-century furniture long since carted across the German border.

"Perhaps if I had lived in a garret instead of a chateau, I would have been a better painter." He opened the door of a café that he remembered from before the war, and they went inside. "As it was, the paintings were mediocre, and the sculpture not even that. If I had been an eighteenth-century artist, I would have been admired. But in the twentieth century, no. My work was correct, but without life."

Paul had no idea whether or not she understood what he was telling her, but felt a great release in the telling. Never before had he been able to admit, even to himself, that his work was without life.

"I am afraid, Claire, that I have no imagination. The unexpected appears only in my life, never on my canvas. God has not seen fit to inspire me." He did not add that God seemed to have lost interest him altogether.

"Well, the bourgeoisie must admire your paintings, anyway," Claire smiled, letting him seat her at a damask-draped round table under an elaborate chandelier, unlit because electricity had failed with the last bombardments. "They love art that doesn't upset them."

What is she? Paul wondered, folding his hands and leaning his elbows on the table, watching her. *A communist perhaps? Or an aristocrat? No, neither one, with that father of hers. Maybe a Huguenot, a French Protestant? Mother would never consent to my marrying a Protestant.* Paul tried to remember Claire's mother, so he could place the girl in some known social context, then gave up, feeling foolish. His mother had taught him too well for even a war to break the patterning. Would he be unable to love Claire if she turned out to be a *bourgeoise* and a Huguenot as well?

His mother's world was gone, Paul reminded himself, glad that it was, if it would have stood between him and this girl, bourgeoise, communist, or whatever she was. *Certainly she does not keep her eyes cast down or simper like the girls I met at parties and balls, long ago in that other life. This one would kiss you on the mouth just as she looked you in the eyes, warm, firm, and altogether present in the act.* Paul tried to keep his eyes off Claire's lips, which were pink and shiny. She wore no lipstick, he gathered, but her mouth was moist. He noticed that between sentences, she sometimes put the tip of her finger at the middle of her upper lip, as if cautioning herself not to talk too much.

Claire sipped the execrable fake coffee. "Did you know people in Paris are raising rabbits and chickens in their bathtubs?" She laughed. "At least no-one's fat anymore."

"Or drunk." Paul lifted his cup and touched Claire's, smiling back at her. "I like this simple new life. Families like mine are probably the better for it. Starting like ordinary people with a fresh canvas. That might be the best way."

Paul imagined that everything in his life from now on would be a palimpsest drawn over the old figures in the past, which were drawn over still other figures old before his birth and farther back, to when his family began. The portraits of his ancestors came to mind, with their long noses, gleaming jewelry, and brocaded costumes that set them apart from the common herd. They had been Catholic as far back as the thirteenth century. His earliest known ancestor, Simon de Montfort, had swept down from the north in 1215 to destroy the heretical southern Cathars, and for his bloody service to Pope and King had been made Count of Toulouse. For the de Montforts, Catholicism was their very identity. Even to contemplate breaking with the Church in order to marry Claire was like wiping his family off the map of France. He was the last of his line, and his mother never let him forget it.

Claire waited for an answer, and when Paul was silent, hurried on in a breathless voice, perhaps afraid that he was a *bourgeois* and was offended by her words. "Anyway," she said emphatically, seeming to hope that she could finish with grace what might have begun with a blunder. "What sort of pictures where they? Landscapes? Portraits? What?"

"Religious, for the most part. I had hoped I could do better than those saccharine madonnas and Infants of Prague one sees in Catholic art stores and churches."

"I'm sure you could," Claire said, with a positive nod. "They're sort of cheesecake, aren't they? Churchly cheesecake. Meant to sell something or other."

"It is a bad day for religion when God has to advertise," Paul agreed. "But yes, advertisement is what they are."

He glanced around him at the darkened restaurant that he remembered as being bright with a dozen crystal chandeliers. Now there was only one, set with flickering candles, a signal of hope that Paris would once again be the City of Light. *At least it did not belong to the Germans anymore,* Paul thought. *The Nazi occupiers are running away with whatever they can steal, and the Americans will not stay. They want only to go back to their ball games and frankfurters.* Paris was a still life, like one of the first daguerreotypes, in which the only thing that registered on the film was what did not move. No gas came through the underground pipes of Paris, and in many parts of the city, no water came out of the taps. Electricity went on for only an hour a day, if that. There was so little food left that the people ate dog biscuits and rats, when they could get them. Meanwhile, the Allies were planning to detour around Paris, an army heading toward another army on a collision course.

Claire leaned back looking at the sparkling chandelier. "Here comes the waiter. No use asking him for a menu. I can't believe there's any food left in Paris."

Paul smiled. "In Paris, there is always food."

"As long as it isn't linden leaves." Claire's nose wrinkled. "Today they said on the radio that it's all right to eat ash or linden leaves. They don't make you sick. Oak leaves make you sick."

The waiter, with an immaculate towel over one arm, bowed and brought them rutabaga soup. He leaned over and whispered to Paul, "And we have a splendid roast rabbit, monsieur, if you have one thousand francs."

"Very well then, let us have the rabbit," said Paul, shaking out his napkin. When the waiter was gone, he sighed. "We used to feed rutabaga to the livestock at home. Now I suppose we should be glad to eat it ourselves."

He looked down at his soup, thinking of the bejeweled party-givers of his childhood, directing servants to pour rare wine for their guests, who looked just like themselves. They had all come through the genetic funnel of upper-crust French society. Every titled person in France seemed to be related to him, Paul reflected, and the portraits that hung on the paneled walls of Champs-de-lys might have hung on the walls of any great house in Carcassonne or Albi. Copies of them did, in fact. He had often met the faces of his own aristocratic friends in faded portraits hanging on the walls of fine old homes. There, they were decked out in renaissance ruffs or eighteenth-century wigs. In every de Montfort generation, the aristocrats were reborn with new names and new garments, but they were the same, always. Paul looked up at Claire, who had stopped talking and was staring at him, one eyebrow raised. This face, at least, was new. He had never seen it hanging in a hallway, over napoleonic décolletage.

"Have some soup," she said. "It came while your thoughts were somewhere else." She dipped her spoon in the thin green liquid and paused. "I'm from Rheims, Paul, and not the fashionable part of it. My father's a career officer. The Leclerqs are nobody special. In fact, my ancestors were winemakers."

Paul felt ashamed of himself. It had been his talk of ordinary folk and their difference from him and his family that had made Claire defensive about living in middle-class Rheims. "I wish they were here now," Paul said. "What Paris needs are its winemakers and its bakers and its craftsmen. The people I come from are useless. I'm afraid to go home and see our uselessness."

"Is it possible to start over?" Claire set down her spoon and leaned forward. "No looking back? Or will we be where we used to be, going through the motions, being alive only the way paintings are, being copies? Isn't that what you said was wrong with your pictures? Maybe it won't be wrong with them anymore, now that the war's changed everything." She put her hand over his, and her eyes shone. "What if we go back and it's all gone? All there was? What then?"

"Well, then we would have Eden," he smiled, shaking his head. "We would live naked in the garden, all children of God. But that is gone too. No more Eden, no more children of God." He sat still, his cold hand under her warm one, remembering how it was to be a child at Champs-de-lys in the old days, when the English governess gave him lessons in her language as they strolled in the gardens. He could still recall her grave precision. "Is this a stone, Paul, or a rock, and why?" she would ask, holding up a fragment of slate from the walkway.

"I miss that Eden of my childhood," he sighed. "I suppose what I really want is to regain it. Perhaps through my children, if I have any, I will someday have Eden back again."

"I've been wanting to ask you," Claire's voice dropped and she took her hands away from his, folding them tightly together. "When we were together on the beach at Dunkirk, I had two children with me. They weren't there when I woke up. Neither were you. It was like a dream, with everyone being real before I opened my eyes. Then they were gone."

"The children went with Henry Harrison, the officer who left me on the beach in the hands of the medics," Paul said, trying to remember the face of the buck-toothed young Englishman leaning over him four years earlier, saying, "You'll be all right, old man. I'm taking the children to England. You can tell the young miss so, if you see her again." At that point, Paul had fallen back to sleep, dreaming he was at Champs-de-lys, showing Claire the governess's stones that were either rocks or pebbles.

"Then I'll go there," Claire said firmly, finishing her soup. "They may be in an orphanage. It's been only four years. They'll remember me."

"If they lived." Paul laid his forearms across the table, wanting to touch her, but uncertain whether or not to do more than reach out. "A lot of people tried to cross the channel that day and died."

"And a lot didn't." Her voice was high and tense. "Dora and Maxi weren't alone. Henry was with them."

Paul thought of the stories he had heard about the boats overturned on the edge of the sea and emptied of their passengers by frantic soldiers who wanted only to get home. And of the boats that were blown out of the water by German aircraft.

"Come home to Carcassonne with me first," he said abruptly, hardly knowing what he was going to say until he had said it. "And I will go with you to England to look for the children, if you want me to."

"Yes, that's exactly what I want," Claire said, brushing her wet eyes with the backs of both hands. "My children."

Carcassonne..............................1944

Later that month, Claire sat beside Paul, celebrating a Mass in thanksgiving for the war's end. The words were in Latin, and Claire felt restless, not understanding what was going on. Paul whispered a running translation in her ear and held her hand, the one that bore an engagement ring with a stone of astonishing size. They were going to be married the following week in this place where Paul's ancestors had been baptized, married, and buried for nearly a thousand years. The wedding would be without the blessing or presence of her father. For one thing, General Leclerq had declared that Paul had an unhealthy attitude toward a soldier's patriotic duty in war, which might carry over to other duties as well. When Claire had asked him to be more precise, the general muttered something about the duties of a man to a woman and then changed the subject, looking embarrassed. General Leclerq had made some inquiries to the French High Command about Paul's military record and had not been satisfied at what he learned.

"There was the matter of his battalion at Courtrai," Claire's father told her gravely, sitting her down on a hard chair in his office and keeping his hands on her shoulders. "Five hundred men lost. No one knows how it could have happened. I suppose young Paul himself doesn't know. What sort of man have you got there, *ma fille*? No better soldier than an Italian. He's probably not good for anything else either. But then he comes from a rich family, and no doubt imagines that his name will take care of him."

General Leclerq put his hands behind his back and strode back and forth, putting his heels down hard at each step. "Be sure that these rich boys, raised by their tender mamas, are spoiled for other women, Claire." He stopped walking and stood in front of her again.

"Whether or not Paul likes war the way you do," Claire said, "he served de Gaulle in the Resistance." She kept her eyes on her father's shiny black shoes that reflected light from the ceiling fixtures. "You have to admit he's brave."

"Spying isn't the same as fighting," her father said, pacing again. "Not at all. His father was a great general in the First War. It's not as if Paul had no example to follow. But he chose not to go to the military academy. And why?" Leclerq stopped in the middle of the room and threw up his hands, at a loss to describe Paul's folly.

"He wanted to study painting in Paris. That's his gift, Papa." Claire knew her father too well to believe that further argument would change his mind or hers.

"Painting in Paris! What sort of man spends his time slopping paint on a canvas when his country is within an ace of invasion? Answer me that!"

Claire had answered him nothing. Her father always tried to sort out the men he was dealing with, assuming that they were one familiar type or another, nobody special except for the military men he approved of. Paul, with all his subtleties of character, could not be fitted into General Leclerq's neatly squared masculine grid. When Claire had brought them together, her father immediately recognized Paul as a reluctant soldier and had found nothing good to say of him since. "That painter of yours," he would grumble. "That bellboy for de Gaulle."

Her father was habitually scornful of aristocrats, and Claire supposed it was because he could not bear to have anyone look down on him. Paul's perfect manners had put her father off from the first, and in self-defense, the general had been as calculatedly rude as he could be on the only occasion when Paul had accompanied Claire on a visit.

So when Paul had wanted to ask the general for permission to marry Claire, she would not agree. Having come of age, she was free to marry whomever she pleased. The general made it clear that he would take no part in the occasion. His family had always been Huguenot and had nothing to do with the Catholic enemy. He would not set foot in a Catholic church, General Leclerq swore, not even to see his daughter married. Claire explained that she would be Catholic in name only, to satisfy Paul's family, but the general just sneered and cursed, turning his back on her. Meanwhile, Paul was making elaborate arrangements with his own family to receive Claire for the first time.

"Receive is such a phony word," Claire objected. "It sounds like I'm going to a tea party."

"Nevertheless, received you will be," Paul said firmly, "like it or not. It is the way such things are done."

They would be married in the little chapel of Champs-de-lys, the family estate. Claire and Countess de Montfort managed to have their first argument over where the wedding would take place. Countess de Montfort expected to marry off her only child in the huge, red-brick cathedral of Albi, making the occasion the first great postwar social event. It was pointedly hoped that the de Montfort wedding could be brought off before the de la Roche ball, planned for October. Paul explained that the conflict was an old story. His grandmother and the previous Duchess de la Roche had been rivals in love, and the two families had been quarreling ever since. When Claire asked what the original cause had been, Paul explained that his grandmother had been jilted by the man who later married the de la Roche woman. For a while after Claire had heard the story of *"l'affaire de la Roche,"* as it was called in Paul's family, she imagined herself like some peasant in the middle of a blood feud among the local nobility, wondering how she was expected to take the affair as seriously as Paul's family did.

The second argument, also at long distance, was over Claire's decision to go to London for their wedding trip. Claire knew it was no use telling her prospective mother-in-law about her lost Dora and Maxi, so she did not try. "Cannes would be acceptable," the Countess de Montfort shouted over the fragile, fading telephone connection. "Or perhaps Ischia. But London! What shall I tell people when they ask where you'll be traveling? London, indeed! It's as vulgar as a trip to America."

That was when Claire first had the idea she wanted to live in America. Later, she could not remember if the idea had pleased her because the Countess would find it appalling. *Perhaps,* she thought, *America is a place where the de la Roches would have no authority over decisions about churches or destinations for wedding trips.* She found herself feeling as her father did about these shadowy society people who always minded their manners and yours. It was such people her mother had tried to copy, reading magazine articles about their social habits and home décor, not being who she was.

As Claire sat beside Paul, looking up at the vast, soaring roof of the Albi cathedral, she seemed to feel its weight and power not as the liberation from the flesh it was meant to be, but as a burden that would crush her if she stayed for too long under it. Listening to the priest's voice say, *"Ite, missa est,"* echoing their dismissal from one end of the cathedral to the other, Claire shivered, hearing him as her mother had heard the voices of her own past, telling her how to come and go through the narrow corridors of all her days.

"No," she said, so loud that Paul and others around her turned and stared. *No,* she said to herself, looking down and pretending to pray. *I won't go through my life fighting old fights and listening to the voices of the dead. I won't hear them, and I won't look back.*

She raised her head suddenly and saw Paul looking at her, lines between his brows, as if he were trying to figure out who she was and where he had seen her before.

He's a stranger, after all, she said to herself, with an abrupt clenching of her stomach and a coldness in her hands. *Here I am, about to marry a stranger who wants me to be like his mother and put on white gloves for a trip to the bathroom.*

She reached up and ran her finger down his cheek, and where the harsh lines were, alongside the straight, thin mouth under its neat moustache, and smiled. Whoever this stranger was, she loved him as an act of faith, and her body shook with a long, sweet tingle from one end of her to the other as she imagined being alone with him and married. *Anyway,* she said to herself, *all people are strangers to each other, married or not. Maman and Papa were strangers their whole lives.* It took the memory of her family's failure at intimacy to make Claire grasp the truth that she could never know any other person as he was. *Only God knows who we are,* Claire thought, *or who we might become.*

"We're stuck in ourselves," she sighed, getting up. "Stuck in our bags of skin. I pray that God will someday take me out of my sinful little self and let me grow."

The organ burst into the shimmering notes of a Bach postlude, and for a moment Claire followed the music into the air, freed from her bag of skin, stranger to nothing and no one. Her fingers moved as if over black and white keys, making melodies only she could hear, and she ached to have her piano back. Paul had promised her one as a wedding present and at this moment, she hardly knew which she desired more—him or the music which had for so long been locked up in her fingertips, waiting to be set free. Already she had new blank music books to replace those containing Maxi and Dora's songs. The first of the new books, she decided suddenly, would be filled with wedding music, dedicated to Paul.

She walked out of the church holding his arm tightly, listening to the bells, her head filled with their echoes. Underneath the dissonant clanging, she could already hear the first notes of a wedding song, and she whispered the words into which the music would be woven: "May the God of Israel join you together, and may he be with you who was merciful to two lost children."

The liturgy was referring, she supposed, to Adam and Eve, but for her, the words meant Dora and Maxi, herself and Paul, every human pairing born in the world. Yet each life was a surprise, a new thing under the sun, because it would be lived for the first time. She and Paul would be a mysterious new union of selves, two beings who over time would dissolve into one flesh.

"I have something for you," Paul said, reaching into his pocket for an envelope which he laid in her hand.

She opened it, then cried out with pleasure. "Oh, Paul! The two vulgar tickets to London! We're going!" She turned quickly and kissed him, holding his face between her hands and looking into his eyes. "Paul, if we find Dora and Maxi, can we take them with us? Can they be our children?"

"If their parents are dead, yes." Paul ran his hands down her back and then pulled away a little, as if he were afraid to be so close. "They could be our children. Our first children."

As he spoke, Claire tried to imagine the as yet unborn others and felt them growing under her skin, lying in her arms, standing beside her with their hands caught up in hers. Until now, there had been only her and Paul. Next week there would be his parents, and then perhaps Dora and Maxi, then others, nameless now but already real to her. It was the beginning of a time in which she would no longer be herself only, but a being borrowed by others, a grain of wheat buried so it might grow and nourish multitudes. There would be no movie marriage for her, no fairy tale in which two people lived in a perpetual state of romance happily young and beautiful forever after. *Good-by to that old dream, and high time too. Instead,* she thought, standing still beside Paul at the foot of the church steps, *we will grow old and tired, misunderstand each other and make up, wonder where to turn for money, worry about children living away from home.* What she was getting into, Claire saw clearly for the first time, not on the silver screen of her imagination, was ordinary life, just like her mother's and father's and billions of other ordinary married people. It was a hard truth, one that she felt unready to face.

All the way to the south of France, Claire found herself looking at Paul as if she had never seen him before, taking nothing for granted, watching the way his face sank into childish softness as he slept, or grew thoughtful as he looked out the window, or tender when he looked at her. She was trying to fix in her mind that vision on the church steps in which every moment was new and to see this man for the miracle of blood, bone, and spirit that he was, a child once, and before that, a single cell. He had been held by a mother, taught to speak and make pictures where there once were no words or images. Seeing all that he was and might be, she would become a good wife to him, a mother of generations, a maker of music. Her cup overflowed.

"He has put in my mouth a new song," she sang softly, remembering the words of a psalm she meant to add to her wedding music. Then she stopped, feeling suddenly shy that someone other than God was hearing her.

"Amen," said Paul, reaching out to take her hand.

If Paul had seemed momentarily a stranger to Claire on the church steps, he seemed even more a stranger at his family estate. His face fell into the lines of a mask, the creases around the mouth deeper, and the eyes sunken. By the time their taxi pulled up the long gravel drive of Champs-de-lys, he looked years older than the boy who slept on the train. In the foyer, she saw portraits that receded down the main hall into what seemed to be an infinity of ancestors, all with faces hard and still as Paul's was now. Claire stood in the middle of the foyer, waiting for the butler to announce them to the Countess and trying to pull down the sides of her brown tweed skirt so it would look longer.

"It's too short," she whispered to Paul, afraid her voice would carry in the vaulted hall. "Will she know skirts are this short in Paris now?"

For the first time in her life she felt socially unacceptable. *Did I really see the matrons of Carcassonne stare with disapproval at my bare legs, or did I imagine it? Will Paul's mother stare too?* Claire looked unhappily down at her white sweater, which had a gray swath across one sleeve from the sooty windowsill of the train. She adjusted the sleeve so it wouldn't show as long as she kept her arm firmly tucked against her side. *I must look like a cripple,* she thought. Perhaps the Countess would assume she had been hurt in the war and did not bear some congenital defect that would be transmitted to the next contingent of de Montforts, and then hang on the foyer walls, a scandal to the family.

"Why are you clutching your side like that?" Paul asked, his soft voice sounding distant and reproving.

So she didn't look right even to Paul. Claire swallowed hard and let her arm hang loose, the dirty sleeve in full view. She was sure the butler noticed it when he returned to take them into the drawing room. The Countess was reclining on her chaise longue, which was placed so that she could see into the garden through tall glass doors. An antique white and gilt piano angled out of one corner. It looked too delicate to be played, but Claire longed to try. This drawing room Paul had explained earlier, was his mother's reception hall and had been done in blue, cream, and gold to match the five-hundred-year-old Aubusson carpet that the Countess had inherited from her mother, along with the many antiques that filled the house. Claire felt for a moment as if she herself were a prospective museum piece, being checked for purchase by a curator who was hard to please and skilled at detecting frauds.

The Countess made the most of her impressive height by waiting to get up until they had come across the room. She was almost as tall as her son, a full six feet, with the same high cheekbones, thick, waving dark hair, and black-lashed hazel eyes. *The hair and lashes are probably assisted by art,* Claire thought, immediately censoring herself for judging another as she feared being judged. *The lines from the Countess's cheeks to her mouth are even more deeply etched than Paul's, no doubt from a lifetime of doing her duty at all costs,* Claire guessed. The woman seemed to be doing that now, as she surveyed her prospective daughter-in-law with an eye to her qualifications as the next matriarch of the tribe, not with any intent to win her love. *Love*, Claire sensed, *is very low on the Countess de Montfort's list of priorities.*

Paul gave his mother a kiss on either cheek. She hugged him briefly, and then stared into his face. "You look almost as old as I do, Paul," she said finally. "It seems this war has turned us all into a collection of mummies."

She turned to Claire and held out her hand. "But not you, my dear. You must have slept through the war and waked up when it was over, like the princess in the fairy tale, with the right kiss." Her mouth smiled, but her eyes looked hard and steadily at Claire, probably not liking this young woman whose face was so fresh and glowing, and who had taken over Paul's life.

"No one in Paris slept through the war," Claire said, looking straight back. "My father was in the Resistance, like Paul, and I worked for him. We got very little sleep, I assure you."

"Well, it did your complexion no harm," said the Countess, patting Claire on the cheek with a cool hand. "And you've certainly kept a trim figure. I understand the girls in Paris ride bicycles everywhere now and are as thin as little boys. Is this true? Do sit down, both of you. I'll ring for tea."

"I rode a bicycle, yes," Claire said, sitting at the edge of a fragile, velvet-covered chair. "No one had petrol for cars and the horses had to be killed for meat." She had a stubborn wish to tell this elegant woman as many unpleasant truths as she could.

"Claire's father is a general," Paul said, setting his chair between the two women. "He was a great force in the liberation of Paris."

"I know of the family." The Countess poured tea into three tiny, blue-flowered Limoges cups. "They are very industrious."

Claire blushed, imagining Paul's mother telling the family solicitor to check on the Leclerqs. *I guess she knows about the wine-making. And that the Leclerqs sold their wine on the streets of Paris.*

Paul seemed eager to change the subject. "How is my father? Your telegram said his heart is weaker."

"Since the Nazis came, he is not himself." The Countess stared into her teacup as if to read the leaves. "You knew, of course, that he was punished for helping a Jewish family escape to the coast?"

Claire caught her breath, thinking that she and her mother had been right to leave Rheims with Dora and Maxi. *Evidently Paul's parents had not run in time. No doubt this large, formidable woman had not been of a mind to leave her precious house with its antiques.*

"No, I had not heard," Paul said, putting down his cup and twisting his hands together.

The Countess's voice had no expression in it, and she gathered her long black shawl around her as if she had suffered a sudden chill. "The Nazis ran a truck over his legs," she said. "The legs had to be amputated. He paid a high price for his principles."

"May I see him now?" Paul stood up. "He knows what happened at Courtrai?"

"From your commanding officer." The Countess nodded toward the door. "You will find him in his study. He receives no one now, but he will see you."

Claire watched, feeling as if she were merely a ghostly presence in the room, unseen and forgotten. *What happened at Courtrai?* she wondered. *Why didn't Paul tell me about it?* She knew only that many of his men died during the German attack on Courtrai, but Paul would say nothing more. From Paul's tight-pressed lips, Claire guessed that he would have to speak about it now to his father, who sat alone, without his legs. *The old man can't blame Paul any more than Paul apparently blames himself.*

"Off you go." The Countess gave him a little push. "I will speak to Claire for a bit. You may as well hear what your father has to say and get it over with." She took the seat that Paul had left and for a moment sat silently, looking Claire up and down.

Claire wished she could imagine this cold-faced woman giving Paul birth, nursing, and upbringing, though one would never guess such intimacy from the tone of the words she had just spoken to him.

Well, my dear," she said evenly, her hands folded in her lap. "Does Champs-de-lys meet with your approval? Is it all that you hoped?"

Claire stared at her. *What does the woman think? That her son is in the clutches of some adventuress?* "I'm glad it's still standing, if that's what you mean. We didn't expect it would be." About to mention that her own house had been blown to pieces by the Nazis, Claire decided not to, after all. *Such a comment might be construed as a bid for sympathy, or a sign that I'm in the market for a new home.*

"The Montforts have a way of surviving everything," Paul's mother murmured, pouring them more tea from the gold-trimmed white porcelain teapot. "You would not believe what we have survived." She was silent a moment, then looked hard at Claire. "There is no money you know. Hardly a franc left. Paul's father invested all he had in *objêts d'art,* which were taken away by the Germans. My poor Henri thought cash would be useless after the war and that art might be the only commodity. A pity that he did not buy diamonds instead."

The Countess laughed a little, but the laugh turned into a harsh cough. "Like our son, he believed that people will always value art enough to sell what they have in return for it. But art is not bread." She sighed and closed her eyes briefly, seeming to be tired of looking at Claire. "If you had hoped to live as well as the previous Countesses de Montfort did," she said sharply, "you were mistaken. Champs-de-lys will be sold in the next few months to pay our debts. Paul will get a little from the sale, but only a little." She returned to her chaise longue and lay down. "We are poor now. Do you understand?"

Claire saw what pained the woman and wanted to reach out to take the hand that lay curled in a fist on the embroidered damask chaise. *Paul's mother doesn't seem so formidable now,* she thought. *She's just an old woman whose husband has no legs and whose home is being sold out from under her. Not so different from my own mother.* She cast about for words that might be comforting.

"Paul and I will get along. In Paris we ate rutabaga soup and rode bicycles. We want to live simply."

The Countess's cheeks turned red and she sat up suddenly. "You cannot know what it is like to live with a man who has no prospects. How will you put bread in your children's mouths? You think Paul will be able to give them what they need? He is his father over again. Nothing but talk and art. At least his father had an estate, an income. Paul will have nothing. Do you understand? Nothing at all." She fell back on the chaise and stared out the doors into the garden, where fall leaves were beginning to drop on the flagstone walks.

"I expect to work hard," Claire said finally, when the other woman kept silent. "Maybe I can earn some money." *I know I sound like the daughter of tradesmen because I am, and do not care.*

"Paul says you play the piano." The Countess turned her head and looked hard into Claire's eyes. "Surely you do not mean to perform?" She put her hands over her face. "Once the de Montforts were patrons of the arts. Patrons, you understand, not performers." The Countess sat up straight and rocked to and fro like a mourner. "We were always the ones others had to please," she said, half to herself. "When you have nothing left, then you must be a performer, pleasing others. Paul calls that being an artist."

Claire turned her back on the other woman and walked over to the piano. "This may be a new sort of world," she said, "but it needs what we have to offer. I'm glad I've got something that's needed. If people give me money for what I do, so much the better."

Letting her fingers run up and down the keyboard, she checked to see if the piano were hopelessly out of tune. *A little off*, she thought, *but only a musician would notice.* Not caring how big a sound she made, Claire crashed into a Chopin étude, letting her hands have their way, remembering what they knew. Forgetting that the melancholy Countess de Montfort lay on the damask chaise longue behind her, Claire gathered up the sound in her fingertips and let it spread across the keyboard until the fragile instrument trembled. Then she played a quiet song, one of those she had made up for Dora and Maxi. As she played and remembered the two children who once sat beside her, she was suddenly unable to go on.

"Keep playing, my dear," the Countess said. "It is very good. Very pleasing."

"I haven't played in a long while," Claire replied, getting up abruptly. "There's been a war in between now and when I last played." She looked out the glass doors and sighed, thinking of her lost life, her mother busy in the kitchen, Dora and Maxi beside her on the piano bench.

Paul's mother crossed the room and laid a tentative hand on Claire's arm. "Perhaps it is not so bad to perform," she said. "Now, of all times, we need to hear music."

When Paul came from his interview with old Count de Montfort, he said very little, just took Claire's hand and led her upstairs to the room that would be hers until their wedding the following week. She wanted to tell him that his mother was no longer acting like a stranger, but he seemed too far away. Claire reached up and slid her arms around his shoulders, wanting him to hold her close to him and go as far as they could allow themselves to go in the making of love. Instead, he kissed her lightly on the forehead, staring somewhere above her. His body was stiff, on guard, unavailable as a stranger's. Whatever his father had said to him about Courtrai, about soldiering, about marriage, was apparently not for her ears.

The whole week before the wedding, Claire waited for Paul's father to summon her for inspection, but the old man remained secluded, holding to his rule of seeing no one but his wife, son, and valet. Sometimes, when she was out walking in the gardens, Claire would see a frail figure in a wheelchair sitting on the upstairs balcony. Once she waved, but he turned away, wheeling himself back through the double doors. *Maybe he has heard that his son is about to marry into a family of vintners and performers,* she thought. That afternoon, when Paul came out to join her on the veranda after tea, Claire asked him whether his father objected to their marriage or was just holding himself aloof for his own reasons.

Paul sat down on a stone bench and held his hands around one knee, rocking a little. "My father always has reasons," he said after a while, keeping his face turned aside, "and he always lets you know them, however unreasonable they are."

"He might be right in this case," Claire said in a low voice, wanting to put her hand on his, but not daring to. *I'm afraid some frowning parent will be looking out a window at us and think me brazen.* “Maybe he objects to me as a daughter-in-law.”

“Not everything is about you, Claire.” Paul said. “”It is I whom he thinks am not good enough. My father says I am a failure and wonders what kind of woman would want me.” He got up and began to walk with long steps down the grand path, as if trying to get away from her, the house, and this strange father of his who thought him worthless.

“But why?” Claire followed along behind him, trying to keep up. “He's the one who's losing Champs-de-lys. He made the bad investments, not you. Maybe he's mad at himself.”

“And did losing the estate bother you? I suppose my mother told you there is nothing left.” Paul stood still, looking over her head at the house behind them. His voice was harsh and distant, like his mother's when she had told Claire they had no money. “Perhaps you assumed that all titled people are rich. Not so.”

Tears gathering in her eyes, Claire stopped beside him and reached up to touch his face. He seemed to be another man than the one who in Paris had told her what made him sad or happy or perplexed. *That other man let me into his deepest heart and made me welcome. This new one, this cold aristocrat, is a stranger.* Claire could hear her father's voice telling her he had known better than she did about what to expect from such people, and for a moment she wondered if he had been right.

“Don't be mad at me just because your father is mad at you,” Claire said, trying to keep her voice steady, so he would not know how hurt she was. “He's just taking it out on you that he's crippled and poor.”

“I am not angry,” Paul said, brushing her hands away. “What goes on between and my father and me is private.”

“Private, private, that's the way of everything here.” Claire kicked some stones out of her way. “Ever since I came to this house I've felt alone. Shut out. Maybe you've changed your mind about getting married. Maybe your mother changed your mind.”

She could hear the hysteria in her tone and hated it. *I wish I could tell him how I need him to stop talking in that awful, alien voice and hold me, not saying anything except that he's sorry.* As she thought back over their time together, she realized that he had never apologized for anything, never admitted being in the wrong.

“That is nonsense,” Paul told her firmly, taking her arm and walking briskly up the pebbled path back to the house. “My mother tries to get her way, it is true. She twists the truth to her advantage, and so do you. I must tell you Claire, that I resent being manipulated and would prefer that you not do it.”

Claire broke away from him and ran into the house, using the servant's staircase to get up her room, so that she would not run into the Countess. She had a bitter taste in her mouth, and spat noisily into the china bowl on her dresser. *I wasn't manipulative,* she said to herself. *How could he think so? I just want to be close to him. I just want to know how he feels and not have him push me away.* She paused in front of the mirror, rubbing her eyes until they burned. *I'll look ugly at dinner if I don't stop crying*. She held a wet cloth over her eyes. Paul might feel she was manipulating him if she appeared red-eyed and miserable. *He must never, never think that*, she said to herself, wondering if it were true that she had done what he accused her of. *Yes, I want him to be sorry for hurting me. Why not? How can I live with a man who turns off his feelings when I open up to him?* She could see his face as it had looked in the garden, deep lines around the mouth and between the eyebrows, engraved by the unforgiving spirit within him. The image brought her up short. *He can't forgive himself, and he thinks I won't forgive him either.* She lay down and pulled a quilt over her to stop her shivering. *I am about to marry a man who wants nothing to do with his feelings. Or mine.* She pressed her face into her pillow until she could hardly breathe.

Early in the evening Paul left a blazing bouquet of flowers at her door, with a note telling her that to him she was just such a flower as these, beautiful and loved. After dinner, they walked again in the gardens, and he kissed her eyes, her cheeks, her lips. *It may be the only way he can apologize,* she thought, *and I guess it will have to do*. That night she went to sleep feeling cold and lonely in the five-hundred-year-old bed of Paul's ancestors.

An old friend of the Countess gave Claire away at the altar because her father was not there to do it. A few of her school friends had come from Rheims to be her bridesmaids. Since no relatives sat on her side of the church, Claire agreed that the Countess should tell the ushers to fill it up with the overflow of society guests. Paul stood at the communion rail, dressed in a black swallowtail coat, his face as still and far away as it had been the day of their quarrel in the gardens.

His hand was cold when he took hers, and his lips barely brushed against her mouth at the end of the ceremony. Claire felt still unmarried as she walked out of the church. In the nave, where a mirror hung, she saw her mother-in-law's tall form reflected as she greeted guests. In the mirror also was her own bright, smiling face surrounded by white tulle veiling. She was surprised at how happy she looked and felt she had already become able to produce feelings on demand, as the Countess clearly did. Claire drank uncounted glasses of champagne thrust at her by waiters.

"My dear, let me introduce the Countess de la Roche," Paul's mother said. "Claire's father is the General Leclerq who helped de Gaulle defeat the Pétain regime," she added, and Claire's mouth closed hard. She realized she was being used as a counter in the great game of *l'affaire.*

"Really!" said the other woman, a stout dowager in lavender silk. "You must be quite at home in society, then."

"No, my father's father was a winemaker in Le Marais," she said to the duchess. "Nothing more."

Paul hunched his shoulders a little and looked away, pulling at her to come with him down the hall.

"It was very good wine," Claire called back over her shoulder, one hand on her pearl tiara to keep it straight. "Our family won a hundred francs for it in a contest."

Claire caught a glimpse of her mother-in-law's pale mouth turned down at the corners, as Paul jerked his new wife through a little door near the front veranda.

"She is about to lose this house," he whispered harshly, "and everyone knows it. Yet you had to cut her down like that. You have a hard heart, Claire, and I am sorry to see it."

She looked down at her pearl-trimmed shoes, thinking she should not have drunk so much champagne. Pastor Vence used to say that indulgence in wine made the tongue flap like a beached fish. Now she had humiliated Paul, the Countess, and herself. *God help me, I'll never take another drink. Somehow wine brings out the worst in me and makes me hurt people.*

Paul left her on the balcony of the ballroom, saying she should wait there until his return. After pulling off her veil and tiara, Claire wrapped them into a ball and wedged it into a big vase. Without the long veil, she could dance, and Claire meant to dance in freedom, enjoying at least those few moments of her wedding that were not prescribed down to the last detail.

As they danced, Paul seemed to forget the insult to his mother. He held Claire tightly and spun her around the room until her head was dizzy. The champagne she had drunk made her feel dizzier still. At the end of the evening, she wilted on his arm, several pearl buttons having burst on the tight bodice of her dress. Paul said goodnight to the guests and half-carried Claire up to their room.

Once it had been his parents' bed chamber, lying between the two rooms in which the Count and Countess de Montfort now lived apart from each other. Paul waited in the hall while Claire undressed. She lay half-drunk and faintly nauseated on the silken white sheets. Paul got into bed next to her after undressing in the dark and began to run his hands tentatively over her. It tickled too much for Claire not to laugh, and she hiccupped, feeling a foul taste in her mouth. "I've never done this before," she said. "Have you?"

Her words sounded fuzzy and she could hardly make them out. "I mean, could you let me know what I'm supposed to do?" Claire spoke slowly and politely, feeling a vague desire to be helpful or at least not get in the way of whatever it was Paul had in mind.

"That hurt," she cried suddenly, the bad taste rising again. "You hurt me."

"Oh," Paul said in a small, disappointed voice, pulling back.

Claire leaned over the side of the bed, saying in a tight voice, "Paul, I'm drunk. Don't touch me." She gagged once, then threw up champagne and canapés all over the hand-woven, antique Flemish carpet at the bedside.

"I'll clean it tomorrow," she whispered, understanding finally that she had spoiled her first act of love. *For sure, I'll never take another drop of wine,* she vowed.

"No, I'll take care of it. Stay there." She heard him moving about in the dark, and then felt him wipe her face and mouth gently with a wet towel. "Goodnight, poor drunk little girl," she heard him say before she fell asleep.

When she was awake in the morning, Paul was holding her close. "Will you be sick again?" he asked, cradling her head in both hands and looking into her face.

"Was I sick?" Claire only half-remembered the night before and decided not to remember anything at all. She wanted to remember only what was happening between them now. *It was a lot better than being drunk,* Claire thought. *Love was better than wine, anytime.* She felt she was drowning in love, dying in it, and coming back to life.

Finally Paul lay down next to her and put his head on her pillow. "Don't you remember how sick you were?"

"I don't remember a thing." She almost believed herself and from then on could not be sure what had actually happened between them on their wedding night. "Only this morning, is all."

"Then that is what I will remember too," Paul said, his breath heavy and deep, as if he had already fallen asleep. "What a good morning it is."

She lay with her head turned toward him and watched the lines in his face become smooth in sleep. *I made a poor start,* Claire thought. *God, help me to love Paul as you love him, not just so he will love me back.* Finally she went to sleep herself, not waking until the church bells rang at noon.

Claire had hoped to meet her father-in-law after the wedding, at least, but not even then would he allow her into his room. He wanted only those who had known him when he was whole to see him now. Those for whom he would be nothing but a cripple, he would not see at all. He had, however, sent her through Paul an antique pearl cross on a gold chain as a wedding gift, for which she thanked him in a note that was never answered.

On their way to Calais, to take the channel boat for England, Paul told her that his father's heart was giving out. A violent arrhythmia had begun on the occasion of Paul's visit to his father's room, just after the couple had come from Paris. This time Claire knew better than to ask what had been said that could have wrenched that tired old heart off its moorings. It might have been the incident at Courtrai, whatever that was, or the marriage, or a disagreement over the bad investments that were making necessary the sale of Champs-de-lys. To bring back the cold, distant Paul who had introduced himself to her in the gardens, before their marriage, was the last thing Claire wanted to do. Ever since they had come from Carcassonne on their way to London, Paul had more and more left behind that brooding other self. During their wedding trip, she had had only a moment's glimpse of the Paul who was an enemy to both her and to himself, and she wanted no more pain than that.

She had dared to ask Paul as they were getting ready to leave the estate, "Are we going to go up and say good-by to your father?"

Paul stopped packing and did not move for a moment. "No, I have already said what I had to say. My father does not care for sentimental occasions, either comings or goings. He would rather just repeat the daily routine so that nothing is demanded of him but correctness. Now, more than ever, he goes through only the motions of living rather than the fact of it." The big black leather bag that held their clothes was closed hard and snapped shut.

"He's angry, then," she said, wanting to back out of the conversation into generalities. "Anger, I've heard, is the only correct emotion for a soldier."

"I suppose it is," Paul replied, starting down the hall ahead of her. "But I am the last person to ask, not being much of a soldier myself, according to my father."

So Courtrai and the lost battalion, not marriage to a bourgeois girl, was the source of Paul's quarrel with his father, Claire thought, resolving to ask no more about the matter. She took Paul's free hand as they went down the stairs and laid it against her cheek. "No one needs soldiers now, anyway," she said. "The war's over."

Paul sighed and the lines around his mouth deepened. "For some men, the war is never over. My father is one of them. Maybe I am too."

The Count de Montfort might not care so much for war, Claire reflected while looking out the window of the train, *if he allowed himself to see the results.* Sitting in his study at Champs-de-lys, he could not, of course, imagine the rubble heaps and chasms she had seen all the way from Carcassonne to Calais. Children played alongside the roped-off wastelands and waved to the train as it passed. Claire waved back, thinking that on the dunghills of war, these children were the flowers. Despite the deaths of young soldiers, women kept bearing children, a triumph of hope over experience.

Claire imagined that perhaps a child was growing in her already, and wondered if after wars, women always had this fierce longing for babies, to balance old losses. She closed her eyes and leaned her head back, letting it bounce against the little white doily on the seat top. *If only the lost ones could be replaced,* she thought, *but lost children can never be replaced.* Claire had once planned to name her first children after Dora and Maxi, but now she decided against it. Handing over their names to someone else would mean that the two children had been given up for dead, and Claire would not give them up. For her there would be only one Dora, one Maxi.

"Now that we are on our way," Paul said, pulling a folded paper out of his coat pocket, "I will show you what the British War Office sent me on Henry Harrison."

Claire reached out and took the letter. "I didn't know you had an answer. Now we can find him, Paul."

"Not so fast," he said, staring out the window. "Henry died in the Normandy invasion."

Claire shook her head silently and put one hand on Paul's knee. *Poor Henry.* She could still see his buck-toothed grin as he gave a refugee child some candy. *Henry was the good sort of soldier,* she said to herself, *the kind that never becomes a general, never sends another man to his death.* She read over the letter from the War Office, shaping every word with her lips because the English was so hard for her to follow.

5, July, 1945

Dear Captain de Montfort:

We are sorry to inform you that your friend, Sgt. Henry Harrison of the 107th, was killed in action on the Normandy coast in the invasion of 1943. He was buried on the beach. As for his family, his mother and sister still live in London at 129 Prince Edward Street. They may be a further source of information for you. No record exists in our files of any children whom

Henry Harrison might have brought with him from France. We would encourage you to contact the orphanages in Dover and London, also the International Red Cross regarding these children...

"At least we know he had a family," Claire said, folding the letter and putting it in her purse. "At least we have a place to start."

Even before finding a hotel room, Paul and Claire went to talk to the Harrison women on Prince Edward Street. They were let in by a tall, lanky woman, who brought them into the parlor of Henry's white-haired mother. She was rocking in her chair by the window, clutching the edges of her shawl together with lumpy, arthritic fingers. Mrs. Harrison seemed unsure whether or not she was supposed to recognize them. At first, she was silent. Only when her daughter had served the tea did she speak.

"Henry told me about his friends," Mrs. Harrison said. "He called them his buddies and liked to talk about them."

Paul put down his teacup and clasped his hands together around one knee, rocking slightly. "Did he ever mention a Captain de Montfort at Dunkirk?" he asked. "Please try to remember, Mrs. Harrison. Did he say anything about helping a girl and two children?"

The old woman's eyes faded under a veil of tears. "Henry was killed on the beach," she murmured. "How could he tell me about people he helped?"

"Mummy, the captain means another beach," Miss Harrison said, stroking her mother's hair back under the lace cap. "Not the one where Henry was killed."

Mrs. Harrison shook her head so vigorously that the cap shifted and released more snowy, fine hair. "No, I think not. But Henry always helped anyone he could," she said. "He was such a good boy."

"Paul, ask her if anyone else might know," Claire whispered in French. "School friends? A girl, perhaps?"

After Paul translated Claire's questions, Mrs. Harrison put one hand on her forehead as if to coax her memory into cooperating. "As a young boy, he went to St. Hilary's School, then, when he was older, Highgate. Then the London School of Economics. Henry was very clever, you know. But he had to drop out after two years, because of the war." She put a handkerchief over her eyes and then stuffed it in her sleeve. "His fiancée married an American officer not long ago and went to Japan. I do not know her married name." Her voice trailed off and she gazed out the window again.

"You have been a great help, Mrs. Harrison," Paul said, standing up. "We will start with the London School of Economics. Perhaps he was in a society of some kind and had friends there." Mrs. Harrison did not answer, and he leaned over, raising her hand to his lips. "Henry's death was a loss to us all," he murmured. "You have our sympathy."

Henry's sister took them to the door. "My brother had no children with him," she said emphatically. "And didn't mention any during the short time he was here. You had better try the orphanages."

That week, besides contacting orphanages in the vicinity of London, Paul ran advertisements in the London *Times* that no one answered. Toward the end of their stay, Paul sat on the bed in their hotel room calling a long list of telephone numbers, while Claire lay down with a damp cloth over her eyes. Since she had been to see the Harrisons, she had developed a pain in her forehead that reminded her of the one she had waked up with on the Dunkirk beach.

"No associations," Paul said, hanging up and making a note on the paper in front of him. "Apparently, Henry was a loner at school. At Highgate, he was on the soccer team, but dropped out after a year. No particular friends there. I will try St. Hilary's again. All I have ever gotten when I've called before is a busy signal. Maybe someone has taken the phone off the hook."

This time a voice answered at St. Hilary's, but after a brief conversation with the person at the other end, Paul hung up. Slipping off his shoes, Paul lay down beside Claire. "The vicar and his family are away in the Cotswolds," he said. "Medical emergency or some such thing. But the secretary assures me that the school has no recent records on Henry Harrison. She has been at the school for some years and does not remember him at all." Paul loosened his tie and folded his hands behind his head. "It seems like the war opened up a sinkhole in everyone's head and all the past just slid into it. Disappeared. No one wants to remember."

"I wouldn't want to either," Claire said, turning over and putting an arm across his chest, "except for Dora and Maxi. They aren't just memories to me. They're part of me. I couldn't lose them if I wanted to."

Paul reached out and ran his fingers through her hair, letting the curling ends wrap around his hand. "Well, you may not see them again, Claire," he said finally, "You may have to give up and say they are gone, along with a lot else."

Claire leaned against his chest and cried. "I'm sick of war," she said. "Sick of losing people. I want to go where there aren't any wars, Paul. I want to go to America."

"To live there?" Paul sat up and looked at her, his hazel eyes wide. "Whatever would we do in America?"

"Start over," Claire said firmly, surprised at how sure she was of what they would do. "Why should we stay here? There's no living to be made, and all people talk about is who their ancestors were. Maybe that's because they don't see themselves as having any future. And maybe they're right. There's nothing to stay here for," she ended, shaking her head.

"It is a sort of life," Paul objected, his voice uncertain. "The only one we know." He ran one finger up and down a valley between two ridges of chenille.

"I want to know something besides this little life," Claire said, putting her face close to his. "Don't you? What kind of artist can you be here? You've told me that you just paint what everyone's always painted. Your children will have no imagination either, and neither will their children. They'll just sit in a tired country with nothing to think about except the feud with the de la Roches and where the servants might have put the marrow spoons."

"You really want to leave? You really want to go to America?" Paul lay back and stared at the ceiling. "I suppose we could use the money from the sale of the estate to get started somewhere else. But America?"

"If you don't like it, we don't have to stay," Claire added eagerly. "We can always come back to France." More and more she felt like going to America was a call from God to let the past go and to empty her soul of all that had burdened it before.

"No." Paul pressed his palms into his closed eyes. "Coming back is not so easy. I would never come back. Homecomings are too much grief."

Knowing Paul's father was on his mind, Claire said nothing, but just ran her hands lightly over his chest as she kissed him. *Since we can't find Dora and Maxi in England,* she thought vaguely as he began to return her kisses and to slip the robe from around her shoulders, *I might as well go to America where so many lost children have gone, maybe Dora and Maxi, too.* Then she gave herself to Paul's love-making and stopped thinking.

When they arrived back at Champs-de-lys, the Countess met them on the front steps of the chateau. One look at her face, damp and red with crying, told Claire that more than dispossession was the matter. Throwing her arms around Paul's neck, the Countess rested her face against his.

"Your father," she said, her voice breaking between her words. "Last night. We couldn't reach you."

Paul half-lifted her back up the steps and brought her into the drawing-room before he spoke. His eyes were bright with tears. "He told me I was killing him with what I did," Paul whispered, sinking down beside his mother on the gold-embroidered brocade divan. "Those were his words, that it was I who was killing him." Paul's breath came in gasps, as if breathing hurt, and he put his face in his hands.

Afraid of saying the wrong thing, Claire said nothing, but stood silently next to her husband, trying to be available in case he wanted her instead of his mother. He seemed to have forgotten she was in the room.

"Your father was not well this whole last year," the Countess said, laying her hand for a moment on Paul's thick dark hair. "He was angry about what the Nazis did to him, angry at the house being sold, even angry about getting old. None of these things were your fault."

"What he said cannot be unsaid now." Paul brushed his coat sleeve across his eyes. "He wanted me to know his feelings, and I do."

"He died right after signing away the house to the de la Roches." The Countess spoke in a low, mechanical voice, not looking at either of them. "The Duchess is buying our home for her son and his bride. You can imagine how she gloated as she signed the papers. She had to be reminded that the sale is not complete until all the money is in our hands. Since the de la Roche funds are tied up in German munitions and chemical factories, the money will not be available for some time.

Countess de Montfort's mouth closed tightly between sentences, so that her pale lips were one thin line. "Did you know that the francs of people like the de la Roches wound up in Swiss bank accounts? They secretly invested with the Nazis. What a scandal. You might guess the de la Roches would be involved." She let her arms drop to her side. "Well, at least we will have some months here, and you can be sure I will spend the time stripping my house of every little treasure. Not for the new Madame de la Roche to enjoy my Louis Quinze crystal chandelier. We will sell it to the bank and put up one of those nineteenth-century brass horrors." She suddenly stopped running on in her breathless monotone and turned to Paul, her shoulders drooping and her voice uncertain. "Where will we go? Where?"

Claire pictured the three of them living in some dreary Parisian rooming house, Paul taking his mother visiting each afternoon and talking with her in the evening about who among their surviving relatives were listed in the *Almanac de Gotha.*

"Paul and I are going to America," she said, her voice sounding too loud, even to her. Then, to deflect Paul's certain anger at her tactless timing, she added in a gentler tone, "You'll come with us?"

The Countess stared at Claire, clasping her hands together, opening and closing her mouth, no words coming out.

"Later, Claire," Paul said, half-turning toward her as if barely acknowledging her presence in the room. "She cannot talk about it now."

"Am I really to lose everything, then?" The Countess said, her voice shaking. "My country, too?"

Claire came over and sat beside her on the divan. "We've all lost from this war, Mother, and the last one, and the one before that. Nothing's left here for any of us. Next time the Germans decide to invade France, I intend to be somewhere else with my husband and children."

"I could go to live with my aunt in Paris," the Countess murmured. "I could visit you from time to time. Perhaps that would be best."

"Come with us," Paul urged. "I want you to."

Claire held her breath, afraid that Paul would insist on taking his mother to live with them in America, carrying her on his back like Aeneas carried his father from the sack of Troy, and afraid his mother would agree. *The old ones are always right there behind you, not letting you forget the past, always reminding you what was lost when we became children without a home, thrown out of Eden.* Even Dora and Maxi had worn their parents' names and carried identifying letters marking them so they could not begin elsewhere as newborn beings.

But it was those names, Claire said to herself later, as she sat alone in their bedroom, that might someday allow the lost children to be found. *Your name, your past are, after all, what tie you to other people, and that's a good thing. In my family, we had no such ties.* She wished Paul were beside her as she finally gave up her father, knowing she would not see him again. *Without the parent on your back, without your name and faith and origin, you're nothing but a random piece fitting nowhere into the puzzle of this world.* That was why the Lebenthals had made sure Dora and Maxi wore their names and their faith like safe conducts. For as long as they knew where they had come from, they would have some sense of where they were going, and they could not be lost.

4

Dora's Journal

London..............................1948

Now that the war is over, maybe Claire has found a new home, just as Maxi and I have. London doesn't feel like home to me, maybe because there aren't any other Jews in our neighborhood. Maxi and I are outsiders. When we're grown up, we'll probably go to America, or maybe Israel, a brand new country. Now, Israel would be a fine home for a Ben-Ari, I think, but Father Jonas says it's full of sand and swamps and marauding Arabs. I asked him how many Jews are there, and he said only about thirty thousand before the Aliyah, when the immigrants started coming last year from Europe. That sounds like rather a lot to me, certainly more than they are in South Kensington. Maybe we will go to Israel, after all.

Maxi says he won't leave England until he at least finishes the sixth form at Highgate, which is the public school he wants to attend. Father Jonas will send him anywhere Maxi wants to go because my brother is a great scholar. He's only fourteen and can read Hebrew better that the pupils in my form read English. Father Jonas is starting him on Greek this term, and a professor at the University of London is teaching him math privately. The professor thinks Maxi should become a theoretical physicist and Father Jonas thinks Maxi should become a biblical scholar. Maxi has decided to become an archeologist. Just now he is making a model of the Temple of Solomon to the exact scale described in the Bible. I'm to landscape the outside when it's all finished, but at the rate he's working, we'll be long gone to Israel by the time the temple is off the drawing boards.

Maxi first got into archeology when we went to stay for two weeks in the Cotswolds, about the time the war ended. We took a cottage near the Vale of the White Horse. Every day Maxi would walk around this chalk figure of a horse that was laid out on the green hill. It was three hundred feet across, so he did a lot of walking. No one knows why the horse was put there or who made it thousands of years ago. But every year, the villagers go out and brush the horse off, picking away the weeds so that the white horse would keep on galloping across that hill forever. The idea of 'forever' always sets Maxi to dreaming.

"Some things last," he would say to me, as we walked together around the chalk figure. "The whole world changes and people die, but they make things like the White Horse that go on and on." He got out the little stone spear tip that he and Father Jonas had dug from a deep pit on Froucester Hill, where it was said that a prehistoric settlement existed long before the Romans occupied Britain. Maxi always carried the flint spear tip with him.

"It's just as if no time had passed, for all this flint knows." He held it up in the sunlight so that its rough-cut facets gleamed. "Eight thousand years ago a caveman carried this around, and now I do. It's all the same to the flint."

"Of course it is," I said, putting some wild flowers carefully in a paper bag, so as not to crush the petals. Later I would use Mrs. Grey's books to figure out what their names were. "Stone isn't alive, not like plants. It can't know anything."

Maxi smiled and put his flint away. "Rocks have been here the longest and will outlast everything else." His eyes were on the horizon, far across the valley. "Rocks are the bones of the earth," he said. "We are only the skin. Not made to last."

Little in Maxi's short life or mine had been permanent, or anything you could count on. So I understood why he loved what could not disappoint him or change. We had thought that once the war was over things would stop changing so fast, but they didn't.

Nothing was the same after Mrs. Grey started losing her mind. She had been walking home from the market at dusk, when one of the last V-2 rockets hit the building next to her. People were blown out of windows and fire burned up the whole block. She didn't come home that night, and when the Civil Patrol found her wandering down by the Thames, she didn't know who she was.

We thought she might get well, but she just sat with her face to the wall, mumbling and crying. Once she pulled out all Father Jonas's books from the shelves and threw them around the room. Another time she ate some rat poison, enough of it to make her turn blue and throw up. By this time, I was taking care of the garden and making meals, as she had taught me to do. At eleven, I was a big girl and could do as much work as a woman. When Mrs. Grey took the poison, Father Jonas decided she would have to live in an asylum out in the country, where doctors could help her get well and where she could see nature, not just city buildings.

So we went on holiday to the Cotswold Hills in August, celebrating the end of the war and delivering Mrs. Grey to her asylum. Poor Father Jonas wasn't in much of a holiday mood. I remember going on a long walk with him over the Ridgeway, a high, winding trail across the top of the hills, like the backbone of some prehistoric beast, as Maxi said. Because rain was expected, we wore our plastic ponchos, which blew straight out behind us like wings. Rain was always expected in the Cotswolds, even more than in London, and we looked forward to tea-time. It was in the Cotswolds that I figured out why English people seemed to have a sort of gentle melancholy about them, even on holiday. They are never really comfortable, what with the damp air and no central heating. Always they're a bit too wet, a bit too cool, to feel in their hearts that things are as they should be. But since they've never known what real comfort is, they expect nothing and take any amount of distress without surprise. Father Jonas was like that, but at times, as on that holiday in the Cotswolds, he could get downright depressed.

"Dora, we may never have Julia back again." He was trudging along, swinging the walking stick he always carried for self-defense. Unlike any other Englishman I have known, he was afraid of dogs and had given Maxi and me elaborate instructions on what to do if one attacked. I remember being put through drills when I had to bend my forearm over my throat and keep my eyes on those of the hypothetical dog, played by Father Jonas, who would growl and snap menacingly.

"Never let them get behind you, Dora," he would say, finishing the lesson, "that's the secret." He had the same theory where his parishioners were concerned, and I would often see our tall, thin Papa held at bay by a churchwoman demanding a position on the vestry. Father Jonas would put his forearm over his ascot tie and keep his eyes on hers, as if he expected her to bare her teeth and lunge. That day on the Ridgeway, I saw no dogs, but Father Jonas seemed to feel as if he were under some invisible attack.

"Until she's well," I said, ignoring his gloomy certainty, "I can keep the house and garden. We'll get along."

"It may be that I can't go on in that parish," Father Jonas said in a low voice. "Perhaps I wasn't called to the ministry after all. It's a silly life, Dora, when all's said and done, visiting old ladies and waving one's hands about during Sunday sermons. I've nothing new to say to them, and they wouldn't listen if I did."

"You have the school," I pointed out, trying to keep my poncho from flying away altogether. "The children need you."

"Do they?" Father Jonas shook his head as he stood looking over the hills, green and rolling as the waves of the sea. "I never meant to teach little children. I was going to be a scholar, teaching at the university. Only I married early and missed the chance. I had thought that perhaps God wanted me to do something, serve some special purpose, and now I don't even know if I believe in God anymore. What sort of vicar can I be, not sure if I believe in God?"

"You sound like Maxi," I said, taking him by the arm and beginning to walk again. "Always thinking that you need to do some big thing just because you survived the war. That's how he feels, you know. Like there must be some reason why he's left over and not someone else. So he thinks he's got to count. You know what I think?"

"What, Dora?" Father Jonas stopped and put his hand under my chin, looking down into my face with a sad sort of smile, his big teeth not looking like an ogre's anymore. "I can never tell what you're thinking, but I always want to know."

"I think you take care of Maxi and me, and we're special. We wouldn't have any kind of life without you, would we?" I felt strong, like a plant with wet greenness rising through me to the top of my head, and I held out my arms, pointing to the hills. "You see how we are only special when someone else thinks we are? You see how no one is special by himself?"

Father Jonas stopped a moment, and then laid his arm over my shoulder as we walked, our feet dampened by the tall, curving grass. "You're saying that my being alone is just an illusion, not real. I'm entangled with God and my parish, you're saying, faith or no faith." He sighed, patted my hair, and let his arm drop. "All right, Dora, I'll stay at St. Hilary's."

In 1950, when I was sixteen, it was my turn to get depressed. I believe it was the first and last time in my life that depression was a word I understood. Maxi had started school at Highgate, where he boarded, and was too busy being a genius to write or visit much. He took special classes at the university in mathematics and chemistry, which he said would be useful for locating and dating archeological finds. His teachers seemed to think they could talk him into becoming a defense scientist. If they had understood that far from wanting to destroy what was on the earth, Maxi wanted to uncover the past so it would never again be lost, they might have saved their breath.

Maxi had told Father Jonas and me over dinner one day, with that faraway look of his, that he wanted to remember as much as God, to forget nothing. The way he could keep numbers and events and places in his memory, you would have thought he was halfway there. Halfway to being God, I mean. I once read a story about an Argentinian who remembered every little thing he had ever seen or heard of. His head was so full it hurt, and he had to lie in his hammock all the time, sick with remembering. Sometimes I was afraid that would happen to Maxi. He used to say that everyone else had a personal past, a family, and a childhood, with photographs and reunions to help them remember, but since he had nothing, there was lots of room in his head for all those facts from books. His classmates called him the Electric Brain, and asked him to do their homework for them during lunch hour. He never had time, though, and spent his lunch hour in the chemistry lab. Since he was carrying university subjects in addition to his fifth form classes, he had to use for himself whatever free time he had. Naturally he had little left for me. Sometimes I visited him in the chemistry lab, learning what I could about what made fertilizers work and why. In fact, fertilizer production became just about the only bond left between my brother and me.

I tried to take up the empty hours with my own schoolwork, the garden, and experimenting with growing vegetables in the greenhouse. My watercress and tomatoes did so well that I could sell my little harvest around the neighborhood. With some of the money I earned, I decided to hire a boy to carry the heavy planters inside for the fall seeding and come over every day to do the watering and weeding.

The first person to apply was Thomas Leighton, who was now studying at vocational school, learning to repair automobiles. He was a big boy still, as he had been when I beat him up in that fight ten years before in St. Hilary's school yard. Now he was better-looking, with a square-jawed freckled face, broad shoulders, and a lopsided, goofy grin. Because he was good at machinery, I gave him the job, hoping I could get him to build a couple of fans that would blow the hot air from the greenhouse into the cold parlor where Father Jonas's fingers turned blue as he worked on his Hebrew texts.

Tom came around every day after he was hired and sometimes stayed for dinner. He liked to talk about the circulating pumps he had in mind for the greenhouse, as soon as the fans were installed.

"No other girl I know has her own business," Tom said one night while we were transplanting tomato seedlings in the greenhouse. "You sure got a lot going for you." He wiped his forehead with one dirty sleeve, leaving a dark streak.

Tom always talked like the men in American movies and sometimes spat on the floor or shifted his cigarette from one side of his mouth to the other. His mannerisms struck me as clumsy, and sometimes I wanted to laugh when he swaggered around, holding his elbows out a bit, moving slowly as if he were too muscle-bound to walk at a normal pace. When he walked that way, he looked to me like a gorilla or a baby who had just gotten himself off the floor into an upright position and wouldn't last long as a biped. But to him, I suppose, the ape walk was a sign of manhood. Perhaps it was so even to me, for I found myself watching him lumber along, his body heavy, swelling with muscular bulk and weight. I probably should not have let him see that I noticed. One night, when Father Jonas was at a church meeting, Tom turned off the greenhouse lights and started kissing me.

At first I didn't move, because the arms around me felt strong and hard, good to lie against, the way water is when you float on your back, not having to move. No one had kissed me on the mouth before, and long, quivering roots seemed to run down my body from the place his lips planted themselves, until my mouth opened up in surprise, letting more kisses in.

"I love you, Dora," he muttered, trying to put his hands where they shouldn't be. "I want to touch you all over."

My hands pushed against his chest, and I turned my face away from his wet mouth. Though I wasn't clear on what exactly I wanted at the time, slowing Thomas Leighton down seemed like a good idea. My hope was to hear something more about how much he loved me and something less about what he wanted to do to me.

"We don't really know each other," I gasped, trying to extricate myself from his tightening arms. "I don't love you yet. Maybe down the line I will. We can talk about it."

Talk was the last thing on Tom's mind. He was like one of his machines, pushing through whatever was in his way, groaning as if he needed an oil job. I was no match for him, and this time it wasn't I who won the fight.

Afterwards, I lay still on the floor, considering the consequences of what he had done. "You might have just started a baby," I said, feeling as though I were talking to someone on the other side of the world. "I guess you never thought about that."

Tom was cheerful and seemed pleased with himself. "Naw," he said. "Prob'ly not. We could go to the movies tomorrow. Want to?"

"Let's get back to the point," I said, pulling my clothes and myself together. "What will I do if there's a baby? Marry you?"

Tom looked blank, then resentful. "Well, we couldn't get married," he said, wiping his sleeve under his nose. "You're a Jew."

My hands dropped to my sides, and I stood looking at him as he buckled his belt. "So was Jesus."

He seemed confused, but finally found some words. "Naw, you're nothing like Jesus. He was holy, not like a Jew."

"You're saying I'm not as good as you are?" I couldn't believe it. Here was this gorilla thinking he was better than Dora Lebenthal, who spoke four languages and ran a gardening business, while he was just a poor shmuck who knew nothing at all.

I was stupefied at first, thinking about how he had said he loved me and then that he couldn't marry a Jew. My hands curled and my nails raked down his cheeks. "You liar," I yelled, kicking him in the knee just as I had when we were kids. "You bloody liar, I'll kill you."

When he fell down on all fours, I kicked his face and pulled his hair with both hands, not noticing that the door of the greenhouse had opened. Father Jonas was suddenly hauling me back, while Tom got to his feet and held both hands over his bleeding mouth.

"Dora!" Father Jonas cried. "What happened? What's he done?"

"Just get him out of here," I repeated over and over. "I'll kill him if I see him again."

Father Jonas sent Tom away, got me upstairs, and sat with me until I went to sleep, stroking my hands and wanting to know what had happened. Time enough for him to know, I said to myself, as I dropped off to sleep, if I turned out to be pregnant. But time came and went and I wasn't. The gorilla child, if it had materialized, had failed to stick, so I didn't have to tell Father Jonas after all. But I didn't forget what Tom Leighton had said before, or what he said afterward, and I was very, very depressed. St. Hilary's no longer seemed like home, and I began to long for a place where no one would humiliate me for being who I was.

It was at that time I began to ask Father Jonas what more he could find out about our parents. Maxi and I had hoped that after the dust of the war had settled, we might get a letter from Germany or America or Israel saying that our parents had located us and were on their way to London. After the first year, we didn't talk to each other about that hope anymore, nor did we run to the post box at delivery time. Being pretty sure Claire had died on the beach at Dunkirk, we didn't even hope for a letter from Rheims. It seemed that by crossing the Channel, we ourselves had died and gone to another world. Except for our bears and the letter pinned to my coat, we had nothing to remind us of our family or country or religion.

Father Jonas had to prepare Maxi for the Bar Mitzvah, since the nearest rabbi lived so far away. Actually Maxi prepared himself, for the most part, and Father Jonas just got him the books he needed or listened to him recite. It was a very small celebration when my brother became a man, for Father Jonas and I were the only ones there, besides the rabbi. After the ceremony, Father took us to dinner at the Cheshire Cheese, but still we missed the feeling of a family party at home, the way I remember it being done in Frankfurt.

"Well, Maxi," said Father Jonas, rubbing his hands together briskly before attacking his Yorkshire pudding. "Now that you're a man, you should be able to decide what you want for your Bar Mitzvah gift."

Maxi pushed his plate away and sat back, pondering, his thumbs circling each other in his lap as they always did when he was thinking.

"Could we go to Frankfurt? The three of us?" He passed his hand self-consciously through the short dark curls on his forehead, then reached back to see if the unfamiliar yarmulkh was still there. "It's probably too expensive, but Dora's put by some money from the greenhouse, and I've been tutoring students in math. We could help pay for the trip."

"You know I wrote to your parents' company at the end of the war," Father Jonas said gently, putting down his fork. "There was no word of them at all. When I wrote to the American Occupation Forces, it was the same. Would there really be much point in going?"

"It's the closest thing we have to a childhood home," I put in, glad that Maxi had voiced the idea. Since the night in the greenhouse with Thomas Leighton, I had begun to feel the need for a place I could truly call home. "We could walk around where we used to live. Ask people what they remember about our parents. Until we're on the scene, we can't know they're really gone."

Father Jonas never could stand against the two of us and didn't succeed this time. We reminded him that we could practice our German, and this educational aspect of the journey to Frankfurt gave him an excuse to surrender. Father Jonas was, as he himself put it, an irrepressible pedagogue and insisted that we read about all the historical sites of the city, so that no time would be wasted wandering aimlessly about.

When we got to Frankfurt, we found that nothing was left of the old city. Our home, on the west side of town, had been buried under one of the many new high-rise apartment buildings. In between the tall, rectangular concrete boxes were pits of rubble. Perhaps one of them, I thought as we walked through our old neighborhood, contained what was left of Maxi's baby cot, of my parents' books, of my antique Swiss dollhouse. Once I bent over the edge of a rubble pit and stared, imagining that I saw a gold bracelet just like the one my mother had worn to parties. But it was only sunlight glinting on a torn piece of gold foil from a cigarette wrapper. A gust of wind blew it away.

In one place near the river, where nothing was left but broken concrete, a playground had been built. Father Jonas sat sipping German beer at an outdoor café, watching Maxi and me climb up the rock pile in the center of the little park. Maxi was drawn to the pile because from the top he could look down into an excavation opened years before by an American bomb.

The remains of a Roman villa were fifteen feet below, and its mosaic floor was in a lot better shape than the houses that used to stand on this piece of ground. Maxi wanted to climb down and touch the mosaic, but the park guard stopped him when he tried. So he and I sat on top of the rock pile, just looking down into two thousand years of history.

"Two thousand years from now," he said, "a couple of children may look into a hole over Friedenstrasse and see the rubble that's left of our house." He paused and leaned his head back, staring at the heavy gray clouds rolling low overhead. "I've seen pictures of the excavations in Jerusalem. You can look down into digs at five thousand years' worth of history as if no time has passed. This floor is nothing to what we could see in Jerusalem."

"Next year, in Jerusalem," I said out loud, not meaning to, not remembering at first where I had heard the phrase. Suddenly a picture of our mother flashed before my eyes. She was sitting at the table in our Frankfurt house and saying these same words in a slow, faraway voice, as if echoing other mothers as they had echoed theirs, back to the time of the Diaspora. That was when Jews had just left a Jerusalem destroyed by the Romans and comforted each other with the words "next year." It seemed for a moment that I was not myself, sitting on that rock pile, but a hollow tube, an instrument out of which at this moment words were blown like music, not my words, not my music, but those of other voices that had come and gone like windblown leaves.

Always it was next year, and always in Jerusalem, as if neither time nor space were real, and we were all everywhere at once, the way Father Jonas used to say God is. A person could never really tell who he might run into next, someone from his past or someone from his future, since past and future are illusions. Only the present is real, Maxi tells me. Where we actually live is now. The thought made me happy, for I felt it proved we would see our parents and Claire again and that nothing is ever lost.

I held Maxi's hand tightly, and we sat not saying anything for a few minutes before going back down the rock pile to find Father Jonas. The three of us walked through the whole west side of the city, finding no landmarks, nothing to remind us of what we had lost except rubble-filled bomb pits. The one building left standing, Father Jonas told us was the I.G. Farben headquarters, where our parents had once worked, and where Father Jonas had made inquiries after the war about where our parents might have been taken by the Nazis.

As we walked up the long drive toward the Farben Building, he also told us that some ugly things had been revealed about this great chemical and drug cartel since the war's end. It was no accident that the sprawling glass giant had been spared bombing, for its interests were closely tied to those of American corporations with voices that the Pentagon listened to. The official reason for sparing Farben was that the U.S. occupation forces would need such a building as a headquarters. Father Jonas, however, was as suspicious of this explanation as he was of dogs. He said it was certainly odd that Forrestal, Roosevelt's Secretary of the Navy, then Secretary of Defense, had also been president of the Vanderzell Oil Corporation, which had been partners with Farben long before the war. Naturally, he and others in high places would protect their financial interests by seeing to it that American bombardiers left Farben alone.

"But how could American companies have helped the Nazis?" Maxi demanded, his face looking as startled as when Thomas Leighton had senselessly attacked him. Maxi was too logical to comprehend violence. Though he was the Electric Brain of Highgate School, where human motives were concerned, he was so dumb he needed a keeper. "Nazis were killing American soldiers. No American would help them do that."

"Money, my boy," Father Jonas sighed, pulling open the tall glass door into the foyer of the chemical building. "Vanderzell was supplying trucks and engines to the Germans all through the war. No matter who won the war, Vanderzell would prosper. Don't forget that this world is run for profit, Maxi, not for God or truth. Now that you're a man, you must remember that. Put it away with all the thousand other things that remarkable brain of yours can't forget."

I had thought Father Jonas was just being his usual pessimistic self, quick to believe the worst of a society that had lived godlessly and allowed his beloved St. Paul's to be destroyed. Later, I was not so sure he was wrong. But at that moment, I could only look around me at the sunlight streaming through the glass and clutch Maxi's hand. Our parents had walked through this door, come to work here every day. Right here, where the metal taps of our shoes rang on the marble floor.

We waited while Father Jonas asked questions at the pharmaceutical division and finally at the top executive offices, where he hoped to find someone who had known the Lebenthals. Each time, he said, it was as if he were asking about the existence of angels or elves. No one had ever heard of them.

"It makes no sense," Father Jonas said, his hands shoved in his pockets as he walked down a tiled hall, head hunched into his shoulders. "They were here only ten years ago. We know that. Why no records and no memories?"

On impulse, he stopped to talk to a stooped, gray-haired lady with a mop and bucket. She was washing the floor outside the pharmaceutical offices.

"Lebenthal?" The old woman raised her head and pushed a lock of hair behind her ear. "Yes, I knew them. Long ago, before the bombs, there were Lebenthals here."

Her eyes were vague and she turned her head from one of us to the other. "They were kind," she said. "I remember how they would give me hot chocolate on snowy days, and sometimes clothes for my granddaughter." Her eyes focused for a moment and she reminded me a bit of Mrs. Grey about to be lucid for a brief time.

"We're their children," I cried taking the old woman's hand. "We've come back!"

"Children?" Her pale blue eyes went vague again, the moisture heavy at the corners. "Don't recall any children."

"Can you tell us who else might have known the Lebenthals?" Father Jonas urged. "Anyone at all?"

"The president of the company, maybe." The woman looked doubtful. "Or the man whose office is in here?" Her mop gestured at the door of the pharmaceutical division chief.

"We've tried them." I shook her arm a little, hoping she wouldn't drift off the way Mrs. Grey always did. "They don't know." In a lower voice I added, "Or won't tell. There must be someone else. Please try to think who. Maybe someone who's not here anymore?"

"Herr Schroeder," the woman said suddenly. "Heinrich Schroeder, over on Sudenstrasse, not far. He was head of the pharmaceutical division, but he's retired now. Herr Schroeder would know about the Lebenthals."

Father Jonas fished in his pocket and gave her a whole *deutschmark*, then rushed us off to the telephone down in the lobby. When we called the only Schroeder on Sudenstrasse, a woman answered coldly, saying that Herr Schroeder was resting. He had recently almost died from a heart attack and was seeing no one. Father Jonas overrode her, saying we would be there shortly.

"It's about the Lebenthals," he said as he hung up. "Tell Herr Schroeder that their children have come from far away, and he must see them."

Sudenstrasse, like all the other streets in Frankfurt, was straight, wide, and lined with tall apartment houses, white and even as rows of false teeth. Herr Schroeder's building was like all the others, clean and bare, the way you would expect a hospital to be, not like a home. The apartment even smelled like a hospital when the old woman who tended Herr Schroeder opened the door for us.

"He says he will speak with you." She stood by the door doubtfully, her hands folded under her starched white apron. "But he's very weak. You can talk for a few moments only."

We followed Father Jonas into the sunny, stark room, over to the bed under high, curtainless windows. On the bed, under a quilt of multi-colored squares, lay an old man with white curly hair, thin on top and falling in wisps over his ears. His skin was blotched with red, and his long thin nose seemed to split his face in two, the cheeks on either side sloping down from the nose like sagging laundry.

"You are the Lebenthal children?" He spoke in a voice that quavered as if blown by a high wind. "You were very small when I put you on the train. Ten years ago, was it? Twelve? Very small, you were. So big now." His eyes closed, watered, and opened again.

"You remember." I felt my breath rush out and realized that I had been holding it a long time. Maxi and I both came near the old man's bed and stood over him. "We were small, yes. Too small to remember very much."

"It was almost too late," Schroeder said, the blotches darkening as he exerted himself. "That afternoon the Gestapo came for your family."

"Aunt Rachel too?" Maxi knew our aunt by name only, but since she was all the family we had besides our parents, he wanted to know.

"I think so. There was a woman who recognized them in the Gestapo wagon." Schroeder took a few deep breaths and began speaking again. "You see, they wanted to question your parents, not just arrest them like the others. That's why we had to get you children away."

"Question? About what?" I sat down on the edge of the bed and took the old man's hands in mine. "Something to do with their work at Farben?"

"Perhaps the Gestapo thought your parents had given information to the enemy. That's why they wanted you children. No parents could disobey the Gestapo if their children were hostages and might be tortured."

"What did my parents know?" I squeezed his hands, trying to push some life into that failing voice.

"So much was going on," Schroeder whispered, the blotches now dark as blood against his pale skin. "Farben was producing poison gas, you see. Your parents knew that. Also, Farben was the secret financial supporter of Hitler. Without Farben, he could never have come to power. Your parents, being highly placed in the company, knew that too."

"The company must have been controlled by the Nazis," Maxi said, kneeling on the other side of the bed, his face close to Schroeder's. "Who could our parents have told without their being caught doing it?"

"Ah, they were idealists, the Lebenthals," said the old man. "As many of us were in those days. They were going to tell the authorities in Geneva about the poison gas. They had prepared a statement for the world press about Farben's support of Hitler and about Vanderzell's support of Farben. I warned them to keep quiet, but they wouldn't listen."

"And because Farben was trying to keep its corporate American friends," Father Jonas said softly, "Farben didn't want Vanderzell's dealings with Hitler to be known."

Schroeder nodded. "So the Lebenthals were marked, not only as Jews but as enemies of the state," he said. "Goering wanted to know what they had revealed to Geneva. When they were arrested, orders went out for the children to be picked up too. I'm happy to see that for once, the children managed to escape. I'm very happy." His eyes closed again and his head sank into the pillow.

"Herr Schroeder," I asked him, my heart seeming to beat high in my throat as I spoke, "what we want to know is, could they still be alive? If they had information the Nazis wanted, could they have been kept alive?"

"I do not believe, knowing what they knew, that they would have been allowed to survive," Schroeder said, his voice thinner and weaker than before. "They were taken to Bergen-Belsen. Very few survived that place."

"Father Jonas kept his hand on my shoulder. "Surely someone must have come back with word of them."

Schroeder's mouth twisted as if he had just eaten something bitter. "The camp records," he said, his breath laboring. "In Israel now, I think. If anyone knows what happened, you might find such a person there. Anyone who stayed in Germany has forgotten. Only the Jews who have forgotten would want to stay."

"Herr Schroeder is tired now," the woman caretaker said, standing by his couch like a guard and pointing at the door."I knew talk would tire him. You must go now."

Maxi bent over the exhausted old man. "Thank you for helping my parents," he said softly, kissing the pale, blotched forehead. "Thank you for our lives."

Schroeder opened his eyes and lifted his arm in farewell. Then the woman in the white apron hurried us all out.

"It's a dead end, isn't it?" I asked Father Jonas when we were out in the hall again. "That's all we're going to learn."

"If there's any more to know," Father Jonas said, leaning his finger into the elevator button until the fingertip turned white. "You won't find it out in Germany. Only in Israel. Yes, I'm afraid Frankfurt is a dead end."

I didn't say anything, but already I knew that Israel was where Maxi and I would go. If either of our parents had survived, they would be there. If not, the records of their death would be. But for now, I didn't say what I was thinking.

We found another dead end when we stopped in Rheims, on the way home, looking for Claire. In that city too, new white concrete buildings were on their way up, or already had filled gaps in the empty, broken streets of the city. Where Claire had lived, an apartment building now stood, and we could hardly remember Claire's narrow, three-story brick house, with its tulip-edged yard. A few small houses remained in the neighborhood and we knocked on doors, asking questions.

"No, I never heard of the Leclerqs," said one young matron with a rosy little boy on her hip. "We moved here last year and hardly know anyone yet."

"Lots of changes here, since the war," another woman said, standing with us on her neatly scrubbed front steps. "It is hard to remember. My mother knew everyone, but she died."

Finally we found an old couple weeding their little garden. They had known the Leclerqs and talked with them. "Claire played the piano," said the old man, pausing with a weed dangling from his hand. "We used to hear her music when the windows were open in summer. Very nice it was, too."

"Do you know if they ever came back here, Claire and her mother?" I asked, feeling helpless and transparent as a ghost touching down briefly to look for another ghost.

"No," the woman said positively, leaning into her shovel like a gravedigger, until the dark earth split under it. "That's for sure. They didn't come back after the war. I heard the mother was killed. The father and brother probably were too, since they served in the Resistance. Anyway, none of them came back here. Nothing to come back to, poor things. We were luckier, eh Papa?"

She nudged the old man, who nodded, looking up only for a moment, his fingers already curling to pull the next weed. When we turned back to wave to them, they were both hard at work again, like Adam and Eve just thrown out of the garden, not knowing how much labor was needed in order to survive, but taking no chances.

One thing I kept with me from what they said. Claire's death had not been reported. So, as we returned to London, I wasn't empty-handed. No one had reported my parents' death; no one was sure of Claire's. One good thing about living in an uncertain universe where anything can happen—there is always hope, and a resurrection is no more miraculous than the sun rising in the morning. Already I was looking East, and though I hadn't yet told Maxi, the words "Next year, in Jerusalem" were to me no longer just words.

5

France to America..................1948

Three years after the sale of Champs-de-lys, Claire was still waiting to leave for America. "By the end of the year," Paul promised. Then, "next year." He and the Countess were in no hurry to leave and the de la Roches in no hurry to pay the full amount they had promised. In keeping with the post-war European mood, the feuding families had turned their attention from manners to money. To survive, Paul began selling off their furniture to dealers from Paris and New York. The Countess's Aubusson carpet bought their groceries for six months, and the sale of the piano, which Paul had held off for Claire's sake, paid for their tickets to America. The Countess insisted on getting a return ticket for herself, having already arranged to spend most of the year in Paris. She would stay in America only long enough to direct them in arranging their new household.

Claire, who had become increasingly anxious about living under one roof with Paul's mother, was so relieved at the Countess's decision that she promptly became pregnant. Because she was afraid Paul would delay the trip if she told him about her condition, Claire kept the news to herself. Just before their departure, when the de la Roches had finally paid Paul what they owed, a letter came from Jerusalem. Claire had hoped from it better news than it brought.

When the letter was delivered, Claire went hunting for Paul through the enormous, half-empty house. Lately he had been hard to find, except when he was helping his mother pack. The Countess was determined that the new owners would have no antique or *objêt d'art* that she could wrench from wall or ceiling. Paul objected that the de la Roches might sue them, but his mother said dismissively that they had the taste of swineherds and would be glad for the chance to install modern hardware from Michigan. No one nowadays, she said, knew the difference, as long as what they owned was shiny. Besides, it was for her grandchildren-to-be that she took whatever pieces of the ancestral home she could. Though they would have to grow up in America, they would turn door handles that had belonged to de Montforts of the past. She was determined that they lose as little as possible by the move. In the end she wore Paul down, and he paid large sums for transporting crates of stuff he would rather have sold.

The letter from Jerusalem came just a week before their ship left Calais for New York, and Claire brought it to the old Count's study, which Paul was using as an office. It had been his idea to write to the British authorities in Tel Aviv, hoping they might have some knowledge of two refugee children from Europe. Two among so many would be a miracle of coincidence, Paul explained to Claire. They had heard that two hundred and fifty thousand European Jews had been interned on Cyprus while on their way to the Holy Land but that thousands of others had actually arrived at their destination, just as the state of Israel was being born. So Paul had written to the British Consul to ask for information about the Lebenthals. The communication from the Consul was as tactful and polite as Claire remembered the British had been in London, but no amount of tact could ease her disappointment.

Claire stood behind Paul, who sat at his father's great mahogany desk, already spoken for by the Mayor of Albi. Over Claire's objections, the Countess had used the mayor's money to buy silk sheets and hand-embroidered baby clothes. Paul read aloud, translating for her:

We have traced Albert Lebenthal and his wife Miriam, but found little. Albert's sister Rachel died under Nazi interrogation in Frankfurt, 1940. The Nazis themselves recorded this death and their records also say that the Lebenthal couple was sent on separate trains to Bergen-Belsen. The Red Cross authorities in Geneva have gone on record with a protest against Nazi treatment of the Lebenthals, claiming that the couple had filed an accusation with their office against the production of poison gas for military purposes by I.G.Farben. The Lebenthals disappeared before proof of this allegation could be communicated to Geneva.

At Bergen-Belsen, the trail ends, as it does for so many. No word at all of any children has reached us. If the Lebenthals had children, presumably they too ended in the camps. On that point we have no information.

"I'm sorry, Claire," Paul said, getting up and putting his arm around her. "It was a long shot, you know."

"Yes, I know that." She brushed one hand over her eyes. "Nothing certain. I hate uncertainty. This letter is no more help than the one from Farben." Three weeks before, they had received a communication from the Chemical Division of I. G. Farben disclaiming any knowledge of the vanished Lebenthals.

"Well, we know why Farben didn't want to admit the Lebenthals had worked for them," Paul said. "They're afraid they'll be in trouble with the occupation forces or the war crimes courts. Someone must have told them about the Lebenthals' letter to Geneva, and they want to weasel out of paying reparations."

"The Nazis would not have let the Lebenthals get away alive," Claire said, clenching her hands into fists. "If the Nazis killed Jews for nothing, you can imagine what they did to Dora and Maxi's parents. But we don't know whether or not the Nazis got the children. Maybe they escaped when the British left Dunkirk."

"You think too much about those children," Paul said abruptly, going back to his chair and riffling through the pile of papers. "It is not doing them any good, you may be sure, wherever they are."

Claire looked down at him, her cheeks as red as if he had slapped her. *One moment, he seems so tender, and the next, he withdraws, observing me critically and from a distance.* It was at such times that he would give her a brief, impatient lecture on the folly of being anxious. *My feelings bore him, and he wishes I would take them somewhere else. So much of my energy is spent dancing to Paul's moods that his indifference to mine is infuriating.* She often wondered if his clinical remoteness had been taught to him by his mother. The Countess had a way of waving off the pain of others, preoccupied as she was with her own, and Paul did the same.

"Do you remember when you were little," she said trying to keep her voice steady, "how your mother acted when you were upset?"

"She would tell me not to be a bore," he replied, hardly looking up from the papers he was signing. "Other people's emotions, she used to say, are as boring as other people's dreams."

"That's what I thought." Claire folded her hands under her apron, in a peasant gesture that she knew would have annoyed the Countess and hoped would annoy Paul.

Her husband put down his pen. "I suppose you mean that I have been traumatized into coldness by my mother. Really, Claire, I would rather you did not play the psychologist with me. Look to that hardheaded father of yours and your trouble with him, if you want to blame the past. He made you over-sensitive."

Pressing her lips together so as not to cry, Claire bent her head and was silent a moment. Again the nausea struck, and she swallowed hard, trying to get rid of the bitter taste. *I want him to stop lecturing, stop keeping me at arm's length, and admit that whatever concerns me concerns him.*

Paul always seemed to act like an entirely separate person, except when they were making love. *So much,* she thought, *for the liturgical ideal of marriage as 'one flesh.'* When they had first met, he had seemed altogether hers, but no longer. Now he belonged to his mother and Champs-de-lys.

Maybe he always will, she thought. Determined to make him feel guilty for hurting her, Claire blurted out something she was not entirely sure of.

"Paul," she said, "I'm pregnant."

He put down his pen and came away from his desk to stand by her. This time his eyes were shadowed with worry, though his mouth was smiling. "Claire! How long have you known?"

"Not long." Claire didn't want to spoil the pleasure of this warm moment by admitting she wasn't sure. Anyway, she was sick to her stomach, and that was unusual enough to make her feel pregnant, even if she weren't. "Our baby will be born in America, if we leave in time."

"How easy it will be for him, Paul mused, looking out the window into the garden. "It will take me years to become an American, if in fact I ever can."

Here he goes, off into his own world again, thought Claire. *It will do him good to have a baby. Take his mind off himself, and that's what's needed.* Paul didn't mind talking about his own pain, but if she complained, Paul wouldn't hear her. He had even seemed just now to have forgotten about the baby.

"You had an English nanny, Paul. At least you speak English," she said, not liking the sullenness in her voice. "I will have to learn it."

He looked at her coolly, seeming to see through her words as he always did. "It is not very becoming of you to resent my advantages, Claire, when you stand to gain from them. Have you any idea how difficult getting started in America would be if we had between us no English and no capital? Especially now, with a child on the way."

She shook her head, staring dully at the floor, ashamed that she could be seen through so easily.

"Here, now, let me explain." Having won his point, Paul gave her a quick hug as he pulled a chair over next to hers. "After all my father's bills are paid, we'll have enough francs left over to make almost twenty thousand American dollars. That is enough to buy a house in American and still have something left to live on until I find a job. Well? Are you pleased?"

Claire smiled, her mouth feeling stiff and unresponsive, still wanting to justify her anger. As Paul went on describing how they would get a big home in America with land around it and call it Champs-de-lys, she remembered what the Countess had said about the impracticality of de Montfort men. In his determination to replace the estate he had lost, perhaps Paul was planning to spend more than he ought to. *After all,* she wondered, *how can he be sure he'll find a job so easily? How many positions will there be in America for elegant counts who paint pictures?* Now that she was planning for a child, Claire was frightened, not sure that Paul could be depended upon. It was one thing to enter the new world as a strong, independent woman, but to begin as a burden to Paul and unable to take care of herself, was something else again.

She felt for a moment the same impotence as she had on the beach at Dunkirk when she realized that she alone couldn't save Dora and Maxi. *At least my mother was able to save me,* Claire *thought. At least she got us to Dunkirk before she died.* A sudden desire for her old home in Rheims, for the small parlor crowded with overstuffed furniture, came over Claire, and with it a longing for her mother's voice, giving advice, taking over, anxious that Claire should be spared any trouble.

"Claire, what is it?" Paul asked, putting his hand under her chin and tipping her wet face up. "Is something wrong?"

"I miss my mother," she sobbed, sinking down in the chair by the desk. "I miss her bustling around and telling me how to do everything."

"Come now, dear one." Paul gathered her up in his arms and held her so that she needed no strength to stand. "I'll take care of you as long as you need it. But that won't be for long, you know. Once the baby's born, you will be yourself again, my strong Claire."

Claire relaxed in his arms, wishing he would take away this burden he had given her of being strong, wishing only to be allowed weakness. In her nausea and lightheadedness, Claire wondered if she would ever again want to decide anything more serious than what to have for breakfast. *At least Paul says he will be there for me, keeping me safe until the baby is born.* But once having known this weakness, this betrayal by her body, how could she ever again be strong enough to make her own way, if she had to? She turned her head to look out the window into the barren garden, watching the leafless trees whip in the stiff wind driving from the distant, snow-capped Pyrenees. *Oh God*, she prayed, *I want to be the way I was as a child, safe and loved. I'm hate being weak, expecting Paul to play God and have no needs of his own.*

Claire sighed, nestling her face against Paul's chest. Just now, when she tried to look within herself for strength, she saw only the probable baby who was growing by the minute, a miracle of exploding cells, holding onto the wall of her womb by a lifeline of her own flesh, breathing and eating along with her, the tiny shadow of herself growing toward the light, and into whose own shadow, in her turn, she would recede.

The Countess was so happy about her prospective grandchild that she broke out the cellar's oldest bottle of Rothschild Bordeaux, though she would not give Claire any.

"The child would become tipsy in the womb," she said solemnly, moving the bottle between herself and Paul. "We must be careful to teach him good habits right from the start. To your health, Claire!" She raised her crystal glass so that it sparkled in the candlelight. "You are a strong girl and will have healthy babies." She turned her glass in her hands, warming the wine. "So many of the de la Roches have miscarried," she murmured cheerfully. "Worn-out stock."

Claire knew her mother-in-law was trying to resign herself to Paul's having married beneath him. *She sees the connection as a necessary evil, like breeding too delicate Arabian stallions with thick, clumsy Percheron workhorses, for the sake of the line's survival. My children will be strong, as I am.* For the first time since her marriage, Claire was proud of who she was.

"We have had little music from you these days," her mother-in-law said, nodding at the piano. "The buyers are coming for the piano tomorrow, and I want to hear you play once more."

I'm glad I have one way of making up for the deficiencies in my pedigree. Claire smiled as she settled herself on the velvet covered piano stool. For the next hour, she played the Countess's favorites. Then, when her fingers had grown flexible as new leaves and her ears sharp as an animal's, she forgot the presence of the other two in the room and began to play the notes forming in her head. *Kindertanzen,* was the name she silently gave the piece as she played. Children's dances. She could see Dora and Maxi, hands joined and heads thrown back, spinning in time to the music as they had danced so long ago in the parlor at Rheims.

The Countess wanted to delay their passage until Claire was farther along in pregnancy, for her own mother had told her that newly conceived infants are easily shaken loose by travel. Claire insisted that the doctor had given her permission to travel anytime, for she was, as he put it, tough as a young mare. *One of the benefits,* Claire had wanted to add, *of being born from common stock,* but she managed to keep quiet. She knew that what her mother-in-law really wanted was to delay leaving Champs-de-lys. The young de la Roches who now owned the house were travelling in Greece until summer, so the Countess felt she might reasonably hang on for a little longer. There was packing to do, she insisted, and more to be bought.

As for Claire, she would have preferred to take nothing at all and to start with empty rooms, leaving behind old cabinets and armoires with their drawers full of memories. Claire brooded silently over their shrinking funds, while the Countess bought everything from monogrammed towels to hand-dipped candles. Her mother-in-law felt that one could get no items of quality in America, and was apparently stocking up on enough necessities to last the rest of her life and theirs.

By the time the ship left for New York, the de Montforts had barely fifteen thousand dollars left from the sale of Champs-de-lys and its furnishings. The Countess, after her orgy of shopping, had collapsed in her cabin, seasick for the entire voyage. Claire stood beside Paul as the ship passed the Statue of Liberty and steamed into the dock area of lower Manhattan. American voices churned around her, as unintelligible as the language of the motors throbbing in the bottom of the ship, and she clutched Paul's hand.

"Will I ever learn to speak English?" she asked, frightened that she was catching hardly a single word, despite Paul's daily instruction. "What if I'm one of those people you hear of who can't learn another language? How will I buy the groceries?"

"I shall go with you to the store at first," Paul assured her, his arm tightly around her shoulders. "You will have the trick of it in no time. *Mon Dieu,* Claire, look at the buildings. So high, and no rubble, no sign of the war."

She smiled, glad to think of her child growing up in a place no bombs had pitted, no mortars smashed. *Never any more violence,* she thought, *nor bombs, nor guns, nor killing. Never again. Not in America.* "People don't live around here, do they?" she asked, repelled by the low, ugly buildings near the docks.

"No. They live in apartments, in the tall towers you see on the skyline." Paul gestured into the distance. "The houses are farther out, miles from here. That is where we will look for the new Champs-de-lys."

Claire frowned. "I wish we could call the house an American name," she said. "Who knows if there are lilies in America, anyway, let alone fields of them? The name might not fit, Paul." She turned to him and laid her palm against his cheek. "Maybe we should just get a cottage in a town, with a little yard for the baby to play in."

"No." Paul set his jaw in the same hard way his mother did. "My children will not be raised in some worker's hut. They will have land around them as I did. Room to grow. America has more room than France. Otherwise, I would not have agreed to come."

He nodded at her expanded middle, as he often did now, including the baby in their conversation. "It is important for children to be close to nature."

Claire sighed and shook her head. What the price of land was in America she did not know, but she was sure Paul overestimated how much land he could get for his dwindling number of francs. He had hoped that northern New Jersey would offer the best bargains. But when they sat in the office of a real estate agent, she caught enough of the conversation to confirm her fear that they had nowhere nearly enough money to buy the grand estate Paul and his mother were looking for.

The first place they were driven to was a hulking Victorian house a few feet from a main road, with two acres of scrub pine around it. Next door was an auto dump, and Claire could smell burning tires. On the other side of the property was a reform school. Claire, who had grown tired and cross after the long drive, said there was probably a leper colony down the road which might account for the three years that the Victorian had been on the market. When Paul opened the screen door in front, it fell off and hung at a crazy angle from one hinge at the bottom. He politely told the realtor that they would consider this place, but that he wanted to see others.

No doubt the realtor hoped that this cultivated foreigner, with his precise British accent, had a good deal more cash than he admitted to, for the man drove them next to what he called a 'colonial,' a tall, brick-fronted rectangle. Columns framed the front doorway, as they did all the other homes in this 'exclusive neighborhood,' as the realtor called it. *Who or what is being excluded?* Claire wondered. *Probably people like me with little money and less English.*

"It's a prestige area," the realtor said, waving his hand at the rolling landscape, with its carefully cultivated shrubbery, lawns, and ponds. "Everybody has exactly one acre around his house. No undesirables, if you know what I mean." He smiled, showing a big gold tooth in front, and lit his cigar, tossing the match onto the fake marble floor of the foyer.

The Countess looked around at the shiny, curliqued brass fixtures and false stone fireplaces, and whispered to Claire, "I would rather live in my great-grandmama's armoire than in this—what you call it—colonial!" She pronounced the word like a curse, making Claire laugh until her stretched belly ached.

Paul and the realtor sat in the front seat of the car, their heads close together over a map. When the realtor began to drive, Paul laid one arm on the seat behind him and told them they were going to a little town called Pine Lake, the last of what the realtor explained were 'bedroom communities,' near enough to Manhattan that commuting was possible. Claire knew Paul would have preferred to buy a house much further west, but he was afraid he could not find a job so far away from the city. The realtor had only one place left to suggest, a house with three acres around it. The place was called a 'handyman special,' a term Claire did not understand. Because the price was only twelve thousand dollars, Paul decided to have a look at it.

They drove up a narrow road on the outskirts of Pine Lake and passed a few small houses close to the shore of a lake ringed with hundred-foot-tall hemlocks. The realtor pulled up to a sprawling, dirty white stucco house with a steeply pitched slate roof, broken in places, and tall casement windows opening onto an overgrown meadow on one side and on the other, a view of the hemlock forest across the narrow street. In back was the lake, far down a sharp slope, below a deck that leaned at an alarming angle over the hillside.

Claire stood in the front yard, listening to a cardinal sing, watching the bird sail past the house and into a white flowering tree where his mate was building a nest. Its caroling cry brought tears to her eyes, and she caught at Paul's arm, pointing silently at the birds. They went around in back and stood on the deck that was supported only by a few wooden piers. Looking down at the lake, they saw a family of ducks that chuckled at each other as they floated by. Paul shook his head, saying to Claire that the whole house would tumble into the lake if the deck were not soon reinforced. They looked up to the top of the house where pointed gables rose high over the glass porch above the deck. The house had dark timbers laid crosswise between patches of stucco, making it look like the Tudor palaces Claire had seen in England.

The realtor took them through the empty house, not trying very hard to sell it. Claire got the impression he had tried too many times with this house, and given up. The plaster walls were chipped, light fixtures had blackened like the peeling wires above them. The basement was ankle deep in water, run-off from the hillside above the little lane, and caulking dropped out of the casement window frames. Paul pointed out stains on the dining room ceiling over the picture window that looked out on the lake, and the realtor admitted that the roof needed patching. While the two men talked, Claire and the Countess went for a second time through the five bedrooms upstairs, opening the doors of closets big enough to serve as dressing rooms, exclaiming when battered brass handles came off in their hands or plaster fell on their heads from holes in the ceiling. *It looks like a house that's been through a war,* Claire thought. *Maybe we can bring it back to life. Maybe it will help bring us back to life, too.*

She found Paul and the realtor downstairs in the kitchen, standing on the cracked linoleum floor and arguing about a stove that did not go on when Paul turned the knob. Claire guided Paul through the side door, where they could see the meadow, thick with buttercups and dandelions stretching up the hill.

"Could it be another Champs-de-lys?" Paul wondered. "I think not." He paused and looked out over the meadow. "So untamed," he said, his brow wrinkling. "No paths to speak of. No gardens."

"I like this yellow meadow just as it is," Claire said firmly. "A garden could be put there in the corner where the sunlight will come early in the day. Paul, Champs-de-lys would not suit as a name. It's too wild for lilies here."

"We will call it Amberfields then," Paul decided. "An American name. What do you think, Claire?" he held both her hands. "Will you like this place? Is it enough for us?"

"You said we couldn't have Eden again," Claire said. "But here it is. This is where I would like my children to be born."

At that time Claire did not know that American children were born in operating rooms. She was surprised and disappointed when the local doctor said he could not deliver her baby at home. They had moved into Amberfields the day after they saw it, renting the house until the papers could be signed that made it theirs. The following day, Paul had taken Claire to the home-office of the town's general practitioner. The doctor, knowing she had little English, patted her on the head, saying "Hello, hello," loudly, as if to a deaf person. After he had examined her, he told Paul she was a regular baby machine, so perfectly shaped was she for this function. "Whish, right down the tube," he chuckled.

Paul grew pale, then flushed, and finally smiled a little, understanding that the doctor had meant no insult. Dr. Fairfax left Claire struggling to make conversation with Mrs. Fairfax while he took Paul through the basement of the Fairfax home and showed him how to install new electric wires.

"You'll learn in no time, young man," said the doctor, delivering Paul to Claire again. "Just remember not to put in your new fixtures until you turn off the current. Otherwise," he winked at Claire, "fried fingers for dinner." *He speaks to us as if we are children or mentally impaired,* Claire thought, *and perhaps we seem so to him.* It was as if he could hardly restrain himself from dandling them on his knee or offering them sweets for being good.

Claire was glad to make her escape from Mrs. Fairfax, a good-natured woman who lectured her about chloroform and other methods of anesthetizing women in labor. From the little Claire could catch of the woman's conversation, no American mother could give birth unless she were bound hand and foot to an operating table and drugged as if for the amputation of a limb. Apparently Mrs. Fairfax had produced five children in these strenuous circumstances, and was sure none would have survived without the sterile, gloved hands of the pediatrician waiting to receive them. The doctor's wife seemed to think babies were alien beings, hardly able to survive in the world without a squirt of blue gentian in their eyes, in case Mrs. Fairfax had lived wildly enough to have contracted a social disease, and a whiff of pure oxygen, in case her babies found ordinary air not to their taste.

Having always assumed that babies found their way into the world without need of such artifice, Claire was alarmed by Mrs. Fairfax's account of American childbirth. Hospitals in America were like resorts, Paul had assured her. Women were put in them to give birth because they needed a vacation. The whole experience, as Dr. Fairfax had explained it to Paul, was a sort of rest cure, in which the new mother had no responsibility for her child during its first week of life and could spend her time reading, listening to the radio, and chatting with her roommates, in one last orgy of self-indulgence before starting her all-consuming career as a mother.

Claire wanted to know what was happening to the baby while its mother was having the rest cure, but Dr. Fairfax hadn't explained to Paul who took care of the baby if it cried or wanted to be fed before the sacred hour decided upon by the head nurse. Claire and her mother-in-law agreed that being an American baby seemed a distinctly unpleasant experience, rather like that of a chicken hatched in a tiny, electrically warmed box and forced to eat chemical pellets.

While Claire and the Countess were discussing the failings of post-natal care in America and arranging the family antiques so that Amberfields did not look so much like a haunted house, Paul was looking for a job in New York. Every night he came home on the bus, walking two miles from the station and having nothing to report for his efforts. During the first week, he explained to his mother and Claire that commercial artists seemed limited to drawing advertisements for the sale of soap and feminine undergarments. The second week, when Claire had sneaked a look at the bank book, she discovered they had less than two hundred dollars left. *Dear God,* she prayed, *let me not have to go to that expensive hospital.*

Paul told them that apparently no corporations wanted a multi-lingual artist to represent them in dialogues with foreign countries. Europe was still recovering from the war. Until it had something to offer the American firms, they would concentrate on their home market. Paul gave up on the corporations and went to see Dr. Fairfax, who sent him to the Pine Lake Superintendent of Schools. Because Paul knew four languages, two of them marketable, the local school system might have a place for him, the Superintendent told Paul. Dr. Fairfax had called ahead of the interview and given Paul his recommendation, which seemed to mean a great deal. Pine Lake was a small, intimate community, having little experience with strangers, especially foreign ones. If Dr. Fairfax had not served as an army captain in the war and felt a sort of military brotherhood with Paul, no doors would have opened.

As it was, Paul was offered immediate work at the Pine Lake high school. He replaced the previous language teacher, who had unexpectedly run off to France with the teacher of art. In the fall, he took the jobs of both reprobate teachers and brought home enough money to fix the roof, pay for the groceries, and buy Claire a used piano.

"Never say we have no money for such things, Claire," Paul said as she stared first at the new piano and then at him. "Just play your music. Play the *Kindertanzen.*"

Claire played, slowly at first, then, as if the children for whom she had written this music were dancing with her own unborn child, in rhythm with her own beating blood and sighing breath. From that day on, she spent hours every day at the piano, hardly noticing the reddening of the fall leaves and the coming of the cold. She wrote a cantata for Christmas, imagining Mary's journey to Bethlehem, the search for a place to give birth, and the gladness of the shepherds in their moonlit fields. She had little to keep her busy except work on her music. Her mother-in-law insisted on doing both shopping and cooking, so Claire would not tire herself with the half-mile walk to the grocery store. The Countess, shocked at the slacks and curlers of American shoppers and intent on setting them a good example, would dress up in a hat and high heels for her shopping trips. Invariably, she would bring back canned frog's legs, tiny jars of Iranian caviar, and filet mignon, along with the oatmeal, milk, and eggs Claire had asked for. *The money might better be saved for a car to fetch the groceries in and drive Paul to the bus station,* Claire thought. She decided to ask her next door neighbor to give the Countess rides to the store until a car could be bought.

The next door neighbor, a plump, talkative young blonde, often put her two small children into an old Ford and jaunted off for a few hours, returning with bags of food, so many that the children were squashed into the corner of the back seat, only the tips of their heads showing. *Such freedom,* Claire thought. *I can't imagine having that much freedom, but good for Charlotte that she has gained it for herself.* Charlotte Webster came over once a week, usually bringing a dessert, and sat dutifully for an hour, trying to make conversation with Claire. Charlotte was from the South, had an earnest commitment to being neighborly, and cooked with great quantities of sugar and fat. Her children were chubby and undisciplined, for Charlotte believed any punishment would inhibit their spunk. The Webster children ignored their mother's mild admonitions, but went in terror of their father who shouted curses at his children and smacked them with his belt.

"My Frederick's daddy used to buggy-whip him good, for every little thing," Charlotte explained. "That didn't make his temper any sweeter. 'Least he doesn't hit me, like one of those redneck Georgians. Frederick's an Alabama gentleman and knows how to treat a lady."

Wondering if she had heard correctly, Claire shook her head at the thought of Frederick, a burly contractor and ex-Marine, being whipped like an animal.

Charlotte rose to reclaim Freddie Junior, who was trying to smother his little sister with the Countess's favorite needlepoint cushion. "Now you make nice, Junior," she said, removing the pillow from the howling baby's red face. "Belinda's a lady and gentlemen take care of ladies. They don't smother them."

Waving to the Countess, who was tottering up the hill with her grocery bags full of snails, wine, and caviar, Charlotte Webster rushed her children off to prepare for Frederick Senior's return from whatever wars he had fought that day with salesmen and homeowners like Paul who were trying to install their own new furnaces. According to Charlotte, Frederick felt that taking Okinawa had been a cinch compared to collecting overdue accounts from his customers. Paul made a point of paying at once for whatever he bought, without haggling, and Charlotte reported during one of her weekly visits that in her husband's eyes, Paul and Claire were gentlefolk like the ones down home, not like the Yankees living all around them. When he saw Paul was walking back and forth to the station in town, Frederick insisted on driving him, saying no man should have to walk up and down that lousy hill every day.

The hill had become more treacherous with the arrival of the first winter snow in mid-December. Frederick Webster had to park his truck at the foot of the hill, leaving Paul to make his way up the road. Paul had to slant his feet to the side, as if he were wearing skis. Claire's baby was expected at any moment, and she was forbidden to set foot on the icy front steps. *I'm too large and tired to mind restrictions*, Claire thought. *Better to sit indoors playing the piano. S*nowflakes fell on the hemlock trees, clothing the branches like white sleeves and covering the lake with windblown mist. Claire watched the scene out her window, happy to be doing nothing at all.

On the day her labor began, so did the heaviest snowfall of the winter. Just after the Countess had called Dr. Fairfax to let him know Claire would soon need to go to the hospital, the wet snow snapped the telephone and electrical wires that served the whole hillside. The doctor had planned to drive Claire to the hospital himself, and the Websters had promised to fill in if the doctor were out on call. No one, however, could go up or down the hill on the day Claire's pains started.

Paul had stayed home, since the school had declared a snow day. He had tried futilely to shovel the road so that an ambulance might make its way up to Amberfields. Not even the town snow plow could get up the hill, which had half an inch of solid ice beneath the heavy, wet snow. Charlotte left her babies with the cleaning woman and came over to deliver one of her pecan pies, drowned in a sugary sauce. Seeing that Paul and the Countess could think of nothing to do for Claire but dab at her wrists and temples with a handkerchief soaked in cologne, Charlotte took charge.

"You say the pains are two minutes apart?" Charlotte threw up her hands. "And Dr. Fairfax is fixin' to get here on snowshoes? I declare, we might as well be in Point Barrow, Alaska. The first thing is, get her into bed. That baby's like to come any minute with pains so close together." She looked at her watch. "When did they start, honey?"

Claire let Paul sit her up on the couch, and then she doubled over with another contraction. *This one was so hard,* she thought, *something inside is surely going to split apart.* "Only an hour," she gasped, feeling the sweat run like tears down her cheeks. "I've heard it can last for a whole day." Her body tightened again and she cried out, hearing her voice as if from far away, like someone else's.

"It cannot go on like this for much longer, can it?" Paul lifted Claire off the couch and looked anxiously out the window. "No sign of the doctor. How about the day bed in the study, Mother?"

The Countess nodded. "*D'accord*. The stairs would be unsafe for her. I made up the day bed yesterday, just in case."

"Paul, try the phone again," Charlotte called from Claire's bedside. "Never mind the hot water I asked for. This baby's coming right soon."

"The phone's out." Paul's face was gray and the lines beside his mouth very deep. He stood in the doorway of the study, not sure Claire wanted him to come in. "God," he said, staring at her, "why does everything have to be so hard?"

"Come, sit with me a few minutes, Paul," Claire whispered. "I just want to hold your hand. Charlotte, get the wastebasket." She hung over Paul's arm, gagging with a nausea so deep it made her wonder if the baby were planning to be born out of her mouth.

"That means the baby's started into the birth canal," Charlotte said matter-of-factly. "Better go get a lot of towels, Paul. There's gonna to be one big mess hereabouts."

Paul ran upstairs and Claire began to cry, clutching at the Countess's hands as the pressure inside her grew, forcing groans out of her that rose to shrieks. "I want Paul," she sobbed "Tell him to come back."

"No honey," Charlotte said, smoothing Claire's damp hair from her forehead. "You don't want him here with you gruntin' like a sow. Close that door, Mrs. de Montfort, ma'am." She raised her voice as Paul came down the stairs. "Paul, you just stay out, hear?"

The Countess grabbed the towels Paul had brought, then closed the door, leaning against it. When Charlotte impatiently beckoned to her to come closer, the Countess unfolded the towels, her hands shaking, and handed them over one by one. Charlotte tucked them under Claire's body.

"Courage, my dear," the Countess murmured faintly. She leaned over Claire, kissing her on the cheek.

"This baby's stuck, maman," Claire gasped. "I can't get it out." She clung to her mother-in-law's hands, straining. The contractions were so close together now that all she felt was one long, uninterrupted pain. *Was this what my mother went through to give me life? And I did not respect her? Please Lord Jesus, forgive me for my pride, and tell my mother I'm sorry.* Her prayer ended in a shuddering gasp and a sudden bearing down that seemed to split her in two.

"I can see the head," Charlotte called from the other end of the day bed. "Push down good and hard, honey. One shove should be all you need."

They heard a pounding on the door and a joyful cry from Paul. "The doctor's here," he called. "Hold on, he's just coming in the door."

"Oh God," Claire cried aloud. "Oh Christ, help me." She bore down with all her strength, hearing her own voice howl again as blood and water gushed out of her, along with a great round weight that seemed to pull all her innards with it. She lifted her head a little and saw Charlotte pick up a kicking mass of shiny flesh, covered with what looked like runny yellow cheese, and wrap it in a towel. *Thank you Lord,* Claire prayed, *for keeping me out of that hospital. My child has been born in his home, as he should be.*

"It's a fine little boy," Charlotte said, laying the baby on Claire's chest. "He's still attached, and we'll just leave him that way until the doctor can finish things off. Mrs. de Montfort, would you take away these messy towels?"

The Countess gagged as she took the soiled towels, and her face turned white. She hurried from the room making odd noises in her throat. Claire suspected that the woman had slight acquaintance with bloody, elemental truths. *Servants had always taken care of such thing for her, I have no doubt*. Despite her cramps, Claire smiled, thinking that America had begun to educate them all.

As the doctor worked on her, Claire kept her eyes on the baby's face. The small head, topped with light, damp hair, was perfectly round, showing no sign of the tight passage which had been his point of entry into the world. His dark-blue eyes were open and looked vaguely in her direction as she murmured to him, brushing his cheek with one finger. The baby's mouth at once started working, trying to suck whatever it was that had touched him.

Charlotte gave Claire a quick kiss. "Better get back to home before Freddie's up from his nap and tries to murder Belinda. I don't know whether that child's jealous, or if he's just got a mean streak like his daddy," she rattled to the Countess as they went out the door.

Holding her baby tighter, Claire felt the need to protect him from the mean streak of Freddie Junior. A great premonitory wave ran over her body as if she herself were the one facing attack. The thought of harm coming to this little red creature who was waving his fists as if fighting off trouble already, made tears come to her eyes, and she promised him silently that no one would ever hurt him. She would see to it, never letting him out of her sight, holding every ugly thing at bay, keeping it outside the kind, happy world she meant to make for him at Amberfields.

"Claire?" Paul's voice was soft and gentle, as if she were too fragile to bear speech. "Are you still in pain?" He lifted one of her hands and kissed it. "So much pain, before."

She looked at him, astonished, as if he were no more than a pleasant neighbor in the room, like Charlotte. *All this time, she thought, I forgot Paul. He's the baby's father, part of him, just as I am.* She smiled at her husband over the baby's head. Strange that Paul had been upstairs gathering towels, while the baby fought through that valley of the shadow of death and tore her body open to let himself out. What Paul had begun nine months before, he had no part in now. No blood had run from him, no contractions had bent him double, and yet he had a son now, with no more effort than a moment's burst of joyful energy. Still, this baby was as much his as hers. She had a sudden vision of Paul trudging off each morning to work, laying in wood for the big stone fireplace, installing the new furnace, and she was suddenly ashamed. *Without Paul, there would be no baby, no home, no warmth in the cold winter.* She looked down at the baby and for a moment she imagined him growing, changing before her eyes, as if the short span of his life had speeded up like a camera gone crazy. He would grow large like Paul, outlive her, unbeatable and strong in the grace of God.

"Would you like to hold him?" She tucked the towel more tightly around the baby. "Here, maman, show Paul how to do it."

She handed her son to the Countess, and as their hands met, had a sudden flash of collective memory in which the Countess herself had once handed Paul to her own mother-in-law and husband. *Already*, she felt with a sudden stab at the center of her body, worse than that of the laboring womb,

I am giving up my son. He doesn't belong only to me anymore. Only a few mild, steady contractions reminded Claire of the time he had been all hers, a holy burden, as Jesus had been to his mother.

She remembered telling Dora that every Jewish girl hoped to bear the messiah, and realized suddenly that for every child born, there was a woman for whom that child was the son of God, whom she would lose to the world. Watching the Countess bend over Paul as he awkwardly held his son, both of them looking closely into the baby's face as if to read the features of their family, far away in space and time, Claire knew what the mother of Maxi and Dora must have felt when she gave her children away to save them from the camps. The faces of the two children, their wide, serious dark eyes staring into nowhere, came back to her, and she turned her face on the pillow, taking long, shaky breaths as she grieved their mother's loss and her own.

6

Dora's Journal

Israel..............................1953

Maxi's decision to study at the Hebrew University in Jerusalem was mine, even though I had engineered it to seem like his. For one thing, I reminded him that only in Israel could we hope to find our parents, if they were still alive. Maxi didn't remember them as I did, and often confused Mutti with Claire. He thought it was Mutti who played the piano and remembered that she had made up songs for us. At first I corrected him, but since his memories were all he had in the way of family, he might as well have as many as possible.

The really hard thing was leaving Father Jonas, especially since Mrs. Grey had never gotten well. Without us, he would be alone. Mrs. Grey sat all day staring out the window at the Cotswold Hills Asylum, whispering and smiling to herself. When anyone tried to talk to her, she grew agitated and had to be restrained. Eventually we stopped going to see her, though Father Jonas himself went every month. Since she wanted no one to talk to her, he just sat staring out the window too, wondering, as he told me, what God wanted him to do with the rest of his life. The parish of St. Hilary's was now very small, and could no longer support the school. In another year, he said, the school would close. What he would do then, he had no idea. Become a wandering scholar, perhaps, and visit us in Jerusalem.

He looked so bleak when it was time for us to leave, that I insisted he come along with us to Israel for a month's vacation. We pretended to be anxious about getting ourselves settled, reminding him that Maxi was only seventeen and I just two years older. Maxi was grown-up young man, and I had already been working as a horticultralist for almost a year. Though Father Jonas had protested, I hadn't gone to university, but instead became certified at the London Botanical Gardens, where I was hired even before finishing my apprenticeship. Since first watching Mrs. Grey in her garden, I felt that nothing was more astonishing and gratifying than to bury a seed and see it work its way up through the soil, then into the air, where it would stretch its stem and uncurl its leaves. One's only real task is to feed it what it likes, prevent it from being annoyed by insects or fungus, and it will become whatever it should become. No meddling is necessary, for God has taught it to unfold of itself. In a way, that's how Maxi and I grew up, and we seem to be the better for it.

Father Jonas just tended the soil, that was all. He was a good gardener and we bloomed in his care. From him I learned a good deal about Jesus. At first I thought that I must not love Jesus, since Jews had been mistreated by Christians. I remembered Thomas Leighton's insult and wondered if all Christians felt that Jews were beneath them, as he did. It didn't occur to me until recently that this shmuck was not a real Christian, while Father Jonas was. As I grew older, I began to feel a bond with the gentle Jew who had forgiven his killers. It seemed to me that other Jews should be proud of him, not turn away as if he were an enemy. He certainly wasn't *my* enemy.

The first few days in Jerusalem Father Jonas spent with Maxi, getting him set up in his room at the university dormitory and buying books for him. I seized the opportunity to go to the immigration authorities, taking the bus to Tel Aviv, and filled out my application for Israeli citizenship. All I had for proof that I was really a Jew was my mother's letter, but it was enough. Apparently I was not the only orphan of the Nazi storm to appear in Israel without genealogical credentials. I kept my plans secret as long as I could, for I didn't want to see how sad Father Jonas would be at my news. While he and Maxi visited archeological sites, I took a trip of my own, to Kiryat Anavim, a kibbutz six miles north of Jerusalem, one of the first experimental communes in Israel. Since I wanted to be near Jerusalem and Maxi, this kibbutz suited me perfectly.

Trying to make a good impression, I had dressed in a smart black gabardine skirt and sleeveless white batiste blouse that showed off the tan I had picked up during those first two days of intense desert sunlight. I wore my only pair of high heels, wanting to look taller than my unassisted five feet, two inches, and not knowing that kibbutz girls were supposed to be above such vanities. Around my long, curly hair, which was a bit too thick and wild, I tied a red headband which matched my nails and lipstick. Inspecting myself in the hotel mirror before I left, I was quite pleased. My cheeks were rosy and my eyes wide and clear. I had practiced smiling in such a way as to keep my upper lip from rising too high, so no one could notice my slightly crooked front tooth. If my face weren't so square at the jaw, I think anyone would have considered me actually beautiful. And it's always been my experience, except in the nasty episode with Thomas Leighton, being thought beautiful does no one any harm when favors are being handed out. So with total self-confidence, I took my beautiful self and offered it to Kiryat Anavim, sure it would be received gratefully. After all,

Israel was a barren garden, trying to bloom again, and I was a gardener. How could we not get along?

Though among the girls of Jerusalem I would not have seemed conspicuously over-dressed, at Kiryat Anavim, I felt out of place the moment I got off the bus. Most of the women my age were wearing khaki shorts and faded blue work shirts. Their hair was either tied under a kerchief or cut short. None of them wore any make-up, and my face, which had looked so beautiful to me that morning, began to seem to my mind's eye as decorated as a clown's.

Waiting for my interview with Lev Harkavy, the director of the kibbutz, I sat in the small, spare outer office and chewed on my lips, hoping the lipstick manufacturer's claims about the indelibility of his product were overstated. Unluckily, my eyes looked made up even though they weren't, because my lashes and brows were naturally so dark. A St. Hilary's teacher had once insisted that I wash my eyes to get the make-up off, and had even marched me into the bathroom to see that I did it.

"No need to paint yourself up like Jezebel," she had said primly, handing me a washcloth. "We'll have no face paint at St. Hilary's."

Now, about to face Lev Harkavy, my hands sweated and wet circles began to spread under the armholes of my blouse, just as they had when Sister Margaret had taken me to the bathroom sink to make me pure. Lev Harkavy opened the door and motioned me inside, hardly looking at me. I followed his tall, spare figure, noticing how faded and patched his denim work shirt and pants were. Either Kiryat Anavim was very poor or its inhabitants were indifferent to fashion. He didn't shake my hand or smile, just went back to his desk and sat down, his pointed dark eyebrows raised in his long, bony face, with its deepset pale blue eyes and heavy creases down his sun-wrinkled cheeks. Because of the gray at his temples and his wrinkles, I thought he must be pretty old, but he was actually thirty-seven. As he told me later, "the sun out here ages a man like war or disease.' Evidently Lev had seen a lot of all three, for his skin looked like the desert when the sand lies in little furrows, as if it had been cultivated by the wind.

"Well, Dora Ben-Ari," he said, looking up at last from the application I had filled out. "You seem to have spent a great deal of time in greenhouses. A regular African violet, ha?" Lev spoke English with an accent that seemed vaguely German. When he said 'ha' at the end of sentences, meaning to be sarcastic, he would raise his eyebrows, which bent in the middle almost into right angles over his cold, light eyes.

"My work in horticulture should be useful to the kibbutz," I said stiffly, in my archaic Hebrew. "I have been raising vegetables since I was a child.

Of course, at the London Botanical Gardens we grew flowers. I grow what I am told to."

"You speak Hebrew, at any rate," he said, not answering me. "Even if you sound like a biblical patriarch. How did you manage to learn such Hebrew in London? Never mind." He spoke rapidly, clipping his words by shutting his mouth in a tight, thin line. "What do you suppose a kibbutz would do with a greenhouse, ha? We grow no orchids here." He looked at me hard, and I was embarrassed at my matching red nails and hair ribbon. "Our growing season lasts all year, not like Europe's. We raise our vegetables under the open sky. If you want indoor work, you'd best go somewhere else. Kiryat Anavim is no hothouse."

My cheeks felt warm, and I pushed my offensive red nails into my palms. "I didn't come here looking for a hothouse," I said, hoping he wouldn't mistake the shaking in my voice for weakness. If I could have punched his long, thin nose it would have given me great satisfaction. He was looking down it at me in a way that reminded me of the tiresome Sister Margaret. "What I want is to work. I've always worked." When he didn't answer, I felt tears rush to my eyes and wanted to make him feel guilty for thinking me a hothouse flower in search of care. "Since I lost my parents in the camps, I've had to make my own way."

"Do you think losing people in the camps gives you some special status here?" His eyes grew colder, and he put down my application. "I myself spent much of my twenties in Bergen-Belsen, doing hard labor. None of my family even survived the cattle cars. Don't tell me about loss," he said, folding his long brown fingers together. "Don't try to tell anyone around here about loss."

Paying no attention to his scolding, I got up and leaned on the desk, my arms stiff as crutches. "My parents were at Bergen-Belsen. Albert and Miriam Lebenthal . Did you know them? They were chemical engineers, from Frankfurt."

Lev Harkavy looked up at me, the lines of his face suddenly not so deep. When he answered, his voice was not as harsh as before. "My first year at Bergen-Belsen," he said, seeming to look through me and far away, "I was sent with other prisoners to carry some furniture from the trains to homes of Nazis in Frankfurt. They had taken the furniture from great Jewish houses in Germany. A man named Albert Lebenthal was sent back to the camp with us in the cattle car. It was Yom Kippur, and he sang the whole *Kol Nidre* from memory. At first he stayed in the corner of the car, by himself, and later others gathered around him. I didn't join them, not being religious. After all, what sort of God would let his people be enslaved by a gang of rabid Nazi animals, ha? Albert Lebenthal's voice carried, a big, deep voice, I remember. He could hardly walk, because the Nazis had done something to his legs, but he sang the *Kol Nidre* in such a voice that some of the men cried."

Remembering my father's long stride and how he used to run with me on his back, I felt my insides shrink and hurt to think of his legs no longer able to carry him. My arms went limp, and I almost fell onto Lev's desk. He stood up and came around the desk, then held me by the shoulders so I could stand straight.

"I think this Albert Lebenthal was a scientist," he said. "Someone told me afterward that the Nazis had wanted him to work for them or give them some information, and he wouldn't. Later, at Bergen-Belsen, the guards took him off the train first, asking for him by name. An old man, who knew he was about to die anyway from a bad heart, tried to pretend he was the one they were asking for, but Lebenthal just put his arm around the man and said the sort of thing we all hope we would say at times like those: 'No, my friend, you have no idea what they would do to you if they thought you were me. I must go myself.' That was the last I saw of Albert Lebenthal, your father, if that's who he was."

I turned around so my back was to him, not wanting him to see my face, stretched wide open like a crying baby's, though no sound came out. After a few moments, I sat down again and asked Lev if he were sure he had the name right.

"No one knew anything for sure, in those days," he said, his voice hard and remote again. "I suggest you go to Tel Aviv, where records are being put together. They have names and death-dates. More comes in all the time, whenever the survivors remember. As you might guess, survivors want to remember as little as they can. Now." He picked up the application and rattled the pages. "Let us decide what to do with this English orchid of ours who wants to play at being a turnip. Becoming a real peasant isn't so easy, ha?" He rubbed his bristly chin and stared at what I had written about my work.

When I tried to protest, he waved his hand, smiling so that his creases deepened, and his teeth shone whitely against his dark skin. "We're running a guest house here as well as trying to turn our little valley into a garden. You'll go to work in the kitchen at first. Everyone does. After a little while, if you stay, we'll send you out to the tomato garden."

The kitchen was the most despised assignment on the kibbutz, but at least it was a place to begin, and I meant it when I thanked Lev for letting me stay. He told me to report in two days to the dormitory, since no single rooms were open at the moment. When I left, he shook my hand briefly and told me to get myself some proper work clothes. Then he waved his hand, dismissing me. At the time I thought Lev Harkavy was one of those power-drunk males, the kind that enjoys being rude to people who don't talk back, especially women. But it didn't take me long to learn that no one on the kibbutz had the leisure for talking around a point. One just comes out with it and toughens up so as not to be hurt, rather like getting on with the bullies in the sixth form at St. Hilary's.

Maxi had always been shocked when people pushed him around, more shocked than angry, for he had never encountered brutishness before he came to England. Mutti had always made him be polite, and he was open-mouthed and astonished before the hateful little thugs of St. Hilary's, who teased him for his accent, his race, and his good marks. I would have knocked them down, but Maxi either stood there, his mouth working in silent argument, or he would reason gravely with them, gesturing to make a point in a professorial way that reminded me of Father Jonas. For me, politeness was only a reluctant artifice, and when chewed out by someone at the kibbutz, I had no trouble chewing them out in return. For gentle Maxi, kibbutz life would not be so easy.

By the time I got back from Kiryat Anavim on the day I met Lev, Father Jonas had left our hotel to go to church at St. Elizabeth's. It was just as well that he wasn't there, for this way I could tell Maxi about what Lev remembered of our father and about my acceptance into the kibbutz. Before he went back to the university, Maxi tried to talk me out of leaving Jerusalem for the kibbutz, but gave up. He hated disagreements, maybe because he'd never yet won an argument with me. I didn't mind putting off telling Father Jonas that I planned never to go back to England. As it turned out, something happened to Father Jonas that night that made him into a new man, not needing me anymore.

He came in from the church meeting so late that the moon was already turning pale in the sky, and the streets were beginning to stir, with vendors setting up their stalls to open at dawn. I put on my robe and went to the room next door. Father Jonas was standing on the little balcony overlooking M'ea She'arim, the Orthodox section of the city. When I came out to join him, he turned with the rapid movement of a young man, grabbing my hands.

"Dora, I may be going out of my mind," he said, his voice full of laughter, but kept low so the laughter wouldn't burst out and wake our neighbors. "Nothing I'm going to tell you makes any sense, even to me."

Had he met some woman and gone crazy over her? His face was flushed and his eyes shone like a man's in a fever. I sat him down on one of the folding chairs, wondering if a doctor should be called.

"Are you sick from the food?" I asked, putting one hand on his warm forehead. "Or have you gone and fallen in love?"

"In love?" He threw back his head and laughed. "Yes, that's it. That's what's happened to me, Dora. I have fallen in love and forgotten myself."

"Well, it sounds very dangerous," I said, wrapping my robe tightly around my legs, which were getting goosebumps from the cool morning breeze. "Someone once said there are three rules for leading a happy life. 'Never give away anything, never sign anything, and never fall in love.' You can't lose if you go by these rules, it seems to me."

"Oh, but Dora," he said, looking up at the pink morning sky, "you can't gain anything either. Only by giving everything away, by loving to your limit, can you live a happy life. It's a divine paradox, you see. Only by throwing away your life, your ego, can you find yourself. That's what I learned tonight."

"Tell me, then. What exactly have you given away?" I asked, not sure now what sort of love he was talking about. Maybe it bothered me a little that he might have committed himself to a woman, for he had been all mine for a long time, and giving him up would be hard for me. The more one loses, after all, the more one hangs onto what's left. Father Jonas would not agree, but it's true, in my experience so far.

"Let me begin by saying that it's God I've fallen in love with, Dora, not with a woman. But loving God means loving all women, all men. You might say I've fallen in love with everything God's made. The sun rising over there." He pointed at the horizon that was turning yellow and deepening the golden color of Jerusalem's stones. "And with those birds flying over us." He looked up and smiled, as if he could feel the wind from the birds' wings on his face. "It seems like I've been stretched in every direction so that I'm full of holes, full of empty spaces, and can pass through the solid world without touching anything, just like a comet's tail or like wind through trees. Ah, Dora, I'm happy, happy."'

As Father Jonas talked, I began to understand what sort of love he had fallen into and was glad for him. Apparently he had not hoped for much when he went with several scholars from the Ecole Biblique to a gathering of charismatic Christians in the Old City. Father Jonas had given up on hope, so he had no expectations as he approached the low stone building with arches like our St. Hilary's and candles set in the windows to show there was something going on inside. A dozen people, housewives, priests, workmen, even a few teenagers were sitting in a circle, praying with their hands raised, palms up. Sometimes one or another would speak. the words rushing out crazily like a lover's. Sometimes everyone was quiet.

Feeling uncomfortably barren of soul, as he put it, Father Jonas pulled up a chair outside the circle and tried to pray, too. As usual, his mind was full of the words of ancient prayers in Hebrew, Greek, and English. Whatever he tried to say to God turned out to be someone else's idea of a prayer. Such prayers suddenly sounded to him like tinkling cymbals, and he wished them gone from his mind. When he had arrived at that church, he had felt God was no friend of his, having taken first Mrs. Grey, then Maxi and me. He had come to feel that he was no friend of God's, either. There seemed nothing to say in this circle of prayer, nothing to do. He felt the way he did when he sat beside his mad wife's window in the Cotswold Hills Asylum, only being there because he loved her, but unable to touch her or speak. At last his mind felt emptied and he sat bereft of words, all he had ever relied on to get him through hard times.

At that moment, a young girl, her face wet and twisted in pain, went to the center of the circle and asked the group to pray for her. She had been molested by her uncle, who had threatened to kill her if she told anyone. Now she wanted them to ask God to heal her hurt body and soul. As she wept, the others stood around her, some touching her shoulders, others touching theirs, until they were a living web of arms and fingers and murmured prayers.

Some prayed in languages that even Father Jonas did not understand and some were silent, moving only their lips. Slowly, unsure of himself, Father Jonas reached out and put a hand on the shoulder of a man at the outermost rim of the circle. At first he drew back, because his hand had begun to tingle and burn as if he had touched a live wire. Cautiously he put his hand out again and left it on the man's shoulder, despite the tingling. What was it? Perhaps the emotion of the group had reached such a pitch that it had drawn him in, by a kind of hypnosis. Perhaps, he thought, some current of spiritual energy was pouring through these ecstatic people who prayed and wept with the unhappy girl.

For Father Jonas, it was the spirit of God, and he was as afraid as Moses was when he looked into the burning bush. Still he found he could not take his hand off the man's shoulder and run from the room, as he wished to do. Though he wanted God's love and always had, Father Jonas was not sure he could give up all he would have to give up in order to love God back. His scholarship might have to go, and maybe his love for languages. For a long time, these pursuits had defined him, made him real to himself. Now he would have to be nothing more than a baby in the arms of God, knowing only love. He found himself clinging to what little else was left of his own identity and will, just as he clung to Maxi and me, even while we were deserting him. When he thought he could no longer bear the burning and tingling in his arm, the girl stood up, smiled and reached out to the circle of friends around her.

One woman embraced the girl and went with her to a corner of the room, where they sat down together. The circle closed and the people waited, their palms turned up, their eyes closed. Father Jonas suddenly had a great pain in his chest, as if the wind had been knocked out of him, and he gasped. His body felt empty, as though he had lost whatever made him who he was. The tears began to pour down his cheeks as they had that morning at St. Paul's, when he saw the ruins of what he had so loved. He felt himself falling over backwards and thought he was about to drop off the edge of a cliff and die. Father Jonas heard a few words in the distance, as if he were already dying.

"He's being slain in the Spirit. Catch him, brothers."

He was not sure how much time had passed, but knew it had been enough to kill what he had been before and resurrect him. A circle of faces smiled down at him, and he lifted his head from the stone floor.

"I never knew," he whispered, as they raised him to his feet. "Forty years a priest, and I never knew what Christ meant by 'born again'."

Like a blind man, he held out his arms as he made his way around the circle, touching each person. He remembered the story of how friends had lowered a paralytic on a stretcher through the roof to set him down before Jesus. Father Jonas's new friends closed in around him, their hands reaching out. Through waves of dizziness, as if he had fallen from a great height and lay broken on the ground, he heard a low, quiet voice inside his head. "Rise up and walk. Dead bones in the valley must live again." Father Jonas knew the dead bones in the valley were his own, so he didn't argue with the voice in his head. "Christ, Jesus," he said, surrendering. "Raise these bones. Have them. They are not mine anymore."

Hands held him as he fell again and laid him gently on the floor. When he opened his eyes, a middle-aged woman with a babushka over her graying hair and a thin man in a bus driver's uniform were leaning over him, stroking his hands and forehead. "Do you want us to sit with you for a little while?" the woman asked.

For the rest of the night he sat with the man and woman who held onto him from either side, like parents with a newly walking child whom they expected would topple at any moment. Father Jonas said he felt like a wet, just-hatched butterfly sitting on a twig afraid to move the wings it was hardly sure it had. And if he could not fly, where would he go? What would he do with himself?

"I'll go home, of course," Father Jonas said, rubbing his eyes which seemed puffy and ready for sleep. "Back to St. Hilary's. For a long time they've needed a priest and haven't had one."

He wanted to go first to the university and tell Maxi how glad he was to be going back to St. Hilary's, but I persuaded him to rest. Maxi and I would come and get him for lunch, when he was more himself. He smiled at that, as if being more himself were a secret joke, but said nothing, only patted my hand, rolled under his quilt, and went to sleep. He no longer needed me to be there. As I walked out into the sunlight and saw it bounce off the golden stone walls lining our Jerusalem street, I stretched my arms, feeling free, like Father Jonas's new butterfly. Maxi was waiting for me, and my heart was light as a leaf in the wind.

When we reached the university dormitory, Maxi insisted on showing me the bookstore and the archeological museum, his favorite places. I was just as determined to take him up to Kiryat Anavim, so he could have his first look at a real kibbutz. As always, Maxi was good-humored and let me have my way. So after inspecting the university, we went to the kibbutz.

"You're really going to live here, Dora?" he said, looking around him at the rows of tables in the dining hall. "In nothing but a dorm? Even the university has a place to go where you can be by yourself. How will you stand never being by yourself?"

"You're the one who likes to be alone so you can study," I said, somewhat on the defensive, for I wanted him to see it was his deficiencies that might interfere with kibbutz life, not mine. "My work is outdoors, not in a stuffy little room."

Maxi sighed and followed me out of the dining hall into the vegetable garden. "Of course it's best for you here," he said, shading his eyes while he looked over the rows of tomatoes. "A choice must be made between living for the group and living for oneself, or so the politicians here seem to think. Maybe it's true that the time has come for the personal self to be forgotten."

"That's what I believe." My hope was that he would believe so too and someday leave his studies for this place. "People have been living for themselves too long. I don't mind sleeping in a dormitory."

Just then Lev Harkavy's secretary came over and said she had been looking for me ever since she had heard Maxi and I had come up from Jerusalem that morning. Lev had given orders that I was to have a room to myself and she was to show it to me. It surprised me that a room had become available so quickly and for so new a member of the community. When I mentioned my surprise to Maxi, he shrugged and said Lev must have his own reasons for wanting me in a private room. For the first time, I wondered if Maxi were a little jealous that I was living on my own, without him.

"Lev Harkavy has no time for romantic nonsense," I said, feeling my face flush. "A kibbutz isn't like anyplace else. We're all working for each other. No one takes advantage."

"You believe everyone thinks as you do, Dora," Maxi answered, turning to survey the plain square room, with its sofa-bed and small table. "If they did, no one would have the need for a private room."

I stood looking out the windows that framed the corner of the room, glad to see that my second story home had a view of the great gorge behind the kibbutz. In the gorge, newly planted olive trees were beginning to grow, and tiny flowers crept out from under massive red-gold rocks. Already I was deciding where I would hang the begonia plant I had bought in Tel Aviv and where Father Jonas's menorah would stand.

"Can I borrow your zebra rug?" I begged Maxi, imagining how sharp it would look in the center of the black tile floor. "Just until I can get something of my own."

"Your own?" Maxi smiled and shook his head in mock sorrow. "Not even moved in yet, and you're talking like an American consumer. Better not let the great Lev Harkavy hear you. He doesn't seem the sort who'd let a snake into his Eden."

What he said about Lev was too true for me to dispute, so I didn't try. Instead, I took Maxi out to the edge of the vegetable field where the kibbutzniks labored in one ceaseless, flowing motion. As I watched, I imagined how hard Lev worked to keep his people busy. These people had no free time to question his rigid communitarian ideals.

"If I were running this garden," I said, pointing at the field, "I could get twice the yield. See how far apart they've put the beans?"

Without turning my head, I knew someone had stopped behind us.

"And what's wrong with our beans?" Lev's deep, abrupt voice asked.

I swung around to face him. My hands shook a little because he looked so stern and sure of himself. "They could be planted closer together if the seeds were placed a full foot down instead of only six inches," I said, drawing strength from Maxi's nearness. "As it is, you're wasting space and water."

"Whoever heard of planting so deep?" Lev scoffed. "Our soil doesn't allow it."

"You could bring in more topsoil from the creek bed," I told him, wondering why he found it necessary to stand so close in order to look down his long nose at me. "That's where erosion has dumped it. By the way, you wouldn't believe how inefficient surface inundation is for irrigating."

"And what would you have us do instead?" Lev asked, his hands waving about as though words alone were not enough to express his disbelief. "You think it rains here the way it does in England, ha?"

"Everybody knows sprinklers are more efficient than flooding a whole field," I snapped, not liking the way he put me in the wrong with Maxi looking on. Before he could hit back, I picked up a handful of soil and spread it out in my hand. "Look at that," I said. "Phosphate poor. Probably not much sulfur or calcium either. Five hundred pounds of single super-phosphate would turn this field around."

I tossed the dirt in the air and walked off with Maxi's hand in mine. "Try it and see if I'm not right," I called back over my shoulder. Lev had not asked who Maxi was, and for some reason I was glad he didn't know this tall, handsome young man was my brother.

Maxi was pretending to blow his nose so Lev wouldn't hear him laughing. "Nothing like the way you go about making friends, Dora," he said when Lev was out of earshot. "If that man didn't have designs on you, you'd be bounced out of here tomorrow for insubordination." Maxi wiped his eyes. "Five hundred pounds of single super-phosphate! Did you see his jaw drop?"

Stopping on the path back to the Jerusalem Road, I stared at him and swallowed hard. Until that moment, living apart from Maxi had seemed as unreal to me as Father Jonas's visitation by the Holy Spirit. All our lives we had slept the night within calling distance of each other, eaten at the same table, fought the same enemies. We were like the children raised among their age-mates on the kibbutz, who hardly knew their parents and caretakers, having only each other for comfort. Just by looking at my face, he knew what I was thinking, and we stood for a moment, our hands on each other's shoulders, forehead to forehead.

"You can't guess what a stroke of luck I've had," Maxi said finally, beginning to move down the path again. "I'll be working weekends on the Jericho dig with Kenyon's crew. One of Father Jonas's friends at the Ecole Biblique got me an interview yesterday. When they heard I could do chemical analyses of metals, they gave me the job."

"We won't be getting together on Saturdays, then?" My voice was tight and strained, sounding like someone else's, as if I were on a stage, going through motions. I was supposed to sound glad, so I tried to.

"Not for a while, anyway."

Maxi bent to pick up a rock, turned it over in his hands as if it might prove to be an artifact, then tossed it away. "Next to Jerusalem, Jericho's the best site in Israel. The oldest city in the world, or close to it. For ten thousand years there's been a Jericho, from the time people first grew grain.

Work is just beginning on the deepest stratum, twenty-three feet down. I'll be part of that."

"No metal down that deep, is there?" I tried to keep my voice impersonal, man to man, following Maxi's lead. Folding my hands tightly behind my back, I took long steps, keeping my eyes on the ground.

"Only stone implements, of course, and maybe some religious artifacts, if we're lucky. The metal I'll be working on came from later levels."

Maxi was already talking like it was his dig, the way I talked about my kibbutz. We had learned to fit in anywhere, like cactus flowers popping up overnight between dew-damp rocks, not wasting time.

"You can come and dig too, sometimes, if you want. And if Lev will let you go." Maxi smiled a tight little smile as though he knew something I didn't, but his eyebrows were drawn together in the middle, making his face look sad.

Later that day, at the Jerusalem Central Terminal, after we had put Father Jonas on the bus to the airport, we said good-by to each other, having little else to say. For a moment it was as if Father Jonas had been our only point of contact. Now that he was gone, we seemed to have lost our mutual past. Then Maxi tucked a bulky bag under my arms and kissed my cheek before I got on the bus back to Kiryat Anavim.

"I knew you loved that zebra rug," he said. "So I brought it for you. And I want you to keep my Ben-Ari bear in your new room. I'll come and visit you both."

All the way back to the kibbutz, I sat holding the stuffed bear close to my heart, not caring that my neighbors smiled.

At dinner in the crowded kibbutz dining hall, I took time off from work to sit at a corner table, near the kitchen door, and eat the food I'd helped to prepare. People were eating fast and talking to each other, wandering around the room looking for their friends. Not having any, I sat alone. Lev was in the midst of a group of men who were gesturing and talking loudly, while he drew a diagram of some kind on the paper placemat in front of him. He glanced over at me from across the room, and I looked back at my plate, turning red as I wondered if what Maxi thought were true. When I looked up again, Lev wasn't with the men anymore, but had come across the room to me.

"Your idea about sprinklers was a good one," he said, straddling the bench beside me. "We'll put them in early next spring, before the dry season hits." He took a carrot off my plate and crunched it between his yellowed teeth.

He was less a dictator than he seemed, I realized, knowing that it would take me a while to get used to the abrupt, casual way kibbutz people spoke and acted. Always I had seemed to myself and others too rude and urgent in my manner, but in the kibbutz, I seemed like a polite princess sleeping uncomfortably on a pea.

"Maybe I spoke out of turn," I mumbled into my mouthful of cold mashed potatoes. "You know what you're doing." I couldn't resist adding, "Best to put the sprinklers on wheels. Stationary ones aren't as versatile."

Lev smiled at me and nodded. "We try to learn from everyone who comes here. So much to learn." He sighed and got up. "How do you like your room?"

"Very much, especially the view. I was surprised." My fork dropped out of my fingers onto the floor, and though I waited, he didn't pick it up. "I mean, at getting a room so soon, let alone such a good one."

"It used to be mine." Lev stretched and his work shirt opened over his wide chest with its matted dark hair. "I'll drop by later to talk to you about your next assignment. A kitchen isn't the place for you."

Washing dishes later, I asked Shana, the girl next to me, what she knew about Lev Harkavy. She was a statuesque blonde who worked fast, rattling the flatware as she dried it and dumped it in a drawer.

"He's a lady's man," she said. "Ever since his wife was killed back in '47, he just goes from one girl to another. Interested?"

"Maybe." I handed her a wet platter and was surprised to hear myself telling a stranger a truth like this one. "His wife was killed, you said?"

"Shot by Jordanians during the War for Independence." Shana stood on tiptoe to put the platter away, after giving each side a quick pat with the towel. "They gunned down some hostages near the border, and she was one of them. Not by accident. They took only the relatives of the best known fighters in the Irgun."

"Lev was one of those?" He had, in fact, struck me as a military man, more used to giving orders than explanations. "A terrorist?"

"We don't say that around here." Shana looked behind her and then leaned closer. "Lev helped to blow up the King David Hotel when the British were dragging their feet about signing the Independence Declaration. Without men like him, Israel would be a despised little corner of Jordan. Understand?" She slapped the damp towel over my shoulder and walked off into the dining room with a long, quick stride.

Lev didn't come to my room until I had fallen asleep. Moonlight was streaming through the curtainless window onto my pillow, and I thought at first that it had waked me, not the short, muffled raps on the door. I pulled on my white nylon robe over my underwear and opened the door. Lev walked in as if the room were still his, closing the door with his foot.

"You didn't wait up for me," he smiled, sitting down on my bed. "You went to sleep."

"I expect to work a full day tomorrow." Cautiously I stayed by the door, figuring that if he were going to claim his room and me with it, I might have to leave in a hurry. "You wanted to talk to me about a new assignment?"

Lev lay back on my pillow, folding his hands behind his head. "You should be working out in the gardens," he said. "Tomorrow, report to Esther at dawn. I've told her about you. Better keep your advice about phosphate to yourself. Esther thinks our soil's as good as Eden's, just as it is." He paused and put out his hand toward me. "Come here."

Closing the loose flap of my robe firmly over one bare leg, I shook my head, staying by the door.

"Then I'll have to come to you." Lev was on his feet before the words were out and had me pinned tightly between his arms and the door. "Such a beauty you are," he whispered gallantly in my ear. "All that pretty hair. Let's see what else."

Slapping his hand away as it pulled at the sash of my robe, I ducked under his arm and stood behind a chair. "You can have your room back," I said, furious at being bribed. "I'll sleep in the dormitory."

"What's the matter?" Lev's voice was reasonable, and he kept it soft so no one would overhear. "I'll be good to you, Dora. Do you think I won't? Haven't I given you my room? Tell me what else you want."

"To be loved," I said, suddenly knowing what it was I really did want and being too tired to hide my feelings. "Not just had. You're used to having. Anyone can see that. Now, do you want your room back or will you go away so I can sleep? Work starts at 6 AM, you said."

His mouth looked thin and stretched as he started for the door. "It's not true that I've only had, not loved." He paused before turning the handle. As he went out, he didn't look back at me. "You can keep the room. I want you to have it."

Over the next two weeks, Lev didn't come close again, but from time to time he would stare at me in the dining room, until Shana noticed and gave me a dig with her elbow as we ate.

"You've got him all bothered," she said, smiling behind her napkin. "I heard from Japhed over in the smoke house that Lev's put in for the room next to yours. Of course, that's just a formality. If he wants the room, whoever's in it will move."

So the next night, only a wall separated Lev and me, and I started lying awake for a long time after going to bed, imagining his tall, spare body lying just a few feet away, without sheets covering it in the heat of early fall. After a few nights of thinking that I heard him breathing slowly, deep in sleep, I got up, put on slacks and a sheer, printed Indian overblouse, then went out walking. Not very far along the path to the gorge, Lev caught up with me and took my arm.

"Your door slammed," he said. "It woke me up."

"The door didn't slam." I shook my head. "You make up stories, Lev, to fit your own view of the way things are."

"Not always." He steered me toward a footbridge over the gorge, and we stood looking down at the olive trees. "Life doesn't tend to fit the story I'd like it to." Lev flashed me a smile that faded when I didn't smile back. He sighed, lit a cigarette, and extended the pack to me.

"No thanks." I folded my arms on the railing and looked out at the rocks, shining where the moonlight struck them. "The air's enough for me."

He breathed in the smoke deeply and let a little out after a while. "A bad habit I picked up in the army. Something to do while you're waiting. I was never much good at waiting." He gave me a significant glance and stood closer, though not touching me. "Waiting for you is hard. How long will it be?" He put his hand on the back of my head, turning my face toward him in one swift, easy gesture.

I pushed his hand away, not entirely wanting to. "Look Lev, I have this weird, twisted mind. For some reason, the idea of making love with a man I don't matter to makes me sick."

"Is it that boy I saw you with?" he persisted, still standing too close. "You're in love with him?"

"No, that was my brother." I reached up and pulled a poinciana leaf from an overhanging tree limb, then stood shredding it carefully, with great concentration. I was nervous at the prospect of telling anyone the secret I'd kept even from Maxi. "Lev, someone attacked me a couple of years ago. Eventually, I suppose, I'll get over it. Find a man who loves me. But it'll take a while."

Because I was so ashamed of what Thomas Leighton had done to me, I couldn't tell Lev the whole truth about that humiliating night. But at least I had told someone my secret. It felt good, like scratching an itch.

"Then I'll have to smoke a lot of cigarettes, won't I?" Lev smiled, and his deep voice was gentle. "To pass the time during this long wait."

"Guess you will." I tossed the remains of the leaf away. "Tell me, why is there no shabbat dinner at Kiryat Anavim on Friday nights? No rabbi?" If there had been a rabbi, I thought, maybe I could have told him about what was keeping me apart from men. "Are we Jews here, or aren't we?"

"We don't need the old rituals to make us Jews. They did us no good in Europe, and they would do us no good here." He took my hand as Maxi often did, and we began to walk back toward the residence hall. "All the tribalism, all the family life, and what did it do but cripple us? We were afraid to protest, walked to the gas chambers because we thought we were protecting our wives, our children. We thought God would save us because we had been faithful to the Law. At Kiryat Anavim, we save ourselves. Our ties are not to family or to rabbis or to God, but to our comrades."

His voice had a hollow, faraway sound like the cry of the shofur when it was blown at the synagogue in Tel Aviv on Friday nights. Because he looked so angry, I didn't say straight out what I thought, but spoke cautiously. Feeling for words was not my usual way, but I didn't want to hurt this man, who had obvious been hurt quite enough.

"My brother and I used to say that because we'd lost everyone we loved, we wanted not to love anymore. We had this silly idea, you see, that if we loved somebody, he would die, sort of like a curse." Since Lev didn't laugh at me or object, I went on more confidently. "And of course, if you don't let yourself love, you don't get hurt when you lose the person. That's only logical. But whoever was as logical as that? Just machines, I think, and even they break down when people don't care enough to tend them."

We were back at the doorway to my room before he spoke. "Will you walk out with me another night, Dora?" He patted my cheek before going to his own room, just as my father used to do when I was a little girl. "When neither of us can sleep? I find I am the sort of machine that needs tending."

Often during that autumn, Lev Harkavy and I took walks in the evening after the others on our floor had gone to sleep. We spoke first about the singleness of purpose that made a good kibbutznik, and about how to improve the food production at Kiryat Anavim. As time went on, we spoke of our parents, who had all been lost in the war. One night, Lev told me about how the Jordanians had shot his wife. She had been six months pregnant. When he talked about the day they shot the hostages, he cried, leaning over the railing of the bridge, holding his head in his hands. I tried to comfort him, but he moved away and went on making harsh coughing sounds deep in his chest. Only when he had finished crying did he let me put my arms around him. I held him for a long time, rocking back and forth the way Claire used to do with Maxi when he cried for his mother.

The next day when we met at breakfast, Lev didn't sit by me as he usually did, but kept away. The next three nights we didn't meet, and I heard

Lev pacing in his room until I fell asleep. On the fourth night, at about three in the morning, he knocked on my door and stood there in his ragged underwear, asking me very formally if I would become his wife.

"It seemed like a good idea," I told Maxi that Saturday when I visited him at the Jericho dig. "So I said yes."

"Lots of things seem like a good idea at three in the morning," Maxi said, scraping carefully around a lump in the dry dirt. "It's a time when people tend to think about all the things they need and don't have."

He spoke as if he knew from experience, and for a while I dug beside him, not saying anything.

"Don't you think it would be a good marriage?" I asked finally, stopping to watch the lump at the bottom of Jericho's eleventh level look more and more like a small body.

"What I think doesn't matter," Maxi replied, bending his face close to the lump and blowing some of the dust away. "He's a bit old, that's all."

I opened my mouth to object that Lev wasn't as old as he looked, wasn't just a father figure as Maxi clearly thought he was. Before I could speak, Maxi shook the last bit of dirt off the object in the hole.

"Dora, look!" He held up a stone figure, nearly a foot tall. The face was delicate and triangular in shape, with features only slightly indented in the stone and had an expression that suggested laughter. The eye slits slanted up and so did the corners of the mouth. The face was smooth and childlike, neither male nor female. One hand held close to the body what looked like a spear. Maxi leaned over and blew on the statue as if to bring it to life.

"Now this," he said softly, "this is a god worth believing in. Child, mother, father, all in one, not like the battling gods we know." He sat back on his heels, one finger lightly on the pregnant belly of the statue. "I've often thought that people make their gods in their own image. Fertility freaks, mighty warriors, gentle martyrs. Here's the likeness of a god who is everything at once."

He reached for his camera, and then paused to look at me. "What sort of people could have made such a happy god ten thousand years ago? They would have been ashamed of us." Then he leaned over the statue, his eyes shining, and seemed for a long time to forget I was there.

Thinking of the pure Spirit who was Father Jonas's God, I had to argue with him. "Come on, Maxi. You can't believe in idols. Not in the twentieth century. God is within us, the Holy Spirit, the Shekinah. Where were you when Father Jonas explained it to us?"

"I like a god you can touch," Maxi said, "perhaps because I'm a scientist."

"You're a pagan, that's what you are," I said clipping him lightly over his ear. "How can a Jew be a pagan?"

"Belief does not come easily to me, Dora," he said with an edge to his voice that made me shut up. "Not anymore."

Maxi took as many pictures as he had film for, and I watched him record the measurements of his find, take soil samples, and finally cradle the statue in his arms as he carried it to the director of the dig. Both of us were aware that he might just have made the single most important find at the Jericho site, but for us at that moment, the god stood between us, like the marriage I was about to make.

That night back at Kiryat Anavim, I wrapped up the Ben-Ari bears that had been sitting on my dresser, and put them away in separate drawers. Lev had laughed at me, a grown woman, for keeping my old toys. Now that we were to be married, it was time to put away my childish things, but I did it as slowly as I could. When I had closed the drawers on these last relics of my childhood, I remembered Claire's song about the Ben-Aris going to Jerusalem, and her voice was in my ears now, breathless and soft as it was when she used to kiss us goodnight, bringing two extra cookies for our animals. Try as I would, when thinking of my mother, I saw Claire's face and heard her voice. As far as I knew, Maxi and I were the only children Claire would ever have, and we owed her remembrance with love.

I put my face against the cool window pane. Beyond the gorge, the distant, humped red hills resembled the curled up ginger cats that used to lie beside the fireplace in Rheims. Nothing is ever lost, I said to myself, thinking of Maxi's stone god, waked from its ten thousand year sleep, of Father Jonas's new life, and of my own. Though I had brought only one suitcase to Kiryat Anavim, I knew I was carrying with me everyone I had ever loved, and that I always would.

7

Amberfields..............................1950

Paul sat on the piano stool, painting a picture of Claire nursing their second child, a newborn son. The image was to be a traditional Madonna, with a veil and mantle, but somehow it was just Claire, her blue-veined white skin standing out sharply against the open red blouse, and a few tendrils escaping from the elastic band that held her pony tail. The baby started to stretch and complain.

"He won't take any more milk, Paul," she said, buttoning her blouse. "He never drinks as much as Timothy did."

"Wouldn't you sit with him like that for a few minutes longer" Paul felt his fingers become stiff and clumsy as they got the message to hurry.

"If only portraits didn't take so much time," Claire said, trying to arrange the baby as he had been while he nursed. "When a baby's finished, he's finished." By now, small John was red and screaming, his legs stiff. He bore no resemblance to the pale, placid Christ Child of Paul's painting, and Paul gave up. This baby was nothing like Timothy either.

In his first two years of life, Timothy had hardly cried at all, perhaps because Claire had been with him so constantly that she could anticipate every wish before he made it known. *Watching Timothy being loved,* Paul felt, *I feel loved myself. I can almost sense the baby's plump, rosy limbs as extensions of my own.* Sometimes he would go against Claire's orders and wake the sleeping boy in the night. He would run his hands over Timothy's arms and legs, which seemed to him like sculptured works of art, all chaos and impurities cut away by some sure stroke.

At such times he envied Claire for being in daylong contact with this marvel of art and engineering, for being able to observe its tiny muscles hardening under the soft curves. Whether or not he loved the child, as Claire so often said she did, Paul was unsure, for he had no words for this unfamiliar feeling. When he looked at Timothy drag his huge teddy bear about the room by one ear or push his wooden train along an invisible track, he felt his own body move, its muscles in sympathetic imitation of the child's. Sometimes he forgot his own body entirely, so alive was he in the movements of this new self, this perfect Paul, born again and suffering from no fault of mind or will, no frailty of form.

Such was not at all the case with John, the newborn. For Claire, John seemed to have displaced both his father and Timothy, who consoled each other after supper, during the interminable nursings, diaper changes, and baths that kept Claire in the nursery all evening. Paul would sit with Timothy on his lap, reading American picture books about animated railway cars, talking tugboats, and neurotic monkeys, which Claire insisted on bringing home from the local library.

When Paul rebelled at this silly fare and went to the library himself, he could find no copies of the books he remembered from childhood, in which mythological figures with horned helmets clashed in combat or sacrificed at ritual fires. What he could remember of the old stories he told Timothy. The child listened indifferently, sucking his finger to ease the pain of teething. Bored with Paul's tragic Norse gods, Timothy piled Claire's picture books in his father's lap and opened them, pointing at what he knew.

"Archeopterix," he said clearly, his finger on some preposterous, long-gone reptile. "Stegosaurus." Timothy reverently turned the page and moved from the Mesozoic to the mammalian period, jumping millions of years, as if he had command of space-time, black holes, and other freakish new phenomena that Paul could make no sense of. He wished Claire would not encourage Timothy to be precocious in the sciences. But she insisted, convinced that American children would someday become beggars in the street if they were not taught to pronounce the names of dinosaurs, parts of engines, and Jupiter's moons. "Carburetor," beamed Timothy, flipping to the relevant page in his supermarket science encyclopedia. "Piston!"

Paul rolled his small son and the polysyllabic science book off his lap. "Now, look at this," he said, taking a book of William Blake's prints off the coffee table. Timothy opened it to a picture of a heartbroken, chained giant, head on bony knees, with tiny human figures around his ankles. Timothy pulled back against Paul.

"Bad!" he shrieked. "Ugly!" Timothy ran out of the room, bawling for his mother, no doubt wanting her to soothe him with pictures of spiny-backed, antediluvian monsters so much lovelier to him than Blake's sorrowful, captive giant.

Paul picked up the book, looking again at the giant and noticed that Blake had named it "America." *Strange,* he thought, *that the land of the free should wind up in Blake's imagination as a prisoner.* Closing the book, he lay back and stared at the beamed ceiling. Paul thought about how it had felt to walk as a teacher for the first time into an American high school classroom, and he drew his knees up, clasping them tightly together, hiding his face against them, like Blake's trapped monster.

He had felt on stage that day, a performer, some sort of clown with a made-up face and over-sized feet, when he had taught his first class in German at the Indian Hills High School. The place was well-named, he told Claire later, for it was full of savages, sullen, cruel-mouthed young brutes, who whispered to each other during the long silences of that first day. Meanwhile, Paul had hunted for his place in the unfamiliar text and watched the hands of the clock crawl toward the end of the hour, when the savages would leave and go about their business of scrawling obscene remarks on lavatory walls or extorting lunch money from younger children.

Some of the boys affected unbuttoned dirty denim shirts and no socks or belts, to look hip, they said. He had heard in the faculty lounge that Californian young people were even stranger than the strangest of Indian Hills students, calling themselves Beatniks, and ridiculing other people's articles of faith. One saw pictures of such youths from time to time in news magazines that spread the word of their revolutionary activities, replete with four-letter words, long-haired anti-heroes, and drugged ecstasies.

For the most part, Paul gathered, the prosaic young of Indian Hills thought about their future as models or housewives if they were female, policemen or construction workers if they were male. The faculty members who taught science classes spoke self-importantly about the space race with Russia and how America must produce better technicians who would produce better hardware, as they called it. No school time should be wasted on frills. Classes Paul taught—German, French, and one course a week in art appreciation—were obviously frills and the students knew it. So they slept, whispered, and chewed bubble gum throughout Paul's attempts to teach them how to communicate in some language other than their mumbled, monosyllabic English.

The football players and cheerleaders sat in back with their hangers-on, who fought each other for seats near their heroes and tight-sweatered goddesses, snatching up crumbs from the tables of adolescent glory. In the middle of the room sat the obedient, vacant-eyed "C" students, who did whatever they were told, moving with slow caution through the school day like sleepwalkers. The "brains," whom Paul privately called the Parrots, sat in front, their pencil points trembling over their notebooks, their bright eyes wide behind their round glasses. Paul imagined them with red crests and yellow beaks, as he imagined the football players with furry shoulders and knuckles brushing the ground.

He had never heard any students except the Parrots volunteer a comment, take issue with a statement, or ask a question, except about the date an assignment was due. To stir them into thought, Paul tried opening each class with some current news item, speaking in simple German and asking them questions to see if they understood the event. He worked his way through the news from Korea, the treason of Klaus Fuchs, giver of atomic secrets to the Russians, and denunciations of crypto-communists. He described the avant-garde writers and artists who complained of their poverty and of the disrespect American philistines showed their angry, inhuman art. Intellectuals mocked the churches' tiresome efforts to maintain simple faith and morals. "God is dead," the intellectual elite proclaimed, echoing fashionable philosophers in Europe. "If it feels good, do it."

And so the message of drugged, godless nihilism spread from west to east, poisoning the well of Judeo-Christian culture. Even if to Paul, God indeed seemed dead, or at best indifferent, he kept his opinions to himself. *Civilization depends on religion-inspired rewards and punishments,* he felt. *Most people, would behave no better than wild animals if they did not believe in heaven and hell. Without God,* it seemed to him, *the Hitlers and Stalins would spawn again, and next time, they would win.*

Paul had listened to the tired neo-philosophies of Europe as a young man and believed they would bring only chaos and old night, a Götterdämmerung that would make Wagner's Ring operas look like musical comedies. The boasts of world leaders, who claimed that carrying the world to the brink of war was the only way to peace, reminded him of the drunken officers in his battalion who used to slay whole German regiments in imagination, while eating caviar and drinking champagne at the officers' club. Paul thought of his innocent Timothy growing up in a world run by rabid warriors, fat old men in centers of power who sacrificed the young, jealous of what they themselves had lost, like ancient priests in Canaan burning infants in the maw of Moloch. Life was cheap to those who had not carried and borne it, as Claire said when justifying her belief that men could not love children the way women did.

In his dreams, Paul often saw hordes of jack-booted soldiers breaking into the homes of frightened civilians like himself, attacking Claire, killing Timothy. On the nights when incendiary bombs and flaming mortars lit his dreams until he woke sweating and sleepless, Paul would go into the nursery and bend over Timothy, who had lost his crib to the new baby and now slept on a low cot. The sight of the sleeping child reminded him of what he had once been, fearless and at rest, without the imagination that churned up sludge from the bottom of his mind. Nothing he read in the papers made him rest any more easily. *I have heard it before*, he thought, *this same demented litany of human error.* Already some enterprising Americans were beginning to sell underground shelters against radioactive fallout, for it was rumored that the Russians had finally cracked the secrets of the A-Bomb, with the help of American spies who felt it was their moral duty to distribute democratically around the world the capacity for atomic destruction.

In the winter of 1950, President Truman, having wrestled all night with the angel of his conscience, decided to build and test a thermonuclear bomb. The result would be a weapon that could incinerate a city with many times the effectiveness of the little device that had turned Hiroshima into a crater full of charred bones. When Paul saw the news in the papers, he went to the faculty lavatory, locked himself into a metal stall, and wept, his mind's eye burning with the heat of fallen stars and the pain of seared flesh. The bodies of his men, skin shriveled from their bones by flame throwers, lying in pitted streets, were as vividly before him as they had been at Courtrai, and Paul tried in vain to drive their image back down into the cellar of his memory.

Sitting at his desk in the classroom, remembering the terrible day the atomic bomb had dropped on Hiroshima, Paul laid aside his books, leaned his chin on his clenched fists, and surveyed the rows of faces that might someday see the things he had imagined. In their own time and place, they would be consumed by the fiery toys of scientists indifferent to the laws of a dead or dying God.

Hardly knowing what he said, he began to tell them the ancient Nordic story of the Twilight of the Gods, half in German, half in English, so they would understand. First, he told them about the mysterious ring that had extinguished all love in the one who wore it, but gave that one mastery of the world. The trouble with this ring was that you might be master of the world but you would die from the burden of being unable to love. For a moment, he sensed that the Norse epic echoed the words of Christ, that love was what would save the world, but he put that message aside, not ready to believe it himself. Even the gorillas of the back row had begun to lean forward in their seats, their jaws quiet, the gum wadded in one corner of their mouths. Paul went on with his story.

"An evil warrior wanted the ring and killed a hero to get it. This hero, who was the last hope of men and gods, was stabbed in the back. His wife had turned against him and helped his enemies bring him down, since she too had been poisoned by the ring. In the end, she found out that both she and the hero she loved had been betrayed. She destroyed herself and threw away the ring. It was no good to human beings anyway, because we cannot live without love. When she lay down on her husband's flaming byre, even the hall of the gods went down in a great burning, because without human beings who can love, there can be no gods and no peace."

Paul ended the story and let his hands fall to his lap. He and the children stared at each other silently for a few minutes. No one chewed gum or wiggled or whispered. One of the Parrots, a plain girl who carried a volume by Nietzsche under her arm, had tears in her eyes and wiped them away on her sleeve.

"What has happened today?" Paul asked finally. "What has happened in our own world that long ago happened in this story?"

"The Cold War?" Someone in the middle section, behind the Parrots, waved his hand and offered an answer for the first time that term. "The Russians saying they're going to bury us?"

"That, yes," Paul said and was silent again for a moment. "But there's more. What did the President say he is going to do?" He wasn't speaking German now, since he wanted the young people to miss nothing.

A boy with the beginnings of a beard and wearing a deliberately dirty denim shirt answered. "The President says the United States can make a thermonuclear bomb big enough to blow up Moscow. The Russians are trying to make one too."

"What will happen to us?" The plain girl with her Nietzsche book clutched to her chest, spoke in a thin, high voice, as if to herself. "What are we supposed to do?"

Paul had never known what he himself was supposed to do in the face of catastrophe, so he had nothing to tell the girl. "That's up to you," he said at last. "It is not something one person can tell another, though everybody tries." He paused and leafed through a few pages of the grammar book. "Now, can anyone tell me the future conjugation of the verb 'to be'? Remember, 'to be' is a great gift, and we should not forget that."

"You're tricking us," said the plain girl, after she had waved her hand for a few minutes, trying to get Paul's attention. "That's an unreal conjugation."

"In what way? Explain." *At least someone remembered something I taught them, after all these months.*

"You have to use other verbs in order to get the future of 'to be' in German," the girl said, her glasses twinkling as the sun hit them. "In German, there is no future tense for that verb."

At her words, Paul sat still and stared out the tall windows. The sun had vanished again between the layers of heavy gray clouds, so like those he had watched over the sea on the Belgian coast before the disaster at Courtrai. *Ever since I was resurrected on the beach at Dunkirk,* Paul thought, *the life I was given has seemed as unreal as the German future tense is to this young American girl.* She had realized the darkness threatening them all by the decision of their president to create a bomb hot as the innards of the sun, by the light of which no life would grow. Sometimes he felt like a ghost, an ectoplasmic cloud hovering over the half-awake students at Indian Hill

High, warning people in a faint voice of things to come because he knew at firsthand the things that had been.

When he spoke to Claire about his fears for the future, she had brushed them off. "America's children are just fine," she said, rocking small John on her lap after tucking her milked breast away. "What is the future, if not these children? You're dreary, Paul, with all your talk of bombs and the twilight of the gods. Who were those old gods anyway, with their plots and poisons? They didn't deserve to live anymore. Christ came to replace them, and a good thing, too."

She bent over the baby with a frown. "Haven't you noticed? John breathes in a funny way. All uneven. He wheezes like Timothy did when he had the croup."

Paul kept his eyes on the principle parts of the French verbs he was correcting, his red pencil poised above the student paper. "What does the doctor say? You take him very often to the doctor, it seems to me."

"Because he doesn't breathe right." Claire walked the baby up and down the room, his blanketed form slung over her shoulder like a sack of laundry. "I wake up in the night thinking I don't hear him breathing, and can't go back to sleep until I'm sure he's started again."

"Claire, this is not your first child." Paul tapped the paper with his red pencil. "You have no reason to suppose that John will stop breathing. For a hundred thousand years human babies have continued to breathe even though their mothers don't watch them do it. John is no different from the others."

"It's easy for you to talk." Claire stopped pacing and stood in front of him, the light from the fire behind her rimming her form like an aura. "Timothy is yours, because he's turning into a boy. John will do that too, someday. Right now he's mine, and no one loves him the way I do."

Paul did not challenge Claire's reading of his love for the new baby, because he knew it was true. Sometimes he even felt that John had not been born yet, so little a dent had the baby made on his imagination. Timothy was enough for him, and other babies seemed redundant. When he thought about how many children Claire wanted, Paul trembled. *Raising the five children Claire talks about would cost more than I can possibly earn. Claire and Charlotte prattle on about five, six, ten babies as if they were so many puppies. Already Claire has borne two children in three years, and she is only halfway through her twenties.* In dreams that woke Paul in the middle of the night, babies crawled out of the closets when he opened doors, appeared from behind the furniture, out from under beds. Dozens of babies, all crying and naked, needing to be clothed, fed, educated. He could hear his mother's voice saying that each child would require a tour of the continent and private rooms at a university.

He would wake up sweating and holding his head, after nightmares about a superfluity of babies. Claire refused to practice birth control. "Tampering with human life at the source," she called it, copying the words of their priest and infuriating Paul. *I cannot bear the idea that Claire discusses the secrets of our married life with the parish priest,* Paul said to himself. Y*es, she is trying to be a good Catholic, whatever her Huguenot ancestors might have believed but still...* Every time he saw Father Echlin in town, Paul would cross the street to avoid having to greet him. He could hardly bring himself to go to Mass for fear of seeing Father Echlin's small, bright eyes on him, the unspeakable sinner who would stoop to tampering with life at its source. Paul had tried not touching Claire during her fertile times, of which he kept guilty, secret track, hovering with his red pencil over the calendar like a boy with a naughty picture. But when Claire curled up next to him, her body soft against his, Paul forgot what time of the month it was. John's birth was the result of one such forgetting, less than a year before, and ever since, Paul had slept on the couch in his study for two weeks out of every month.

Claire often tried on those occasions to urge him back to their bed. "I'll be good," she said humbly, sitting beside him on the narrow sofa bed. "No touching. It's just that I want you near me."

"Whoever made up these ridiculous rules?" Paul groaned. "I think they hate sex," he said. "That's why they became priests in the first place. If deep down, when a man hates and fears women, what better place for him than the priesthood? It's a good place to hide."

"They're not hiding," Claire said, drawing the corner of his blanket over her bare shoulders, "they're sacrificing. What kind of a faith asks no sacrifice?"

"I thought Jesus said God wants mercy, not sacrifice," Paul answered, wondering if she would repeat his words to Father Echlin, and come back with stories of how the blasphemous patriarchs of Israel had spilled their seed on the ground and were slain by Jehovah in the interest of family values. "I suspect Jesus would have found absurd the logic that says both abortion and prevention of birth are equally mortal sins. If nobody's there, how can you kill him? Ask Father Echlin to answer that."

"Someone just like Timothy or John could be there, don't you see?" Claire argued. "In God's mind, the new life is there and by stopping it from being born, we commit a sort of murder. I can understand that, and I wasn't even born Catholic like you."

Paul saw that their conversation was going nowhere. He merely kissed Claire's palms and folded them together, away from him. *She's against practicing birth control because she wants a big family,* Paul knew, *not for doctrinal reasons*. Sighing Paul turned over on the sofa bed, his back to her, not saying goodnight when she left his study. He felt such anger rising in his chest that if mild Father Echlin had appeared before him at that moment, Paul would have shaken him until the priest's rimless spectacles fell off.

"It's not as if I wanted other women," Paul said crossly to the invisible presence of Father Echlin. "I just want to make love to my wife without having to worry about how to pay for somebody's college education." He punched his pillow a few times, muttered into it, and finally subsided into sleep.

While Claire attended Father Echlin's Friday night services during Lent, Paul was left in charge of the sleeping babies. On the third of these occasions, when Father Echlin was scheduled to talk about the wisdom of Divine Providence, Claire had almost decided to stay home. Small John, now two months old, had suffered one of his wheezing attacks that afternoon. Although Dr. Fairfax had said the baby was in no danger, Claire had her doubts. Before leaving for church, she hung over the baby's crib, wondering to Paul if she should take John with her.

"I'm sure he's better off in his own bed," Paul said. "It's cold tonight."

"Then promise me you'll look in on him every half hour." Claire let him walk her to the front door, but her steps were slow.

Paul put his arms around her as she stood in the open doorway, the ends of her lace scarf raised gently by the wind. "Of course. Now, run along and hear all about the wisdom of Divine Providence. It would do us both good to believe in it."

Paul closed the front door. As he put Timothy to bed, he noticed how slim the child's body seemed now that it was no longer padded by bulky diapers. The two years of his life had been so brief that Paul suddenly felt as if he and the child too were ephemeral as mayflies. Only a short while ago, Timothy had been as small and unformed as John, and yet out of that flaccid bundle of newborn flesh had come eyes bright with questions about the constitution of trees, lips that spoke hypotheses and truths, and a body so open to learning new and astonishing things that Paul would not be surprised if by the following week, the boy were able to fly.

"My prayers," Timothy reminded him. "You need to be here when I say them, like Mama."

Paul knelt beside the cot with his son as the boy said his short prayer, made the sign of the cross backwards, like a Greek, and closed his eyes as soon as his head hit the pillow. For a few minutes Paul stood over him, his eyes on Timothy's face. Just so his father must have looked at him, a nexus of possibilities, and just so his father must have shaped him, naming birds and stars and telling him why the hands of the clock moved. Even then, Paul had felt that time, as the clock taught it, was unreal, and that Timothy had been alive in the old Count. *Is this what Claire meant when she argued that we see only the life that has been conceived and carried to fullness, while God sees the potential life and longs to bring it home to himself? Perhaps the definition of God,* Paul thought, kissing Timothy good night, *is the sum of all the possibles. Perhaps God lives in a dimension that subsumes all the others, so that every form of life is fully present to him in a single now, whether it has been born in the flesh or not.*

He had a quick vision of many points of varicolored light, stars of different magnitudes crowded together and pulsing like living tissue, all radiating from a center that folded inward like a woman's birth chamber, the inside hidden, dark, and full of futures. Each point of light was a different color, as if a painter had overlaid thick, quick brushfuls of violet, white, and yellow on each other. Suddenly his fingers felt the presence of a brush and his mind was on the palette where the colors were mixed. *Tonight I will paint,* Paul thought, *paint for the second time since I came to America.*

Pausing in front of the baby's room, Paul listened a moment, thought he heard the rustle of plastic pants, and hurried on. He ran down to the cellar, his steps light as a boy's, and brought up his easel and paints. For this project he would need the biggest canvas he could find. The only one that would serve was already spoiled at the center by an abortive attempt at a Madonna and child. *Where those two figures are,* Paul thought as he set up his easel by the fireplace, *will be a sort of fishnet, shining with scales and water drops, plucked from behind by an invisible hand that draws the whole surface gently backward into itself, swallowing the mother and child in a mouthful of light.* He smiled as he began to work.

When Claire came back three hours later, Paul had not moved from the spot by the fire. His canvas was half-covered with bright points of layered paint that seemed to glow with half-buried light. One point merged into the next, and yet each was distinct. Each was touched by all the others in an endless trembling, like the electric waves between cells moving faster than the mind could comprehend. Paul's hand was working independently of his thought, or rather, as he tried later to explain, his hand became all that he was, and he had no thought left.

"Father Echlin was really good tonight," Claire said, pulling off her scarf so fast that a lock of her dark auburn hair fell across her cheek, reddened by the wind. "You had the feeling that you could almost see your own life the way God sees it, like a comet that visits only once. But for God the comet is always there, spreading light." She came closer to Paul, looking at the painting.

"Kind of like this," she said. "I like the way you've gathered up the light, Paul. It's different from anything you've done before. The canvas seems to be moving as if it's alive." She tossed her scarf and coat on a chair. "I'd better go look in on the baby. He's been on my mind all evening."

Paul walked away from his painting, studying it as he moved. *I'll call it Creation. It's a new beginning for me.* He tossed another log on the fire, and the hearth blazed like the colors on his canvas.

"Paul!" Claire's cry was hardly a name, more a sound torn out of a machine by something gone wrong in the gears. "The baby's dead!" Her footsteps pounded down the stairs, and Paul heard her calling Dr. Fairfax on the phone in the hall. As she waited for the doctor to answer, she covered the mouthpiece with one hand and called out, "Paul, you didn't take care. You promised, and you just sat there painting while John died."

Feeling as though he had been caught in the act of murder, Paul felt naked and cold before Claire's accusing eyes. From long ago, he could hear his father's voice blaming him for what he had failed to do and his mother's for what he had done wrong. Their voices mingled with Claire's, and his chest hurt as he held his breath.

"You're a cruel man." Claire's words were cried out with a force as final as damnation. She slammed down the phone and rushed into the living room. "You let our baby die. Look, this is how bad I think you are." She seized the painting and threw it into the fireplace, where the wet oils immediately caught fire and sent sparks into the air.

His breath choked him and he opened and closed his mouth, unable to defend himself with speech, just as he had stood before his general, torn up inside like the bodies of his bleeding, lost men. *I failed them all because I did not love enough,*" Paul thought, staring at the canvas that twisted like a curling body in the flames. *Just as I did not love my men or little John enough, and because of me they are dead.*

"No," Paul cried, and ran out the door, his breath searing his throat as it finally burst out of him. "I loved them. No one can say I didn't."

Dr. Fairfax pushed past him into the house, followed by the ambulance driver, but Paul kept going. He ran out into the fields of dried yellow weeds and lay down in the midst of them, like one more plant waiting for spring and resurrection. Long after the ambulance scream had shrunk away in the night, he lay shivering in the remains of last year's buttercups.

"Crib death," Dr. Fairfax told him later. "No one knows why it happens. Suddenly the baby can't breathe anymore. He seems to forget how to live. No one's fault."

Despite the doctor's words, Paul felt the baby had died because his father had not loved him as he loved Timothy, and had not sat with him body to body, willing him to breathe and live. He knew Claire blamed him, whatever the doctor's verdict, and he was ashamed.

As the months went by after John's death, Paul slept in his study, afraid to go near Claire. She spoke to him in a faraway voice, as if they lived on different continents and communicated by telegrams. Timothy had become perpetually naughty and threw temper tantrums whenever he didn't have his way. He appeared to know that the adults around him wanted calm and would do anything to get it. When he stamped his foot and demanded candy, Claire gave it to him, mechanical as a sleepwalker, not seeming to notice what she did, though Paul glanced at her in surprise. They had agreed never to give their children sweets, but Claire seemed to have forgotten. She went through the motions of her life, being polite to Paul, too generous to Timothy, and hardly spoke to Charlotte, during the once-a-week visits. When Charlotte's son hit Timothy, Claire would pick up her child and hold him tightly, saying nothing.

At last, halfway into the summer, Paul spoke to Father Echlin about Claire's condition, and the priest came to see them. He tucked his cassock around his legs as if he were cold, and Paul could see the man was nervous, out of his depth. Claire looked like a thin, angry goddess, thirsty for blood, and Paul felt as nervous as the priest.

"I hear that you play the piano, Claire," Father Echlin began, staring into his coffee cup, no doubt trying to construct some aphorism on the wisdom of Divine Providence in the matter of dead babies. "The parish needs an organist. Could you play for us?"

Claire stared at him, probably remembering that it was on the night this man had spoken of God's care for his children that John had died, and she had become a stranger to her family.

"You might play Father Echlin the marriage anthem, Claire. We haven't heard it in a long time." Paul had little hope that she even heard him, but wanted to support the priest's kindly effort.

Looking at her hands as if she had forgotten what use they might be put to, Claire got up slowly and sat down at the piano. At first, her hands fell heavily on the keys, making sound but not music. Then they found their way into the rich chords of the anthem. When it was over, she sat staring at the keyboard with a surprised look on her face.

"For Dora and Maxi," Paul urged, finally able to hope that the dry, dead time was over. "Play the dances you wrote for them."

Claire's face was still at first, then as she played the *Kindertanzen,* again, her mouth began to move, as if she were talking to Maxi and Dora and to John, who had not lived long enough to draw music out of her.

"She must become our organist," Father Echlin exclaimed to Paul. "We have no one like her."

"I don't know much about playing an organ," Claire said slowly, as if she were only now aware that the priest was in the room. "I used to practice on the church organ in Rheims, but that was a long time ago. I could try again. Yes, I believe I could."

When the priest had gone Paul took Claire upstairs. She leaned against him and cried, saying John's name over and over again, mixing it with the names of the children she had lost at Dunkirk. Paul lay beside her on the bed and reached out to stroke her body. Claire responded slowly, as though she were reluctant to wake up from a long, healing sleep. Paul kissed her until she kissed him back, until to one music they did one dance.

Nine months after Father Echlin had asked Claire to become music director for St. Michael's, Julie Louise was born at home, as Claire insisted. The little girl was named after Paul's mother, who had recently died in Paris, too suddenly for Paul to be at her side. Timothy was disappointed that Julie was not a brother, and asked if John were ever coming back. But Paul took the baby girl in his arms and put his face against hers, knowing her as his own from the moment he touched her. He held the child whenever he was allowed to, staring into her round, perfect face as if it were the center of that lost painting which Claire had thrown into the fire and he had never sought to recreate. Julie stretched her small body under his hands and drew in her breath for a mechanical, colicky cry, all unaware that she was for Paul central to the web of life, the point at which the whole universe was drawn into God.

Shortly after Julie's birth, his mind full of images of Claire's empty, waiting body, Paul went to a doctor other than the familial Dr. Fairfax, and had his vas deferens sealed off so that it would send no more children to stand between him and Claire. *One more child,* he thought, *even one as wonderful as my Julie, would finish me off.* And so he sat under local anesthesia while a doctor tied off the vessels of life and sewed him up. Claire did not know Paul could have no more children because he was afraid to tell her. At times, when she held him in the night, moving her body under his as if to draw life out of it, Paul felt the same cold, helpless sorrow that had caused him to stand weeping in the streets of Courtrai.

About the time of Paul's operation, a strange sickness settled over Indian Hills High and over the whole country, from what Paul could gather. Persecutions and witch-hunts were dissolving the fabric of trust, so that society itself was becoming a tattered rag. The sickness did not come home to Paul until his principal called him in after a series of parental conferences.

"Paul, you know we feel you're a good language teacher," the principal began, spinning his pen between his index fingers. "But being good at your job isn't enough anymore."

Feeling as he had in the old days when he was told by his father that he had not come up to the standard expected of him, Paul sat straight, digging one thumbnail into his palm, so he would not notice pain elsewhere.

"We're in a state of siege," the principal went on. "The communists are swallowing country after country and spies are in the Pentagon itself." The principal dropped his pen and vaguely moved his hands in the air. "No one trusts foreigners, these days. You told that story to the kids about the end of the world, about peace always being better than war. Some of the parents came to me, nervous about your being foreign. Understand, Paul. The communists want to bury us and we're all scared."

When Paul did not answer, the principal began to talk very fast. "I have to ask for your signature on this loyalty oath." He took off his glasses and polished the lenses vigorously, looking at Paul with unfocused eyes.

Paul stared at the words of the oath until they blurred. *Perhaps,* he thought, *the destruction of the world had to come before a new creation. 'Things fall apart. The center cannot hold.' The lovely, ordered world I knew as a child will be trampled by barbarians screeching their ugly music and rude words. Honor has become a quaint notion. It is the end of the world, or at least the end of civilization, and I grieve that I have lived to see it.* He laid the paper back in front of the principal and shook his head.

"God knows I am no communist," he began, remembering his fear of the invading Russians. "God knows, I do not believe in brain-washing or dictators. I only want…," here he paused, finding it hard to tell the pale, plump principal that he did not care about teaching frills to the youth of Pine Lake. "I only want to protect my family and paint pictures. That's where my loyalty lies." His voice broke, and he had to stop for a moment. "As for signing this paper, I cannot. That is something no honorable man could do."

Having lost his job, Paul came home to find Claire giving piano lessons to a pupil, while Charlotte tended Timothy and Julie next door. The family would have enough money to buy the groceries, thanks to Father Echlin's weekly check, paying Claire for directing the choir and playing the organ on

Sundays. The recording Claire had made of the choir singing her marriage anthem on one side and the *Kindertanzen* on the other, had recently been bought by a nationwide music firm that sold religious music. It had already brought in five hundred dollars in royalties. Only the week before, the record had been played on a New York City radio station. Claire had received a commission from the Cathedral of St. John the Divine to write a liturgy of reconciliation. Paul was trying not to envy his wife's success, but he was beginning to feel unnecessary. Not only could he no longer produce children, the children Claire wanted, but he could not even produce a paycheck. *At least we can sell off the rest of Mother's antiques in an emergency,* Paul thought as he came in the front door and stamped snow off his boots. *The past is all I can count on to get me through the ordeal of the present. I cannot find anything in myself adequate to the task.*

Without telling Claire about the lost job, Paul went off to Manhattan the next day, a portfolio of his religious paintings tucked under his arm. *More baggage from the past,* he said to himself. He headed for the Marcus Art Gallery on the fashionable upper East Side, near the Metropolitan Museum of Art. He had read in the New York *Times* that new artists were welcome to show their work at the gallery after 'a free evaluation of its quality' by Mr. Marcus, the proprietor.

The gallery was a small one, with paintings stacked one against another, leaning against every available wall, table, and crate. Yehuda Marcus, a plump, balding little man, sat on a bar stool over his work table, examining Paul's paintings with a jeweler's lens, then standing back to look at them with his naked eye.

"We have too many paintings already, as you see," he said, gesturing around the gallery. "I had hoped to encourage unknowns. Who would have guessed there are so many of them? Just now, I have come from Israel, with dozens of canvases. Where to put them?" He shook his head and the jeweler's lens fell out of his eye, hanging like a monocle from a cord around his neck.

"They have terrible technique, these Israeli painters, but their work is alive. It jumps off the canvas, so to speak. A pity the paint will crack in ten years. They were too impatient, you see, to mix their paints properly. Now you, young man," he said sincerely to Paul, who leaned forward, clasping his damp hands together. "Your work is not alive, you know." He beamed a kindly, anxious smile at Paul, evidently not wanting him to despair in the manner of rejected artists. "The figures clump about like statues, all heavy and stiff. You should have tried sculpture, perhaps."

"I did." Paul began to gather up his paintings and to stuff them back into the big leather portfolio. "Nothing came of that either."

"Not so fast." Mr. Marcus put out his hand over one of the canvases, the half-finished portrait of Claire and John. "You see here and here," he said, pointing with his surprisingly slim white forefinger. "Excellent detail, precise workmanship. In this hair curling on the mother's neck, this crease of the baby's arm. Not often do we see technique like yours these days. You studied in Paris?"

"At the Conservatory, yes." Paul had heard so little praise of his work that he immediately distrusted the small man. "My paintings were not highly regarded, I'm afraid."

"But in technique," Mr. Marcus persisted, leaning forward. "There you excel. Surely they must have said so." When Paul nodded, Mr. Marcus went on. "The Metropolitan Museum has asked me to recommend to them artists who could serve as restorers in their workshop. Until now, I have found no one to recommend. Would you like to try for such a position?"

"I would, gladly." Paul relaxed in his chair, suddenly so relieved that he doubted he could stand up. "Let us hope they agree with you."

"From your mouth to God's ear," the other man said. Seeing Paul did not understand, Mr. Marcus explained it was a prayer. "May you get what you want, is all this prayer means. You were in the war?" he asked abruptly.

"I served in the French army, then in the Resistance," Paul said, not minding the question as he usually did. "And you?"

"You might say I served at Bergen-Belsen," Mr. Marcus said, fingering his jeweler's lens. "Burying the dead, comforting those about to die. I recorded their names in my head, so someday, if I survived, I could at least give tribute to their memory. It kept me alive, I think, the task I took on myself." He poured two cups of tea out of an elaborately carved antique Russian samovar and handed one to Paul.

"And after the war, you went to Israel with all those names still in your head?"

"Yes, I joined the other survivors in Jerusalem, and together we wrote out hundreds, thousands of names and all that we could remember about each person's last moments and last words. That was all the survivors came away with, you understand—their memories. It perhaps gave some comfort to them. At least, it gave comfort to me." He sighed and stared at the paintings on the wall behind his visitor, as if seeing into a far distance. "Have you children?"

"A little boy and a newborn girl." Paul knew better than to ask the same question of Mr. Marcus, imagining the answer he was likely to get.

"Ah, then, you must have a gift for this new baby, something beautiful for her to look at, so she will become an artist like her papa." He rummaged in a carton and pulled out an irregular piece of leaded stained glass, with the Star of David at the center and held it up.

"There," he said. "All the way from Jerusalem, this comes. Broken, but beautiful, is it not? Perhaps we too must be broken to be someday beautiful. It must be that God has some reason for suffering, and what better reason than beauty?"

Mr. Marcus patted Paul on the shoulder. "Go now and see about the job," he said. "I will call ahead to say you are coming. We survivors must help one another, after all. That, perhaps, is another reason God saved us."

Back at Amberfields, as he told Claire about Mr. Marcus and the new job that he had been given at the Museum workshop, Paul leaned over Julie's crib with the gift from Jerusalem. The baby flailed her hands, wanting to touch the sparkling glass. When Claire reached out to touch the Star of David, Paul knew she was remembering other children, not her own. He hung the Star near Julie's crib, in the window, so the red light of the setting sun could stream through the glass like lifeblood.

8

Dora's Journal

Israel........................1956

Lev thought it would be good for me to work in the infants' house for a while before our baby was born. It wasn't clear to me whether he hoped I would learn something about children and be a better mother, or whether he wanted me to get my fill of child-rearing before it became something personal. Knowing Lev and his devotion to communal values, the second reason was probably closer to the truth. It was hard for me to leave the garden to Esther, who had been critical from the start about my use of French intensive cultivation. Esther had more on her mind than our contest over how best to grow tomatoes, as I learned from Shana, my old partner in the kitchen.

Shouting above the wails of babies in the infant house, where she had come to visit me on her lunch break, Shana leaned closer to me. "Esther's doubled the distance between all the tomatoes you put in. By the time Lev caught her at it, the transplanting was done."

"And to move them again would be hard on the plants," I shouted back, putting down the baby I had been changing. It began to howl as soon as it left my arms, but I had to rush on and change the messy diaper of the baby next in line. "The tomatoes will have to stay where they are. Such a waste of work, though, and fertilizer too. What gets into Esther, anyhow?"

"You don't know?" Shana steered me out on the porch so we wouldn't have to shout over the din. "Lev and Esther used to be an item, before you came on the scene."

I tried and failed to visualize tall, thin-faced Esther, with her manlike cap of pepper-colored hair, being intimate with my husband. "She wasn't the only one, you said?"

"But she was the main one," Shana looked around to see if anyone were near enough to overhear. "Esther survived all the rest, until you. I think she expected that someday he'd get around to marrying again, and hoped he would choose her."

"So she moved my tomatoes in revenge?" It was hard to believe anyone would torment innocent plants just to show me how she felt about my husband.

"Not so much revenge," Shana explained. "An act of war, rather. That's why Lev moved you off garden duty until the baby comes, just to keep you and Esther apart. When is the baby due?" She patted my swollen belly.

"In less than a month, I think. I'm more than ready. He kicks all night and sits on my bladder all day. The doctor says he's enormous, a nine-pounder at least. There's talk of sending me to Hadassah Hospital for the delivery."

My tone was nonchalant, but underneath, I had my worries. Here was this infinitely large baby growing bigger in me by the minute, and who must, on some day of reckoning, come though my small finite pelvis, over which the doctor shook his head, mumbling ominously about calipers and centimeters and forceps. Still, since Hadassah Hospital was in Jerusalem, only six miles away, my delivery was not a subject I brooded on.

My mind was busy with a scheme. I would try to make an end run around Esther by appealing to the agricultural committee. Over in Degania Kibbutz, a commercial greenhouse had been built and was turning a profit. I wanted to build a greenhouse that would give us year round leafy greens, paid for by avocados we could sell abroad.

Until the baby was born, however, this project would have to wait, as would my plan for a potash plant, which would supply just about all our fertilizer. Mostly, though, I wanted the birth over with, so Lev and I could be close again. It had been a long time since we had shared a room. Lev lost all interest in me as a love object once my pregnancy had begun to show. Instead, he hovered anxiously about me, and would have carried me from place to place if I had let him. Remembering what happened to his first wife at the hands of the Jordanians, I was not surprised at his anxiety now. Still, I was restless, wanting love more than protection. Lev seemed to be the sort of man who could give only one or the other, not both at once, and so was not of much use to me during this breeding time.

When Maxi phoned to say he had made another find in Jericho, I insisted on visiting him, over Lev's protests. Being pregnant made me feel trapped in my shapeless, heavy body, and the whole kibbutz seemed like a cage. Jericho, by contrast, was a broad stretch of plain with steep red hills rising in the distance. Maxi showed me the houses they had reconstructed with the same old style, foot-crushed brick that had been mixed eight thousand years ago with straw and water. The stream that had made Jericho an impregnable fortress still flowed, and Arab girls still carried water jars on their shoulders from Jericho to their villages.

"Think of it—we're standing on the very ground where the whole Neolithic revolution began. Right here, humans moved from hunting and gathering to growing plants for food." Maxi pushed his straw hat back on his head. "You'd have been right at home back then, Dora. A fertility goddess who raises food in her garden. In those days, women were the channels to spirit, maybe because they were used to carrying life. How about you? Channeled any spirits lately?"

Maxi liked to tease me about being superstitious just because I believed in God. I didn't rise to his bait. "Only Lev, who's turned phantom on me," I said. "Always in Tel Aviv, being political, never with me."

"That will change once the baby comes." Maxi bent down to check a lump of earth by the side of the path, to see if any treasure were inside. "Lev's a hunter, not a farmer. He's a throwback to the old stone age. Like most males, I think, he would rather roam around hunting and fighting than stay home to weed the garden. Your Lev goes to Tel Aviv and makes a speech that sets Arab-Jewish peace talks back by twenty years, and why? Because he's a hunter, that's why. His god is the spear."

Maxi and Lev had always argued about politics, and there was no making peace between them. Maxi thought all the hawks, with their insistence on pre-emptive strikes against the Arab enemy were primitive barbarians. Nazis in yarmulkhs, he called them, which for my gentle Maxi was strong language. Lev, on the other hand, felt that Maxi lived in a dream world of fertility statues and old clay pots and knew nothing about the Arabs' unchanging intention to push all Jews into the sea.

"It's human nature," Lev argued with Maxi, on one of my brother's rare visits to the kibbutz. "The only answer to force is force, and there's an end to it, ha? When someone tells you straight out that he intends to bury you, you either lie down in the grave or hit him with the shovel."

Maxi, being a dove, had given up and gone to pour the coffee, but Lev had not persuaded him. Now, working at his dig, he explained to me that men could survive almost anything but the loss of their principles. While he wasn't an observant Jew, Maxi at least held to Jewish values. He had even come to believe that the Bible was right about Jewish history, though he had once thought the whole thing was a myth.

"See this oven?" He pointed to the fenced-off area nearby. "After I uncovered it, we carbon-dated it to the thirteenth century B.C.. The blackened layer shows it was in a fire, very likely the fire Joshua's men set to destroy Jericho, once its walls had fallen."

"They were warriors, then, like Lev," I said. "And had a warrior god."

"Yes, and the warrior god, the great Patriarch in the sky, still rules the West, you know. Jesus never stood a chance." Maxi's eyes were focused far away, as if he had forgotten I was there. "Jesus, Yeshua, would have ruled by love."

"Love doesn't rule," I said softly under my breath, so Maxi wouldn't hear me. "Love only serves."

Maxi was still talking about the triumph of the wrong kind of God. "Of course, the prophet of love wasn't allowed to get away with his pacifist message. The hawks were in charge then, as they are now."

Arguing with Maxi, as Lev said, was like spitting in the wind. You hit nothing you aimed at and had better not start in the first place, unless you liked having a face full of spit. Lev was pleased, though, that Maxi had won the archeology prize at the university for the second year in a row, because of the Joshua find, as the oven was called. Lev often referred in public to Maxi as his brother-in-law, getting what political mileage he could from the family connection. He hoped to be elected to the Knesset and needed all the publicity he could get. Sometimes I wondered if our marriage had not been part of his public relations campaign. He liked to bring reporters to our room to take pictures of pregnant me, sewing baby clothes. My brother was not pleased that Lev had appropriated his scholarly fame for the Hawks' cause, and the two had exchanged hot words on the subject.

For this reason, I was sorry that Lev insisted on meeting Maxi and me at Beit Sahur, a village outside Bethlehem, where the sparse fields suddenly turn into desert. Lev planned to escort me back home because Arab guerillas had been active in this border area. When we met him at a kibbutz near the village, he and my brother didn't have much to say to each other. Maxi clearly hadn't missed the implication that only Lev and not he could protect their helpless, rotund Dora. If I had been less drowsy, and the cramps in my lower abdomen any less sharp, I would have left the two of them wrangling and taken a bus to Hadassah Hospital by myself. During the pregnancy, I had become passive and lumpish, not insisting on my own way as Lev said I usually did. We stopped briefly in the dining hall of the kibbutz and had only just gotten into our fish dinner when the sound of firing began, followed by the heavy thump of mortar shells landing nearby.

"Everybody up," shouted a man at the head table. "To the shelters. Visitors follow along. No questions will be answered at this time."

No questions were being answered half a day later, when we were still packed into the shelter and could hear the explosions over our heads, just as they had while we learned Hebrew from Father Jonas during the London blitz. Only this time, instead of conjugating verbs, I was seriously engaged in the business of giving birth. For the first hours of labor, I pretended to sleep, curled up with my head on Lev's lap, all the while thinking that my cramps were the result of spoiled whitefish.

After a while I groaned, and Lev leaned down anxiously. "What?" he asked. "Are you hurting?"

"These are pretty bad cramps," I said to him, trying to keep my voice down. "Not stomach cramps, I think. Probably labor pains. I never had them before, so I don't know."

Suddenly a vise seemed to close around my belly, and I held my sides together the way one does when laughing, sure they were about to split. Only I wasn't laughing, because the pain was shooting from one side of me to the other, as if trying to break out. When this thought occurred to me, I realized that of course it—the pain, the baby—was trying to escape. The baby was nothing but a poor, maddened, crushed little thing being squeezed like a tomato, his head pounding against the pelvic ring which the doctor had said could never let it through. Each time his skull ground into my bones, I shrieked, feeling both his pain and mine.

By this time, the others had given us a curtained-off area in the shelter so I could have some privacy while I screamed and vomited and strained as if trying to evacuate all my bones. After what seemed like days, I asked Lev how long we had been in this hole under the kibbutz, and he said it had been twenty hours. Our radio contact with Jerusalem had broken down early in the attack, and the Israeli Defense Force had no idea that the kibbutz had been under fire for a day and a night. Finally some scouts were sent to alert the army station fifteen miles away, because we were running out of ammunition. By this time, also, I was running out of strength. When I screamed, the sounds came out like breath underwater, bubbling in my throat. Lev leaned over me, holding my shoulders as I writhed against the baby's attempts to slam his way through the other end of me. Maxi was talking to the midwife, all we were able to find for the job at hand, since this kibbutz was too healthy to support a doctor.

"You don't have forceps?" Maxi was saying. "Then I'll go over to the kitchen and get the canning calipers. We'll improvise. She's got to have help."

Whatever it was Maxi fought his way through the mortar shelling to find was not enough. The midwife tried again and again, shoving the tool into me. "I can't reach the baby's head," she told them finally. "It's stuck just above the pelvic ring. No chance it'll get through on its own.

"Well, what do we do, then?" Lev held me close against him. "What happens if the baby's stuck?"

"We wait for the woman to die," said the midwife, "so we can cut her open and try to save the child. It happens this way sometimes, if there's no doctor to do a c-section."

"That's unacceptable." Maxi got out some of his archeological tools, and I watched him through a red haze, every blood vessel in my eyes broken. "Sterilize this one and this. We'll break the pelvic ring open. It's the only way. An amateur caesarian would make her bleed to death. At least broken bones don't bleed."

"You don't know what you're saying," the midwife argued, sitting back on her heels. "She'd probably never walk again."

"She may not even live," Maxi cried suddenly, his voice breaking. "Do you know exactly where the weakest point of that bone is?"

The woman nodded and took the instruments, as another shell struck just above us, making the light flicker.

"Well, then, break it." Maxi held my legs apart while Lev held my shoulders. "Do it fast. She can't take any more. There's too much blood lost already."

I heard his voice from far away and then felt the baby lurch in me.

"He's turned," the midwife said. "The feet are down."

"Now," Maxi said, his voice tight and low. "Break the bone now before the baby's head goes down again. We may be able to save him yet."

The midwife pounded inside me with the implements and my body shook, resisting breakage. I kept pulling back, deeper into Lev's arms, trying to escape the hands and the steel. The pain drove me out of my body, and I seemed to float up to a corner of the ceiling, from where I looked down at the bloody scene below.

At that moment, I felt a presence with me, as if I were being held up by invisible arms in an embrace so tender that I surrendered to it, holding back nothing of my willful self. I looked behind me, thinking to see Father Jonas, for the presence felt like his. Words reverberated in my mind, which had become a great empty room, with nothing of me left in it. The voice I heard sounded something like the sea, slow and rolling and comforting as it swept me up and bathed me until I felt washed clean for the first time. *You do not know me now, but soon, beloved, you will know me as Yeshua. When that time comes, you will remember this moment and thank God for the suffering that has brought you close to me.* I knew then that I would live and dropped back into my flailing, anguished body.

"Yeshua," I murmured, "don't go. Stay with me."

"You need to press harder," Maxi ordered the midwife, and then helped her open the excavation instrument that was trying to dig my baby out of this tomb that was his mother. "Hold her tightly, Lev."

Though Maxi and Lev said later they had heard nothing, in my own ears, the crunch of the bony ring breaking was louder than the mortars. As the broken bones parted, the baby began to drop down and the midwife guided him out. He slid into her hands, she said afterward, like a pea from the pod.

I was afraid to see the child, afraid his head had been punished into idiocy, afraid he would die under my eyes, but the midwife held him up, a big, red, shouting boy, his head a bit lopsided, but no worse-looking than other newborns in the infant house. Yeshua had apparently blessed him too, and saved his life as he had saved mine. That is when I began saying that I was not lucky, but blessed.

"Let me touch him," I remember whispering, before I passed out from the pain in my broken skeleton. "Let me touch this fine boy who the Lord God has given me as my redemption."

"She must be delirious," Lev said. "Dora never talks like this."

"Maybe not to you," Maxi replied shortly. "There's more to her than you are ever likely to know, unless you…"

His voice faded, and I didn't wake up until an ambulance, having arrived with an army detachment, had me halfway to Jerusalem. Lev was at one end of me, carrying our baby, and Maxi was at the other, helping the orderly to hold ice packs against my broken pelvis.

"Maxi," I said, my lips hardly moving, "thank you for the baby. I love you." Then I passed out again. Later, from what Lev told me, I realized these words were not the most tactful ones I might have chosen. But at that time, Lev was forgotten, and Maxi's hands were all I could sense, along with the voice of Yeshua delivering me into life again, out of that darkness in which for twenty-four hours I had gone down and nearly drowned. Like the sun, I had died and returned to life at dawn.

In Hadassah Hospital, where I was to spend two months recovering, the doctors were interested, in an academic sort of way. "A lot of tubes got torn loose during the breaking of the bones," observed the head of Obstetrics. "No more babies for you, miss, as I suppose you'll be glad to hear." I wasn't glad and didn't answer him.

Another doctor, an orthopedic surgeon, operated on the pelvic break, mending it with plastic clamps. "No worse damage than a good head-on auto collision might have done," he said cheerfully. "You'll be up and about before the baby learns to smile. Young bones mend fast."

My favorite doctor was the pediatrician who insisted I have baby Benjamin beside me whenever I wished, which was all the time. "She's been through so much to get him," the doctor said. "We must let her have the fruit of her labor."

So as my pelvic bones mended, I nursed Benjamin, cuddled him, watched him move his lips in what seemed the beginnings of a smile. He didn't know I couldn't sit up, couldn't change his diapers, couldn't move below my waist, trapped as I was in a cast that kept me even more helpless than he. Together we watched the sun rise and set as he pulled at my breast, his fists pounding wherever they landed. We woke in the night together and whether or not he was hungry, I let him nurse, wanting him to have more than he asked for, more than he needed, until he lay back, his mouth dribbling milk, with a gaseous burp, blessed past my comprehension. He looked the way I had felt when Yeshua spoke to me and brought me back from death.

Already I was planning how to keep Benjamin with me once we were back at Kiryat Anavim. Yeshua had given him to me, and I was not about to give up this gift from God, my one and only child. When Lev came to see me and wanted to take the baby to the infant house, I pretended to be in extreme pain and held Benjamin tightly. I would go nowhere without my baby, I told Lev. He sat down stiffly in his chair near my bed, being a stranger, not knowing what to do with this new, non-communal Dora.

Maxi understood and told me to let him know if the kibbutz people tried to take my baby away. I didn't believe they would, and smiled when Maxi warned me. But once Benjamin was two months old, and I was cured of my broken bones, the rules of Kiryat Anavim came down on me like the walls of Jericho at the sound of Joshua's trumpet. The word from the executive committee was that I could visit Benjamin in the infant house no more than two hours a day, during the general visiting period. Furious and balked, I asked Lev if the order were his, but he avoided my question. One thing Benjamin and I had going for us. When he wanted to be fed or was about to cry from loneliness, I heard him at the edge of my mind and ran to him. The *metapalets* who were so strict with the other mothers turned their backs when I came to care for Benjamin. They all knew the story of my famous delivery under enemy fire. While the other infants lost contact with their mothers before they learned to sit up, Benjamin and I stayed close.

About the time the baby started to walk, Lev insisted that he was spoiled. Other babies were left to cry. If they wailed for half a morning in their loneliness, no one comforted them except for the accidental touch of another infant. This way, Lev explained, they would grow tough, like good soldiers. But when Benjamin cried for me, I heard him somewhere inside me, and ran across the fields, my hands on my aching pelvis. I would throw my arms around this little being who called me out of myself, who could always call me and be answered.

The other parents of the kibbutz, who were bored before curfew time and gladly put their babies down, celebrating their freedom from childcare, did not know that I came back to Benjamin for the rest of the evening. Lev spoke to me of duty, of our comrades' need of us, but I hardly heard him.

Feeling Benjamin's arms around me, I was home, while Lev's arms felt comfortless and strange.

Perhaps Lev seemed like a stranger because he was now spending most of his time in Tel Aviv. He had been elected to the Knesset, and I knew more about him from the newspapers than at firsthand. He had explained to me that it would be easier on us both if he were away until I was well enough to resume our conjugal life. That Lev had gone celibate for eight months was improbable, given his history, but it was not until I talked to Esther about the transplanted tomatoes that I began to realize Lev had not been lonely while I was out of service and being repaired.

Esther was checking my violated tomatoes for aphids when I went to confront her. Of course, I was concerned at this time about her treachery in the vegetable department, not the marital one.

"Yes, I moved them." Esther's voice was clipped and cool. She hardly looked up at me when she spoke. She kept her face down close to the lower limbs of the plants, as if like a frog she were planning to catch the aphids on her tongue. "No one knew your method of cultivation. How were we to carry it out while you were sick?"

"All you had to do was weed and water, as you do with any vegetables," I said, my voice as low and cold as hers. "Nothing to it. And you knew I would be back again before the harvest."

"We didn't know that," Esther said, her head still down, as if the tomatoes absorbed all her concentration.

"Maybe you thought I would die," I said nastily, "and you would inherit the orphaned tomatoes, not to mention my husband?"

"Lev was afraid you might die from the way your baby came." Esther straightened up and stood a few feet away from me, as if she expected blows from my clenched fists.

The thought of Lev confiding to Esther all the intimate secrets of my internal geography struck me as a betrayal even worse than allowing my tomatoes to be moved. Remembering what Shana had whispered about the relationship between my husband and this tanned, whip-thin female, I burst out, "So you and Lev sat around in the evenings discussing my health?"

"We've always been close," Esther murmured, an insulting lilt to her voice, "and he's been lonely. Make of that what you want to."

Her tone maddened me, and I said more than I should have. "I make of it that you've had Lev to yourself all this time, the way it was before I came. Just remember," I told her, coming closer, "he's my husband and the father of my son. You're nothing special to him."

Esther's head turned rapidly to the side, as if she had been slapped. "You use the word 'my' a lot, don't you?" she said. "Lev has noticed that too. 'My husband, my son, my tomatoes.' It's unbecoming in a kibbutznik."

Face burning, I ran back to the infant house to hold Benjamin, my baby. There it was, that word again. Lev and Esther were right, and that was why I'd had no answer for her. My cheek rested on Benjamin's wiry curls, and the lump in my throat slowly went down. All my life I had lost whatever mattered to me. Naturally, if someone wanted to take what was mine, I would fight. If Esther wanted a battle, she would get one, and she would lose. My hand curled so tightly around Benjamin's fat pink fist that his mouth stretched, ready to cry. "No one will take anything away from me again," I said aloud, meaning Benjamin and Lev and my place at the kibbutz gardens. "Never again. Just let them try."

They certainly tried. When I continued to visit Benjamin and even took him to the fields on my back, strapped in a little canvas contraption Maxi had made for me, the kibbutz was outraged. They all gathered to consider a formal censure. I stood before them, feeling like I was a criminal in a courtroom.

"We have rules," the chairman of the executive committee told me, scowling at me over her glasses like a judge at a delinquent child. "What sort of molly-coddled brat are you trying to raise, anyway? Everyone knows a kibbutz child must learn to depend only on himself and his comrades. Long after you're gone, they will be there for him. It is selfish, Dora, to make him dependent on you and selfish to deprive your own comrades of your energy."

Looking down at the gray tiled floor of the meeting room, I felt ashamed, for it was true I had spent less time with the agricultural committee and the gardens than with Benjamin. "Well, then," I replied, being as polite as I could, so as not to alert them to my sinful obsession with what was mine, "I'll spend twice as much time at work as I do now. Will that be enough?"

"And will you keep the infants' house rules like the rest of us?" said Sol, a tall, red-headed, skinny man who had been one of my great supporters on the agricultural committee. We two had, over Esther's protests, changed the entire irrigation system. Now the fields were nearly twice as rich as they used to be. For this success, as for much else, Esther could not forgive me.

"We need you on the job, Dora."

"And will have me," I promised, eager to get away because it was time to feed Benjamin.

My breasts were getting too full for comfort. He had been nursed for a year, and the *metapalets* had ordered me six months ago to wean him.

Benjamin still nursed as fervently as a newborn and sucked his hand desperately when I was slow getting unbuttoned. He would not be forced to the cup before he was ready, I had long ago resolved. He would not have to suck his thumb like so many of the sad-eyed five-year-olds I had seen in the pre-school. Their caregivers slapped the offending hands away, for it was thought unwise to let a child enjoy some selfish, lonely act. The kibbutz was determined that children find their happiness only in cooperation with others. Benjamin's pleasure was in me, and mine in him, but since he couldn't talk, and I was ashamed to, our guilty co-dependence remained our secret.

"We cannot allow that," the chairman said. "No one has such a privilege here." She was a friend of Esther's and could be expected to give me a hard time.

My voice was even and strong, for my trump card was in my hand, ready to go. "I've told you the job won't suffer. You have my word. But if I don't have the time I need with Benjamin, I will take him and leave. You know my husband's position in the Knesset. I don't have to explain that your forcing me to leave would be bad publicity for him."

The committee members clustered in conference, casting glances my way as they talked. Finally they sat down again. The chairman glared at me as she spoke. "If you can manage to see your child discreetly," she said, "we will give your plan a chance. You can instruct the *metapalets* to give him a nap during the late afternoon play hours. That way, you could stay with him all evening, in your free time."

Their offer was accepted, though never in so many words did they give me permission to be the mother I was intent on being to my son. Already I planned to sneak over to the infants' house, well before work in the morning, to feed Benjamin and play with him. My lunch break would be spent with him too. I knew that with my threat to leave hanging over them, I could be sure no one would argue with my choices. Even if I had to leave Kiryat Anavim, I would always have a home with Maxi. So I couldn't lose, a position which greatly satisfied me.

From that time on, Benjamin was put to bed early so he could stay up late with me. While my comrades spent their evenings arguing politics over coffee or playing ping-pong, I sat in the empty playroom of the infant house with Benjamin, showing him picture books, teaching him to put one block on another, until he could build a tower as tall as he was. Late at night, when everyone was asleep, I carried him out to look at the stars, our heads thrown back and mouths open, as if to eat their light. The desert stars were close and many, so bright that our two joined bodies cast shadows on the dry, bare ground. Benjamin would point at them and then look at me, his round face beaming, too pleased to say the word for what he saw, though he had long since learned it. Then I would take him to his crib, change his diaper, and stay by his side until he was asleep, his hand loosening around my fingers and finally falling, palm up, open to whatever was being given to him in his dreams.

Lev was home more often now, so he knew my free time was being spent in this illicit affair with my son. Sometimes he would be smoking in bed, having waited too long for me. My heart warmed quickly to him, for I was still drenched with love from the hours with Benjamin. As always, the sight of Lev's long, hard body excited me. Lev seemed content with what I gave him, though we seldom talked anymore. He would go off to Tel Aviv, replete and virile, ready to make his hawkish speeches and shake his Paleolithic spear. If he still spoke to Esther, their talks must have been of an impersonal sort, for I had drained him of everything but his anger and his ambition. Those, I figured, she and the Knesset could have. As for myself, I had Benjamin.

True to my word, I fulfilled my obligation to the gardens and the agricultural committee, even taking over the chairmanship, with the help of skinny, admiring Sol. Esther had tried to marshal a conservative faction against me, but I had rolled over them all, with my figures on the prospective rise in fertilizer costs.

"Why can't we just keep buying fertilizer from the West?" came the plaintive voice of one of Esther's creatures. He was an old man and had come from Spain, where agriculture was still, as Maxi would have said, in the early Neolithic age.'

"Why not?" I stood up and walked back and forth before the chairman's table. "Because that fertilizer depends on oil, and the price of oil depends on Arab whim. We have to be prepared for a rise in price that puts Western fertilizers out of our reach."

"What do you propose, then?" Reliable Sol stretched his long legs under the conference table. It was the right question, and launched me on my speech.

"A potash plant on the kibbutz to supplement our compost piles. The profit from last year's tomato crop will pay for the initial phase of construction. Here, I have copies of all the figures. Would you pass these around, Sol? Lev says he can get us a government loan for most of the rest, and Leumi Bank in New York will bridge the gap." I didn't tell them that the Israeli bank had also promised me personally a loan of $400,000 for a commercial greenhouse as soon as the phosphate plant had produced enough to serve as collateral.

Esther and her faction fumed and argued, but my figures on the recent rise in the price of oil carried the day. Sol and I had a celebratory cup of coffee after my victory and were partners at the weekly folk dance in the dining hall. Sol's brown eyes sparkled in his homely, freckled face and his hands sweated as he danced, always trying to hold me too tightly when he whirled me around. I left him drooping disconsolately on the outskirts of a wild hora to go for my evening visit to the infants' house. Benjamin toddled into my outstretched arms, and we danced a hora of our own, there under the stars. Then we walked together through the rows of vegetables.

"Food," said Benjamin, touching a tomato, no doubt remembering that he had seen one on the table. He turned to me and put his hand over my breast laughing. "Food!" Laughing too, I lay down on the ground on my back, pulling my sweater up to my neck, letting him lie on me and take out of both breasts what little milk was still there. He had been weaned, finally, and it seemed as if he knew as I did that this was the last time for us.

Later, when I went back to my room, my body throbbing from Benjamin's attentions, Lev was there, having come back from Tel Aviv on the late bus.

"You were at the dance, I heard," he said, crushing out his cigarette. "You danced with that admirer of yours. Have you forgotten me, Dora? Sometimes I think you have." He pulled down the sheets, then rolled me into the bed next to him.

"No, Lev, I remember everything. I spend too much time remembering, since you're not often here," I said reaching for him, thinking of Benjamin and of Maxi, their faces collapsing into his as he came close. Lev put his mouth over my heart, but I pulled it up quickly onto my lips, where it belonged.

The next day Maxi appeared, as if he knew he was being thought of. He arrived during the evening, with the girl I was afraid he was going to marry. These were the hours he knew I would be with the baby, so he came directly to the infants' house. He swept Benjamin up in his arms and held the baby as we all went for a walk around the grounds.

Carolyn Freiberg, the girl Maxi had brought with him, walked with me under the orange trees, while Maxi carried my son ahead of us. She was from America, a slim, delicate-faced girl with brooding, deep-set gray eyes that looked as if she were about to cry at any moment.

"I love the idea of community," she said, speaking rapidly, in a high voice like a little girl's. "I love the idea of a kibbutz. In America we're so separate from each other. People are murdered in their homes and it takes a week for the neighbors to notice." She laughed nervously, twisting her handkerchief like a bandage around her fingers. "And that's only because of the smell." She stopped at the ravine and looked at the olive trees below, glistening in the moonlight, their boughs ripe with oily fruit. "Community is a better way."

"You wouldn't love the work." I leaned over and pulled some fungoid leaves off an orange tree, trying to remember exactly which tree it was so I could tell the morning work crew where to spray. "I get up at five a.m. for a few hours with my baby, then work straight through the day with only a half hour for lunch. We don't get many Americans here." I was looking first at Carolyn, and then ahead to Maxi's back, wondering what he saw in this scatter-brained girl.

"Oh, but America's changing," Carolyn said, her words coming faster, as if she were afraid no one would listen if she didn't hurry up and finish. "Everyone knows we're ruining the land, stinking up the air. All those divorces, you know?" She waved her hands, appealing to my moral sense in a dramatic non-sequitur. "I mean, nobody's happy anymore. They just want money. You should hear the commercials on TV. My God! Everybody wants two houses and two cars and to smell like chlorophyll. We even have green toothpaste that causes cancer in rabbits. Isn't that sick? I mean, why should we smell like plants? We're people, after all. Chlorophyll, my God!"

She was certainly very nervous, I thought, trying to imagine how Carolyn would do in the middle of an air raid. Pretty, to be sure, with her long blond hair, heart-shaped face, and delicate, bright-red lips, which never stopped moving. But not strong, perhaps because she had not needed to be. Carolyn had studied in Paris and wanted to teach French literature in high school. Her father, who owned a big department store in New York, had sent her first to Vassar, then, at her insistence, for a year of study at Hebrew University. That was where she had met and fallen in love with Maxi.

"We have this great idea, Maxi and I," Carolyn said, lurching against me as her high heels became entangled with a strand of barbed wire fencing. "We can live here at the kibbutz and work in Jerusalem, teaching. I mean, I don't want to live in a city. The pollution, you know?" She leaned her face close to mine, looking desperate. "Nothing's clean in America. My God, so much soot sneaks through the windows, you could grow turnips on the sills. You go around your apartment stalking two-inch long cockroaches with biceps. In the night, you can hear them working out, getting ready to carry off the brisket." She flexed her arms vigorously in illustration, and then went on talking.

"You never know what you're going to find on your kitchen floor in the morning. As a present, the day I left for Israel, you know what my cat left in front of the stove?" She paused, her gray eyes wide. "A rat so big and mean it should have been given a draft card and sent to Korea." She laughed wildly and teetered ahead on her tiny pointed shoes to catch up with Maxi. "Let me hold the baby now. I love babies!"

Benjamin shrieked in alarm and spat up, flinging the remains of his lentil soup, odorously diluted with hydrochloric acid, all over Carolyn's white linen suit. She had to go back to my room to clean herself up and lie down for an hour, requiring intensive care from Maxi during her recovery. So I didn't see much more of her that day. Because it was the baby's time for feeding and changing, I left my guests in Lev's hands, telling him to explain to them what accommodations might be available for prospective part-time kibbutzniks.

After all, we ran a hotel and were used to transients, Lev said, rather peevishly, I thought, not pleased to hear him refer to my brother and his girl-friend as if they were temporary as fruit flies. Lev charmed Carolyn with compliments on her high heels and elegant alligator bag, though he would have made fun of me if I had owned such things. He took her arm cautiously as they started off to look over the unoccupied rooms and listened to her long, nervous jokes about urban life in America. No doubt, from the way he was laughing, she was telling him about the comparative militance of cockroaches in New York and Paris. Although too nervous, Carolyn certainly was a clever girl, I said to myself, as I rescued Benjamin from the communal potty, where he sat with his pants hobbling his ankles. He had fallen asleep there, having been forgotten by a feckless *metapalet.*

Again I took Benjamin out after his meal to look at the stars, describing to him the heroic fauna of New York apartments. Although I couldn't be clever like Carolyn and make Maxi or Lev laugh, Benjamin appreciated whatever I said, smiling back at me. In just this way had Maxi and I smiled when Claire told us stories and sang us songs. If she had somehow lived through Dunkirk, she might now have children of her own who were smiling at her the way Benjamin was smiling at me. As I remembered Claire, I forgot about Maxi's strange girl friend and was at peace. Benjamin lay against my shoulder with his face upward toward the sky, and I thought of nothing but Yeshua, imagining his light shining through the stars, those tiny holes in the fabric of heaven.

9

Amberfields..............................1963

On the deck behind their house, Claire stood with her son Timothy, now fourteen years old and taller than she was, and watched the night sky reflected in the still lake. It was hard for her to know where she should begin their conversation. Timothy had recently turned from a bright little boy into a surly stranger, who wore his frayed blue jeans perilously low on his narrow hips, demanded pizza for breakfast, and without asking permission, had electrified his expensive classical guitar.

She chose to begin with his report card, for Timothy had received his usual high marks for achievement and low marks for effort and conduct. His grandmother would have said it was not the report card of a gentleman. When Claire told him so, Timothy laughed until he choked, almost swallowing his wad of gum.

"I don't get it," said the boy sullenly in a cracking voice, as he picked obsessively at a promising bump on his handsome, cleft chin, so like Paul's. "If I can achieve without trying, what's the big deal? So I don't have to try. What's wrong with that? 'Snot my fault that other people gotta try and I don't."

"I beg your pardon?" Claire said coolly, stiffening at the word 'snot,' which Timothy had been enjoined never to use. She relaxed when she realized he was offending not by his language but only by his diction, which had grown careless since he had entered the local high school. "If you didn't chew gum when you talk, Timothy, I'd understand you better."

In what he apparently regarded as a conciliatory gesture, Timothy pushed the pink wad into the corner of his mouth. "Yeah? Okay," he said in the manner of his idols on phonograph records. He had learned from them to make these essentially agreeable words sound like a sneering challenge. "Sure wish you'd call me Tim, like everybody else does. Timothy sounds like one of those names out of the Bible or like a pet mouse."

"I'll try." Claire took a deep breath and held the splintery railing tightly with both hands. "Look, Tim, you've had a lot of freedom. Too much, maybe, if there can ever be too much freedom. I used to think not, but now I wonder. Your teachers say you have no discipline."

"I thought they were supposed to discipline me," Timothy said, with exaggerated stupidity. "I can't help it if they don't do their job. They want us to turn out like them. Finks." He pronounced this word more carefully than the others, obviously liking it. "Nothing but finks, like all the old guys around here, with their ties choking their Adam's apples. They want everybody to suffocate just because they're doing it. Businessmen. Finks." He went on rumbling and picking.

Timothy had a way of going off the point that reminded Claire of Paul. She knew she was being diverted into one of her son's favorite areas of moral outrage but steered toward it anyway.

"Really? Lucky you, to have finks for parents, so you can take guitar lessons and go out for pizza. When I was your age, I was dodging bombs and taking care of children. Maybe you ought to find a job to pay for what you want. How would you like that?"

Timothy mined his chin furiously and squinted at the porch light, a way he typically avoided eye contact. Claire longed to slap him.

"No, honest," he protested, conciliatory once again, perhaps because the matter of a part-time job was looming. "I think it's hip that you're into music and Dad's an artist. I'd really puke if he sold toilets like Freddy's dad. I mean, toilets!" Timothy made retching noises. "But still, you and Dad just do old stuff." He shuffled one foot repetitively, like a bull pawing the arena. "I can't even play my friends that record you made in New York, because they'd puke. Freddy said so. He heard it, but I made him promise not to tell the other guys it was religious."

Charlotte's son, two years older than Timothy, had become the younger boy's moral authority. Freddy, who let his eyes hang half-closed and kept his lips in a perpetual sneer, affected a resemblance to Elvis Presley. *The boy has sold marijuana to fellow students, smoked it himself, and now wants Timothy to play in his rock band, an activity I'm sure will start him smoking too,* Claire worried. *The band is not what I had in mind when I mentioned the part-time job.* She stood with the breeze blowing her scarf behind her and kept her eyes on the reflected stars shining in the lake, trying not to cry. She had been proud of her record until she knew her son was ashamed. It had been made at a Manhattan synagogue during last year's Yom Kippur. A rabbi had commissioned the work, a Kol Nidre, after hearing a broadcast of her "Song of Elijah." Claire had written the Kol Nidre in honor of Dora and Maxi, whose names were in the program, and had thought of them as she wrote the notes that spilled out more like a cry than a song.

"I wish you wouldn't keep saying 'puke,'" she told her son. "I wish you wouldn't pick at your face like that. You'll scar yourself." When Timothy did not respond, she went on. "Freddy's bad for you, Tim. That crazy music of his, staying down at the pool hall till midnight, all of it's bad for you.

Until the next marking period, you'll stay in the house after dinner every night. If the marks get better, we'll see about giving you more freedom."

"Aw, come on. The guys and me are just getting our band started. We're going to do really big stuff. I gotta keep seeing Freddy, Mom." Up and down the scale Timothy's voice slid, as if by the dramatic range of his whine he could convince her to take back her curse.

"You heard me." Claire was struck by how much she sounded like her mother, and she stopped short, remembering. *But my mother never had reason to take such a tone, for no Freddy Webster with his marijuana and filthy Elvis Presley records lived next door in Rheims*. "Go do your homework. Now."

Timothy collapse into apologies, tears in his eyes. "Honest, Mom, I liked your song. It was only Freddy who thought it wasn't hip, not me."

She knew he was going to ask if he could go next door and watch slack-jawed popular singers gyrate obscenely on the Webster's television set. Paul had thrown theirs out the door the year before, when he caught Timothy and Julie watching "The Outlaw." Paul had never been loud or violent with his children before, and little Julie had wept in terror when she heard her father shout, "I will not have this trash in my home." Claire had had a sinking sense that she was being firm too late. *I can't bear to see a child of mine being vulgar.* "Vulgar," she said aloud, wondering. *My mother's word. Nobody says that word anymore.*

Timothy muttered something under his breath and slumped off, hands in his pockets.

"What's that you just said to me?" Claire heard herself sounding tiresome as a siren and felt Timothy go far away, halfway around the world in a giant leap, like an astronaut on the moon.

"Sugar!" Timothy called back over his shoulder. "I said 'sugar,' okay?"

Claire did not answer him, but went in the house by another door, feeling as if she should do what mothers in the old country did, put on black and mourn the son who was no longer hers.

Paul was sitting at the piano, turning the pages of Julie's music, as the eleven-year-old girl worked her way through 'Für Elise' with wooden competence. The faces of the two were close together and moved rapidly from light to shadow to light again in the flickering blaze of the fire. Julie's heavy, waist-long red-gold hair was tied back with a blue ribbon. Remembering her own insistence on short hair, Claire had offered Julie a beauty parlor appointment on her eleventh birthday. "Everybody likes long hair now," Julie answered indifferently. "I guess I'll leave it the way it is. I don't really care."

Nothing seemed to move Julie to care except the opinions of her father, who was available so seldom that his opinions were largely unknown. Claire sat down on the couch and flipped through one of Timothy's magazines. It was devoted to electronic imitations of real instruments played by human breath and touch. Every now and then she looked up at Paul and Julie, who had pre-empted her piano. The new liturgy commissioned by the Cathedral of St. John the Divine would have to wait until Julie had exhausted her repertoire. Certainly, if it had to wait until Julie had exhausted her father's attention, the liturgy would remain forever unfinished.

Claire put down the magazine and studied the two as if they were strangers, feeling for the moment that they were. Paul's body was relaxed as it seldom was, curved in the same posture as when he made love, which was seldom too. The hard lines of his face had gentled, as though by the contagion of Julie's soft, lineless skin. Claire's hand reached up to her own face automatically and touched the dents around her mouth and at the edges of her eyes. Once she had had skin like Julie's and taken it for granted. Now she watched her daughter, noticing what had been lost. Julie's round face, with large, pale blue eyes and pink cheeks was too still and perfect. She was like one of Paul's pictures, not quite alive, though a good likeness of the real thing. The child's head bent forward a little, and Claire could see the outline of her daughter's thin, aristocratic nose, like a shadow of Paul's.

Already, Julie's beauty had registered on the pubescent males of Pine Lake. Boys of Timothy's age, with cracking voices, called her on the phone, and hung up abruptly when Claire told them Julie was unavailable. Other girls were intimidated by what they called her 'hipness,' and wanted her advice before they would wear a new coat or pair of jeans. At the boy-girl parties which Paul reluctantly allowed Julie to attend, after pressure from Claire, Julie was known for refusing to kiss the boy her spun bottle pointed to and simply sat with him silently in the kissing room for the required three minutes. Still the boys seemed glad when they were the ones chosen by the bottle.

"It's too easy for her," Claire fretted to Paul after Julie had gone upstairs. "She doesn't have to care about anything."

"Why should she?" Paul asked, perhaps remembering having had the same attitude in his own youth. "A girl as beautiful as Julie doesn't have to care. Already she has what everyone wants—acceptance and admiration. Lucky girl."

So you're smitten too? Claire stared at Paul. *Why is he so in love with this pretty doll of ours?* Claire found herself hoping Julie would grow a pot belly and heavy cheeks before her head was addled with all this unearned praise. A girl's good looks could curse her, if they were allowed to shape her life.

"I wish Julie looked like Belinda next door," Claire said, tossing aside Timothy's magazine, infuriated by the picture of a Beatle engagingly posed with his electric guitar hanging down to his thighs. "I wish she had freckles and crooked teeth and one of those haircuts that looks like a duck's tail."

"Claire, you're jealous of your own daughter." Paul threw another log on the fire, making sparks fly in a sudden swirl up the chimney. "Shame on you. Don't you realize you're a hard act to follow? Julie is not going to compete with you. She'd rather just pretend nothing matters to her. I'm kind of tuned into her lifestyle."

Claire frowned, annoyed at Paul's tone and choice of words. Lately, since he had been teaching evening art classes in lower Manhattan, he tended to speak in this unfamiliar voice, very knowing, very modern, and to her ears, very fake. It was as if he mistrusted his own past and had put on a mask through which he talked to her in a language she did not recognize. *Is he as little at home in America as that? Was I wrong to bring him so far away from where he felt rooted and himself? My husband is going native,* Claire decided, watching him through narrowed eyes, as one would watch a wildcat or dangerous maniac.

"Paul, Julie's never going to be a real person if she doesn't find something to care about," she said, putting the screen over the fire that he had heaped high with wood. "Every time I ask her to do anything, she looks in the mirror before she does it, as if she's making sure she can't fail, in that one department anyway. Don't you see?" Claire knelt down at Paul's feet and rested her arms on his knees. "She'll just wind up belonging to some man, as she belongs to you now. Julie's even smarter than Timothy, only she won't push herself. Julie never pushes. Never."

"What kind of life do you have in mind for her?" Paul asked, drawing back and taking Claire's insistent hands in his to keep them still. "You want her to be a musician like you? Get famous? What good is that to a woman or to her husband?"

Claire looked at his face, red in the firelight, deep shadows beside deeper lines. She had never considered how Paul might feel about her music being performed in New York, recorded and reviewed in newspaper arts sections that did not mention his name.

"Well, I guess her husband should be glad," she said, standing up, tying the sash around her robe with a hard snap. "After all, how could she do it without him?"

Paul looked into the fire, not at her. "If they don't do it together, it had better not be done," he said, his fingertips touching each other in a steeple.

"A man doesn't care what a woman's credits are. He just wants her to love him. And comfort him. Especially comfort."

Suddenly Claire remembered Julie and Paul curled up together in each other's arms weeping over the assassination of President Kennedy. Julie had not understood what was going on but wept because her father did. Claire had felt scornful of them both. *Paul was a believer in Camelot,* she said to herself, *in some vision of knights righting the world's wrongs. Even the Vietcong in Indochina were dragons to be slain, like something out of his Viking legends.* Julie and Paul were believers in myths, forgetting themselves in the tales of heroes larger than life. The stories Timothy had refused to hear from his father, Julie heard gladly, sharing his world as Claire could not.

The next night, when Julie and her father sat down at the piano after dinner, Claire gathered up her music and a blank book for composition, put on her new maroon turtleneck sweater and slammed out of the house. She was headed for St. Michael's and the organ, where she could practice without interruption. She walked along the side of the main road that took a sudden twist into town just a fifteen minutes' stroll from Amberfields, not turning her head as the headlights of cars lit her path and then passed, leaving her in the dark again. The cool air made her skin feel tight and stiff, as if her body were in a suitcase of thick hide, locked up against all that was outside it. Never had she felt so conscious of the weight of her flesh, even in pregnancy. She felt alienated from the ground she walked on, the trees she passed, the air she breathed.

Just as Timothy and Julie and Paul weren't hers anymore, but were off on their own trips, packed up in their own bags of skin, so had everything around her become separate and strange, as if she were a visitor from another planet. She looked up indifferently at the sky, remembering for a moment that once, long ago, she had enjoyed seeing blue-white stars hanging together in the dark, glowing with an unreflected light. Now they were only to be passed by and forgotten, no part of her.

Having turned down the main street into town, Claire stopped under the streetlight by the pizza parlor and looked around her. Loud young people in jeans lounged against the walls, their chins red with tomato stains and zits. They pulled up the cheese from their pizza slices in long elastic strands, which they noisily vacuumed into their mouths.

On a bench next door, in front of a closed, derelict gas station, sat Freddy Webster and her son Timothy, their electric instruments plugged by a long wire into Freddy's old Ford. They were surrounded by a crowd of young people who were writhing and clapping, rolling their heads on their necks as if they were caught up in a religious revival. Timothy saw her, but averted his eyes. She knew better than to acknowledge any connection with her son. Only Belinda Webster, a small, thin girl almost bisected by her tight jeans, waved at Claire, then went on clapping and shaking her narrow, childish bottom. The music sounded to Claire like empty tin cans being dropped on the cement at rhythmic intervals. The beat pounded in her ears like a jack hammer at work. If there were words to these attempts at song, Claire could not distinguish them.

"So ugly," she murmured, crossing the street and walking past a store window full of television screens all in motion at once, each with a different picture. On one, a housewife held up an aerosol can and smiled glassily as she sprayed a pot. *The spraying seems gratuitous, since the pot already gleamed immaculately,* Claire thought, *as my pots haven't done since they were bought fifteen years ago.* Paul said Claire's pots looked like they had been unearthed from an archeological dig and carbon-dated early Neolithic. *I doubt that even the magic aerosol spray could redeem them.* Claire sighed and looked away.

On another screen, an obedient, fresh-faced boy and girl celebrated the soundness of their teeth with their proud parents, for whom these youngsters seemed to have a cheerful, uncomplicated love, unlike the natives of Pine Lake. She stood for a moment and watched, as a handsome, laughing couple in evening clothes stapled bogus Roman tiles to their family room ceiling. The activity apparently had an erotic significance for them, since they kissed each other fervently once the last tile was stapled into place. Claire watched the kiss, her own lips moist and parted. She remembered that she had not been kissed in quite a while and that she very much missed it.

"No telling what'll turn some people on," said a warm male voice close to her ear. "Is this how you spend your nights when there's no choir practice?"

Claire turned around and saw Brian O'Hara, star baritone of the St. Michael's choir. He was a burly, bearded man with tiny, twinkling eyes that seemed to watch her from deep inside his head. He was not a member of the church, for he openly declared that religion was a crutch for the weak. He liked to sing, however, and appeared regularly at Claire's choir rehearsals. During the day he was an advertising man in Manhattan, but what he did during the evenings was a mystery. Since he was a bachelor in his forties, it was said among the women of the parish that he was up to no good, and given his wicked, mocking smile and his atheism, Claire could well believe it.

"These advertisements all assume everyone wants to be loved," Brian O'Hara said, taking her arm and walking on down Main Street. "What if you're a loner, like me? I don't want people to love me and try to take me over. What I need is a product that guarantees privacy. Let us call it 'Horrid.' For those who can't bear the endless tedium of intimacy and long to be free from the smothering closeness of others."

Claire giggled, thinking of Timothy and the repulsion she felt whenever he begged her for money and attention, breathing his oppressively sweet bubble-gummed breath in her face.

"About now, I'd buy it," she said. "No one should engage in family life until well protected with Horrid. I didn't know that when I was young, but I do now."

"What a shame people marry before they know," Brian said, opening the side door of the church for Claire, after she had turned her key in the lock. "Of course, once they know, they never marry."

"Is that why you're single? Claire asked, thinking *here's a man who ought to be unhappy but clearly isn't. He acts a lot happier than I feel, but doesn't care if he's loved. Maybe I should take lessons from him.*

Brian leaned over her and switched on the light, illuminating a circle around the organ. "My dear child," he said, hovering for a moment with his face near hers, "have you never heard that a man who is faithful to one woman is unfaithful to all the rest? I love women far too much to marry any one of them."

Feeling herself lean toward him in a sort of involuntary tropism, Claire pulled back suddenly. *Calling me his dear child sounds so phony, not like the Countess used to sound when she said the same words.*

"Did you never love anyone?" She busied herself turning on the organ and setting up the music, trying not to notice that her body felt as though it were being melted in a hot bath. *Surely he has the desire to love with his whole heart,* she thought. *Maybe he's been waiting until he found someone he did not want to repel with Horrid.*

"Not until lately," Brian stood behind her, his hands on her shoulders. "Play 'None but the Lonely Heart,' why don't you? It suits the occasion."

Claire did not much care for popular songs, but obliged Brian so she could hear him sing in his clear, pure voice. His lips were close to her ear as he sang about feeling alone and sad. Her hands trembled on the keys. *He's singing the words to me,* she realized, *and has been singing to me for a long time.* She remembered now how she had looked up from the music during the Sunday service and found his eyes on her and how he had put his coat around her shoulders when the church was cold during rehearsals. It occurred to her that he might be lost without someone to turn him gently from his mockery of marriage to a new life. *Then he might find some good woman and love her the rest of his days. Maybe I should introduce him to Charlotte, now that she's about to divorce Frederick.*

"You should find someone to love," she said finally, feeling as if she were making a kind of sacrifice, giving him up to a virtuous, unknown woman who would teach him what it was not Claire's place to teach him.

"Maybe I have." Brian hung over her, playing the organ at either end of the keyboard, his arms outside her arms, his body arching over hers. "I have been loving for some time. Hadn't you noticed?" He sat down on the bench beside her and turned her face up to his. "Claire?"

Without knowing quite how it happened, Claire found herself in the arms of Brian O'Hara, his sudden embrace scattering her music on the floor. The kisses that forced her mouth open were not so bad, but when he started pulling at her clothes, Claire drew back.

He knelt down, still holding onto her skirt zipper. "We can go in the coat room if you aren't okay with having sex in the church." His face was hot and red and his hands, having given up on the stuck zipper, were trying to work their way up under her sweater.

"I don't want to go in the coat room," Claire cried out, appalled not so much at Brian's searching hands but at where she wanted him to put them. "I want to go home."

Brian ignored what she said, occupied with other matters. He kept murmuring, "What's this? What's this?" as if he had never touched a woman before.

"We can't do that here," Claire burst out, pushing his hands away.

"Then come to my place," he said, his red face so close she felt her own cheeks burn. "I've imagined taking you there. So many times."

Claire closed her eyes and nodded, not trusting herself to speak until she had swallowed down Paul's name, which had risen to her lips whenever Brian's hands stirred her.

"Go outside," she said finally, knowing that she needed time alone before making another move. "I'll come out in a few minutes. If we leave together, it would look funny. Go on."

When Brian had slipped outside and closed the door, Claire locked it behind him and went back into the church, up close to the altar where she could no longer hear his discreet rappings. She knelt at the rail and stared at the red sanctuary light hanging over the altar to signify the presence of God. After kneeling silently for a while, with no thought left in her brain, Claire prayed, *Lord it was not his love I wanted, not Brian's. Don't let me be fooled. I don't want to be a silly romantic. I know whose love I want. Paul's. Yours.* Love for God and love for Paul suddenly seemed to be the same thing, requiring nothing from her but being attentive and available. *It should have been easy, but it isn't. I don't know how I got so far off track. It's not where I ever meant to be.*

She waited a while, hoping God would let her know in some dramatic way how much he wanted her love, too. When nothing happened, Claire put her face against the rail and wept. *I don't want to lose Paul, and I don't want to lose you.* She ignored the rapping on the door, not noticing when it went away.

Claire knelt for a little longer, not knowing what to say to God any more than she knew what to say to Paul these days, after he came home from New York smelling of other people and looking puzzled when he saw her, as if she were the last person he was expecting to see. *Maybe that's because he's seen me so often that now he doesn't see me at all.* She looked up at the crucifix over the altar that bore a glowing byzantine image of the transfigured Christ, his arms out. She had seen the image so often that she no longer saw it, any more than Timothy or Paul saw her when she reached out to them. *How easy it is for us not to see the familiar, not to feel the love that calls no attention to itself and is always there.*

She stood up and lit a votive candle, her hands unsteady, then held her stiff, cold fingers over the flame until they seemed to turn transparent in the light. When she left the church, the streets were totally dark except for a beam of light streaming from a church that was a few blocks away. It was small and white, with no stained glass, only simple golden panes through which the light poured from inside, turning the sidewalk in front of the church into a yellow brick road. As she approached the church, she noticed a sign saying "Evangelical Free Church. Here, Jesus is Lord."

Free, Claire thought. *How lovely to be free and not tied to the past, to all our stupid mistakes.* Music from a dozen voices rolled toward her, carrying her like a wave. The voices were singing unfamiliar songs about Jesus calling over the sea and walking in the garden alone. Claire stopped outside the church door, her heart beating hard. Though she did not know the music, it spoke to her as had the cries of her infant children. 'Christian, follow me," the voices sang. And Claire opened the church door, ready to follow where the voices led her.

She slipped into the back pew and set her music down beside her. As the people sang, they raised their arms like children wanting to be lifted up. Claire remembered lifting Maxi and Dora and her own children and she raised her arms too. *O Christ,* she cried within herself, *I'm so tired of being foolish, willful Claire. I want to be yours. I give up.* Hardly knowing what she did, Claire got to her feet and walked down the aisle toward the minister. When she reached him, she did not look up into his face. She no longer even thought of her children or Paul. Into this garden she would have to walk alone except for the Lord who had known her before she was born. She had been pinning her hopes on phantoms, on mere human beings, all her life, and suddenly, now, her vision opened to a vast sky of light and stars, and in the center of the light, the form of Christ, arms stretched out, was waiting for her. Like a rush of wind, Claire felt his Spirit in her like an animating flame. She sank to her knees.

The minister bent over her, raising her up. "It's done," he said. "Love the Lord with all your heart and lean not on your own understanding. Trust in him."

"I will," Claire said, hardly breathing. "And I will never forget again. God help me."

The next day over coffee, Claire confided to Charlotte her romantic adventure in the church, stammering as she tried to explain why she had half-wanted to go into the coat room with Brian O'Hara and how glad she was that she hadn't. She wanted to say that she had been suddenly surprised by the sense that the love of God, like her husband's love, was ordinary as air, nothing like an adventure, but common and unappreciated as drawing your breath in and out. Claire could not speak of her encounter with Christ in the little church, for even a single word, she felt might shatter the delicate vessel within her that carried the Holy Spirit.

Charlotte interrupted with a story of her own, taking Claire's moment of temptation in the church as her text for the day. "He was just trying to seduce you, honey. It didn't mean a thing to him," she declared. "That's how they are." She took another Linzer torte from Claire's cookie sheet. "Alley cats, every one of them."

With tears, Charlotte began to describe the infidelity of her husband Frederick. He had thought the children were still in school and she still in Alabama, visiting her mother. Frederick had been apprehended in the family room removing the Avon Lady's bellbottom pants. Charlotte had fainted, and the Avon Lady, mindful of her franchise, had taken off in her beat-up Pontiac.

"I swear Frederick never had cause to cheat," Charlotte wept. She peeled off some paper towel and blew her nose so hard her veins stood out. "I was as good a wife as anybody."

"Men must need new worlds to conquer," Claire said, mechanically stroking Charlotte's head, fingers working around the curlers. "They get tired of us. We look so old." She got up to pour Charlotte some more coffee.

"You think your Paul has some little lady friend in New York?" Charlotte sniffed hard and stared at Claire.

Claire gave the possibility some thought, laying her index finger over her mouth. "He might. I keep getting these phone calls from his girl students. Their voices all sound the same. I don't know who these girls are."

"He's got girl students?" Charlotte noisily sucked up her coffee. "Then he's unfaithful. The young ones are what they want. You wouldn't believe what these girls will do, and for free."

Claire remembered the childish, light voices on the phone, and all the times when the wire had gone dead, no doubt because Paul had not been the one to answer. Closing her eyes, she tried to imagine how Paul looked to the girls at Parsons School, his thick hair standing on end, his long body bagged in old pants with paint stains, and his face worn as a guru's, engraved with all the imposing power of pain endured and overcome. She knew from Timothy how the young obeyed the authority of suffering. The poor, the beaten, whoever was in pain, all these sufferers were admired and had songs made about them.

Too often she had found Belinda Webster in Timothy's room, telling her sad story of the day. Timothy would lock the door before consoling her, and Claire was sure from the smell that came through the crack, that they were smoking something other than tobacco. For all she knew, Timothy took Belinda into his extravagant Patagonia sleeping bag, comforting her for the way her father cursed and hit her when she came home late. *Paul should speak to him about Belinda,* Claire thought. *She's practically our daughter, she's over here so much. Suppose she gets pregnant? Would Paul finally talk to Timothy then?* But Paul was busy in New York City, speaking to the girlish telephone voices and had no time to give advice to Timothy about conduct in sleeping bags or anything else.

"Paul, I'm wondering what you did to get your handkerchiefs smelling like no perfume I would ever use," Claire said to him one day, Charlotte's suspicions still in her head.

Her husband sat on the couch before the fire, his hand busy with a sketch of their daughter. "I don't know what you mean, Claire," he said in the faraway voice that always made Claire angry. "Don't create drama. You've got nothing to worry about."

Claire stood in front of the fire warming her hands, which were suddenly cold. "All I'm worried about is that I'm thirty-eight years old, running out of eggs or hormones or whatever keeps a woman young, and I'm not making any more babies. The doctor says there's nothing wrong with me." She felt a rage rising in her worse than the sickness of their first night together. "Paul, why is that? Even when we used to make love a lot, there were no more babies after Julie."

"Once I asked you," Paul said, holding his sketch at arms' length, examining it. "You said you'd accept them. I would have to accept the cost. God's will, you said. So I had an operation."

When she stared at him, the sleeve of her nightgown falling off her bare shoulder. Paul put aside the sketch and stood up. "I would have told you, but you thought I should be man enough to care of as many children as God sent. And I couldn't be, that's the truth." His voice turned creaky, like Timothy's when the boy was heading for an emotional crash. "I couldn't be what was wanted."

Claire pulled her sleeve back over her shoulder, still staring. Her husband had been afraid to admit his fear of her. "I shouldn't have expected so much," she said, her voice choked, "but I so wanted lots of babies and now it's too late." She ran out of the room, up the stairs, hoping Paul would follow her.

When he stayed where he was, Claire began to fume and mutter to herself. She pulled open Paul's desk and went through the papers in his bottom file drawer until she found a few torrid letters from a girl named Meredith who lived in Greenwich Village with some boy she claimed was too childish to understand her. Apparently she wanted Paul, with his long freckled legs and his great mind, full as it was with useful information about how to make painted skin look real. *Of course they think Paul is strong like their fathers,* Claire thought, *full of power under his lined cheeks and stained pants. I should have made him wear a wedding ring too tight to get off in a romantic emergency.* These girls had no idea that Paul's breath in the morning was often stale from pipe smoke, that he liked to paint in a tattered, baggy track suit, and that he made helpless, involuntary faces when the mailman brought notices of checks he had bounced.

Suddenly she realized that Paul was standing behind her, his breath coming in quick, shallow gasps. He pulled the letter out of her hand. "These girls mean nothing to me, Claire. I hope you're not going to try to make me feel guilty. That doesn't work, you know." He started toward the door.

She knew that guilt was the last thing her husband needed more of. Instead, what he needed was the kind of love that she had experienced in the church the night before. "Paul, please," she cried, "don't go. I need you." Something deep within her spoke with the irresistible voice of truth, and Paul seemed to hear it.

He turned around, sat down in his worn leather chair, and pulled her down on his lap."I thought you didn't need anyone," he said. "You didn't act like it."

"Maybe not all the time." Claire brushed her tears away with the backs of both hands. "But I need you now. More often than you think." She put her face against his shoulder. "The children are so far away. Timothy says my music makes him puke."

"And his music does the same to me," Paul said matter-of-factly, stroking her hair. "Timothy is an idiot, just now, like most teenage boys. You know the critics say your music is good, and so do I. Don't listen to that ridiculous boy."

"You liked my Kol Nidre?" Claire felt panicked for a moment, utterly laid open to his opinion. *If he says he frankly doesn't like it, I'll never write another piece of music.*

"It's your best work so far," Paul said, standing her up firmly before him. "If I could paint as well as you make music, I'd be a lot happier than I am." He leaned over his phonograph and turned it on. "See? Your record's always here."

The Hebrew words and her own sorrowful melody rang in Claire's ears and she stood still. *I remember how Paul threw himself over Dora, Maxi, and me, saving our lives.* That same Paul now put his arms around her, and swayed her to the music that had been born out of her love for two lost children. She held onto him, glad that she had found him again.

"Now," he said, his voice gentle as if he had seen into her soul. "Forget Timothy and go back to your music."

"I haven't time anymore," Claire lamented, not yet wanting to give up being comforted. "Julie's always practicing."

"Then I'll sit with her while you're making dinner. She'll practice earlier, and you'll have the piano all evening. If you ever need help, Claire, just ask me."

"I was too proud to ask." She wrapped her arms tightly around Paul, the two of them so close together that they seemed to be one body, moving slowly and gladly as if it had always been one and had never been apart. "Yes, I want your help. I want you."

They lay down together on the study rug and took the whole night to comfort each other for what had been lost and to celebrate what had been found.

10

Dora's Journal

Israel...............................1967

As soon as Moshe Dayan became Minister of Defense, Lev said cheerfully that war was inevitable. He told me that we were already at war without knowing it and that peace was an illusion. Everything he said cut two ways for me, being just as true of our marriage as it was of Israel and the Arab states. I watched him walk up and down in our room, his brown, muscular arms folded over his chest, his high forehead, even higher now that the grizzled hair was receding, was cut with lines that met over his heavy eyebrows.

We saw each other so seldom that I was sharply aware of his aging. Other married couples hardly seemed to notice the coming of wrinkles and gray hair, so kind to the process of growing old is the mere fact of physical closeness. Already, at thirty-two, Carolyn had wrinkles around her eyes and mouth from the attack of the desert sun on her fair skin, but Maxi has said she looks to him as she did when he married her ten years ago. Those two were never apart, so they didn't look at each other like strangers, as Lev and I had been doing for so long.

Seeing myself in the mirror before which Lev was walking and orating as if he were addressing the Knesset, I noticed that aside from a little more weight around the hips and two rather becoming streaks of white hair from either temple to the back of my head, I had not changed much. Perhaps Lev had noticed too, but he never said so. No doubt he didn't want to call attention to the difference in our ages. Lev did exercises to keep his body young, and I had caught him peering anxiously at his craggy features in the mirror, searching for new fault lines in the geography of his face. He liked to think of himself as a soldier, and it was important to him that there be another war before he was too old to fight in it. At least, that's what Maxi said. Ever since Maxi became such a famous scholar, I tended to accept everything he told me without question, but about Lev, perhaps he was wrong.

"If the war is fought now," Lev was saying, "Benjamin and the other young ones won't have to fight it ten years from now. And this war won't be fought with atomic weapons. In ten years, twenty years, who knows? A single hydrogen bomb could kill everyone in Israel. Such a small country can't afford atomic warfare. So we must fight now."

I sat mending a sock, pulling it tight around my olivewood darning egg, made by Benjamin in the shop. "It's said that you were the one who's responsible for Eshkol's choice of Dayan as Minister of Defense. That to make it happen, you told the doves he was the only one strong enough to keep the peace. Maxi says that because the doves believed you, they threw their support to Dayan. Were you lying to them?"

Lev stopped walking and stood over me, his face grim as a bulldog's. "Did Maxi say I was a liar? Do you say so, ha? Can neither of you see that we are no safer now than we were during the partition of '48? Things are no different. In the eyes of the Arabs, we aren't real. Israel is not on their maps. They see themselves walking through us as if we were shadows." He leaned down, putting his face next to mine, speaking louder than he needed to. "For them we have no right to exist, you understand?"

"That's just Arab propaganda." I slipped the mended sock off the egg and pulled on another, hardly looking up, not wanting to see his tight, angry face. "The Arabs know the Brits already gave them a Palestinian state, a lot bigger than ours. Instead of spending all that money on a war, why not just pay refugees to settle in Jordan?"

"Can't be done." Lev shook his head and began to pace again, whirling at the end of each pass as though he resented being caged in a room so much smaller than the parliamentary chamber. "You can't change Arab thinking. They're ignorant nomads, straight off their camels. The technological world is beyond them. They belong back in their tents and their tents belong in Egypt or Jordan or wherever they came from a hundred years ago. Most of them are no more 'Palestinians' than we Jews are."

I laid the darning aside and got up to stand in his way, so he wouldn't pace anymore. "How about their children? Their minds can be changed. We can educate them."

Lev's harsh laugh mocked my words. "Remember when we passed a law to keep Arab children in public schools? Their parents rioted. Wanted their brats to be on the street begging or in the madrassas, where they learn nothing but religion and how to kill Jews."

"Maybe the madrassas could be required to teach other things too. Why can't we change the Arab children? We're changing our children on the kibbutz." It was true that we were raising a new kind of person here. I felt on sure ground as I took this stand, thinking of Benjamin and of Maxi's two young ones, Yael and Joel.

Already, at twelve, Benjamin was in charge of his age-group's olive grove and working nearly twenty hours a week at the olive press. Yael and Joel were raising a small herd of goats, their group's project, and had presented the kibbutz with twenty quarts of feta cheese only the previous week. We had heard about children in the West who owned cars and fought against their elders because they wanted even more freedom and toys, but our children were not like that. They had no television, so they saw no luxuries. Even if they had, no one would have known what to do with them, for the children's rooms contained no more than beds, chairs, and study tables. Their food, clothing, and books all came from a common stock, so they had no reason to envy others and no reason to hang onto anything as their own. Because I disliked in myself the habit of guarding what was mine, perhaps I exaggerated the virtue of selflessness in others.

"You must admit," I added, when Lev did not answer me, "We're raising a new kind of child, nothing like ourselves."

"Because they are being raised without religion," Lev retorted, moving the argument to an arena where he could be sure of making me angry enough to fight. For some reason, he always felt closer to me when both of us were angry, not just him. At least I couldn't help noticing that only when we had been fighting did we make love. Lev was a hawk, all right, even in the bedroom. Because he was so often in Tel Aviv, we had little time for making either war or love. This particular evening, if my husband had love in mind, he would have to get me angry soon, for he was due to leave in half an hour.

"Religion has nothing to do with it," I snapped, giving him the fight he wanted. "The children of an Orthodox kibbutz are just like ours. And they have something ours don't."

This might be the perfect moment, I thought, to tell Lev I was taking Benjamin to Rabbi Meir in Jerusalem every week to prepare him for his Bar Mitzvah. I had to do some ground work first. "If you raise a child as an atheist," I said, "he's not going to be a Jew, not on the inside."

"The God of Abraham, Isaac and Jacob wasn't much help when six million Jews were murdered in Europe," Lev countered, picking up my old brass menorah and turning it nervously in his long fingers before he put it down. "Maybe God doesn't know the difference between side curls and crew cuts, ha? Or if he does, he doesn't care."

I moved the menorah away from him to the other side of the dresser. "If the Jews still survive after five thousand years," I said, remembering what Father Jonas had told me in the cellar of St. Hilary's while bombs fell overhead, "and are still themselves, it's because God knows who they are and so do they. A Jew who forgets is finished. His children won't be Jews at all." I took a deep breath. "It's because I want my son to know who he is that I'm taking him to Rabbi Meir in Jerusalem for his Bar Mitzvah instruction."

"Without telling me first? Isn't he my son too?" Lev's face was red, as if he had held his breath too long.

No love-making tonight, I sighed to myself. *Only fifteen minutes before he has to catch the bus to Tel Aviv.*

"Rabbi Meir's so Orthodox he wants no state of Israel at all." Lev was shouting now. "You've taken Benjamin to that fanatic?"

"He's the greatest rabbi in Israel," I said, not telling him that Maxi was my authority. "A real holy man. For Benjamin, only the best. No going through the motions. It's going to be a real Bar Mitzvah." I tried to appeal to Lev's pride in this son he knew so little. "Rabbi Meir says Benjamin could be a great Talmudic scholar. He told Maxi that he never saw such a student as our Benjamin."

"So Maxi put you up to this?" Lev grabbed the menorah again and held it tightly. It had been tactless of me to mention Maxi, knowing how jealous Lev was that Benjamin turned more to Maxi than to himself for fathering. "Maxi told you to take my son to an Orthodox rabbi?"

He threw Father Jonas's menorah on the floor so hard it bounced and some of the hands fell off. "You had no right, Dora, no right." He stood over me glaring and panting as I stooped to pick up the pieces, just the same careful way I had picked up the keys of Claire's piano so long ago. "Rabbi Meir is no friend of Israel, and he's a personal enemy of mine. Maxi must have known that."

"If Rabbi Meir were your enemy, would he instruct your son?" I went to answer the knock at the door, not sure how long the person outside and been listening to us yell at each other. "You look all around you for enemies, Lev, and never look where the real enemy is."

I stopped talking, surprised at seeing Esther in the doorway. She was an enemy all right, but not the one I meant.

"Lev?" Esther looked over my head, ignoring me. "You have ten minutes. I'll drive you to the bus."

"On my way." Lev grabbed his jacket and gave me a brief, mechanical hug. "I'll call you shortly."

It was a ritual with him to say that, perhaps one left over from his days as a bachelor playboy. I had learned to discount the words. At the window, I watched him walking to Esther's truck, while she held his arm tightly. I wished I had not brought up the matter of the Bar Mitzvah and that I had ended our fight in the usual way. The bed seemed very empty when I lay down on it, and thinking of the weeks Lev expected to be gone made me feel empty too. I tell asleep hugging my pillow and dreamed that Lev came back in the night to make up.

Late the next afternoon, while I was in the office going over the accounts of our flourishing new phosphate plant, Carolyn came bursting in with news that made me wonder if Lev would ever come back.

"Oh God, we're at war!" Carolyn cried, struggling to keep her fine, flying blond hair and her shaking voice under control. She was three months pregnant and was even more nervous than usual. "Dayan sent the army against the Syrians on the Golan Heights. More troops are on the way to attack the West Bank. Turn on the radio and you'll hear."

Carolyn tucked her hair back under the wide stretch band she wore to hold it down. "This is just like Pearl Harbor in reverse," she said. "We're knocking them out before they know what's hit them. Remember that stupid little town of Quneitra? Somebody told the Arabs there that the Israelis were coming, and they all took off, flapping their robes and croaking doom. Fifty thousand people gone overnight. My God!' She waved her arms wildly, and then collapsed in the chair, hands over her eyes.

My first thought was for the kibbutz. The highly inflammable phosphate plant was half underground, well-protected from enemy fire, but my new greenhouse, which now produced tomatoes and lettuce for the whole region, as well as for export, could be destroyed by slingshots, let alone Russian artillery smuggled to the Arabs.

"How close is the fighting?" I asked, trying to put the books into a metal box, without letting Carolyn see my hands were shaking.

"Six miles away." Carolyn pulled down her khaki skirt over her knees and gripped the hem of it. "Near Jerusalem. And our troops are already fifty miles into the Sinai Desert, heading for the Abu Rudeis oil fields. The Egyptians are throwing away their arms, running back to Cairo. People are making these awful jokes about it." Carolyn's eyes sparkled in anticipation of telling a story. "Cairo calls Moscow saying, 'Israeli soldiers are raping Egyptian women.' Moscow calls back, 'Good. In twenty years you'll have a decent army!" She giggled until she had to struggle for breath.

"That's not funny, Carolyn," I said, thinking it sounded like Lev's sort of joke. "Rape isn't funny at all."

"I guess not." Carolyn suddenly put her head down on the desk, sobbing. "You'd better know now. This morning Maxi signed up for duty in the Sinai, as soon as he heard about the war. I begged him not to. I told him I'd kill myself if anything happened to him, but he left anyway. Yael and Joel went with him to the army transport truck. I couldn't bear to see him go."

Patting Carolyn's shoulder, I closed my eyes, trying to be with Maxi, seeing him in the belly of a tank, bouncing over the hot sand. Because Carolyn was crying, I was not free to cry myself, but kept swallowing a lump that seemed to close my throat, a hysterical bulb, the doctor called it. One thing I was sure of. If anything bad happened to Maxi, I would know, just as I had always known when I had been out in the field and Benjamin had cried with hunger at the infant house.

"What about Lev?" Carolyn sat up and wiped her eyes. "I didn't think to ask. Would Lev go into combat at his age? I mean, being a member of the Knesset, would he have to?"

"No, Lev wouldn't have to," I said, staring out the window to where the sunlight shone on the greenhouse, hurting my eyes with its reflected shining. "Yes, he'll go. He didn't tell me, though. Maybe he told Esther." The thought of Lev leaving for the war, without any love from me made me choke on the lump that was stuck in my throat.

"Should we tell the children?" Carolyn clutched my hand. "How can we tell them we may all be dead tomorrow?"

"Well, we certainly won't tell them that," I snapped at her, pulling my hand away, "because it isn't true." I began walking around the office, my arms folded across my chest, just as Lev walked. If he were dead or dying, I thought. I would want to remember everything he did, so I could do it too. And Maxi, I thought suddenly, envisioning Maxi's long-jawed, spectacled face. If I never see him again, I must remember everything about him. Who would do what he had done for me? Who but Maxi would love me better than I loved myself?

The lump seemed to get bigger, and I tried to clear my throat of it, making loud rasping noises like sobs. Maybe it would have been better, I thought, if I had never loved anyone but Yeshua. I had loved my parents and Claire, and look what happened to them. Now it was Maxi and Lev who might die today. I loved them both, and they were out in the desert being shot at. And Benjamin? My heart almost stopped for a moment, afraid to love Benjamin for fear he would be lost too. So many lives outside my power to save. To take my mind off them, I began trying to save what I could.

Opening the door to the next office, where my assistant worked, I called out, "Run over to the greenhouse, Sarah. Tell Shana to send everyone she can find in the fields to bring canvas sheeting with them."

Five years before, I'd started laying wide, dark green strips of canvas between the rows of vegetable so the weeds would not get sunlight. "And tell Sol to get fifteen foot poles ready to prop canvas over the greenhouse roof. We'll try to block any falling debris before it hits the glass. Nothing much we can do about a mortar shell, but we'll do what we can."

My head lifted suddenly when I heard the siren, so like the one in Germany that made Mutti drop her fork and speak Yiddish. "I'll be at the shelter soon. Tell them that."

Carolyn was still sitting at my desk with her face on her folded arms, her shoulders shaking. She was the one adult at the kibbutz who shouldn't be on duty during a war. "Go down with the children to the shelter," I said. "You'd be good for them. Make them laugh. Go on, Carolyn."

Before she had gotten across the yard to the bunkers, where the children were filing in, shelling began from the hill overlooking our little valley. My office window shattered, and as it did, I dived under my desk, not moving until the mortars stopped twenty minutes later.

The first rounds had hit our residence and dining halls. From the window, between jagged pieces of glass still stuck in the putty, I saw our medical staff hunched over stretchers, picking up people who had not made it to the bunkers. From overhead came the sound of planes, swooping low over the Arabs' hilltop mortar emplacement, firing non-stop down at them. Our planes, then, I thought, glad someone had retained the presence of mind to call the military airstrip five miles away, when the shelling began. No more mortars from those particular Arabs, at least. In case of further attacks, I put the metal box containing my business ledgers under a trap door in the floor, feeling as Mrs. Grey must have when she brought her Hummel figurines down to the shelter under St. Hilary's.

It is said that you can tell what matters most to people by what they save at times of crisis, but in my experience, one mindlessly saves whatever comes to hand. I saved what I could in hopes that it will stand in the eyes of God for all the rest, for my son, whose name I was suddenly afraid to say, even in prayer, for fear he might already be lost. Please, Yeshua, please, I said silently, knowing Yeshua was as close as the breath in my body. Ever since I had first seen him in what was almost my hour of death, Yeshua had been my secret friend. Even Lev and Maxi did not know about my love for Yeshua.

Benjamin was not lost, after all, but came to look for me in the office even before our planes had finished cleaning out the Arab mortar nest. He stood framed in the doorway for a moment, looking at me on the floor as I recovered the ledgers from below. Benjamin's dark hair was close cut except for two longer patches over his ears. He was trying to grow side curls for his Bar Mitzvah, to please Rabbi Meir. His face was shining with sweat, and his yarmulkh, also a new acquisition, hung to one side, barely attached by the hairclip he had borrowed from me. Before he spoke, I took in all he was, with the same feeling I had at his birth, stronger for the knowledge that he was a miracle, that I could more easily than not, have lost him before his birth, were it not for Yeshua.

Perhaps Yeshua had some purpose for Benjamin's life beyond just being with me. I was coming to realize that he was God's son, not mine, and that I would have to surrender him to the future God had designed for him. The Bar Mitzvah would be only the beginning.

I looked at Benjamin with new eyes, knowing he belonged to God and to himself, not to me any longer. Benjamin was stocky, with square shoulders and my square jaw and olive skin. He had Maxi's large, dark, deepset eyes that seemed to look through, not at, whatever he saw. His lips and nose were wide, and his ears stood out a little from the side of his head. No one would have known from looking at him that this boy was not a wrestler but a scholar, already gentle and wise as Maxi, whom he resembled in spirit more than he resembled anyone else. But nobody could be sure who Benjamin was, for to each of us, he was a different person.

With Lev, he was silent and strong, talking only about the level of production he expected from the olive grove. With me, he was vulnerable, confiding his need for privacy in the kibbutz, which gave him every gift but the one he most craved, solitude for prayer and study. With Maxi, he shared his love for mathematics and his questions about the gods men worshipped ten thousand years ago. And with Rabbi Meir, he was a student of Jewish law, but more than that. Rabbi Meir told Maxi that Benjamin was one of those like the great Rabbi Akiva, who would never stop his search until he felt the embrace of God. I too was sure of that, remembering the night long ago, when we looked at the stars together, and Benjamin did a child's clumsy dance, holding up his arms to heaven and singing.

I remembered asking him why he sang. He stopped, considered, and then told me that it was because he heard in his head the song the stars were singing to him. Since then, he had occasionally said he sometimes heard the sound that rocks and trees would cry out if they could. As did the stars, even rocks and trees seemed to Benjamin to be alive, which is perhaps why he was never lonely, even during the times he camped out alone in the olive grove. He would have understood the presence of Yeshua in my heart. Someday I would tell him about Yeshua, but not now.

"I wasn't sure where to find you." Benjamin said, bending down to kiss my cheek. "We'd better go see Aunt Carolyn in the infirmary. A shell hit next to her as she was running for the bunkers. They say she's lost the baby."

"And Maxi's not here to comfort her." The bulb in my throat seemed to burst under the blow of this loss. For so long we had all hoped there would have been another child, and this one seemed to belong not only to Carolyn, but to the whole Ben-Ari family. Another Benjamin, or Yael, or Joel this baby might have been. We had all been waiting for the new Ben-Ari, whose life would make up for so many lives lost in so many places. This newly lost Ben-Ari would be a Wailing Wall for all the others, where Jews stood to remember what was gone. Poor Carolyn, I thought. She had been so proud of being pregnant, perhaps the more so because she knew I could never be pregnant again myself.

"Yael and Joel are safe?" As I had begun to do lately, I was relying on Benjamin to tell me what was going on.

"I put them to sleep in the bunkers last night," Benjamin said, pulling me to my feet with that quick, fluid gesture I remembered Lev making in the early days. "For some reason it seemed like the safe thing to do."

"Did you know last night that the war was about to start?" I wondered if Benjamin had the same sixth sense about Yael and Joel that I did when he was an infant and in need. "How did you know?"

"Father must have let something slip when he said good-by to me." Benjamin shrugged. "I don't remember. But yes, the children are safe in the bunker. We'd better go to Aunt Carolyn now. She must be in a bad way."

Carolyn was indeed in a bad way. We found her in the infirmary, pale as the sheets that clung to her damp body. Plasma was dripping into her arm from a plastic tube over her bed. Her breath came in uneven jerks, as if she were crying, though her swollen eyes were dry.

"I want Maxi," she whispered to us when we spoke to her. "Bring him back. Tell him what happened to our baby, and he'll come back."

"Carolyn, there'll be other babies for you and Maxi," I said, shaking her a little, but gently, so the tube wouldn't pull lose. "Don't make yourself crazy thinking there'll be no more." I thought I was offering the ultimate comfort, the words I would have wanted said to me, the words that never will be said.

"Not if Maxi doesn't live through the war." Carolyn opened her eyes wide. "I'm so afraid he won't come back. It's like he's dead already." Sobs shook her body, and she rolled her head from side to side.

"Mother, wait outside," Benjamin said in his soft, steady voice, so like Maxi's. "Let me sit with Aunt Carolyn a while."

Benjamin had a way of asking that even Lev couldn't say no to, so I sat for half an hour in the hall until my son called me back into the room. Carolyn was sleeping, her face relaxed, with a slight smile, and her fingers curled around his thumb.

"She'll be all right now." Benjamin gently disengaged his thumb and left the room with me. "She just needed quieting."

"What did you say to her?" I asked, wanting to know how anyone could calm Carolyn down when she got into one of her frantic states. "I never know what to say when she gets that way."

"Nothing much." Benjamin held open the infirmary door for me. "I just sat with her and prayed without words."

He wouldn't tell me more than that, and I let the matter rest, knowing Benjamin never wanted to talk to one person about his relationship with another.

We found Yael in the bunkers, her arm tightly around her brother, where Benjamin had left them. Beside her was one of her age-mates, a big sturdy boy named Dan, who was never far from Yael, silent as a sentry on watch. The other children had gone back to their classrooms, but Yael said she wouldn't leave the shelter until Benjamin told her to. For a moment, seeing her with her arm locked fiercely around Joel's shoulders, I saw myself with Maxi, long ago when we were in the basement of St. Hilary's, trying to sleep during the Blitz, after Father Jonas had given us our lessons and put us to bed.

Yael had her mother's fine, pale yellow hair, that shone like a halo around her delicate, pointed little face. Her dark brown eyes, slightly slanted at the outside corners like the eyes of Maxi's man-woman statue, shone too as if she expected to do battle and would do it well.

"Is it over, Ben?" she asked. "Can we come out now? I told Dan and Joel every story you ever told me, but only Dan could stay awake. Joel got bored and went to sleep before I even got through the parting of the Red Sea."

Yael had inherited the same extraordinary memory that made Maxi and Benjamin the students they were. She seemed to forget nothing she had ever seen or heard, and often, Maxi said, wept in his arms at night, remembering some small incident on the playground. Other children occasionally taunted her because her father worked at the university, not in the fields like the other fathers. This touchiness was Carolyn's part in the child. Without her mother's sensitivity, Yael might have been just another tough, grown-up kibbutz youngster, not caring much about anyone's feelings, her own included.

Joel, on the other hand, was a perfect little kibbutznik, demanding nothing, sharing all he had, never complaining. Already he wanted to be a soldier and had pointed out to us with pride that twenty-five per cent of the Israeli Defense Force was composed of people from the kibbutzim. He would be one of them someday, Joel told us, and he practiced drilling every day with one of the wooden rifles in the playroom. He was not clever at school like Benjamin and Yael, but he could draw the other children into his plans on the playground and make them laugh or fight. Whenever a swarm of children played on the broken-down American tank in the schoolyard, Joel was in the lead, sitting at the wheel as if he were a conquering general driving across the desert.

Meanwhile, as we later learned, his father was in an operational American tank searching for Eyptian troops in the Negev. The war, only six days long, was over, and Maxi's unit was not so much pursuing the enemy as trying to rescue retreating Egyptian stragglers from the desert sun. Maxi told me about them soon after he returned, with some rough words for Lev, who had tried to carry the battle all the way to Cairo. On hearing the ceasefire order from Eshkol in Tel Aviv, Lev had objected, urging his men on, furious with them for obeying the voice of the prime minister instead of his.

"We turned back as soon as the orders came," Maxi told Carolyn and me, as we were all sitting on the infirmary terrace. "I found a dozen Egyptians who didn't know where they were, only that they were half dead from thirst. They thought I was one of them because of my Arabic."

Maxi's single point of vanity was his gift for speaking Arabic in the classical manner, not like the Arabs in tent villages but like the scholar he was. "One poor fellow was out of his head, shouting that he would kill any Jew he saw, but he calmed down once I gave him water and a shot of Demerol. We delivered them to the Egyptian border, which was not as dangerous as it sounds. The ceasefire had been signed already. No thanks to your husband, I might add. Lev was determined to conquer Egypt and Syria both, sort of like General MacArthur trying to lunge across the Korean border into China, all on his own. Thank God for Eshkol's sanity. Now the world should know we fought this war in self-defense, not for conquest."

Maxi was restraining himself, not wanting to get into the matter of annexation, which Lev was pushing for in the Knesset even at that moment. The only annexation Maxi approved of was Jerusalem and its eastern suburbs. Even Jerusalem, he hoped, would be run as an open city, not barred to anyone who wanted to worship there. For years, no Jew could cry at the Kotel, the Wailing Wall, and we wanted to be sure that in the future, anyone who wished to could mourn as his ancestors had in that place of cosmic sorrow.

As for twenty-six thousand square miles of conquered Sinai desert, no one knew what should be done with it except hawks like Lev, who wanted to add it to Israel. Maxi and I were embarrassed at the idea of winning so much land in war, for all we wanted was to live without being ambushed from the Golan Heights or the West Bank, to raise our tomatoes and our children without being shot at. Churchill once said the greatest thrill in the world was being shot at and missed. It was a thrill we Israelis were well acquainted with and could gladly do without. Despite Lev's pressure, the Knesset wound up annexing only East Jerusalem and holding the West Bank, the Golan , and Gaza until we had some guarantee the Arabs wouldn't use them to invade us again or to smuggle terrorists into our cities.

The great moment of the war, from Benjamin's point of view, was when General Goren, the chief-of-staff blew the shofur at sunset on Friday, after the army had taken the Dung Gate of Jerusalem. Because the blowing of the shofur made the Arabs uncomfortable, it hadn't been done under the Turks or the British. Now, however, the melancholy voice of the ram's horn sounded over the valley as it had thousands of years ago, long before any muezzin had ever called the faithful to prayer. On the day Jerusalem fell to our army, Benjamin received a shofur of his own as a gift from Rabbi Meir for having memorized ten pages of the Torah in a week. My son went around Kiryat Anavim on the Sabbath, blowing that horn till his cheeks hurt.

After the Six Day War, we could once again go through Old Jerusalem, closed to us for twenty years, and Maxi took the whole family on a tour through the places he planned to excavate as soon as the government confirmed his appointment as chief archeological consultant for the Jerusalem dig. He wanted to prove that the Wailing Wall was not part of the Temple of Solomon, but of another wall around the hill on which the Temple once stood. Rabbi Meir thought this theory blasphemous and had already had sharp words with Maxi over his plans. Besides, the Arabs would have their robes in a twist because they didn't want any proof dug up that Jews had been in Jerusalem for three thousand years. The verbal battle seemed silly to me, for it should have been enough for us all that we had our wall back, whatever its use millennia ago.

The words "next year in Jerusalem," which my mother had said to me so often when I was a child, suddenly became real for me when I laid my forehead against Ha-Kotel to weep for all the people I had lost. I wept for Claire, as well as for my parents and the members of my family I had never known, never would know, unless Father Jonas was right about there being another life after this one. For Lev, too, I said prayers, because he was raging like a madman over not winning the annexation of Judea-Samaria, as he called the conquered territories. They belonged to Israel, he said, and would have been ours, if not for the British betrayal of their own Balfour Declaration. He was too angry to speak to Maxi or me. In his mind, it was people like us who were weakening Israel to the point of ruin.

"Blame yourselves if there's another war and we lose it," he had said to me as he left Kiryat Anavim for Tel Aviv, to rejoin his warrior friends for a spear-shaking session. "It will be your fault."

So because he seemed like someone I had lost along with the others, I prayed for Lev, speaking to Yeshua and God at once, since for me, there was no difference between them. At that moment they seemed close as the cool stone wall was to my cheek. The sun seemed to stand still right over the crowded little square with its cracks and weeds between golden bricks. Closing my eyes, which hurt from all the brightness, I saw the brightness still. The chinks in the wall were stuffed with tiny rolled-up paper prayers, *mezzuzot* at the door of heaven, Rabbi Meir called them, and mine was one of these, asking that these people I had lost might somehow live again, at least in Benjamin and me.

It seemed a miracle that a week after the ceasefire had been signed, a letter came from Father Jonas saying that he had retired from St. Hilary's and was obeying a call, as he put it, to come to the Anglican church and monastery in Jerusalem, where he meant to stay until his death. Mrs. Grey had died in her asylum a few years before, and he was free to leave England. I counted up his years after I had read the letter, and was surprised to realize that he was now seventy. The last time I had seen him, he was still a strong man, glowing with his recent mystical vision in the upper room of St. Elizabeth's church, sure of what he should do for his parish, now that God had done so much for him.

When I learned that he was to arrive the next day at Lod Airport, I was afraid, thinking that he had come weak and frail to Jerusalem in order to die, that I was about to lose still another one whom I had loved perhaps too much. It was a surprise, then, to see him get off the plane, tall and thin, his shoulders stooped only a bit, and his gray hair only a little gone at the temples. We had said good-by over fourteen years ago, but when I saw him and put my arms around his neck, we were where we had always been, as if no time had passed. Benjamin had been saying to me lately that time was only an illusion made up by our brains because we couldn't handle the enormous Now of God. I didn't believe him until I held Father Jonas and heard his voice in my ear, saying my name over and over.

Benjamin, whom I had brought with me to meet this man who was a sort of grandfather to him, stepped up behind me, holding out his tanned, square hand. "I'm Dora's Benjamin," he said, putting his other hand on Father Jonas's shoulder. "We're very glad you've come."

Father Jonas looked at the boy's broad face, glowing with sweat and good will. After a few silent moments, he put his arms around Benjamin and held my son as he had held me. "Dora's Benjamin," he repeated. "Will I be in time for your Bar Mitzvah? It was your mother's letter about the Bar Mitzvah that decided my coming. Other things too, but I don't yet know all of them. God has a way of surprising me with joy, now that I let him." He laughed as we walked with our arms linked together. "Maxi will find me a poor scholar these days, I'm afraid," he said. "I think I know nothing much anymore."

"But you're a very good priest, anyway," I told him. "How will St. Hilary's do without you?"

"They aren't shepherdless, I promise you," Father Jonas said, holding open the truck door for me. "I left them in good hands. Sometimes, toward the end, I felt hardly there, almost transparent, like this glass." He thumped the windshield and smiled, his teeth just as big as I remembered.

Benjamin put the luggage in the back of the truck, and sat down between us in the front seat. "Imagine, mother, that he's in both places at once. That's more like it," He turned to Father Jonas and said in his strong, new man's voice. "Lately it's seemed to me that we shouldn't be so sure about where anybody really is. How do we know where the waves of energy that make us up begin and end? I think they begin and end in God." Benjamin's eyes were round and shining as they were when he and Maxi had their long talks after dinner.

Father Jonas folded his hands around one knee and stared at the road ahead, which vanished under us as we looked. "We're like waves flowing into other waves, aren't we? And finally we break on the shore of God."

"You two ought to sit down with Maxi," I said, steering the truck around the pothole in this road that to the others might be an unsubstantial whirl of subatomic particles, more empty than not, but to me was all too real. "I know, Father, that the new physicists say matter is only energy held together in a pattern for a little while, like a snowflake, but I don't feel it that way. You and Benjamin may choose to believe you're whirling protons, but to me you're people I love."

"Dora," Father Jonas said, reaching out to touch my cheek carefully, with respect for my negotiation of potholes in the material world. "You are a grower of fine vegetables and this fine boy and we will forgive you for not feeling you're an infinitely expanding wave in a finite universe. It's too much an act of faith, even for most scientists. What you do requires a faith of its own kind, and you have it."

Even though I could not understand this cosmic leap of faith Benjamin and Father Jonas were talking about, I was glad they were making it together. Maxi seemed glad too, when he spoke to them after dinner, all of us sitting around a table in the noisy kibbutz dining hall, one end of it still open to the air, thanks to Arab shelling. Yael sat beside Benjamin, Dan behind her as always. Her blond head was on my son's shoulder, her dark eyes first on one speaker, then another, listening to them talk about the new theories that matter was not what our senses told us it was, but full of empty spaces, pulsing with energy and movement. She understood more than anyone but Maxi knew, for he himself had been her physics teacher every night, after her age mates had gone to sleep.

Carolyn had grown silent and bored at the scientific talk, having told her favorite story about the war, that Secretary U Thant of the U.N. had said, when asked who started the war, that he didn't know, but would like to knock out the other eye of the man who had done it. Even Father Jonas knew the power of Lev's friend Dayan, with his brave black patch over the lost eye, and we all laughed, I with some uneasiness, because if Lev had been here, he would have been angry at the laughter.

Benjamin and Maxi leaned forward, their heads close to Father Jonas as he questioned them about the find at Jericho, which to him was more important than taking the whole Sinai Desert. Father Jonas dipped his pita bread into his bowl of soup. "Your article says this statue is all gods in one, like nothing else that's been found."

"It might represent the first inkling humans had of the one God," Maxi said, pouring us all more tea. "The statue's left hand, the one holding the spear, points down to earth, at incarnation and matter perhaps. The other is turned up, toward the release of flesh into pure energy, or so I like to think. It reminds me of what you used to tell us of your Christ."

"First the Incarnation, then the Resurrection," Father Jonas murmured, swirling his tea in the cup. "And we are made of matter and energy, flesh and spirit, dying and being born again greater than we were."

"All this creation is going on at once," Yael said, in her calm, detached voice, "like ocean waves, each beginning where the one before it left off." She joined hands with Maxi and Benjamin, as if to demonstrate how connected their energy was.

Then we all put down our cups and linked hands, in the circle she had begun, hardly knowing why we moved, but moving as a single soul.

Into this joining of one body and one spirit Lev came suddenly crashing, his voice hard and thin, separating us like a knife blade.

"Dora, come with me. We have to talk. No, don't ask me to join you." He raised his arm, then dropped it, as if cutting us off from one another.

Letting go Benjamin's hand and Carolyn's, I left the others and joined Lev by the door, feeling like a multiple amputee without the rest of that circle from which I had just been taken. "What is it? We didn't expect you back so soon." I wanted to hold him close to me, but was afraid to reach out because he had for so long seemed far away."

"No, I'm sure you didn't. I'm just here to pick up the rest of my things." Lev raised his heavy eyebrows in a triangle over the bridge of his nose, managing to look like an angry bird of prey. "Go back to your family.

What am I compared to them? If I had a family, maybe I'd feel as you do." He was blaming me for making a family apart from him, though he himself had drawn the lines.

"You have one," I insisted, staring at his Adam's apple, which worked up and down like a teenage boy's. "You don't want it, though. You want to be off by yourself making war all the time. Why can't you live here with us, Lev?" I put a tentative arm around his neck, but he brushed it away. "You helped make this kibbutz, and it's yours too," I said, my voice as hard as his. "Everything is here, but still you go away."

Lev put one hand over his mouth, not soon enough to stop me from seeing that his lips trembled. He looked at me for a few moments, and then ran outside. I could hear the door of a truck slam and the engine start. Then Lev was off, gone across the country, back to Tel Aviv, where he would again try to convince the Knesset that it should by force turn the conquered territories into Israel. Out of many he would make one, on the plane of matter, if on no other. It was the only kind of oneness he could understand. Leaving the others to talk, I went back to my room, which had once been Lev's, but was not anymore.

Father Jonas came after me, and we sat at the window together, staring at the rising moon for a while, not saying anything. Finally he took my hand and kissed it, then held it to his heart.

"You are not alone, Dora, even if your husband goes away."

"I know. Yeshua is always with me." The words burst out of my mouth before I could stop them. "He is the friend that carries me and all my lost ones in his arms. Without Yeshua, I would have died, and Benjamin too."

Father Jonas looked surprised, then happy. "Dora, he said. "How did you come to know Jesus?"

"Yes, my Yeshua is the same as your Jesus,"I said, pulling my hand away. "But I'm not a Christian like you. Being a Jew is just fine with me."

Father Jonas was back in his comfort zone, being a teacher. He crossed his legs, folded his hands on his lap, and spoke to me as he had when I was his pupil at St. Hilary's. "Dora, the Jews were Christ's first followers. Always there have been Jews who kept both the old faith and the new expanded one, seeing them as a single continuum."

"Like the waves flowing into each other that Yael was talking about?" I said, beginning to get his drift.

"Exactly like that. And you can be a Jew who loves Jesus, or Yeshua, as the messianic Jews call him, without giving up Judaism."

It was just as well Lev had gone away, I thought, since he had a hard enough time with my being a Jew, let alone being a believer in Father

Jonas's Christ. "So I'm not the only one? Other Jews believe in Yeshua? Here on the kibbutz, I don't hear about such things."

"When you visit me in Jerusalem," Father Jonas promised, "I will take you to meet some Jewish believers. They are not easy to find, since they know the Orthodox don't consider them Jews anymore. They could be expelled from Israel, so they keep a low profile."

"I can do that," Dora smiled. "I've kept a low profile all my life. It's something Jews learn young how to do."

"Then it's settled. When you come to Jerusalem for Benjamin's Bar Mitzvah, we'll slip away and go to the place where the messianic Jews meet. You should be aware that they keep kosher laws and live as austerely as the Orthodox do."

"It sounds rather grim," I said. "Like a meeting of the kibbutz's disciplinary committee."

"Not at all," Father Jonas laughed. "They do Davidic dances when they worship. You'll find them full of joy, and they will fill you with joy too. You'll come with me?"

"Yes, Father, I believe I will." My heart suddenly felt lighter. There was, I realized, life after Lev, after the loss of Benjamin to his new manhood. "I love Yeshua, and I love to dance. Sounds to me like a good religion."

The next day, when I heard that Esther had left the kibbutz to live in Tel Aviv, I locked my door and wouldn't come out, even to say good-by to Father Jonas, who was leaving for his new residence at St. Elizabeth's monastery in Jerusalem. My latest loss was one I wanted to mourn only in the company of Yeshua, whose tenderness felt like the remembered arms of my mother and of Claire.

11

Amberfields..............................1967

Timothy is not a son to be proud of, Paul thought, glad that neither of his parents was alive to see their grandson appear on national television with his hair grown to his shoulders, holding up a sign that accused his country's leaders of being swine. True, he was only one of a howling young mob that crowded the screen during the riots against the Vietnam War. *But how did Timothy manage always to be out in front, and so near the newsmen's microphones, into which he shouted his unmanly opinions?*

It was also true, Paul had to admit, that despite the demonstrations he led, Timothy kept his scholarship and his standing at the top of Cornell's junior class. Paul was uncertain about the subject of Timothy's study, for the boy's college transcript lately contained nothing but credits in something called fieldwork. Paul had a picture in his mind of Timothy wandering barefoot in the meadows of upstate New York like a Renaissance shepherd, but was told that the field was community organization. *Apparently my son is being given college credit for instructing angry people on how to confront their government in various unpleasant ways.* Paul had given up wondering what constituted education in this anarchic age. He had given up trying to understand Timothy.

One of his son's recent successes had been a protest against pay toilets in a major New York City bus terminal. He had led in a hundred students who had occupied all the stalls of the terminal rest rooms, until the desperate manager had summoned the police. Timothy had delightedly added a letter to 'sit-in' in order to describe his exploit in the most shocking way possible. To Paul's embarrassment, the term had appeared in a national magazine with the de Montfort name attached.

What Claire had once called precocity, in the days of their son's recognition of dinosaur names and engine parts, had become disorderly conduct and felonious assault, according to the police who had arrested Timothy two days before, on charges of burning his draft card and attacking a police officer. Timothy had hit the officer with his protest sign because the man had just beaten his best friend unconscious with a nightstick. The friend was in a coma, and Timothy was in jail.

Paul sat alone in his small office at Parsons School of Design, watching the lights of the World Trade Center wink on in the accumulating dusk and wondered how he had managed to lose his son. *Timothy has been sliding away, down some black hole into an alternate universe, for the past ten years,* he realized. *I've been losing him ever since I took this job in Manhattan and left our son to be spoiled by his mother.* Paul had to admit it was not just his departure for the city that had caused Timothy's decline into oafdom, as Claire put it, but to his own defection. He had abandoned his family and had caused Timothy's ruin.

To be honest, Paul said to himself, *I can no longer blame the loss of Timothy on Claire's radical theories about child-rearing.* Nor could he blame it on the bad influence of Freddie Webster, chief source of soft drugs in northern New Jersey until he had been busted two years before. Timothy had been out of town in college at the time and on his way to an equally criminal career as an anarchist. Paul remembered saying words to his son like "failure" and "disgrace," and shifted in his office chair as if he were sitting on thorns. Those were his father's words, and he was saying them in turn to his own son. *If Tim knew about my affair with Meredith Simon,* Paul knew, *he would have a word for what his father is—a hypocrite. And he would have been right.*

Until Claire had found the letters and cried in his arms, Paul had allowed Meredith, a plump, aggressive young art student, to coax him into intimacy. She had not even locked his office door behind her. At first, Paul was terrified at the probable appearance of the academic dean, the head of the art department, or the cleaning lady. In time, he forgot to be afraid and began to enjoy himself. *I was faithful up till now only because I had no opportunity to stray,* Paul realized. It occurred to him to wonder if God minded, but God had been remote from him for so long that Paul had come to feel he was free to do anything he felt like doing. *Not so different from my son, I suppose,* Paul had to admit. He had rationalized his adultery by saying that Claire was busy with her work and had mislaid him for months, not seeming to notice the loss.

After a time, Meredith said she wanted to move in with someone other than her current young man, who suddenly had no money to pay the rent. She thought Paul might want to share the apartment, having become tired of his wife and all, as the girl put it. In her mind, Paul's domestic arrangements were as casual as her own. He had begun to act and talk more and more like one of her generation, dressing in tight jeans and talking in short, hard barks like a seal, saying "yeah" and "all *right*," being hip. Very often Claire had laughed at him for it, and Julie, lovely Julie, had once dropped her hands from the piano keys and stared at him, her blue eyes icy and critical when he talked in the style of young New York hippies.

Having no wish to confess his sin to Father Echlin, yet feeling the need for confession, Paul went to see Yehuda Marcus in his gallery on Manhattan's upper East Side. *Marcus was the only man who ever helped me,* Paul thought. *Maybe he can help me now.* Since Paul had begun teaching in the evening division of Parsons, after restoring paintings at the Museum all day, he no longer dropped by the gallery. Mr. Marcus, now in his late seventies, still wore the same jeweler's glass around his neck and sat on the same bar stool, but his round head was now bald as a stone. Much of the fat had melted away under his pale skin, which drooped emptily under the stubble on his cheeks.

"Come in, come in, Paul," he beamed, climbing down from his stool to put his arms around Paul's shoulders. "So long it has been. You are maybe too famous now to visit your old friend? Have coffee, have some halvah." He pushed a bowl toward Paul and set a pot of water to boil on his little stove.

"No, not famous," Paul said, dropping onto a chair and putting his head between his hands. "Just getting by, actually. My wife is somewhat famous as a composer, though."

"Ah, your wife." Marcus clapped his hands. "It is her Kol Nidre, then, that I heard on the radio? You must be very proud. Such a beautiful talent it is to discover music. I do not say create, you see, because the music is all around, waiting to be found. We ourselves, in a manner of speaking, are made of music, of invisible vibrating strings. Did you know that?"

Marcus peered at Paul over his small round glasses. "We are all symphonies, each unique, each vibrating, just as our tiniest atoms whirl in circles to their own song, like dancers doing the hora." He picked up a crystal goblet and ran his finger around the rim until the glass shivered and sang. "You see? Everywhere is music."

"I don't hear much music anymore." Paul stared moodily at the singing goblet. "By the time I get home, it's evening. Too late to do anything but argue with my son, if he's there, and go to bed."

Marcus's heavy eyebrows drew together and his mouth was grave. "I see that you have a problem with this son. And what man does not? You think your father was pleased with his son? No. Every man is as unhappy with his son as he is unhappy with himself. You are no different."

"It's true, I'm unhappy with myself." Paul was surprised to find that his eyes were wet, and he blew his nose hard. "And with Claire."

"You have reason to doubt your wife?" Marcus asked directly. "This is why you are unhappy?"

"No. Claire is only busy. It is I who am unfaithful."

"Oy, so." Marcus sat down in his rocking chair, saying nothing more for a few moments. "You work so hard. How is it you have time for this new woman? Or do you mean to leave your wife so that you can have the freedom you want?"

"I couldn't leave Claire and Julie and Timothy," Paul groaned. "But Meredith will find another man if I don't move in with her. She told me so."

"Then after all, you would be with Claire again." Marcus spread his hands, smiling. "But this time you will be all there. No woman wants a piece of a man, you see. So give her all yourself, just as when you were first married. Then it was a matter of glands, as it is with this girl of yours, but now, at your age, it is a matter of faith and will." He patted Paul on the arm. "You are a grown up man, no longer a silly boy fighting his mama, *nicht wahr?"*

"We don't seem close anymore," Paul objected. "My wife has changed, and I don't know how to find the other Claire, the little one who needed me. Is it so wrong to want her needing me? Once I wanted her to be strong, like my mother, and now I want her to be my little Claire again." He knew the words were foolish as soon as he heard them coming out of his mouth, but was too miserable to be embarrassed or take them back. "We are so far apart that we hardly hear each other when we talk."

"Let me explain to you," the old man said. "Sometimes very smart men need to be told a truth. Once even Einstein had to be told a thing he did not know. Here is what his friend told him. Take two particles that were once together, like you and your wife long ago. Look." Marcus took a piece of halvah from the bowl beside him, and then pulled the soft candy into two pieces. "Now two pieces, two shapes, yes?"

Paul nodded wondering what a broken piece of candy had to do with Einstein or with him.

"Watch what happens when I put them over the heat." Holding a piece in each hand, Marcus leaned over the pot of boiling water. "You see? They both melt, because they are the same thing, whether apart or together. What Einstein learned from his friend was that two particles, if they were ever one, will never forget it. Always they will behave as if they were still connected, even if they are taken to opposite sides of the world. They are entangled forever. Einstein did not know that, and I think you did not know it either. Am I right?"

When Paul nodded again, Marcus arranged two cups on the counter and poured them full of tea from his battered old samovar. "As with these little particles, so it is with our lives. So we are with the God who made us. Someone we once loved is never lost to us. If I did not believe that…" He wiped his glasses and paused a moment. "If I did not believe that, how could

I live anymore? You see how we drink the tea, each from his own cup. But it came from this one pot, yes? Nothing, my dear Paul, is truly separate. We think so only because we cannot touch the web that holds us together, just as we have no ears to hear the music all around. Just as we have not the sort of eyes that can see God."

Paul went from Marcus's gallery to the phone booth, where he called the school, cancelling his class. He wanted very much to go home. That had been the night Claire found the letters from Meredith. Claire had cried, her arms around him, and he had wondered why he ever wanted Meredith's sprawling, heavy body, or her slack mouth on his. Since that time he had given up all but one night class at Parsons and come home on schedule. But the damage had been done. Timothy was a stranger, and Julie was preoccupied with her books and her music, which seemed to protect her from the outside world. She said very little to Paul, even when he began coming home every night. It had been a long time since he had wandered with her in the meadow, picking the lightheaded dandelion seeds and blowing them away.

Now Julie was eighteen and had recently brought home a young man, a farmer in the area south of Pine Lake. She disapproved of Timothy's radical politics, his dirty clothes, and his language. Instead of a hippie like her brother, she chose for herself a man Timothy despised as a square and a crypto-Nazi. Paul despised Charles Frazier too, but for different reasons. The young man's presence in their lives painfully reminded Paul that Julie was not his anymore. Then too, Charles had no education, for all his wealth, and to Paul's mind owned too many machines. At last count, Charles had in one of his barns a Lincoln Continental, an English sports coup, a two story camper, a pick-up truck, two snowmobiles, and a twenty-five horsepower speed boat which Timothy mockingly referred to as the Queen Mary. Probably to impress Julie, Charles had bought a small, twin-engine plane, which had a barn all to itself. He had recently returned from service in Vietnam as a Green Beret and felt that the country owed him the luxuries he had for two years done without. *One of these luxuries,* Paul reflected bitterly *is Julie*. While Paul was busy blaming Charles for the change in Julie, Claire blamed their daughter and tried to talk her out of marriage.

"You haven't given yourself a chance to grow up yet," Clair said to Julie, who was helping in the kitchen before the dinner at which Charles was to be present. "You aren't yet who you're going to be someday. Maybe you could ask the minister to pray with you before you decide."

"I've prayed," Julie said, "and I think the Lord wants me to bring Charles to him."

Although she still attended St. Michael's with Paul on Sunday, Julie had begun going to Claire's evangelical church on Wednesday nights. The two of them spoke in a Protestant language that Paul found strange and disturbing to his peace. *In my church,* Paul thought, *unless people are nuns or monks, they talk about normal activities, not prayer and Bible study.*

"But can't you do that without marrying him?" Claire reasoned patiently. "You have your own life to live."

"I'm not like you," Paul heard Julie murmur. "I'll never be famous or anything. What could I do that you haven't done already?"

"So you're going to settle down," Claire said, rattling glassware and dropping the silver, suddenly losing her temper, "before you've tried anything else. It's such a waste, then, giving you all we've given."

"Daddy doesn't think so." Julie's voice was soft, but stubborn. "He doesn't think I have to amount to anything. Why do you think so? I'm not going to compete with you. I can't."

"Someday you may not have Charles to take care of you." Claire swung open the door to the dining room so hard it banged the wall. "Men can die or run away. Remember that."

The doorbell rang and Paul let Charles Frazier in, trying to organize at once his own hostility, the acceptance of a dozen roses, and the shaking of a large moist hand.

"Julie told me to come early," Charles said in his deep, room-filling voice. "She said I should talk to you. We want to get married, and I'm supposed to ask you if it's all right. What do you say?"

Paul surveyed the tall, blond man who stood in the doorway of Amberfields, his arms now emptied of yellow roses and crossed belligerently over his wide chest. Above his square chin and straight, finely chiseled nose, pale green eyes glittered, and his blond brows drew together over them. He looked to Paul like one of Hitler's advertisements for the Aryan race.

"I have no idea what my daughter wants," Paul said, wishing he could club the young man alongside his handsome head, letting him know that Julie was too precious, too much possessed already, for sale to him, whatever the price.

"She wanted me to tell you I could support her and any children. How about I sit down?"

Paul showed him to a couch in the parlor and took the roses away to the kitchen. "Julie is only eighteen," Paul said when he came back, one thumb bloodied by thorns and wrapped in a tissue.

The young man leaned forward, his large hands clutching his thighs. "What does she need college for?" he asked. "I'll take care of her. My father's a millionaire. He's got hundreds of acres in Passaic County. You know how much that's worth? I know I'm not a college graduate, but neither is Julie. What I'll give her is security. And a good outdoor life, so she'll get out of those books of hers. Julie won't want for anything."

"I don't know what to say." Paul poured the insistent fellow a drink and sat watching him from across the room. "Julie is the one to decide."

Julie had, in fact, already decided, and the date was set for the following month, just after her graduation from high school. When she heard how soon the marriage was to be, Claire had been furious, having expected Julie to wait at least a year. So quick a marriage was suspect, since it implied a reason for haste. She demanded that Paul speak to Julie, urging her to delay the wedding. Perhaps, Claire reasoned, as time passed, so would Julie's interest in Charles.

"Do you really want someone to own you the way this man would?" Paul asked Julie as they walked in the fields, pale with spring flowers. "Really sure?"

"I only want to be loved and have my own place," Julie said, bending down to pick daisies as she talked. "The way Mother has hers. Is that too much to ask? A family of my own and being the mother of it is all I want."

"And Charles is the man to give you that?" Paul took her by both shoulders and turned her toward him, watching the sunlight tangle in her bright hair. "What will you talk to him about? The man has nothing on his mind but cows and machinery."

Julie pulled away from him, her eyes looking coolly into Paul's. "At least he'll be there," she said. "At least he'll be all mine." She began to walk back toward the house, and Paul watched the stride of her long, slim legs, tightly encased in blue denim, and the tail of red-gold hair swing across her back.

"I've never needed much talk," she called to him over her shoulder. "Charles will do as well as anyone."

Like Timothy, Paul felt, *Julie thinks I abandoned her. And did I remember her when I was rolling about on my office floor with Meredith? Now my daughter is about to become the property of a green-eyed stranger who raises cows.* Even worse, this stranger owned an airplane in which he planned to fly Julie and her prospective children to tasteless places like Las Vegas.

Julie had met Charles at a 4-H Club exhibition. She had been exhibiting her needlepoint, learned from her grandmother and applied to the production of a thoroughly American quilt, which the judges pronounced a museum piece. Charles, who at twenty-five was an established gentleman farmer, had attended the fair as a judge of livestock. Seeing Julie in the booth behind her quilt, reading Pascal's *Pensées* in French, Charles had lingered to find out who she was. Julie had told Claire about the encounter, and Claire had told Paul, her voice low and worried, because she was sure this man meant to carry off her daughter like a prize cow.

"You'll ruin your pretty eyes if you read too much," Charles had said, leaning over the quilt frame, his face at the same level as Julie's. "I sure would hate to see you do that."

"I've always read a lot," she replied, hardly looking up. "My eyes are just fine."

"What's it about?" Charles persisted, shoving his way into the booth and looking over her shoulder. "The book, I mean."

"I'm at the place where Pascal says how he feels shaky inside when he thinks about how small we are compared to God and creation." Julie held up the book, and pointed at the page. "Back then, people had just figured out that the earth isn't the center of the universe. Like everybody else, Pascal was scared that humans didn't matter."

Charles smoothed his thick blond hair. "Are you scared about things like that?"

"Sometimes." Julie closed the book and held it close to her chest, against her pale blue tee-shirt. "I should think about God more than I do."

"No," Charles took the book from her and tossed it on the shelf. "You should come to the square dance with me."

Against such self-assurance, Julie was helpless, despite the minister's warning against what dancing close to a man could lead to. She forgot about God while in the arms of this rich, handsome young man whom all the other girls hoped would marry them. So far, he had been engaged five times, or so the girls claimed. The papers had carried news of these phantom engagements at the request of the hopeful families, but nothing had come of their maneuvers. Charles Frazier had been looking, he said, for a Christian girl, who did not, as he put it, solicit sex, and who wouldn't try to run a man's life.

He danced with Julie that night and as many nights thereafter as he could talk her into, holding her close to him and asking if she were ready to join him in the back of his truck, where he handily kept a mattress and a bottle of vodka, no doubt for the girls he had encouraged to believe were his fiancées in the making.

Julie explained that she couldn't go into the truck with him because she was a Christian. "The only man in my bed," she told him finally, as she broke away from him at the doorway of Amberfields, "will be my husband."

Charles started hanging gloomily around the house while Julie played the piano. He turned the pages of her music when she nodded at him and sat as close to her on the piano bench as he dared. Paul watched the pair over the top of his new reading glasses. He had taken to sitting in the living room to read instead of in his study, ever since Charles Frazier had started courting his daughter. After a while, the two young people talked to each other as though he weren't there, and Paul began to understand why this coarse-mouthed, thick-headed young man, who could have married any number of girls, was so taken by Julie. Her cool indifference was to him as much a challenge as the killing fields of Vietnam.

"I'd like to read for a while," she said to Charles, closing the music book. "You'll have to go away now."

"Why? We could take a walk." Charles insinuated himself between her and the door. "The moon's full tonight."

"I never get any time to myself these days." Julie reached around him and turned the handle. "You're always here."

"Such a beauty you to be sitting alone." Charles leaned both arms against the door, imprisoning her between them. "My beauty. That's what I call you in my mind."

Charles is growing sentimental in his frustration, Paul thought. *Any minute he will fall on his knees, raving like a drunk.* In fact, Paul was quite sure Charles had fortified himself with liquor before his arrival at the house, and he wondered if Julie knew why Charles so often slurred his words or maundered on about how beautiful she was.

Julie looked up at the hall mirror and smoothed her hair. *Not so much out of vanity,* Paul thought, *but because she can never be certain that she is really as lovely as people say she is.*

"I like silence," she said, pushing Charles's arms away. "Too much talk makes me tired. I'm tired now." She opened the door and sent Charles on his way.

Paul resisted the impulse to talk to her about her young man's defects, since Claire had already said so much. So Julie went alone up to her room, which overlooked the fields and the lake. Paul had built a window seat for her years ago, which they had often shared. Now he imagined her sitting in the moonlight, thinking without words, as she described it. *What Charles wants,* Paul suddenly realized, *is to keep her from thinking at all and never closing the door between them. The more she withdraws, the more he wants to take her over like one of his superfluous vehicles.* In time, no doubt Charles would win, for he seemed to Paul a very determined sort, not used to losing what he set out to have. *But what will happen once Charles has*

Julie to himself and can no longer be sent away? Paul wondered and hoped Julie would wonder too.

The wedding day arrived and Julie, wonderfully decorated by Claire, appeared at the church door, her face still and remote as a statue's. She hummed the wedding march under her breath as Paul walked her down the aisle. Charles stood waiting for her, his broad face flushed and pale by turns. *This bull of a man is about to go over the slim, lovely length of my daughter inch by inch, taking whatever he wants.* Paul hated the fellow.

That night, imagining the scene at the Miami resort to which Charles had flown his bride, Paul lay in Claire's arms and wept, remembering how he had bathed and dried that fragile, perfect daughter's body when she was small. *Now it is being used by a panting fool with no idea of all that went into the creation of this Julie who used to be mine. Not mine anymore,* Paul reminded himself, turning over and pushing his wet face into the pillow. *Charles's now.* He fell asleep thinking that Timothy should have been there, so that together they could have stopped Charles before he made it to the church. Or perhaps they might have locked Julie in her room and barred Charles from the house on pain of great bodily harm. But Timothy was in jail, serving his time and could not come to the wedding.

The day after the newly-weds had left for Miami, Paul went to Washington with his lawyer to take Timothy out of jail and bring him home. Timothy had spent the first night of his captivity in a large cell with six other men, mostly drunks. But a few were toughs picked up on suspicion of armed robbery. Paul heard the whole story on the way home.

After cutting off his long hair, the police had shoved him into the cell saying, "Come and get him, guys. He burned his draft card. Won't go to war like a man." The policemen laughed as they locked the door. At first Timothy was dizzy from hitting his head on the concrete floor where he had fallen. He propped himself up against the wall and looked at the three thugs, who had tossed their newspapers aside and were advancing on him. As he scrambled to his feet, a memory of his life at Amberfields flashed across his brain, in which long walks by the lake alternated with studying in front of the fire and hearing his mother sing as she cooked a chicken dinner. When he opened his eyes and saw the three men reach out to grab his arms, Timothy felt a violent wrench that reminded him of the first time he had dropped acid and freaked out, screaming that the couch was a dinosaur.

He seemed to be in two separate worlds at once, one green and good inside his head, and one black and filthy, where his body was. As the men threw him back down on the floor, pushing his face hard against the concrete, Timothy screamed once, in disbelief that he fallen from Amberfields into this dark place. After that he was silent, biting his lips as he struggled to protect his face from blows. No one would come if he called. Timothy de Montfort, who had never known what it was to call and not be answered, knew for the first time what it was like to fall among thieves.

They punched him in the jaw and back and stomach, telling him that it was what he deserved for burning his draft card. They would have kept on, he thought, until they killed him, but for a man in an upper bunk. This tall black man, powerfully built around the shoulders, climbed down from his bed and stopped them. His voice was strong and his hands curled into fists hard as stones. Timothy's attackers backed away as he spoke, except for one squat bald felon who gave Timothy a vicious parting kick in the groin.

"Now, tha's jus' enough, man," his rescuer said, putting his coat over Timothy, who lay curled up on the floor, not caring that they saw him cry. "You stop with that boy, hear?" He bent over Timothy and stood him up.

"Hurt's, don't it?" he said, putting Timothy's arms into the coat sleeves, gently as a mother. "I got creamed by a gang myself once, when I was a kid. Up on a Harlem roof, it was. And it do hurt."

Timothy nodded and kept his eyes on the floor, stained with his own blood. "Who are you, anyway?" he mumbled, trying to take a breath, but feeling the very air hurt his lungs.

"Call me Josh." The man put his arm around Timothy and led him to a bunk. "Now you jes' lie down and sleep. I'll take care. Say some prayers now, and be grateful to the Lord you ain't dead meat."

Timothy slept beside his Samaritan and had terrifying dreams of being almost swallowed by a tidal wave. At the last minute, strong arms pulled him out of the water, and a voice told him he was safe as if he were in his mother's arms. In the morning, when he woke up, Josh was propping him against the wall and holding a bowl of oatmeal under his chin. Timothy tried to raise his hand to take the spoon, but could not move. As Josh fed him, Timothy heard the man's deep voice as if it were coming from far away.

"Lord Jesus, bless this boy."

"You're a good man," Timothy murmured, trying to get his swollen lips around the words. "How come you're in here?"

"Some little gal say I the dude that mug her," Josh said. "She mistake me for one of my brothers. But if the Lord want me to suffer in his place, amen to that. Say, man, you want me to give you a healin'?"

"You can do that?" Timothy would have laughed at the man yesterday, but today he was broken in so many places that he was open to believing anything. He looked into Josh's shining, liquid dark eyes. "Yes, I believe you can."

Timothy heard the man softly praying over him. The words seemed to him almost like a foreign language, almost like singing. Now and then, in his daze, he heard a few words he understood.

"May you have faith in the Lord who make you whole right now," Josh murmured.

Perhaps the soft words were lulling him to sleep, Timothy thought after a while, for he hurt less than before. He put one hand up to touch his face and realized his lips were not as swollen as they had been. Moving his tongue experimentally, he found that his teeth were no longer loose in his mouth. A peace settled over him that he could not understand, and he smiled thinking that perhaps after all, God was love, as his mother had so often told him. Josh used the word 'love' many times in his healing prayer, and Josh seemed to know a lot about God.

"I'm better now," Timothy said, reaching down to touch his stomach. It no longer ached from the kicking. "Thank you."

"Give God the glory," Josh said, raising his hands in blessing over the boy. "And never forget, man, God love you and forgive you pride in those recent doin's."

Holding his hands tightly together in prayer, Timothy swore that he would never forget and that he would never again be proud of himself for being a noble protester of injustice. He had acted out of pride, not love, and his actions had led to nothing. He went to sleep holding Josh's thumb, as he remembered holding his father's when he had been very young.

The next day, when he woke up, Josh was gone, but his words still rang in Timothy's ears like music, and Timothy found himself thanking God in breathless, broken prayers he said from his heart, not from memory. He was still saying prayers when his father and the lawyer arrived. During the drive home, Paul listened for the most part, for Timothy suddenly had a great deal to tell him.

"We'll agree not let your mother know about the beating," Paul said after Timothy had described his day and night in jail. "She took it hard that you were arrested. Like Freddy, she said. You heard that Freddy was jailed for drug peddling?"

"Belinda called me about it. Mrs. Webster's all strung out, I heard. Won't let Freddy ever come home again." Timothy put his hands behind his head and stared at the car ceiling. "Does Mom really believe my arrest was like Freddy's? Didn't you explain to her about standing up for what a person knows is right?"

Paul was unsure about what Timothy felt was right. "I explained to her that a protest isn't the same as a criminal act done for gain," Paul said, trying to remember the moment news had come that Timothy had broken the law. "But your mother felt that hitting a policeman was going too far. I agree with her."

"I guess I do too," Timothy said, his head bowed. "I tend to get carried away, don't I?"

"You belong in school, Tim, using your brains, so someday you'll be able to make changes in the world. Just now, you're too young to make decisions on foreign policy."

"Could I do any worse than Lyndon Johnson?" Timothy tapped the picture of the president on the cover of a news magazine that lay between them on the seat. "He lied to us about our ships being attacked in the Gulf of Tonkin. He's bombing innocent people, poisoning even their soil with chemicals." He folded the magazine and creased it hard down the middle. "We've had a hundred thousand casualties in this war and no one even knows how many Vietnamese are dead. I guess they don't count."

Paul laid a hand on his son's knee. "You've done your part against the war, Tim. Let other people do the protesting from now on. Next time you may wind up with a cracked head like your friend, hooked to a respirator. Don't do that to your mother and me."

He wished he could tell Timothy how much it hurt to see one's child suffer, how to his parents he would always be a small, bright-faced boy who named the animals in books.

"Nobody ever really hurt me before." Timothy's voice was high and thin for a moment. "I didn't know how it is to be hurt. What I want to do for the rest of my life is keep as many people from being hurt as I possibly can. I hope you'll understand."

"I do, a little." Paul was embarrassed because he felt no such call as Timothy's. *I felt it in my youth, he* reminded himself, *when I fought against the Nazis, but it's been a long time since I was young.* "You aren't going back to the university then?"

"Yes, but I'll take off sometimes." Timothy pulled a notebook out of his duffle bag and flipped it open. "See? Phone numbers of everybody who counts in the peace movement, all the way across the country. I've been talking to them. We're going to get a hundred thousand people to protest on the steps of the Pentagon, October twenty-first. One for every soldier who's died in Vietnam."

"And you'll be there too, I suppose?" Paul sat defeated, wondering how he would tell Claire that Timothy was going on a march right to the doors of the Pentagon.

"No choice." Timothy snapped his notebook closed. "The Nazis murdered Jewish civilians, and we tried as criminals the men who did it. Then we wondered why nobody had spoken up for the Jews. Well, my kids aren't going to have to wonder where I was when Vietnamese babies were being fried in napalm. I'll be able to say I was out in the streets, trying to stop the killing."

They ate dinner in Toms River, at a local café. Over fish and chips, Paul tried half-heartedly to talk Timothy out of protesting the war. *My own father encouraged me to fight the Nazis,* he could not help thinking, *while here I am, telling Timothy to go home and hide because his parents cannot bear to see him risk his life.*

"I was always proud that you fought in the Resistance," Timothy said, wolfing down his lunch. "Did your dad tell you to go home and listen to the French National Symphony while the Nazis gassed kids in ovens? No? So don't tell me to quit. Everybody's got his own Nazis. My particular Nazi is Vanderzell, the oil tycoon. He and his friends practically own the government. They make money off war and they love it." Timothy flipped open his notebook. "Now, if you'll excuse me, I've got to get on the wire to California. We're going to bring in the whole Berkeley campus on a flying carpet."

Paul heard his son making plans on the telephone in the corner of the café. "That you, Jerry? Tim. I've got five buses coming out of Chicago. Think you can do that for Berkeley? The Grateful Dead will do a show for us? No kidding! Tell 'em they'll have amps like in the Houston Astrodome. Folks'll hear 'em all the way to Saigon."

Paul left to call Claire from the phone outside, uncertain how to tell her that not only was their son going to continue landing in jail, but that he was taking other students with him. He glanced back at Timothy, who had hunched the phone between his mouth and shoulder so he could write in his notebook as he talked. *It's been a long time,* Paul thought, *since I cared so much about anything but my family.* He felt a moment's stab of envy as he watched his son at work.

Claire could not understand, for above all, she had wanted to raise her children in peace, escaping tragedy. *But we were wrong,* Paul said to himself as he dialed. *No one escapes. Each time it's a different kind of tragedy in a different place. No use trying to guess where and jump the other way. One might as well be like Timothy and just jump in. At least there's some honor in that, while there's none in being carried out of your home feet first when you're old.*

Paul thought about how he had tried to get his men out of Courtrai, and then closed his eyes, not wanting to see anything but blackness. *Perhaps there is another way to fight,* he thought. *Perhaps this war in Vietnam is another kind of war, not like the ones my father and I fought against the German invaders. It is not a just war. Perhaps Timothy is a leader of men in his turn, this time for peace.* As Paul talked to Claire, cautiously telling her as little as she would let him, he decided suddenly that he too would march on the Pentagon, alongside his son. *This time,* he told himself, *no Courtrai. This time, Timothy will not go to jail alone.*

The leaves were falling early in Washington that autumn, Paul noticed as he stared out the window of the bus. Timothy's organization had hired it to bring some of the hundred thousand demonstrators to the country's capital.

"A dry summer makes for an early fall," he commented to Julie, who had insisted on coming with him, though she was five months' pregnant.

A dry summer it had been, with cracked ground and pale blue skies empty of clouds. American farmers cursed like their fellow farmers in Southeast Asia, who stared at their wasted rice fields still stinking from the clouds of Agent Orange that had withered both crops and children.

Julie had a news magazine on her lap, spread out before her slightly rounded belly, and was staring at the picture of two Vietnamese babies who were missing the arms and legs they had been born with. She pointed silently at one mother's face. The woman's mouth sagged open like a stroke victim's.

"It may not have been Americans who did it," Paul said, feeling somehow that Julie blamed him for the limbless babies, since he was over thirty and a voter. "The Viet Cong burn villages too, you know."

"They wouldn't be burning them if we weren't there," Julie said, her eyes dropping to the picture again, as her fingers traced the outlines of the babies' broken bodies. "Yes the communists are just as bad, of course. But at least they're not foreigners. Would we want foreigners coming here and burning up our towns just to save us from a revolution by our own people? I don't think so. But I don't know much about these things, Charles says."

Paul put his hand over hers. "Why did you come, Julie? You're no radical like Tim. You and Charles haven't been married very long and you're pregnant. Shouldn't you have stayed home with him?"

She disengaged her hand. "I wanted to be away for a while," she answered, avoiding his eyes. "Charles doesn't own me. Just because he's for the war, I don't have to be. Tim's my brother, and I need to be here with him."

Though he wanted to ask why Charles had not brought her to the bus station, Paul was reluctant to push her into complaint, just as he was reluctant to ask how one of her cheeks had become inflamed enough to half-close the eye over it. *Perhaps,* he thought, *Julie's new willingness to stand against her husband's opinions is the result of whatever had happened to her face.*

The swelling had receded by the time the Friday night speeches at the Lincoln memorial were over. When Julie went off to the north parking lot of the Pentagon to hear the Saturday morning speeches, she covered the redness with make-up and the swelling belly with a flowing, Indian-print hippie blouse, so that she looked like any other girl on the long march across the Arlington Bridge into enemy territory.

They waved to Timothy when they saw him dash by, megaphone in hand, as he kept the crowd from drifting apart. He was followed by Belinda Webster, who always stayed as close to Tim as she could get. At lunchtime, the two came over to Paul and Julie, their faces set as hard as those of the young MPs who lined the strip between the marchers and the pale yellow walls of the Pentagon.

Rhythmic cries rang out from the crowd: "Hey, hey, LBJ, how many kids did you kill today?" As they repeated the refrain, the forward ranks swayed toward the wall of soldiers.

"Some of the radicals are pushing to go over the fence," Timothy said. "Everybody's still in the parking lot or on Washington Boulevard. It's too soon. We'll get creamed. Look at those marshals." He gestured at the white-helmeted older men behind the lines of young soldiers. The marshals were slapping their batons into their leathered palms, looking around for anything else available to slap. "They can't wait to get at us."

"Let's go," cried small Belinda, rubbing her hands together. "Let's tell 'em we're just trying to stop a war, not start one." She danced on the toes of her frayed sneakers, hardly able to keep still, and her skin glowed under her freckles.

Timothy put an arm around her, holding her still. Paul had a sudden insight. *These two are more than friends. Belinda might be my daughter someday.*

"They won't hear us," Tim told the girl. "They're soldiers and out for blood. The thing to do is keep people from getting crazy, so they won't get hurt. We've got nothing to fight back with except one thing. That's what Josh says."

Paul was curious. "And what did Josh say you have?"

"A God who loves justice," Tim said. "You can get crucified following him, but it's the only way to go."

With the uneasy feeling that his son had overnight become a Jesus freak, Paul said, "One crucifixion is enough. Let's get out of here now, Tim, and go home."

"What would Jesus do?" Time smiled briefly, and his eyes seemed to look through his father. "I think he would try to save lives and take the consequences."

He turned around at the sudden sound of cheering and shook his head. "They've started going over the fence. I've got to make them go back." He started running, Belinda close behind him. They headed for the high fence which was being scaled by young men with knotted ropes.

Paul had put out a hand to stop his son, but Julie took it. "No use," she said. "Tim won't give up and he needs us. We'll go too."

As Paul watched, Timothy climbed the fence and then stood on it, his legs trembling as he balanced himself. He shouted through the megaphone first at the crowd to go back to the safety of the parking lot and wait for the others, then to the soldiers, who were facing the charging demonstrators with leveled rifles.

"We aren't armed," Timothy cried. "Don't shoot. We're only trying to stop you from being sent to war. We don't want you to die in 'Nam. That's why we're here."

He turned his megaphone toward the demonstrators, who stopped when they heard him, leaving a breathing space between themselves and the military police. "Sit down," he called out. "It's going to be a long night. Just sit down and link arms. Nobody's going to hurt you."

Timothy waited until the crowd had obeyed than climbed down inside the fence, joining the rest in the front line. Paul and Julie found a flattened area of fence knocked over by some of the demonstrators and made their way toward Timothy. They sat down at the forward edge of the crowd that surged in after them, linking arms with their neighbors. Surrounded by young people, Paul was conscious of the lines on his face, the gray at his temples. *What am I doing sitting here on the Pentagon lawn? Am I a good example or a bad one?* He had always despised people who tried to imitate the young, and despised himself for the interlude with Meredith, when he had forgotten how old he was.

True, Belinda kissed my cheek and Timothy hugged me when I arrived, but they thought I was supporting the cause. Only Julie knew that his personal cause was staying near enough to his son to protect him with whatever authority middle age and graying temples had to protect one's child in these uncertain times.

The night with its fall chill came on, and still Tim and the demonstrators sat cross-legged on the ground, arms linked. Some hotheads, however, had charged into the building in search of draft records to destroy and been clubbed or jailed or both. To prevent the soldiers from weakening at the sight of shivering youngsters singing "God Bless America" and stuffing flowers in the barrels of their guns, the marshal rotated the MPs every half hour.

"The MPs look more scared than the kids," Paul said to Julie, who had shrugged off the jacket he tried to lay over her shoulders.

"They're scared because they're wrong," she replied. "And they know it." Julie stood up, stretching, and watched some other girls put wreaths of flowers around the MPs' necks.

Suddenly her head turned toward a marshal who had reached between the soldier's legs to grab the foot of one girl. Paul's eyes followed hers, and he saw the girl dragged off behind the lines to be hit on the head with a white baton. Other girls screamed and ran back to the line, but Julie hurried forward, holding two fingers up in a V for victory, then laying them on a young soldier's lips.

"We're doing this for you," she said, so loud and clear that her voice sounded larger than Tim's with his megaphone. "Because we love you and we don't want you to die in 'Nam."

The young soldier, perhaps stunned by Julie's beauty and angelic greeting, put his rifle by his side and looked as if he had no idea what he was guarding or why.

"Dad!" Tim yelled over the heads of the crowd. "Get her out of here!"

But a marshal had pulled Julie behind the MP line, and Paul stood in pain, grabbing his own middle, as the man swung his club hard against Julie's stomach, doubling her over. By the time Paul straightened up, she was gone, and the crowd had locked him into itself by its body weight.

The other demonstrators had begun to stir and mutter. Paul saw Belinda turn and bump against a soldier. She froze, then drew back quickly, but it was too late. The frustrated marshals and MPs were determined to make an example of someone. They dragged Belinda up the Pentagon steps, striking her on the head and torso with their nightsticks.

Timothy, his arms pinned behind him by his friends, struggled futilely to run forward as the crowd began singing "We Shall Overcome." Their voices rose over the shouts of the soldiers, who were trying to herd the protesters back outside the Pentagon fence. A marshal called over the loudspeaker, offering amnesty to those on the steps who would leave without making more trouble, all but the leaders. Paul fought his way to Timothy and held his son by the shoulders.

"Julie's hurt," he cried, shaking Timothy. "We've got to find her."

Timothy paused for a moment, his eyes red at the rims, and then threw down his megaphone. "All right," he said. "I'll quit. It's over."

They sat side by side in the government bus that carried them to Ocaquam, the minimum security prison to which the leaders of the demonstration were taken. Paul kept his arm around Timothy's shoulders, which shook as the boy wept over Belinda's beating. He did not tell his son exactly what had happened to Julie.

"What are you going to do now?" Paul was almost afraid to ask.

Timothy sat up straight. "I know better than to protest anymore and get my people hurt or killed," he said, his voice steady, his face looking like a much older man's. "Next time I fight these guys, I'm going to be above them, not in front of them."

"You're not changing sides, are you?" Paul thought of Julie, who never changed sides. She was always on the side of love. He was unsure about Timothy, despite the miraculous attentions of his friend, Josh. "Not going to turn into one of them?"

Timothy shook his head. "I'm going to beat them at their own game," he said. "Someone's got to stop the way the oil barons and the munitions makers have bought the government. More violence won't do it. This time, I'll go to law school. Georgetown's offered me a full scholarship. Didn't tell you before because I didn't know if I wanted to go." Timothy ran his hand over a new crew cut. "I used to be afraid I'd get soul-sick like the other suits if I had credentials and went into politics. Now I don't think so."

Paul didn't think so either, after he had seen Belinda, who died from her beating before Timothy got out of Ocaquam. Standing over the small girl, Paul remembered her as a child, holding up her bag for Halloween candy and collecting for UNICEF when she was older. He felt as if he should make some priestly gesture over her as she lay dying, but knew none to make. By the time he had decided there was some purpose for religious ritual in extreme cases, Belinda was dead from a ruptured spleen.

A few rooms away, Julie was recovering from the loss of her baby, another casualty of a marshal's baton. *So easy to end a human life,* Paul said to himself, surprised at the ease of murder. *So hard to bring it into being and full growth.* He remembered Claire's bloody deliveries, and thought about the years when these small, fragile lives had been held, watched over, seen through nights of teething and croup. All this labor of love poured forth so that a general could someday order these children into combat to die in the economic interests of Vanderzell oil. The oil barons, Timothy had informed him, made money on war no matter who the winners were, just as Krupp's munitions factories and I.G. Farben had made money from both sides during the second Great War.

Paul prayed silently over the anesthetized body of his emptied daughter, *Bless the poor children killed in the name of money and power. Bless Belinda and my grandchild and all the children lost in this long war, our life*. He remembered the pictures of broken Vietnamese infants that Julie had shown him on the bus. "How old I must be," he said to Claire when he phoned her, "that I have seen so much death. I had no idea I was so old."

The war ended, like most wars, in an exchange of insults and promises by old men who had let young ones die in battle in order that they themselves might die in their beds with tubes up their noses. The oil barons and makers of armaments went on amassing their fortunes at the expense of young lives and quietly buying up congressmen to support their wars. The Americans left Southeast Asia and the North Vietnamese put their heavy yoke over the men who had fought against communism and would end by slaving for a new master, their muscles rising and falling in hard labor as they always had, no matter who their leaders were.

Timothy went through law school in two years, his eyes on the men who had killed Julie's child and Belinda. They would get what was coming to them, Timothy said to his father, and he kept his notebooks ready for the moment he would bring Vanderzell and company to justice. For Paul it was enough to take Julie home to New Jersey and deliver her to Charles, who was full of talk about business deals and cattle. He had no desire to hear about the March on the Pentagon, and no sympathy for it, either. *The loss of his child seems not to disturb Charles at all,* Paul thought. *If anything, Charles seems relieved. Julie is the one who wanted a baby. Charles belongs to the Reserves and might have been one of those MPs at the Pentagon, if he had been ordered to serve.*

As it was, Charles was responsible only for Julie and his livestock.

"Something's wrong between Julie and Charles," Claire said, rolling up her tangled attempt at knitting a baby garment. "He doesn't like her being pregnant again. Too soon, he says."

Julie was indeed pregnant again, and her husband had come out strongly for abortion, appalling Claire and Paul. "Julie's too young," he argued."We're both too young to be tied down with a kid." Charles had in mind to make a trip to Venezuela, where he hoped to sell the semen of his bulls and dance with Julie at nightclubs. Julie was unwilling to go and had said so. Her stand had prompted a battle that ended in her flight to Amberfields.

"Why doesn't Charles want children?" Claire asked over dinner, when Julie was sitting across from her, very pregnant, very miserable.

"He wants to be free," Julie said. "Sort of like Timothy used to feel. He doesn't want to be trapped."

"What did he get married for?" Claire slapped her napkin down beside her plate. "Why do men get married if they don't want children?"

“I don’t know what they want.” Julie suddenly put her face in her hands and began to cry. “To be important, maybe. To be in charge. I don’t know. It’s so different from what I want.”

Claire sat beside her daughter, holding her around her swollen waist, saying something softly into her ear, while Paul sat alone, feeling separate and guilty for being of the gender whose primary interest it was to hurt women and children.

“I remember hearing Charles say he wished there would be a war so he could fight in it.” Paul wondered at such avarice for blood. “Was he just trying to talk like a tough, or does he mean it?”

“Oh, he means it, all right.” Julie leaned her face against her mother’s shoulder. “He thinks we should have stayed in Vietnam. That’s why he was so mad when I went on the March. That was when he first…” She sat up and put her hand to her cheek.

“Hit you?” Paul finished for you. “And has he hit you since?”
“I don’t want to talk about it.” Julie pulled away from her mother and sat with her hands clenched in her lap.

Claire reached out and stroked her daughter’s hair. “After the war I felt the same way,” she said. “It hurt so much to see my mother die. To lose Dora and Maxi.” She glanced at Paul. “For the longest time I couldn’t talk about it. When something matters as much as Dora and Maxi did to me, you can’t take the risk of talking about it. No one else could care as much, so talking makes you lonely.”

“I felt that way when I lost the baby.” Julie wiped her eyes. “You’d think hurt would draw people closer, but it doesn’t, except when they pray.”

Hearing her daughter’s unspoken wish, Claire bowed her head and clasped Julie’s hands. They were both silent for a long while.

Paul sat outside their charmed circle and reflected that women mourned the losses of war personally, one by one, while men saw so many die at once that they had to learn impersonality or go mad. Mr. Marcus, who had just gone back to Israel for one of his mysterious tours of duty, as he called them, said that women must become as strong as men and men must become as tender as women, if the human race were to survive. This shift happens quite naturally, Marcus said, once you become old. Paul sat looking at his red-eyed, pregnant daughter and suddenly felt very old, very tender, and not nearly as strong as he wished to be.

12

Dora's Journal

Israel..............................1973

I can't believe that I am almost forty, and am glad to say I don't look it. Officially though, I am almost a crone, which allows me to purvey a bit of folk wisdom once in a while. Only Maxi's teenage daughter Yael, would listen, since my Benjamin is beyond my wisdom or anyone else's. My one child is grown, ready for service in the army, and I feel old enough to insist on my right to die first, before he does.

Although he doesn't know it, Lev is to be blamed for how I feel. He could have been here at the kibbutz, making me forget that I am imminent crone, but he's cutting a swath in the Knesset, living with Esther or whoever the woman is now. Lev is, after all, a warrior, a patriot, and can be expected to act like a leader of men. Women are very foolish to marry such men, I tell Yael. They're in love only with their reputations. Ideology is a curse, a real curse, I say to her, because it lives only in the head. No telling how much damage ideology has done to bodies, its natural enemies. It certainly hasn't been very good for mine. Sol tells me I'm love-starved, but he has his own reasons for saying so.

Sometimes I think of myself as one of Maxi's Paleolithic women, who has seen all there is to see. I am someone whose child has grown up and left, whose husband has gone to fight in the wars or maybe off to hunt wooly mammoths. And so I sit toothless by the hearth, gumming bearskins into clothes and casting fateful bones on the dirt floor, hoping to learn what's next, if anything. Women of my age, unlike the young ones, want to be alone, once they're crones, and it's a good thing too, for what man would want us? To Maxi I wrote, have you any crone-lovers among your friends to whom you could recommend me on the occasional nights when I sit by myself, chewing over home truths and bearskins and reading the bones? Well, it may not be so bad being old, for I never know when someone may have left outside my cave the haunch of a gazelle or a handful of daffodils, out of ancestral piety.

I just checked outside, and no one has. Left anything, I mean. After having heard Maxi talk so much about remains, I tend to think that something is always left, the way he says matter turns into energy and energy into matter, wasting nothing. What is left for me is my own dry bones. I feel how hard they are and how strong, how bare. For a long time, since Lev went to Tel Aviv with Esther, I have felt stripped, like a tree embarrassed by winter. Lev writes now and then, but the words are hollow as outworn ritual, and I feel him wandering ghost-like around my mind. His letters sound mournful, the kind I would put into the cracks of the Wailing Wall, being too proud to let anyone know how depressed I am. Yeshua seems far away and silent.

The Wailing Wall is especially real to me lately, since Maxi has charge of it. The Israeli Antiquities Authority is determined to find artifacts that prove ancient Jewish presence in this land, and they believe Maxi can find what they want. He has his doubts that the Orthodox would allow his new excavation, and he took me off with him to see Rabbi Meir. The rabbi, Maxi felt, would think well of me because I had made sure my son had an Orthodox Bar Mitzvah. His hope was that I could incline the rabbi to accept Maxi's digging for treasure in the shadow of the temple wall. Having Yael along might remind the rabbi that the young have a stake in building knowledge, so Maxi had brought his daughter.

Rabbi Meir stroked his white beard and said. "You don't have to dig up the Holy One. He's not in the ground, but here." His finger tapped the Torah in front of him. "Why do you look for him in the ground?" The rabbi never said the word God, out of respect. Just "Ha-Shem" or "Holy One."

"It's not God I'm trying to dig up." Maxi settled the unfamiliar yarmulkh on the back of his head. "God is already in my mind, understand. I just want to know what people believed about him before we Jews came along. What they loved in the way of God thousands of years ago, before Abraham."

Yael sat beside him, her brown, slightly slanted eyes intense, for she too was always eager to find out whatever was true. "My father's found an old cave at the bottom of the dig," she said, "where the earliest humans were. If there was a religion before ours, would it be wrong to know what it was? Would God mind so much?"

Yael was talking about a cave far below the foot of the temple wall. It had been home to some prehistoric man who had left chipped flint tools by his hearth when he died. Now Maxi wanted to dig away the rubble above and around the little cave. He believed it was next to a primitive temple built to the old gods, before ours was known.

"A religion before?" Rabbi Meir's voice rose in anger. "No more than a fertility cult. The mother goddess had no love for persons. She loved whomever she bore, and made no distinction between good and evil. What use is such a faith? Adonai, blessed be he, gave his children the Law, seeing each man for what he is, righteous or unrighteous, responsible to Adonai. We have no need for this mother goddess. Men are already eaten up with lust. Would you have them know more of the goddess than they do now? More abominations?"

"We need to know all there was," said Maxi steadily, his arm around Yael, "in order to understand all there is. The Antiquities Authority will not fight you and the Orthodox community on this issue. But Rabbi, we need to know the history of the land God gave us. Our dig is as much an act of faith as your study of the Law."

"You speak of faith, but you want proof," Rabbi Meir gripped his knees under his black caftan. "What kind of faith is that? If you believed as our fathers did, you would not want to undermine the wall that is sacred to them and to us."

"Is a wall the best metaphor for our religion?" Maxi asked gently, "or is digging? On this point, we differ. You believe the Wall must stand between our people and everyone else, so we won't lose what we are and have been. I believe it takes digging below the walls to find out who we were and will be, once we are united with all humanity in God. We won't be less ourselves for that, but more."

"My cousin Benjamin thinks we have to dig down for the truth inside us," Yael said suddenly, her high voice so light it seemed to ride the silence. "He says there's only one kingdom, one place, and everyone lives in it already without knowing where they are. By digging down deep within themselves, they can know."

"Is that was Benjamin says?" Rabbi Meir's finger moved in the dust on his desk, and he made some Hebrew letters as he thought. "Well, it may be so, then. We must not worship this Wall or make it into an idol, after all." He thought a little while longer, rubbed out the letters, then blew the dust away. "You will not harm the Wall as you dig?" he asked, his eyes meeting Maxi's. "We must insist on that."

Maxi's word was apparently good enough for Rabbi Meir, because the next day the director of the Antiquities Authority called my brother and told him to go on excavating around the little cave. Benjamin and I went over to the dig for the occasion, which I remember very well because it was the day before Yom Kippur, October 6th, when the war began. Of course, on October 5th, no one knew about the war except the Arabs who were planning their attack. All Jerusalem was preparing for the solemn holy day, the Day of Atonement. Benjamin, who had continued to observe the Law taught to him by Rabbi Meir, planned to stay the night in Jerusalem, so he would not have to travel on Yom Kippur. He wore his new army uniform to the dig, as he had worn it everywhere, since the time it had been issued to him.

Benjamin was sorry his paramedical training had obliged him to miss the talk with Rabbi Meir. He questioned Maxi about what had gone on, as we crossed the great sunny square in front of the Wailing Wall.

"So you think the oldest religion had oneness at its root?" he asked his uncle. "Not many gods?"

"I think the many came later." Maxi took us down to the ground level area of the excavation and then to the rough stone stairway that led through the strata of the past, down a hundred and fifty feet. "Creation began, I believe, with The Eternal One in the eternal Now."

"I get it," Benjamin said, a smile bursting on his face like the sun through clouds. "First comes simple oneness, like the point of energy that began the Big Bang. Then comes complexity like all the galaxies. It's like that in all creation, isn't it?"

I thought of how we begin as a one-celled creature and progress to a galaxy of cells that make us complex humans. That much I could follow, having born life myself.

"So I believe. It takes all our lives to reach back and find that oneness with which we began, where we find the simplicity of God. Lots of work, lots of digging,"

"Like your work here," I said, looking around me at my brother's dig.

Maxi's assistants had cleared away the rubble around the rough stone square next to the cave. The temple, as Maxi called it, had two pillars that no longer supported anything. Up above, there had been many layers, filled with clay gods. Down here, I felt only the presence of Spirit and told Maxi so.

Maxi swung the beam of his flashlight around the primitive temple, its light bouncing off the rough facets of rudely cut stone. We followed him into the cave, ducking our heads low under the lintel. In the rear of the cave was a hearth backed by a rough stone altar thousands of years old. Benjamin reached down to pick up an implement that lay in the blackened dust near the hearth. "What did the maker of this tool think God was, I wonder?"

"We can only guess from his art," Maxi said, "from finds like the statue at Jericho that was both human and animal, female and male, all creation gathered into one Being."

"Rabbi Meir says God is the same, yesterday, today, and forever." Benjamin walked over to the altar and laid his hand on it. "Maybe so, but our knowledge of that one Being unfolds in time. Change is the nature of all that lives, and since God lives…" He stopped short as a slight shudder passed through him.

"What is it, Benjamin?" I put my hand on Maxi's shoulder to keep him from walking on. "What's wrong?"

"I just had a strange feeling for a minute," Benjamin said, his brows drawn together in a straight line, like mine. "It touched me like a cold hand." He leaned close to me. "I think you'd better go back to Kiryat Anavim tonight, Mother. Don't stay here in Jerusalem. I've got to go check in with my unit headquarters."

He broke into a run, and then called to Maxi over his shoulder. "I'd put that Jericho statue back underground for a while longer, if I were you, Uncle."

Maxi and I stood staring at each other for a few moments, remembering that Benjamin had guessed the coming of the other war six years before. Of course we were always expecting a war, and never had the tension between Israel and her Arab neighbors been as great as now. In Israel these days one did not have to be clairvoyant to know a war was on its way.

"You've heard that the Russians have set up their SAM missiles in Egypt and Syria? The Prime Minister announced it yesterday," Maxi said in a low voice. "Now they can knock our aircraft out of the sky. They needn't be afraid to attack."

"Lev knew this would happen." I remembered the night my husband had argued that unless we fought the Arabs to the death while we were still stronger than they were, we would lose the next war. Maybe Eshkol should have let Lev do what he wanted, I thought. Drive the Arabs all the way to Cairo and Damascus, taking and holding every foot of land between the two. As we left the excavation and entered the square in front of the Wailing Wall, I said as much of this to Maxi as I dared.

"That wouldn't have stopped the Russians," Maxi said, his eyes narrowing in the sudden sunlight that poured down on the square. "They mean to make Israel the first battleground in their war against the United States. The Jews are only stand-ins for the real enemy."

"Father Jonas thinks we're living in the End Times," I said. "He thinks God will take us up and leave the warriors to battle it out in the hell they'll make of earth."

"And what happens to all the innocent people that get stuck here because they didn't know the God of Abraham?" Maxi shook his head. "No, we must each look within ourselves to find the divinity that we share with all the others. Only then can humankind be one and at peace. I believe that day will come. I must believe it or despair."

"Well, I can certainly see where Benjamin gets his notions," I replied tartly, thinking that Lev had been right about Benjamin spending too much time with my brother, the Rabbi, and Father Jonas. At least the army might serve to ground Benjamin in the real world, I thought, stopping with Maxi at the door of his museum.

"You're leaving the Jericho statue in the museum?" I asked him. "After what Benjamin said?"

"Nowhere safer. We have a bullet-proof, glassed-in pedestal set up for it in my office. And you, Dora? Are you running back to Kiryat Anavim because your son says you should? Or will you stay with us for the holy day?"

"I'll stay. Tell Carolyn Father Jonas is coming too, and that I'll bring the chicken."

As I said good-by to Maxi, the urge to go home came over me. I suddenly wanted to be with Shana and Sol and the rest in the kibbutz who had become my family, now that my husband, brother and son were elsewhere. Carolyn and Maxi had been living in the university apartments for the past four years, coming back to the kibbutz only on weekends to see me and their children, who had refused to leave their age-mates. Benjamin was stationed at the training camp south of Jerusalem, and Lev, of course, had been gone for a long time. Now only Yael was close to me, for Joel had become a big boy very early and spent no time with women. Still, I longed to go home, and would have, if it didn't seem the act of a coward. That's one name nobody's ever called Dora Ben-Ari.

Besides, there was much to be done at Kiryat Anavim. We had run the irrigation sprinklers into the greenhouse and the system was over-extended. The well we had depended on for so long was beginning to go dry, and only the winter rains, heavier than usual, had saved us from losing the spring crop. Water pressure was down and my avocados were doing poorly, developing brown patches on them that would probably put off the buyers in Haifa. I was glad for once that Esther was in Tel Aviv, since she would have reminded everyone that the greenhouse and extension of the water system had been my idea. Because I had recently been invited by the Minister of Agriculture to set up greenhouses modeled on ours at two neighboring kibbutzim, the failing water supply was an embarrassment for me and for Kiryat Anavim. Maxi had once said there might be an underground water supply somewhere near the foot of the *tel* on our land. He was sure the flat-topped hill was the site of an ancient town, many-layered like Jericho, but the dig there had been disappointing. The town turned out to be nothing but a village, after all, with few artifacts of value. The dig had been abandoned, but the search for a new water supply continued.

Where there had been a village, there would be a well, unless it too had died over the centuries. In desperation, I had given in to Benjamin's idea of bringing a dowser to the site. He was due to arrive from Scotland any day. I paid for the dowser myself, out of money given to me by Father Jonas. We had no need for money, since Benjamin's college education would be free. As soon as he left the army, he would begin his studies in mathematics and physics at Hebrew University in Jerusalem.

I suppose he will become a scholar too, like Maxi, and live in Jerusalem, for the kibbutz seems to him too small and crowded a world. In wanting to leave the kibbutz, but in nothing else, he reminded me of Lev, although each of them has his own idea of what freedom is. For Benjamin, to be free is to have no walls separating him from others, to walk around without a skin, as he puts it, letting the world bleed life into him and him bleed life into the world. For Lev, to be free was to be alone, at least that's what he had said the last time we talked on the phone over a year ago. I had not seen him since, so I was surprised when Carolyn told me that Lev had called, wanting me to meet him at the King David Hotel, where he was staying that night. It would have to be late, I told him, since Father Jonas and I had plans.

After our family dinner at Maxi's, Father Jonas and I slipped out to end Yom Kippur in the company of messianic Jews. We had to drive, since the nearest group met in an industrial park on the outskirts of the city. No name was on the door of the loft above a sweater factory where the messianic Jews worshipped, but Father Jonas said they called themselves Beth Shalom, in honor of the Prince of Peace, my Yeshua. Once upstairs, we found two folding chairs at the back and set them up as part of the semi-circle of chairs around the bimah, where they kept the Holy Scriptures. About two dozen people were there, mostly younger than I. They all wore prayer shawls, and the women had their hair covered with scarves pulled down to the middle of their foreheads. They dressed very much like the Orthodox people of Me'a She'arim, the quarter of Jerusalem that's worth your life to drive through on Shabbat. Young toughs in black suits and side curls throw rocks at your car and once even overturned an offending vehicle. Here at Beth Shalom, the young men did not even look up as we entered, so intent were they on rocking back and forth as they read their prayers. This davening, along with the clothes, made the place seem just like the Orthodox shul, not at all like a church.

I sat behind the women, Father Jonas behind the men. He seemed right at home and whipped out his own prayer book, rocking away like the others. Feeling alien to the scene, a mere onlooker, I sat straight up in my chair and did not open the book that one of the women handed to me. The loft had a high ceiling, but was stuffy from the lack of windows. At least it was immaculate, having obviously been scrubbed the day before. I could see damp streaks on the concrete. On one of the walls hung a large painting of a blue Star of David surrounded by a ring of words in Hebrew that read, "Arise, shine for your light has come." The words, I knew, were from the prophet Isaiah, for Father Jonas had often said to us as he called us awake in the morning at St. Hilary's. I understood now that the light who had come was Yeshua, but Father Jonas, respecting our Jewish heritage, had never actually said so.

Expecting to see a cross or statue in the sanctuary, as in Father Jonas's church, I was surprised to see only a menorah inside a fish, carved into the olivewood pedestal of the bimah. The fish looked more like a dolphin, but I was sure it meant ICHTUS. Father Jonas had taught me that the fish was a secret sign for my Yeshua, his Jesus Christ. As in the ancient days of persecution, modern messianic Jews had to hide their faith from the authorities. Probably the service I was watching was more like one in the first century than any modern Christian church would have offered, since almost all the original Christians were Jews. In fact, I had learned that the followers of Yeshua weren't even called Christians in the beginning, just Jewish believers. Thinking of this comforting truth, I relaxed a little. As Judaism and Yeshua had come together in my small self, so they could, apparently, come together on a larger scale, as part of Jewish life in Israel.

The rabbi was a man of forty, with a black and gray beard and a Star of David around his neck. A small, discreet cross was inside the star. He was that rare bird, a rabbi who had given up his Orthodox congregation, Father Jonas said, when he came to believe in Yeshua. Rabbi Noah Halpern had told his synagogue members that he could no longer serve them and why. They were glad to see him go and take his heresy elsewhere. Now, to make his living, he taught Hebrew to Russian immigrants and lived alone in a screened off corner of Beth Shalom's loft. He had a beak of a nose and large brown eyes under heavy black brows. Tall, and on the thin side like Maxi, he was an arresting presence, especially when he spoke in his deep, velvety voice.

"We will now read from the *B'rit Chadasha*, the scriptures of the New Covenant, from the letter of St. Paul to the Hebrews. 'Learn to be patient, so that you will please God and be given what he has promised.' What has the Lord promised? That faith will be rewarded by the Presence of God in our deepest hearts. Abraham had faith and obeyed God. He was told to go to the land God had said would be his, and he left for a country he had never seen. We too go to a place unseen, a country within ourselves where the Holy Spirit, the Shekinah, dwells in radiance. And Yeshua is here in this Holy Land. He is the one who renews God's Covenant within us. To Yeshua, the Mosiach be glory forever and ever."

My heart felt so full as the rabbi continued speaking that I was afraid it would rise up in my throat and choke me. Here was a Jew who knew Yeshua and loved him as I did. I wiped my eyes with the backs of my hands and kept watching this man who like me had bridged two worlds. And all around us were others who had taken Yeshua into their Judaism and into their hearts. I was suddenly as much at home as if I were in the community room of Kiryat Anavim.

"The Hebrew word Yeshua," he said, looking at me, maybe thinking I didn't know the name, "means salvation. We call our Lord Yeshu, or Joshu, by that name because he is the salvation of his people." His eyes turned away from me and closed in prayer. "Yeshua, incarnate Word of God, be our light in the darkness, enlighten our hearts to desire only you. For in seeing you, we see the Father. Glory to you, Lord, for your eternity in this fleeting world, glory to you for calling us into being, and glory to you for curing our pride of heart by suffering and by forgiving those who cause it. Amin."

I was not especially thankful for the various pains I had undergone in my life, but was curiously touched by this tall, gaunt man's intense belief in the value of suffering. Suddenly I understood that all suffering, even the loss of my parents, was not wasted, just as the suffering of Yeshua on the cross had not been wasted. All of it, all, was part of the human cycle in which we build our strong wills only to melt them away in love and self-forgetfulness. In some mysterious way I had not yet grasped, suffering could become a doorway into unselfish love. I had a vision of my father singing the Kol Nidre to his wretched, helpless brothers in the Nazi cattle car. "Blessed are the meek," Father Jonas used to say, using the words of Yeshua, "for they shall inherit the earth." I had as yet seen no sign of that inheritance, but then no one could say I had learned the lesson of humility, however often it had been taught to me.

The whole group was singing softly in Hebrew the words of a song I did not know, something about a lost lamb and a shepherd who spent a long time looking for his poor animal. When the lamb in the song was found, my heart seemed to open like a flower, and I breathed deeply, feeling that I was the endangered lamb and that now I was saved from the dark, sad places I had hidden in for so long. Looking up at Rabbi Noah in that moment, I saw his eyes on me again, so warm and tender I would have cried, if I hadn't been Dora Ben-Ari and ashamed to cry in public.

The service was over, and people put away their prayer shawls in cabinets against the wall, while a few musicians got out their guitars and cymbals. So there would be dancing after all. Lev would just have to wait a while. I stood in the circle of worshippers, my cheeks flushed and my foot tapping, waiting for the Davidic dancing to begin. Though the steps were familiar, the words were not, and I had to pay close attention. These songs were not just in praise of Israel, the land of plenty, but in praise of Israel's Messiah. My heart warmed to the beat and the words. It seemed to me that my whole body became a harp, and the hands of King David played it as if he were dancing in front of the Temple. When Rabbi Noah grabbed my hands and whirled me around, I hardly knew at first that it was he. Before he whirled on to the next dancer, he flashed me a smile so shy, sweet, and melting that it brought tears to my eyes. It was an embarrassing moment, since my hands were too busy to wipe the tears away, and I was afraid someone would see them.

Father Jonas and I left Beth Shalom at midnight, and he insisted on walking me to the King David Hotel. He was pleased that I wanted to return to Beth Shalom soon, and said I had made a new friend in Rabbi Noah. "A very good friend," Father Jonah insisted, saying that the Rabbi had asked him about me. I was too intent on getting to the hotel to take much notice of what Father Jonas was saying. Lev had probably gone to sleep by now, I thought, and had no doubt left orders not to be disturbed.

I need not have worried. As usual, I found him lying in bed, bare-chested, smoking and sorting through official papers that were propped up on his bony knees. The bald spot on his head had grown larger, leaving more room for the wrinkles above his brows, but otherwise he looked the same as the last time I'd seen him. Because my hands wanted so much to touch him, I had to keep them busy smoothing down my hair, which the wind had blown out of the combs that held it back in a middle-aged bun.

"Dora, let me look at you," he said, getting up and letting the papers fall to one side. "You're not a girl anymore, I see." He took me by the shoulders and looked more closely. "Your hair is different, and you're wearing glasses."

"Without them I couldn't see your wrinkles," I said, smiling. I wanted him to know I was not the only one who had changed. "Why did you call? It's been over a year now."

"If I say it was sentiment that made me call, you won't believe me. But that's what it was, all the same." Lev put out his cigarette and sat me down beside him on the bed. "For some reason, I feel the need to hold you tonight." He sighed and lit another cigarette, coughing as he drew on it. "Maybe because I'm afraid we're about to have another war."

"Benjamin told me it isn't safe to stay in Jerusalem." I tried to keep my eyes on my hands, which were folded on my lap, but my gaze kept moving to Lev's body, half-bare and all remembered. "Did you tell him that?"

"No. We've all been instructed not to tell anyone." Lev inhaled heavily and coughed again, then put out the cigarette impatiently, as if it were not what he had wanted, after all. "But when the Prime Minister hears from Kissinger that this time we must surrender everything we took in '67, we know we must stand alone. If we surrender the Golan Heights, we're done for. And the West Bank is our wall against the rest of the Arab world. If we don't keep the Bank as a barrier, they'll come charging over our border the way they always have."

"Benjamin thinks the Russians have warned the Americans to back off. And Maxi says we'll have to give back the oil fields in the Sinai." I sat gloomily picking the lint off my red cashmere sweater, which Carolyn had brought me from Bloomingdale's in New York. "I suppose we'll have to offer the Arabs whatever they want, if America gives up on us."

"What the Arabs have always wanted is to put an end to us. This time, they have a chance to do that. The SAM missiles from Russia are ready to go."

He stopped talking for a moment and put his mouth against my neck. "And the Arabs are blackmailing the West, threatening to cut off their oil if they help us. This war may be the last one for Israel. Dora. I'm afraid. It came to me suddenly that if this country is lost, so is my little piece of it—you and Benjamin. That's why I called you here. Need you here."

I knew Lev wasn't afraid for himself, having often dared death. It was Israel's death he feared, not his own. Afraid myself, I put my arms around him and forgot that he had ever left me, so much he was with me at that moment.

We woke up late in the morning, and I pulled my clothes on quickly, not wanting to be late for the Yom Kippur services. Lev held me as I tried to put on my stockings, not letting me move.

"I want to come back to Kiryat Anavim, Dora," he said, his face so tight against my back that I could feel the air streaming between his lips as he spoke. "If Israel survives this war, if I survive it, then I'm coming back. Will you be there for me?"

"I never left." My hands dropped to my sides. "It was you who left, wanting more room."

"How much room does a man need? Tolstoy said only enough room for his coffin." Lev's voice was light, all of a sudden, the way it had been when we courted twenty years ago. "I'm too old to be a soldier anymore, Dora. I'll leave that to my son."

"You'll laugh at me, but I will say it anyway. This return of yours is an answer to prayer. If I told you to whom, you would laugh at me even more."

"Tell me, Dora." Lev gently touched my wild hair, as yet unbunned. "I won't laugh at you."

The words stuck in my throat, since I was afraid to bring out my precious Yeshua only to have him mocked by cynical Lev. "I've come to believe that the Mosiach we Jews have waited for so long has already come and we missed him, not entirely by our own fault. Two thousand years ago the Sandedrin thought Yeshua was a false prophet and would fade away. But he didn't fade away. I think the verdict of history is in, by now. Yeshua was the greatest Jew who ever lived, greater than Moses, greater even than Abraham, and he's ours, our Mosiach. Lev, I know him in my heart. He's as real to me as you are."

Lev scratched his receding forehead. "Well, Dora, you must also know it's dangerous for an Israeli to hold this belief. The authorities would think you'd become a Christian and don't belong here."

"But if Jewish atheists are accepted all over Israel," I argued, twisting my fingers in the black hair on his chest, "why aren't Yeshua's people accepted as Jews? We follow all the Jewish laws. We don't wear Christian crosses or light Christmas trees. We are still Jews, as was Yeshua himself."

Lev was taking me more seriously than I had thought he would. "I can't argue religion with you, Dora, since I don't believe in anything except Israel. I only know it would be safer if you kept these beliefs of yours quiet, better both for you and for Benjamin. Will you do that for me, Dora?"

I nodded. "And can you have Benjamin assigned to a safe place?" My hands curled up into fists, and I ground them into my thighs, thinking suddenly of my Benjamin damaged beyond repair by a mortar shell at the front.

"You know I can't do that." Lev's voice was gentle and he stroked my hair in that fatherly way he knew I liked. "There's no place really safe. It was all I could do to get him into the medical corps instead of the infantry. He could have claimed he's an Orthodox student and gotten off with no military service, but Benjamin wouldn't do that. I asked him, but he wouldn't."

"I didn't know. Thank you." I turned around and put my cheek against his.

"For you, I did it, even more than for Benjamin." Lev fished around for my shoes under the bed. "Now you'd better go. You'll be late for services. There's a lot to pray for, on this particular day."

I kissed him lightly on his bald spot. "You don't believe in prayer. You don't believe in anything, remember?"

"Well, it may be time for me to believe in something or other." He tried to reach for a cigarette, but the pack fell on the floor, where he let it lie. "It may be time for me to come home."

He didn't walk me to the door, just gave me a little salute from the bed, as I looked back at him. In his own way, it seemed to me, Lev was observing the Day of Atonement, though he would not have admitted it.

He was not the only one for whom this Yom Kippur was a day of reckoning accounts. All over Israel, as we gathered for the services, we were also gathered for a mourning of more than our sins. I walked the short distance to the Sephardic synagogue of Ramat Eshkol, passing old Orthodox men in their long white keitels, the shrouds they wear representing their death day and young soldiers wearing prayer shawls over their uniforms, keitels of a sort for them too. My heart was heavy as I thought of Benjamin. He and Maxi met me on the steps, having sent Carolyn and the children inside while they waited. Before they saw me, I stood watching the two of them, my tall, slim brother and my stocky son, their faces serious as they stood in the shadows talking, probably about the war Benjamin and Lev were sure was about to start. Both looked up startled, as two of our Phantom jets shrieked overhead. Odd, I thought, since no vehicles should be moving on this holiest day of the year.

"At least they wouldn't attack on Yom Kippur. They wouldn't be so stupid," Maxi was saying. "It's the only time of the year when the authorities know exactly where every soldier is and could mobilize quickly. So we have one more day of peace coming to us." He turned and saw me. "Dora! We thought maybe Lev had convinced you to be a heathen for the day."

"Not at all." I couldn't help blushing, embarrassed that they knew why I was late. "Lev's decided to come home, back to Kiryat Anavim."

"I'm glad for you, Dora." Maxi took both my hands and held them tightly, but his face didn't look as glad as he said he was. "Perhaps this time he'll stay."

Not wanting to argue Lev's sincerity when I wasn't sure of it myself, I didn't answer, but took Benjamin's arm to go into the synagogue. I was supposed to sit with the women, but decided to sit with my men on the border between the sections. People already had too much to worry about to care where I sat. The rabbi had already begun the service. Though I sat between Benjamin and Maxi, I felt alone, as the words reminded me that in fact I was. I wanted to be in the little congregation of Rabbi Noah, looking into his luminous, consoling eyes. For a moment, my throat closed up in fear and my tongue seemed to swell in my mouth, as I thought about how much I stood to lose from this war. My son, my brother, my husband, whose living bodies, today so close to mine, could be blown away tomorrow like leaves in the wind. Then I would have no one, and the thought of having no one gave me the same metallic taste in my mouth that I remembered on that day in Frankfurt when we were taken from our parents. My hands crept into Maxi's and Benjamin's, but already their flesh felt cold to me.

"Adonai," the rabbi cried out, bending forward, "dust am I in my life, yea, even more so in my death. Behold me like a vessel filled with shame and confusion."

I reclaimed my hands and put them over my eyes, not wanting to see the people who might soon be lost, these men of mine. Rabbi Meir once said to me that we are never alone because we are members of the community of Jews, because God knows us by our names. Father Jonas is never alone either, because he is a cell in the Body of Christ. Rabbi Noah is part of both bodies, but I am just Dora Ben-Ari, friend of Yeshua, with my small family on both sides of me and a husband already gone to his tank battalion on the Golan Heights. If there were a web of life, I was not part of it, or at least at that time did not feel I was.

"This is all I have, God," I prayed, not caring if God heard me whine and beg. "Don't take them away." I was ashamed of my prayer and of my fear.

"Be not afraid of sudden fear, neither of the desolation of the wicked when it comes…"

The rabbi's words were cut off by the sudden wail of air raid sirens, and the doors were thrown open by three uniformed men.

"We have a list of names for the rabbi to read," one of them called out as he strode down the center aisle. "Everyone's being called up. We've been attacked."

The rabbi had read only three names when a young man near us stood up, ready to leave. His father, who was sitting next to him, stood up too and held his son in such a close embrace the young man couldn't break away. I could feel the man's tight, low sobs as if they were caught in my own throat, and within myself I was already crying for Benjamin.

The rabbi's voice was gentle as he stopped reading the list and spoke to the father.

"You have to let him go," the rabbi said. "Today his place is not here. Send him up to me for a blessing."

So the father let go of his son, and the boy bowed his head, receiving the rabbi's hand and words. "The Lord bless you and keep you, the Lord make His face shine upon you and give you peace."

The young man went away, and the rabbi continued reading, saying Benjamin's and Maxi's names without a pause, as if they were like any others. Only Carolyn's small cry from the front row marked the reading of my brother's name. I turned to hold Maxi briefly and hard, not able to say good-by.

"Stay with Carolyn," Maxi whispered. "Keep telling her I'll be back." He was working his way through the seated crowd before I could answer.

Benjamin gave me his prayer book and a quick kiss on the forehead. "I'm only a medic, Mother, don't worry. They leave medics alone, you know."

I remembered his unit was assigned to the Golan Heights, so I was as worried as I could be. Benjamin ran off, his prayer shawl still around his shoulders, and caught up with Maxi at the door. After the list of names was read, and the men were gone, I came up to the front to sit by Carolyn and the children in one of the many empty seats. Carolyn was shaking and tears ran down her cheeks, while Joel tugged mercilessly at her hand.

"Mother," he hissed at her, "Don't make such a fuss. Nobody else is carrying on like an opera. Stop it, Mother."

Yael said nothing, just kept her eyes and mouth closed, but her hands twisted together in her lap.

"Shut up, Joel," I said fiercely, pushing him away from his mother. "You just shut up. Your father isn't like anyone else, that's why your mother is the only one crying. If you knew how special your father is, you'd be crying too." I put my arm around Carolyn, and she rested her head on my shoulder as the rabbi went on with the service.

His voice was almost drowned out by the noise of the sirens and the tanks that shook the building. Police loudspeakers called out orders to disperse and take shelter, but we and the rest in the synagogue stayed on, wanting no other shelter than this one.

Not until we were back at Maxi and Carolyn's apartment late that afternoon did we turn on the radio to hear what was happening, feeling that we already knew as much as we could stand knowing. In between the bulletins, the radio played incongruous snatches of classical music, so that orderly baroque quartets alternated with news that Egyptians had crossed the canal and the Syrians had penetrated the Golan.

The Egyptians had put together a great tank force of two thousand vehicles, the radio newsman told us, adding that it was believed they would soon attack our cities by air, once they had knocked out our Phantom jets. Joel cheered as another new flash interrupted the autumn movement of Vivaldi's *Seasons*, reporting that five Syrian missile boats were sunk by Israeli-made missiles used in combat for the first time.

Our planes were holding supremacy in the sky, keeping the Arabs from getting any closer to Israeli cities, but by the second day, we had lost a third of our Phantoms to the Russian SAMs. Joel kept track of the losses in his school notebook. Since the enemy tanks outnumbered ours twelve to one, all we had to protect us was the air force. The loss of each plane was a disaster.

"We should have hit them first," Joel grumbled, as he recorded another lost plane. "We knew what was coming."

"Your father explained why not." Carolyn kept her head bent close to the radio, as if trying to hear behind the words. "Politics. It wouldn't do for us to hit first a second time. The Americans might be tempted to give us up for supplies of Arab oil. Don't count on any American when it's a matter of his car or you."

Joel was silent, deferring to his mother's firsthand knowledge of American priorities.

"Listen," Yael said abruptly, holding up her hand for silence. "The Syrians have come through the Valley of Jezreel. Jerusalem's directly in their line of attack." She got up, tucking her blouse neatly into her jeans. "I'm going with some kids to help black out headlights," she said, dropping a light kiss on her mother's forehead as she went. "You'd better tape the windows and get some water in our buckets. Looks like we're in for it. Come on, Joel."

Like the other women not on active duty, Carolyn and I volunteered the first day of the war to serve as truck drivers, mail carriers, or whatever jobs were emptied by the sudden disappearance from Jerusalem of all men under fifty-five. Even the retired Israeli ambassador to Russia was driving a garbage truck. The Archbishop of Galilee volunteered to join him.

It wasn't until the next night that we heard about the battle for the Golan Heights, where I knew both Lev and Benjamin were. The first terrible two days, when our thin line of men along the cease-fire boundary almost failed to hold, went by without catastrophe. Lev's squadron, which had been overrun in its bunkers, surfaced again, to everyone's surprise but mine. I knew Lev was a survivor, like me. Being survivors was just about all we had in common.

Only once during this time was Lev able to get a message through to me that he was going to the defense of the Binot Yalacov Bridge over the Jordan, where all the Syrian tanks were headed. Benjamin was in the same detachment, he said, trying to cheer me up. Lev would keep an eye on him. Of Maxi down in the Sinai, we had little word, except that his division had driven the Egyptians back across the canal and was methodically wiping out the Russian SAM missile bases west of Suez. Apparently Maxi's division had neatly avoided confronting a huge Egyptian force assembled to defend the Canal on the East Bank and crossed over by night somewhere else, leaving the Egyptians to sit on the bank with nothing to do but wonder where the enemy had disappeared to.

"How about that?" yelled Joel, dancing around the room when this news came. "Father's headed for Cairo."

Luckily, Maxi never got as far as Cairo, for by the twenty-third of October, a cease-fire had been signed, and he was on his way home. That same day I had a telegram from Benjamin in the Golan Heights that he had been wounded. For a medic, as it turned out, Benjamin saw more combat than most. His tank was hit during an early Syrian surge into the Golan, and he had been the only survivor of that attack. "The Syrians kept coming," he said to me later, his eyes wide with surprise at the redundancy of Syrians. When I asked if they were better fighters than they used to be, Benjamin said it wasn't that they were so good, but that they were so many.

As Benjamin wandered in the battlefield trying to stop all his blood from running out the hole in his elbow, he saw an Israeli halftrack in the distance, picking up the wounded. Calling out and waving, he ran toward it. But the halftrack, under fire from an approaching Syrian tank, took off before Benjamin got there, and he was left alone again. The Syrian tank that chased the halftrack away was suddenly hit by a random mortar shell from the other side of the hill and blown apart. When Benjamin stopped to look, he saw a Syrian soldier with a smashed jaw bone and a leg half-gone, the sole survivor of the enemy tank crew. He turned to go on, but could feel the man's eyes following him. So, despite his own injury, Benjamin lifted the Syrian on his broad shoulders and carried him five miles, back to the Israeli-occupied part of the Golan Heights. His only regret was that he never learned if the man lived or died.

Benjamin told me all this at the kibbutz, after I had inspected the extensive damage to the greenhouse from Arab shelling, and after hearing from Carolyn that the only Jerusalem casualty had been the museum wing that contained Maxi's office and the precious Jericho statue that made no distinctions between all forms of life.

As soon as Benjamin's wound was dressed at the Golan medical base, he let me know he had survived and was learning to live with a stiff left elbow. He also let me know that Lev had been killed at the Binot Yalacov Bridge. Holding the bridge had stopped the Syrians from coming over the border and kept the Golan for Israel. So although this war had not, as Lev had thought, been the last one for the Jewish state, it was the last for him. He would have been glad to know that holding the Bridge was what won the war for Israel.

I was later informed that Lev's Israeli Centurion tank had been blown in two. The turret was found on one side of the road and the rest of the vehicle on the other. Of Lev, there was nothing left, only his charred Uzi, which Benjamin brought home to me, along with burned scraps of his uniform. Apparently everyone in the tank was blown to pieces instantly. They had been outnumbered twelve to one but they had killed twelve enemy soldiers for every man they lost. Knowing that statistically twelve Syrians had died at Binot Yalacov because Lev had been there gave me little to be glad about.

For a while that day, I sat by myself in the room he and I had shared and got used to the idea that whatever his intentions, this time my husband would not be coming home. Sol and Shana and some of the others tried to open the door to bring me dinner, but they seemed to me like strangers, their voices striking all the wrong notes in my ears. I wanted Yeshua's comfort and cried his name over and over into my pillow, but his voice was silent.

Only when Benjamin arrived did I open the door, and then we sat together, not saying anything. What I finally said surprised me, but didn't seem to surprise Benjamin. "Mother," I cried, "Father. Claire. Lev. Is no one with me of all the ones I've lost? Why is no one with me?" At that moment I seemed to be a little girl again, and all my life as a grown woman and a mother fell away.

When Benjamin said to me, "I am," my eyes opened, and I thanked the Lord who takes away and who gives. I thanked Yeshua, in the person of my son, for bringing me back to God. Holding Benjamin's face between my hands, I gazed at it as if he were as new to me as when I saw him just born.

13

Amberfields...........................1973

Timothy de Montfort had started a war of his own, which he told Paul was against the military-industrial complex, his old enemy since the day of the Pentagon March. Paul felt his son was, as usual, taking on too much. But he sat in his worn, overstuffed chair by the fireplace, listening while Timothy explained to him that the Yom Kippur attack on Israel began with the interference in international affairs by American corporations like Vanderzell Oil. According to Timothy, the official line was protection of Israel, but that was only to please the Jews and their conservative Christian friends. Privately, he told his parents, the industrial interests despised Socialist Israel and would be glad to see the oil-rich Arabs destroy it. Israel would be sacrificed any time the military-industrial complex instructed the U.S. government to do it. If not for the outpouring of international sympathy and Israeli blood, the Yom Kippur War would have been the end of the Jewish state.

"You mean the American government was colluding with the oil companies?" Paul knocked his pipe empty against a marble ashtray that had been his father's. "Come, Timothy. The attack was a move by the Arabs, like the oil embargo, to turn us against Israel, and it failed. Don't tell me about some government conspiracy to make money for the oil corporations. There's some decency left in the world, whether or not you believe it."

Timothy walked around the room, his hands locked behind his back as Paul had seen him do when he conducted his first trial as a junior district attorney three years before. Now he was busy winning his case before his parents, and had already won Claire. She sat transcribing her new oratorio, the *Passion of St. John,* as she listened to her son's summary of his case against the government.

"So the government is really working for the multinational corporations, not for us?" Claire closed her music book and stared at Timothy. "Is that what you think?"

"You go too far, Tim," Paul murmured around his pipe stem. *I did too, when I was young,* he thought. *My friends and I were sure both World Wars had been engineered by the munitions industry. Yes, I remember thinking that way when my men were being shot down at Courtrai.* Later he had heard that Krupp and Farben were in league with American oil and munitions industries to keep the profits flowing along with the blood. He and other cynical young people might have been right, but no one would ever know for sure.

Pulling a chair up next to his father, Timothy perched on the edge of it. "Vanderzell isn't just the king of oil, he's hand in glove with the chemical corporations too. They run on oil, you know. You can thank the lot of them for those gas queues you sit in for hours. Remember how Eisenhower warned the country to watch out for the military-industrial complex?"

Paul had been in the middle of his affair with Meredith Simon at the end of Eisenhower's presidency. *The intensity of my private life rather eclipsed the public sphere and history was lost on me,* Paul thought. *But not on Timothy, who apparently was able to make adolescent love in his sleeping bag even while taking notes on the evening news.*

"Yes, of course," Paul said, suddenly recalling the phrase used by the earnest, bald-domed commander-in-chief, who had also been in the midst of an affair, if Paul recalled rightly, with someone named Kate.

"Eisenhower added 'beware the governmental connection with that complex,' but his advisors made him take that part out." Timothy began to pace again. "That's why they'll need the next president to be nothing but a smile and a reassuring voice. Maybe an actor. The poor guy won't even know who he's working for." He sat down beside Claire on the piano bench. "But I know, and I'm going after them."

Claire started and her glasses bounced on the bridge of her nose. "Tim, you could get into trouble. I'm afraid for you."

"I'm already in trouble." Timothy stood up and went to the door, then leaned against the frame as if he were suddenly tired. "I've written some reports about the dumping of waste chemicals in Buffalo," he said." If anything happens to me, I want you to take them to my Manhattan attorney. His name is on the envelope."

"What do you mean, 'if anything happens,'" she cried. "You're not mixed up in some criminal thing, Timothy?"

"The people who dump the chemicals are the criminals, not me. I think I can prove they're making poison gas for the American government, but you're not supposed to know anything about it. So don't ask." He went outside to his car, and Paul received Claire, trembling, into his arms.

"What's he got himself into?" she whispered. "Could it be true, what he says? Or is he just getting revenge for Belinda? He told the pastor at my church that he'd forgiven the people who killed her, but has he?"

"Timothy's still very young," Paul said, not certain that was the reason he son was so dogmatic. "He needs to have a reason for everything. I used to feel the same way. It takes some living before you give up on reasons."

"Have you given up?" Claire tipped her head back to look at him in the gathering dusk.

"On looking for reasons, yes." Paul recalled what it had been like to believe you could control your life because you knew the reasons for what had happened to you. "But only on that."

Two weeks later, someone from Timothy's office phoned Amberfields. Paul heard the young voice of an environmental lawyer asking if the family still had Timothy's secret papers. Paul asked the man to call back, giving him a chance to think before he acknowledged what his son had given him. His hands sweating, Paul opened the manila envelope he had hidden behind a bookcase and studied what Timothy had written. *I wonder if the military-industrial complex has silenced our son,* he thought, unwilling to voice the fear aloud to Claire.

"Acrostyleosis" was one of the words that turned up in Tim's report on mysterious illnesses near the upstate chemical dump. The words seared into Paul's brain as he remembered the soldiers his father had described dying of exposure to toxic gases in World War I. "Acrostyleosis rots the bones of the fingers and causes brain tumors," Timothy wrote. "People get it from drinking more vinyl chloride than nature intended." Paul leafed forward a few pages and learned that the state investigative agency contacted by Tim's environmental protection division had refused to run tests on the local water. *So,* Paul thought, *someone has been paid off and the case was quashed. Chalk another one up for the industrial-military-government complex. Timothy has been tilting at windmills, and is likely to get caught in the blades.* Paul wiped his damp hands on his khakis and went on reading.

An outraged and honest agent in the state environmental department had passed Tim a report that verifying Tim's hunch that vinyl chloride was to blame for the sick children in the blue collar area around the dumpsite. He had also handed on a letter from the offending company that if the state prosecuted, the company would take its operation somewhere else. *I can imagine how the city officials would regard the consequent tax and job losses. What I can't imagine is how far they might be willing to go to stop a crusading young lawyer from going public with what he knows.* Paul did not share either the phone call or his worries with Claire, knowing she would tell him to burn the envelope and its contents.

The next day, Paul took the envelope to Larry Keim, the Manhattan lawyer who had called the night before. "What do you think has happened to my son?" he asked the burly young man behind a desk that overflowed his small office. The man's eyes darted about, and he seemed unwilling to look at Paul.

Larry Keim hitched up his pants, which had sagged far enough below his large belly to be a matter of concern. "Can't say. It's a dangerous case, and Tim knew that when he took it on. Now that the whole operation's set to be exposed on national TV, Tim's in the spotlight. It's not the safest place to be, if you catch my meaning." Keim hitched up his pants again and then began rearranging the piles of papers in front of him, not looking at Paul.

"You think someone's going to try to silence Tim before the EPA hearing? Do you think someone already has?" He laid the envelope on Keim's desk and leaned forward, swaying a little, trying to insinuate himself into Keim's shifting visual frame. "Should I call the police? The FBI?"

"No, for God's sake." Keim dropped his pen on the floor, fished around for it, and came up red-faced and huffing. "We can't trust any government official in this business. Who knows which ones have been paid off? We'll put our own people on it. The organization hasn't got much money, you know, but we've got a lot of smart young people who work for us because they love their country."

Keim got up, walked around the room, and turned his head to look at Paul nervously under lowered eyelids. "Look, Mr. de Montfort. We want ordinary citizens to know when they're being shafted, so they can defend themselves. It's what Tim's laying his life on the line to do." He tapped Paul's envelope with his pen point.

"If anyone's after Tim, I gather they'd also be after this vinyl chloride report." Paul wondered if Tim had given him the only copy. *Maybe I should have xeroxed it,* he thought. *Maybe Tim expected me to do that.* "You'll keep it safe here?"

"It's my job to see that the papers get into the right hands just before the hearing. Tim's pulled the stuff together. The rest is up to me."

"Tim told me to trust you with his work," Paul said, standing close enough to Keim to hear the man's rapid breath. "But what about my son? What am I going to tell his mother? She's half out of her mind with worry."

"Don't you think I care what's happening to Tim?" Keim's face was pink, and he wiped perspiration off his forehead with a paper napkin. "Hey, man, I'm setting up his congressional campaign. That's how much I care."

Paul shouted over his words, hardly hearing. "Tim's no public figure to me, understand. He's my son, and I want to know where he is."

Keim backed off and sat down at his desk again. He put his arms out stiffly in front of him, gripping the edge of the desk, as if to barricade himself from Paul. "You don't ask questions when you're in the middle of a war, and that's what we're in. Tim's a soldier and took his chances."

Paul felt rising in him all the rage against his superior officers that he had suppressed at Courtrai. He grabbed the other man by the collar. "That's not good enough," he snapped. "Either you get Timothy back to us by tomorrow night, or I go to the police. The FBI too." He let go suddenly, allowing Keim to fall forward.

"Okay, okay," Keim said, straightening his tie. "I'll do my best. Just don't call the police."

"You heard what I said." Paul turned to leave the office, calling over his shoulder. "Tomorrow night."

He and Claire spent that evening in front of the fireplace, unable to sleep. By midnight, Claire had stopped pacing and crying and sat down at her piano, her head bowed for a while. "Don't laugh at me, Paul, but when I prayed for Timothy, I felt God answer. Timothy is all right. I'm sure of it."

"I wish I could be, too, but God isn't on speaking terms with me." Paul warmed his hands around the bowl of his pipe, staring into the glowing center, and wished that he could see something of more comfort than tobacco leaves turning to ash. *Of course,* he added silently, *I don't ask God to speak. If I never ask, I can't be disappointed.*

Claire began to play the piano slowly, the chords low on the keyboard, swelling higher, and then falling back like the sea. Paul was suddenly reminded of the sound made by the crowd in front of Notre Dame, praying for the life of Paris at the end of the war.

"I'm writing a new piece," she said. "It's called *A Thanksgiving in Hard Times*." Her eyes closed as she concentrated. "It will be dedicated to Timothy, and he will live to hear it. 'Exultamus Deo,' it begins. 'We will exalt you, O God.' I wish we could still use Latin. An awful thing, the loss of a word like 'exultamus.'"

Near dawn the phone rang. Claire's sheets of music lay scattered on the floor beside the piano bench, and she had fallen asleep on the couch. Paul reached the phone after one ring, and the cold pipe fell out of his mouth, its dead ashes on the carpet. Claire was beside him a moment, tipping the receiver toward her so they could both hear.

"Dad?" Tim's voice sounded far away. "I can only talk a minute. This call could be traced."

"Are you all right?" Paul shouted into the phone, making Claire jump, but afraid his distant son would not otherwise hear. "Where are you?"

"I was fine until Larry called. Listen, don't tell the Feds or the police anything. I'm just lying low, is all, till the telecast blows by. Didn't want to say before, but I had some threats. You don't want to know what they were, so don't ask."

"How can we reach you?" Claire was yelling too, and pulling at the receiver to get more that her share of Tim's voice. "What if there's an emergency?"

"An emergency?" Tim said the word as if trying to penetrate a foreign language. Paul guessed that for his son, the word had no meaning, living as Tim did on constant alert, like a soldier at the front. "Just call Larry. He'll know how to reach me. Gotta go now. Take care." Timothy put down his end of the connection before they could say good-by.

Paul and Claire stared at each other over the receiver. "He's all right," Paul said, still shouting, wanting Tim to somehow hear him.

"Exultamus!" Claire clapped her hands and danced barefoot around the room, leaving little toe prints of gray ash from Paul's spilled pipe in the circles where she had been. "Exultamus Deo. Glory be to God!"

Over the next weeks, Tim's telecast came and went, almost ignored in the storm over President Nixon's possible impeachment, then certain resignation. Only the members of Tim's political party seemed to notice his media triumph. On the strength of it, the party decided to nominate him for a congressional seat in 1974. The young nominee, however, was nowhere to be found, and the press had to be satisfied with interviews of Paul, Claire, and Julie. Like Tim, they had too much on their minds to be of much help in selling newspapers.

A war was going on in the middle of his own family, and Paul wished he could protest it as he had the war in Vietnam. *But for domestic wars, there is no march on the Pentagon,* Paul thought, *no draft card to burn.* Instead, he would sit alone in his study and mourn his age, which disqualified him for a fist fight with Charles Frazier. *Back in Europe, my age would have assured me patriarchal status, some authority that would make Julie admit Charles is beating her or to make Charles stop it.* But in America, each man was a king, living inviolate behind the closed doors of his castle, shielded by his guns and guard dogs, and no one could call him to account. No court or pope could punish him, unless someone else behind the walls of his castle complained. And Julie was not one to complain.

"Has she spoken to you about Charles?" Paul asked Claire finally, unable to be silent after Julie had left with five-year-old Annie, whom Julie had refused to abort when Charles demanded it.

Julie's jaw was swollen on one side, and she limped slightly. She claimed to have run into a door, but Paul had heard too many such excuses to believe her. Sometimes, when she had stayed away for too long, he had dropped by the sprawling stone house where the Fraziers lived on their three hundred acres. Almost always, Julie had conspicuously run into something or fallen down stairs. Paul was sure she was avoiding Amberfields so she would not have to explain her bruises.

"Not a word from her." Claire put the pot roast on the table and sat down without serving it, as if she had forgotten about the dinner. "Julie thinks it's her spiritual duty to carry her cross. It almost seems like the more Charles hurts her, the more she loves him. Father Echlin says she's a saint, but I say she's sick. You should talk to Charles, Paul. It's gone too far."

"Maybe Tim could go with me to see Charles," Paul said, taking up the knife and making a few futile passes at the roast. "This is no good. I need a sharper one."

"Tim can't leave Buffalo right now." Claire got up and found another carving knife. "The governor's meeting with him and the toxic waste dumpers tomorrow. It's your job, not Tim's."

Paul supposed it was. *Like carving the roast and finding a faulty fuse in the dark, and climbing up on the roof to patch leaks, talking to Charles is my job because I am a man. Yet Charles is far more likely to listen to his mother-in-law and far less likely to knock her down.* Paul had a great distaste for entering any physical fight, especially one he knew he would lose.

"We should insist that Julie leave him," he said. "Charles isn't going to change because I tell him to."

"I told Julie to come home to us and bring Annie with her." Claire picked up the pieces of meat as he carved them and laid them on their plates. "But she said Charles threatened to kill her if she leaves, and Annie, too. Julie believes him."

"She's stubborn, that's all," Paul sighed. "Always was. Once she believes she's doing the right thing, she sticks to it. Charles calls her a Christian martyr."

Paul found out what Charles called his wife because little Annie, her round pink face wrinkled at the brow with questions, asked him what a martyr was.

"Someone who gives up his life instead of giving up God," Paul said, not sure he had gotten Father Echlin's theological subtleties into this definition.

"Are you sure a person has to die to be a martyr?" Annie asked, her wide blue eyes urgent. She tucked a lock of her straight brown hair, horse-tail thick like Charles's, behind her ear. "Mommy won't have to die, will she?"

Paul took his granddaughter on his lap and rocked her against him. "Of course not, Annie. Your mommy's very well. What makes you think she might die?"

"Martyrs die, and daddy calls her a Christian martyr," Annie explained, her voice so clear and loud that Paul was afraid Claire would hear it in the next room. "And sometimes he…"

Annie stopped and ran her finger across her lips. *Claire's gesture when she had said too much,* Paul thought suddenly. *Claire is just as much a part of this child as Julie and I are.* His arms tightened around the child. "Go on, Annie," he said. "What does your daddy do?"

She wriggled down from his lap and stood on her tiptoes, ready to fly out the door. "Mommy says not to talk about it." She had on Julie's faraway face now. "So I can't."

Paul sat alone for a while after Annie had run into the kitchen to see if the brownies she and Claire had made were ready yet. After brownies came a piano lesson and dinner. More and more often Julie left Annie with them when Charles was home from his trips around the country selling bull semen. *Julie wants to keep her daughter out of Charles's way,* Paul realized, *but she would do nothing to help herself, except go to Mass at dawn every morning, before Charles gets up for breakfast.* "I need the Sacrament," was all Julie would say about it when Paul asked. "I look forward to it."

For some time Julie had been attending both St. Michael's Catholic church and Claire's Evangelical church, not seeming to see any problem in her dual allegiance. "I want as much church as I can get," she would say when asked. Paul had to leave it at that, since no specific complaints or explanations were forthcoming.

Now he sat watching Claire eat her roast beef, unable to eat anything himself. *If only Claire had not taken Julie to church so much,* he thought, *the girl would not have been brainwashed into thinking a wife is supposed to be a man's servant. If only Claire had been an ordinary housewife, maybe Julie would not have been afraid to compete with her. She might have grown to be more a person in her own right.* He stared at his wife, catching himself at his old trick, one Claire had often pointed out to him, of needing to blame someone else for whatever unpleasantness occurred in his life. *Of course,* he thought, ashamed that he was still blaming Claire as he used to, *it was I who had an affair at the time Julie needed me. If there is any fault, it is mine.* And he picked at his meat, wishing he could make the sign of the cross or say the *mea culpa* as Julie did, getting comfort from these small, ritual acts. *My fault, my fault, my most grievous fault,* Paul said to himself, knowing he needed to say it to God.

The phone rang, and when he answered, he heard Julie's voice, thick and blurred, as if she were being smothered. "I'm at Chilton Hospital with Annie. Emergency room," she said. "I think you'd better come."

Paul tried to get her to say more, but she hung up. His hands shaking, he held Claire's coat as she shrugged into it. Twice he lost his way to the hospital, though he had taken Timothy there a dozen times with broken fingers and cuts that wouldn't stop bleeding until stitched.

Still, he was unprepared for seeing Julie's face, caked with blood, despite the pad a nurse had fastened over a split-open forehead. Julie's nose was crooked, Paul noticed, and she kept sniffing. When she forgot to sniff, blood ran down into her mouth.

"Annie," was all she said. "She's probably going to lose her eye. They're operating now."

"Claire reached out and took Julie in her arms. "My God," she wept into her daughter's hair. "What did he do to you?"

"He was trying to hit me again," Julie said, her voice steady until she spoke of her child, "but Annie came between us. She tried to stop him, and he threw her against the coffee table. Her eye hit the corner."

"Why?" Claire groaned, rocking Julie back and forth. "Why can't we help you?"

"You can now." Julie seemed to be giving comfort, not receiving it, and Paul saw her shift in Claire's arms so that it was she who held her mother, not the other way around. "I can't let him hurt Annie again. We'll stay with you until we can find a place of our own, if that's all right."

The surgeon came out, pushed her mask up over her paper cap, and beckoned to them. "I did what I could," she said. "The eye couldn't be saved. We did some plastic surgery and in a few months, we can give her an artificial eye. She's lost her binocular vision, but no one will know it by looking at her." She nodded at Julie. "Now your turn, Mrs. Frazier. You could use some plastic surgery yourself, it looks like. We'll need photographs of your face now, before treatment. I'll call a nurse to take them."

"Will you testify in court, doctor?" Paul asked. "We want to get the child away from her father. And to get protection for Julie. "

"Of course." The doctor took another look at Julie, shook her head, and went back to check on Annie, who had just lost an eye for love.

"We'll need a lawyer," Julie said. "Can you call one now?"

Before Paul could answer, she had fainted into his lap, her broken nose bleeding all over his khaki pants. Paul called Timothy, the only lawyer he knew, and Timothy left the case he had made nationally famous on television to come down and attend to Julie's.

In their living room at Amberfields, the family held a council of war. Paul cursed his helplessness as he looked at his wife, daughter, and granddaughter huddled on the couch. *It was my job to protect them*, he thought, *and I've failed again. What are the rules in this kind of war, anyway? No Geneva Conventions seem to apply to families.* He didn't sit down, but paced the room alongside Tim, which made him feel like he was, in some small way, being effective.

"The court case should come up before Annie gets her new eye," Tim said, his voice as cold and hard as if he knew none of them personally. Tim was fit as an athlete and as focused. He had taken karate lessons for the past seven years, perhaps as a consequence of his prison stay. *I wonder if this Oriental discipline of his has made him as hard inside as he is outside*, Paul asked himself. Since Belinda's death, Tim seldom laughed, except when he played with Annie.

Tim put his hands on his niece's shoulders and turned her face toward the light. "And no bandages. I want the judge to see what happened. Julie, you should wear that white nose guard. Leave the bandages off the forehead so he can see the stitches." Timothy's voice broke suddenly, and he got up, turning away from them. "We'll take that guy for every cent he's got." Paul knew he was thinking of the violence against Belinda and was on another march for justice.

"No," Julie said. "We won't do that. Just a divorce. And two hundred a month in child support. Medical expenses too. That's fair." She was making entries in her notebook, then looked up. "I wonder, does Charles have visiting rights if he pays support?" she asked. "If he does, forget about it. Annie mustn't ever see him again."

"I'll do what I can." Timothy too was making notes. "Judges like to give a man something for his money. Otherwise he may fink out."

"It's a chance I'll take," Julie said. "Annie mustn't see him." Hearing a rattle at the back door, she spun around, her hand on her throat.

"Open up." Charles voice carried through the room as if it were wired to speakers. "I'm going to talk to my wife."

None of them moved, their eyes on the door as it trembled under Charles's blows.

"Does he have a gun, do you think?" Timothy asked, tossing aside his jacket. "This type usually does."

Julie shook her head. "He doesn't think he needs one. No. I'm sure he doesn't have a gun."

But when Charles had forced the door open, the broken chain skittering across the kitchen floor, Paul could see the snub-nosed revolver in the man's hand.

"Get out, all of you," Charles ordered, his reddened eyes half-closed. "Julie, stay put."

Paul exchanged a quick glance with Tim, then threw himself in front of his daughter, so that his body was between her and her husband.

Tim swung one foot against Charles's gun and his right arm against Charles's throat. The man went down on all fours, choking. Tim kicked him over on his back, then clamped his fingers around Charles's neck.

"Stop it!" Julie cried. "You'll kill him, Tim. Let him go." She came closer to her husband and eyed him as she would a mad dog. "Charles, I'll be going away from here with Annie," she said. "You won't see us again. It's no good looking at Amberfields next time. We won't be here."

She reached out and then let her arm fall. "I believe you are in God's hands. I hope you will come to believe it too." She turned to her brother. "Tim, you should phone the police to take him home. He's very drunk. The police should be notified that he was here against the restraining order, shouldn't they?"

Paul was surprised to hear his daughter reminding her lawyer of details to be taken care of, for she had always left details to others. Now it seemed to be Julie who controlled the room, her voice calm and low.

When the police had taken Charles off their hands, Julie's composure wavered enough that she sat shivering for a few moments in Paul's arms before spending the next two hours telling her family the story of her marriage. It was all Paul feared it might be, but there were things he had not suspected as well, things he would rather Claire had not heard.

"He's very sick, you see," Julie said, turning down a third cup of tea. "I think it was from the war. Charles did such a lot of killing in Vietnam. That was one reason I wanted to go on the Washington march, to undo what Charles had done, if I could. He told me that once he and his platoon machine-gunned a whole village full of people. The ones that wouldn't come out of their huts were burned up inside. Charles was sprayed with some chemical over there that made him dizzy and depressed. We asked the VA hospital to tell us what it was, but they wouldn't."

"Agent Orange." Tim nodded. "The big drug companies don't want the government to go public about their experiments in chemical warfare. Bad for their image as laxative-makers and all that. Once we blow their cover in New York state, though, it'll all come out. Agent Orange is only one poison. We're killing our own people with polluted water and food, right here and now in this country. That's what I'm trying to stop."

He snapped his fingers. “Julie, why don’t you and Annie come up to Buffalo with me, at least for the summer, so Charles can’t find you? The minister of my church runs a shelter for battered women and their kids. You could stay there or with me. How about it?”

Julie glanced at her father, an old gesture with her, to see if he approved, but turned back to Tim before Paul could speak. “Good idea,” she said. “Tomorrow I’ll need a police escort to go back to the house and get our things. You’ll take care of that?”

“I’m on my way,” Tim said, locking the front door behind him as he left.

“We’ll all go with you to get what you need,” Claire said.

“No. Just the police escort. Charles mustn’t see you helping me. I’ll go upstairs now.” She turned to Claire who had gotten up to follow her. “By myself. I’ll be all right.”

Julie had always seemed to Paul a fragile branch, but now she was a full, blossoming tree that no storm could break. He watched her go, marveling at the change.

Claire rocked in her chair, in and out of the moonlight that striped the rug. “Remember when I said we were escaping Europe and its wars? Remember when I said America would be safe? How naïve I was.”

“We came where the cutting edge is,” Paul said, suddenly seeing what they had done as he had never seen it before. “We left history behind us. Perhaps that’s not a safe thing to do.”

“I guess it’s some comfort that we’re the first to be at the place every other country will have to be sooner or later,” Claire said looking up, the moonlight filling her eyes. “I wonder what comes next, when you’ve gone beyond history?”

“The Japanese and Germans are getting there. Maybe the Israelis, or so my friend Marcus says.” Paul lit his pipe, hands still shaking. *Good that Claire knows enough not to talk about what Julie just told us of her marriage. I couldn’t bear it.* “We’re moving past what people used think reality is. Only saints and great artists know from experience that nothing is solid, just swirling electrical charges following laws no one understands.” He sighed and began to clean his clogged pipe, glad for something to do with his hands.

Men like Yehuda Marcus knew too, he was sure, though Marcus would claim neither artistry nor sainthood for himself. Paul remembered sitting with the old Jew just before Marcus had left for his yearly trip to Israel. They had talked about life on the cutting edge of history.

“We Jews know how it feels to need a safe place to stand,” Marcus said, blowing on his hot tea and sipping noisily.

"And the rest of us?" Paul was thinking of Tim and his radical utopian friends on the Eden express.

"You forget," Marcus said, his glasses having steamed from the rising heat of the tea, so that he looked blind as a seer. "Like Jews, you Christians, our children, live in history and are carried by it as are fish in a river, going home on a grand scale whether you like it or not. Your great priest-philosopher, Teilhard de Chardin called that home 'the Omega Point,' where everything finally converges in pure spirit. Cosmic Zionism, I call it. But I am not swept by such an upward wind. I am one of those who goes home out of choice."

"To Israel, you mean? Does it help to keep revisiting the past?"

"By emptying myself of what I remember about those years in the camp, I become a new man." He thumped his chest with mock pride. "I take my place in the front lines of the historical process."

Paul pointed at the notebook Marcus always kept beside him, the pages closely written. "You still remember new names and faces after all these years?"

"Remembering is not what is hard," Marcus laid his hand over the page, spreading his graceful fingers. "What is hard is the forgetting, you understand." After a little silence, he went on. "But I will not forget to take your wife's album with me to Israel, as I promised. There is a Christian priest in Jerusalem who would appreciate her music. I met him last year at Yad Vashem, where he was being honored as one of the Righteous Gentiles for saving some Jewish children. Now a eucalyptus tree on the path to Yad Vashem bears his name. Since a tree left to itself lives longer than a man, this honor is an immortality of sorts, *nicht wahr?* Like your wife's in her music."

Mr. Marcus closed his notebook and laid it into an old leather portfolio that he tied with ribbons, like a holy book. Then he picked up the portfolio and held it to his heart. *Wrapped in this old man's arms are the lives of martyrs*, Paul thought, *and the smoke from their bones has risen to the sky. We breathe them as we breathe the dust of stars. Their names will live in memory, the way Dora and Maxi live in Claire's music.* As Marcus raised one hand to his friend, more in blessing than farewell, Paul was struck by the immortality of martyrs and the grace of saints.

14

Dora's Journal

Israel............................1981

I had taken a day off from the latest water crisis at Kiryat Anavim, hoping that a talk with Father Jonas and Benjamin would help me forget it. As I stared out the bus window at the stretches of black road and reddish sand, I thought about the Scottish dowser I had brought in seven years before. At first he had seemed to succeed, and everyone was talking about how the fellow had struck water from a rock, like Moses. The agricultural committee, though skeptical at first, was glad to take credit for the dowser, who had found a stream running down the hill three feet under the surface.

"We did it!" Sol cried, throwing his cap into the air, then dancing me around in a circle. "The committee will get the digging started today. A new well! A new irrigation system! We're in business again."

Maxi just stood by the dowser, frowning a little, shading his eyes with one hand as he looked first up the hill, then down at the base. When I saw him, I pushed Sol away and came over to see what was wrong. Sol joined the men who were already digging where our posthole had opened the stream to the air. They had laughed at me when I brought in the dowser, but they weren't laughing now. I felt like Bernadette of Lourdes, surrounded by the disbelief of bishops and the miracle of healing water.

"What's the matter, Maxi?" I wanted him to be glad too. "We've got a winner, and you're not pleased?"

"You know how these streams are," he said, rubbing his jaw and looking again from the top of the hill to the base. "A year or two and they dry up, just when you've got the irrigation system going. I don't trust it."

"Maybe it's the same stream that fed the original well," I said. "The one you're always saying had to be here under the *tel*."

Maxi shook his head and kept walking, his eyes on the ground, as if he expected to see the ancient well open in front of him. "No, that well would be twenty feet down, at least. So would any stream that feeds it. I'd like the dowser to keep looking, but the committee will overrule me."

"Don't worry so, Maxi," I said, giving him a hug around the middle, feeling good and saved. "We've got the water now, when it's needed. Who knows what will happen next year? The moment is all we've ever had, yes?"

He nodded, but something about the lines between his eyebrows made me think he didn't agree. As it happened, he was right, though not about how long it took for the stream to dry up. For seven years it flowed, and the fields turned green again. We even sprouted a small forest of orange and olive trees up the side of the *tel*. I was proud to show it off to my friends, especially Rabbi Noah Halpern. His approval meant more to me than anyone's except Maxi's, especially when accompanied by a surreptitious squeezing of my hand when we walked among the trees.

Rabbi Noah came out to see me every month and offered an Orthodox Shabbat service to those few who wanted it. Nothing was said about his devotion to Yeshua or my own. My fellow kibbutzniks would have thought I had gone quite balmy or that I had betrayed my roots. At the time, it was still considered unthinkable to have a common cause with the Christians who had given us so much grief in the past, with their persecutions and pograms. Israelis seemed to have forgotten that Jesus and his original disciples were Jewish. I kept quiet and did not remind them.

Noah and I were more than friends, less than lovers. After his first wife had left him, he was afraid to care about anyone again, and was comfortable just sleeping alone on his little mat at Beth Shalom. I, for my part, never wanted to love any man because he might love someone else and leave me. I had lost my father, Lev, and Maxi. That was quite enough to sour me on relationships. Sometimes I had dreams in which Yeshua appeared and pointed to a man in the distance, someone tall, who wore a dark coat, but I could never see the man's face. If it was Noah's, I didn't want to know. Both of us were content with handholding and occasional whispered confidences. We were best friends and that was enough for us. I wished he would come to live with me at Kiryat Anavim, and he wished I would come to live with him in Jerusalem. But we were like Jews and Arabs on opposite sides of the Jordan, disputing over who would have the river's limited, life-giving water.

Now, after a long drought, our stream and well were drying up, just as Maxi had said they would, and Kiryat Anavim was again under a death sentence. We didn't know how long we had. But one season without rainfall would mean the end of the grove and the vegetable fields. The cafeteria and our residence halls had their own small wells, but they couldn't feed the whole irrigation system.

That morning, when I left Kiryat Anavim for Jerusalem, Yael had been at the site of the disappointing stream, with an armful of apparatus from the university physics department, carried for her by Dan Dworansky, her age mate and best friend. Dan was a tall, hairy boy with thin hips and thick shoulders, whose swarthy, cheerful face looked to be handsome under his full beard, mustache and shoulder-length waves of hair, but too little of the face showed for one to be sure. Yael walked ahead of him, delicate and erratic as a butterfly, her pale yellow hair flying around her head, and her bright eyes hidden behind large, round sunglasses.

"I think Dad's right about that well," she said to me, holding her blowing hair back with one arm curved around her forehead. "My hydraulics professor says to work out some charts showing where the shallow stream started and where a deeper main stream might have hit the water table below the foot of the hill. We might find the spot, if his plan works."

The two of them walked off together, and I watched them set up their apparatus at the foot of the hill, where the measuring would begin. Dan stayed close to Yael, working beside her as if their bodies were extensions of one another's. Always they had been together. I remembered seeing them with a few other babies in the same play pen. Even then Dan had made sure no one pushed Yael down or took toys away from her. When as a little girl she cried in the night, the *metapelet* told me, Dan would climb out of bed and go to comfort her. The *metapelet* would find them together in the morning, Dan's dark head buried in Yael's corn-silk hair, and her thin, pale arms tight around his brown shoulders. They had shared a room through their adolescent years, with another girl and boy. Only Carolyn, anxious as always, was afraid they were making love and that Yael would become pregnant. The rest of us were sure that like all children raised together, using the same showers and toilets since childhood, these two would, for lack of mystery, have no erotic feelings for each other.

Now, watching Dan arrange himself beside Yael in such a way as to block the sun from hitting her, I was not so sure. These children might not know with their minds that they loved each other, but their bodies knew. Thinking of Yael's desire to become a chemist and Dan's to be a farmer, I grieved for them in advance of the fact, knowing how it had been for me when Lev went away to the city, his head full of himself and his ideas. Dan would be emptying what he was into the land, even while Yael's head would be swelling with what her professors poured into it. Sometimes, when she came back to the kibbutz for a visit, she would sit by the window, brooding and remote as a pregnant woman, while Dan massaged her neck and shoulders, brought her glasses of fruit juice, and whispered with her as the rest of us talked about politics and the water supply. Though Yael, like Maxi, had a room in her head that was furnished only with ideas and figures of a sort unfamiliar to the rest of us, she was like me too. Her body lived and grew on the thin soil of the kibbutz, far from where her mind was fed and watered.

So half of her lived at the university with her parents and science professors. The other half lived at Kiryat Anavim with Dan and me and her age-mates. Though she and I never spoke of her split life, we were close. When I had my bad moments remembering Lev and how far the two of us had gone in different directions, Yael would put her arms around me and lay her face on my shoulder. Sometimes my whole body would jerk and strain as if being hit by the shell that had destroyed his tank, and Yael would say nothing, only hold me and breathe the way I was breathing, in big gasps, feeling what I felt. The jerking and gasping went on for some time. Although my mind knew Lev had been killed, my body had to get used to it slowly. Sol Stein tried to help and sometimes stood by my bedroom door for an hour saying goodnight. Since I thought my twitching and sighing would make poor company for his body's simple needs, I sent him off and went to bed by myself, shuddering all alone until I fell asleep. Only when I was with Rabbi Noah did these signs of distress disappear, but I was with him all too seldom.

After the short bus ride to Jerusalem, I found Father Jonas at St. Elizabeth's. The sight of him cheered me almost as much as the sight of Noah always did. Father Jonas was talking to a quick, bald little American named Yehuda Marcus, who had come to Israel to give the authorities information about war criminals. Father and Mr. Marcus were sitting on a balcony over the garden between the priest's residence and the church. Their bodies were sprawled on easy chairs and their heads were close together. They looked like old dogs lying nose to nose in the sun.

I was sorry not to find Father Jonas alone because I had meant to talk to him about Benjamin, whom I was afraid was no longer any kind of Jew I could recognize. He had gently refused to go with me to Jewish services, saying he wanted to get beyond sectarian religion and into a new age of peace between people of all faiths and no faith. It sounded to me something like the teaching of the Ba'hai temple in Haifa, but I didn't understand all that much of what he told me. Maybe I didn't want to understand. I had hoped to ask Father Jonas to reason with my son, but now, with the old American on the scene, I realized that the matter of Benjamin's apostasy would have to wait.

"Dora," Father Jonas called, waving me to a chair beside him. "Come and meet my friend Yehuda Marcus, from America. I've been asking him about your parents."

I pulled my chair up close to the bald old man and leaned forward, my elbows digging into my knees. "You knew them in Frankfurt?" I asked, not bothering to shake hands or be friendly. "In Bergen-Belsen? Where?"

"Easy, Dora, easy," Father Jonas, reaching out to touch my shoulder. "I was going to play you a tape Mr. Marcus brought of a friend's music. The song was written for some Jewish children the composer rescued during the war. Sit down with us a little while and hear it."

"Later," I said dropping a quick kiss on his hand, then turning again to the small, tired Mr. Marcus. "What do you know about the Lebenthals? I've heard nothing but that they arrived at the camp in a cattle car and that my father was very ill."

Mr. Marcus lay back in his chair and closed his eyes tightly, as if the sun were hurting them. "They came to mind only when Father Jonas asked," he said, stretching one hand over his eyes like a bandage. "It's so hard to remember at this distance in time, you know. Still, I can't think how I could have forgotten this one until now. Albert and Mimi were well known in Germany. They had a reputation, unlike the rest of us. The others were not special, and no one takes notice of those who are not special."

He opened his eyes and stared at me, as if he thought I might be one of those upon whom ordinary people are wasted. "Albert Lebenthal was special, and we all knew it. Even the Nazis seemed to know. The Red Cross sent representatives to the camp to ask after him, but by then it was too late. Albert Lebenthal was dead."

"You were there when he died?" I had a sudden, aching memory of Lev, on the cattle car with a man who sang the Kol Nidre all the way to his grave, and my whole body gave a lurch, bracing for impact as it always did when I thought of Lev being hit by a mortar shell. "Was he in pain? Was it a fast death?" I could feel Father Jonas gripping my hand, his fingers tightly woven among mine.

Mr. Marcus spoke slowly, with long pauses for his memory to knit itself together like a broken bone. My father had come to the camp as a sick man, despite the strength of his songs in the cattle car, where he sang as a cantor for the last time. After that, he apparently did not sing. He fought. My gentle father, who was too weak to walk without help, had gotten himself in even more trouble with the Nazis by leading a revolt against them in the death camp.

Marcus said the Nazis were caught completely off guard. One of my mother's friends worked in the Krupp explosives factory near the camp. This friend used slave laborers to smuggle in tiny bits of dynamite and charges. The workers carried their contraband from the Krupp factory to Bergen-Belsen in carts full of garbage and excrement and corpses. No one, not even the Nazi guards, wanted to check those carts too closely. Then my father would sit up at night, his fingers working from memory in the dark, and make little bombs with empty bean tins as casings. Others hid the bombs all over Bergen-Belsen, but especially near the crematoria.

The revolt began when my father gave the signal to spray gasoline over the gas chambers with a disinfectant sprinkler. The rebels threw my father's bombs into the gasoline and blew up the death chambers. While the Germans battled the flames and tried to repair the telephone and electric lines cut by the prisoners, three hundred men escaped into the forest. My father, of course, was not one of them, for he couldn't walk, let alone run. He sat on the ground watching the flames, his hands stained with tell-tale grease from the bombs, until the Nazis took him back to his cell. Other prisoners, under torture, told who the leader of the revolt was, so my father was tortured too.

Mr. Marcus would not say how, when I asked him. He had been given the job of cleaning up the cell before my father was taken to the gas chamber. He found my father lying on a bed of straw and pushed straw over his almost naked body to keep him from freezing. When my father was offered water, he refused, since there wasn't enough for everyone, and the children were crying for what little there was. When Mr. Marcus was bending over him, my father pulled him down close, surprising the other man with the strength he had left, and told him to let the International Red Cross know that Farben and the American members of the chemical cartel had been experimenting with poisonous substances before the war. Mr. Marcus, if he lived, was supposed to go to the authorities and urge them to make my father's testimony public. Then the guards came and dragged him away. What happened to my mother, Mr. Marcus never learned, but he believed she had been murdered at the same time because of what she knew about Farben.

"It was as if no one wanted to know the truth," Mr. Marcus said. "Once the war was over, forgetting was in the air. No one since has wanted to remember. To this day, there are those who believe the Holocaust never happened. That it was something made up by Zionists. If six million dead could be forgotten so easily, how much easier to forget one man's story about illegal chemicals?"

"They shouldn't be allowed to forget," I found myself clenching and unclenching my fists, thinking my father and mother had died for nothing if no one knew their story. "Otherwise it will happen again."

"Yes!" said Father Jonas, who sat with his arm around me, for I kept leaning to one side, as if I were about to fall over. "If people can ignore what happened to six million Jews, they can ignore anything. Have we altogether lost our sense of the sacredness of life?"

"Next may come the death of hundreds of millions in a nuclear war," Mr. Marcus said, looking even smaller and more tired than before. "Already the generals in Washington talk about how many millions of people can be lost without ill effect to the nation's economy. But you've seen the Americans riot against the Vietnam War. Perhaps the final atrocity will not come, after all. Perhaps because the Holocaust has touched the imagination of the whole human race, we can never again be blind to such suffering. Yes, I believe it was not for nothing. I must believe it."

After the war, when Mr. Marcus went to Geneva, no one seemed to have any records of my father's letters to the Red Cross. The records, they said, had been destroyed for lack of corroboration, along with the other depositions against the chemical cartels. Farben had even managed to salvage all its assets, Marcus finished, lying back with his eyes closed. They had put their money under false names in Swiss banks and were back in business with their Western colleagues in the Vanderzell Corporation even before Japan fell to the Americans.

Father Jonas worked his fingers together until his knuckles were white. "I too believe that God does not waste the suffering of His people, anymore than the suffering of Christ was wasted."

"He was, after all, a Jew." Mr. Marcus stood up. "Perhaps someday my people will remember that he was one of them." He shook hands with Father Jonas. "Now I will leave you both. They expect me at Yad Vashem."

Turning to me, Mr. Marcus said, "Your father's story will go into the records, now that you've brought him back to mind. You see, even I forget, and I was a witness. We must forgive those who have not seen for their failure to remember." He patted my cheek and went slowly away, as if Yad Vashem and the past were not at all where he wanted to go.

Although Father Jonas wanted to sit with me as I moved through the shock of how my father died, I needed a man who was not a father to me. It seemed somehow disloyal to grieve for one father in the arms of another. So I asked Father Jonas to drop me off at Beth Shalom for a while. He thought I shouldn't be alone, so he rang up Rabbi Noah to be sure he would be there when I arrived. I was glad of that, since Noah and I were closer than Father Jonas or anyone else knew.

I must admit that I fantasized quite a bit about Noah Halpern, imagining myself walking in the gardens of the kibbutz with him, arm in arm, or sitting in the moonlight with him beside the well, speaking of God and God's toys, the stars. For Noah's sake, I had begun to dress, eat, and generally live as an Orthodox woman, which was not easy at the kibbutz. I tied a scarf over my wild hair and wore long-sleeved, calf-length dresses even in the hot sun. While people stared, I said my prayers over the halachic food I had prepared myself. If the secular atheists at the kibbutz could call themselves Jews, then I could too.

Beth Shalom was conducted as an Orthodox synagogue, though we prayed in the name of Yeshua and read from the New Covenant writings as well as the Torah. It was comforting to me to follow the practices of my ancestors, as it was to Noah. We believed that by living as they had, we were keeping alive the legacy of those lost in the Holocaust. After all, they had not been killed by Christians, but by pagan Nazis who hated all religion.

Noah found me in the back row of the Beth Shalom worship space. Now there were a good many rows, since the congregation had grown over the seven years since I had joined it. Noah sat down beside me, his large hands lying on his knees. His beard now matched the gray at his temples, but his face seemed no older than when we had first met.

"Father Jonas said you were grieving over news about your father's death," Noah began, not looking at me. It was hard for him to overcome the old Orthodox rule not to look directly at any woman except one's wife. Since he had no wife, he was apparently doomed to see no woman at all. I found that fact vaguely comforting, since I would not have liked sharing Noah with any other female.

"I had known for many years that he was dead. But just now I heard the details." My voice faltered. I had not realized before this moment that I wanted sympathy, pity, or any form of love I could get from this shy, gaunt man who blazed like a fire on Shabbat and faded into cooling embers for the rest of the week.

"Dora, I'm sorry for your pain," Noah said, raising one hand as if to put it on mine, then letting it drop back in his lap. "I would comfort you if I could, but only God can do that."

"I wouldn't mind if you tried," I said, bending a little and turning my head so I could look up into his face. "Your comfort would mean more to me than anyone else's. Yeshua speaks through you, or so it seems to me."

"Does it?" Noah suddenly forgot the rules of Orthodoxy enough to look straight into my eyes. "And for me, Yeshua speaks through you. Your words are written on the stone of my heart, Dora, and the letters burn. Do you understand me?"

"I'm not sure. Why have you not married again? Why do you live alone like no other rabbi? I've always wanted to ask."

Noah looked down at his hands and flexed them. "I was married long ago, but she left. I was so poor, you see, and no longer had a congregation. Never again have I asked a woman to share my poverty. Why would any woman want to sleep on the floor in the corner of a synagogue?"

"If she loved you, I think she would." My face flushed, and I realized that as usual I was saying more than I meant to.

"But there might be children, and then, how would we manage without money?"

"Sometimes it's too late for children," I said, casting my eyes down at my lap so I would not look as bold as my words.

"Sometimes, it is just too late." Noah sighed and stood up.

Suddenly he reached out, and in a very unorthodox fashion, grabbed my hands and pulled me to my feet. "Dora, I would ask you to be my wife, if there were any chance you would leave Kiryat Anavim for me."

My cheeks burned and I left my hands in his. "I don't think I could abandon my home," I said. "I'm needed on the kibbutz. Couldn't you come and live there with me?"

Noah shook his head and smiled sadly. "What would I do on a kibbutz? They would not even consider me a Jew, because of Yeshua. Orthodoxy is not to their taste either."

"You're right about that," I sighed. "We'll talk about this again, Noah. I would very much like to be your wife, but the logistics are beyond me."

Noah did another unorthodox thing and grabbed me, holding me close against his heart. "We can find a way, if Ha-Shem wills it," he said. "I pray he does."

I was thinking it was Noah who would have to find a way, but said nothing. Maybe Yeshua would work another miracle for me. As I have said before, luck had nothing to do with my survival and flourishing. I call myself blessed because Yeshua, not chance, has saved me.

Father Jonas was waiting for me when my taxi arrived back at St. Elizabeth's. We sat together for a while in the church, surrounded by the sumptuous, alien art of his tradition. I couldn't pray there, but Father Jonas prayed for me, holding my hands.

"Benjamin will meet us here in a little while," Father said, trying to take my mind off the way my parents had died. Since I was waiting until I was alone to mourn, he was successful. "He's at military intelligence doing some sort of aeronautical calculations for them. Wouldn't say what for."

Benjamin had been trained as a mathematician and now served in an army intelligence office because of the injury to his elbow. So it was no surprise to learn that he had once again been called in to calculate flight patterns allowing our surveillance planes to avoid Arab radar and their ground-to-air missiles. At least that's what I thought Benjamin was doing. Not until sunset that day did we learn what was really going on.

Of course everyone had been nervous lately about the Iraqi nuclear reactor, Tammuz 1, which we had heard was about to go hot. No one agreed on what to do about it. Just the evening before, even Maxi and Father Jonas had argued about Tammuz 1, and to my knowledge, those two had never argued about anything. We had been at a party for Joel at a Jerusalem restaurant, in honor of his first air force assignment. The argument didn't start until after dessert, but it had been brewing all evening. I guess our family was reflecting the tension throughout Israel over the Iraqi reactor.

"We have no right to interfere with another country," Maxi insisted. "The French built that reactor for research, not war."

"You've read what the Iraqi government said publicly last September, when Iran tried to destroy that reactor," Father Jonas reminded my brother. "The Iraqis said not to worry. They'll use this thing against Israel, not Iran."

"Just saber-rattling," Maxi said. "You know how the Arabs are, always dramatic. And they're afraid the Iranians might attack them again."

Father Jonas wouldn't give up, and in his hawkish moments reminded me a bit of Lev. "You're enough of a scientist to know that this Tammuz 1 doesn't need to be fourteen times as powerful as most research reactors. Yet it is. And the French gave the Iraqis exactly the grade of uranium suited to nuclear weapons. What could little Israel do against even one hydrogen bomb? A whole population could be held hostage by Baghdad. Is that what you'd want?" He put his hand to his throat.

I couldn't help remembering Father Jonas's lectures on avoiding attack by dogs. "Don't let them get behind you, Dora," he used to say, just as he was saying now.

"I want Israel to act justly." Maxi got up to leave, hating disagreements as he always had. "What good is survival, if you have to be as bad as your enemies in order to win?"

"Survival is always good," I put in, sure of my ground on that point at least.

"So you understand, Maxi, it's survival we're talking about." Father Jonas tried to close the gap between them. "There's no choice. That reactor has to go. Believe me, the world will be glad of it. No one wants to see H-bombs in the hands of madmen. Today Israel, tomorrow New York. That's how the Iraqis think."

Carolyn jumped up to follow her husband. "My God," she said shrilly, "Is no place in this world safe to raise a family? Come on, Joel. You need to rest up for tomorrow."

So that was the end of the argument and the party. Father Jonas and I walked back to St. Elizabeth's together. We went up to his room to have a last glass of tea before going to bed.

"I'm afraid for Joel," I said, sitting down at Father's balcony table. "He's been practicing bomb-dropping in the Sinai. Flying one of these new F-16s."

Father Jonas turned his head quickly to look at me, his white eyebrows coming together over his long, thin nose. "Did Joel tell you that? F-16s are light fighters, not bombers. I don't understand."

"When Joel mentioned them at dinner, Benjamin shut him up." I poured myself the rest of the tepid tea from Father Jonas's pitcher. "He seems to watch over Joel, trying to keep him quiet about military matters. Maybe trying to keep him safe."

"The two boys are closer now than they used to be. That's good." Father Jonas had always felt headstrong Joel would benefit by being closer to his older cousin, and I agreed. But then everyone gained by being closer to Benjamin.

Now that my son was living in Jerusalem, away from the kibbutz, a dozen young people from Kiryat Anavim and elsewhere had moved to the Arab quarter to be near him. After work, they would gather at night for a communal meal and prayers of some kind. I wasn't clear on what sort of prayers these were, since they had no words. They all sat around on the floor for a few hours, and at the end they would chant and hold hands. Benjamin said they were meditating, but I couldn't figure out what they were meditating *on*. Empty silence didn't seem to me something to share with your friends. Why not just talk together as ordinary friends do? I couldn't understand Benjamin anymore.

Now seemed as good a time as any to ask Father Jonas what was going on with my son and these strange, silent meetings of his. I put down my glass so hard it almost cracked in my hands. "Look, Father. My son is a Jew. I don't want him switching over to some New Age religion. He talks a lot about how God's love is in us all. There's no Jew or Gentile, in his thinking. 'All religions point to the same God,' he says." I leaned over and held Father Jonas by the shoulders, looking hard into his eyes. "Can't you talk to him?"

Father Jonas reached up and took my hands in his. "Benjamin's on his own path," he said.

"It's true that he still keeps Shabbat." I thought of all the Friday nights when Benjamin would draw the family together, saying nothing about his path or whatever it was he thought about, just being there at Maxi's and Carolyn's helping his aunt prepare the Shabbat meal. Joel and Yael always came with me from the kibbutz for that Friday night in Jerusalem, loving to be with Benjamin as we all did.

"But Father," I burst out, not wanting to give up on my son's soul. "Some of the friends he prays with are even Arabs." I thought of thin, shy

Kamal, who sometimes came to Maxi's back door asking for Benjamin. I wondered if on other nights this young Arab amused himself by learning how to make Molotov cocktails or throwing rocks at Israeli patrols. Yet Benjamin would hold Kamal in his arms whenever they met and pray with him in their strange, silent way.

"Let him go, Dora," Father Jonas said, patting my hand. "He's not yours anymore."

"If not mine, then whose?" I remembered giving birth to Benjamin in the midst of blood and broken bones. If he didn't know who he was, a Jew, an Israeli, Dora Ben-Ari's son, then my life meant nothing at all.

"God's, I believe," Father Jonas said. "Yes, I think you can be sure Benjamin is God's man. I am."

"God's? Or sure?" I had to smile, for something in his words sounded to me as inside-out as Benjamin's.

"Both." Father Jonas put his hand on my head as if in blessing, and then went to answer the doorbell.

Benjamin came in behind him, his lips held tightly together. "You should be told," he said, after coming out on the balcony to join me. "Fourteen of our bombers are on their way to Iraq. The Prime Minister just announced it. They took off from the Sinai base at 4:40 this afternoon."

"Tammuz 1?" Father Jones hurried to his radio. "That's the target, isn't it?"

"I can say so now." Benjamin sat down on the balcony floor and leaned his head against the railing. "It's a big risk," he said. "Baghdad is over a thousand miles away. We have no provision for aerial refueling. The planes have time for one run. Then they have to come home. There should be just enough gas in their tanks to get them back."

"They're using the American F-16s?" Father Jonas was fiddling with his radio dial, trying to get the latest news.

"We changed them around inside so they're bombers, not just fighters," Benjamin said. "Quite a project. We had only a few weeks till that reactor went hot."

"And what if it had?" It seemed to me that one could bomb a hot reactor as easily as a cold one.

"Once it was hot, our attack would lay a radioactive blanket all over Baghdad," he said. "Unthinkable. It was now or not at all."

"What about civilians?" Father Jonas was taking out his rosary, already praying, no doubt, for the Iraqis who might be in harm's way.

Benjamin shook his head. "It's a Muslim holiday," he said. "No one will be on the site, and we're hitting only the reactor itself, not any administrative buildings."

"That's why Joel's been in the Sinai," I cried, grasping what all Benjamin and Joel's secrecy had been about. "Bombing practice. You hid the truth from me."

"Neither of us was allowed to talk about it." Benjamin passed one hand over his damp forehead. "Would you go with me to tell Aunt Carolyn? Joel gave me the job, but I could use some help."

So Joel had left us for a suicidal mission without letting his parents know. The thought of telling Carolyn where her son was made me wish I could have been on the plane with Joel. Anything would have been better than having to tell his mother what we would have to tell her. Of course, at the time we knew very little. Only later did we hear how it had gone with him.

Everyone on board Joel's plane, the middle plane in the formation, had feared that he might be called back. Five different dates had been fixed, and then cancelled, so that by now, the men felt their mission must be the subject of jokes among the Arabs. When the Jordanian tracking station at Malan picked up the Israeli jets ten minutes after they were in the air, Joel began to swear as he looked down at the bare, rocky red hills under them.

"They know exactly where we are," he said to the radioman next to him. "You know Arabic. Bull your way through."

The radioman was a lieutenant and Joel only a private first class, but no one was ceremonious about rank in this citizen's army. Israeli soldiers were disciplined only by the situation at hand, Maxi had told me years ago. They were all in combat to save their families and their homes, not to build some officer's ego.

So the radioman, his faced dripping with sweat that splashed on his instruments, told the Jordanians that this plane was full of Saudis on a secret peace mission between the Iraqi and Iranian governments. He signed off with an extra flourish, saying that peace was to clear the way for a united stand against the infidel Israelis, all of them dogs, with pigs for ancestors, and of whom monkeys would be the descendents. This improbable evolutionary prospect made the Jordanians cheer and ring off without asking any more questions. They relayed nothing of the flight to the other Arab tracking stations. Their bond with fellow Muslims did not extend to a common air defense command.

The setting sun at their backs, the planes headed over the Iraqi border, screaming through the air at four hundred miles per hour, low to the ground, and weaving to avoid both Iraqi radar and anti-aircraft fire.

"There it is," said Joel suddenly, nudging the radioman.

They both leaned over, pressing their faces against the window to see the sprawling concrete complex, turned red by the sun. Then Joel sat back and studied the instrument panel in front of him, getting ready for his part in the bombing run.

"Do you see anyone down there?" The radioman kept peering out and wiping his face. "I'd hate like hell to kill somebody. It's one thing if they're shooting at you, but like this..."

Joel had no time to answer, for their plane banked, then shot almost straight up before it levelled out, ready for its run. The first plane, its wings shadowing the ground, fired two of its computer-aimed bombs. They punched holes in exactly those places on the dome into which Joel and the other bombardiers were to drop their charges. Joel leaned forward, his eyes on the instrument panel, his mouth moving silently as he counted. His plane swept low over the reactor, but he couldn't see the holes with his naked eye until after he had passed over them. Following the computer's instructions, his fingers had pushed the red buttons that dropped several tons of explosives straight down into the secret, lethal depths of Tammuz 1.

Behind them, as they climbed, Joel could see the cupola's roof collapse, burying the reactor's core under a heap of broken concrete and steel beams. Flames rose up, immolating what was left of the elaborate machine that President Saddam Hussein had boasted would send nuclear bombs against Israel.

Now the only problem was that Joel's plane might not have enough gasoline in its engines to get its crew home. They couldn't very well make an emergency landing in an Arab state. The pilot turned the plane westward and did not look back at the column of smoke rising over the place where once had stood Tammuz, named for an ancient Mesopotamian boy god who used to die ritually every year. Joel and all Israel could only hope that this time, the boy god would stay dead.

I could imagine what Joel was thinking during this ordeal, but none of us dared say anything for fear of frightening Carolyn. We had all trooped into my brother's apartment behind Father Jonas, who had been given the unpleasant task of telling Joel's mother what was going on. He sat beside Carolyn as he told her the news that her son was flying over Arab territory on a preemptive bombing strike. She said nothing at all, which was unusual for my sister-in-law, but when she stood up to get us coffee, she fainted into Maxi's lap and had to be carried to bed. Maxi sat with her, cradling her in his arms, and I closed the door on them, feeling a surge of jealousy that no husband was beside me to hold me up at bad times.

We all sat in the living room the whole night, drinking coffee until our hands shook. Only Father Jonas stayed calm and tried to take our minds off the passing time and the silent telephone. He played the tape brought from America by his friend Yehuda Marcus, but I hardly listened.

"Yesterday St. Elizabeth's offered a formal commission to the woman who composed this Kol Nidre, a Mrs. de Montfort," Father Jonas said. "We want her to write an Easter Liturgy to be performed next spring when the pilgrims come. Marcus thinks we might be able to get Mrs. de Montfort and her family to come here for the performance. Dora, perhaps you could ask Rabbi Meir to propose the woman for one of those Righteous Gentile awards? It seems she saved some Jewish children during the war."

"Maybe you should ask Benjamin to talk to Rabbi Meir. The Rabbi gets on better with men than with women," I said indifferently. My mind was not on the music or on Father Jonas's Easter plans.

"Can't you turn that dirge down?" Carolyn called in a high, shaky voice from the other room. "He's not dead yet, for God's sake."

A mournful Kol Nidre was the last thing she needed to hear just now, we realized, and Father Jonas leaped to turn it off. "Let's try the radio again," he said. "Maybe some news of the raid has come through by now."

He twisted the dials, getting static at first, then a voice. The Prime Minister must have just released his account of the bombing, for the commentator had already begun giving a history of the strike: Iraq had never signed the armistice agreement after the Partition 1948, and so was still at war with Israel; by 1975, the Iraqi dictator had tipped his hand, boasting that his reactor was "the first Arab attempt at nuclear arming." I had innocently thought that unless somebody was shooting his way over our borders, we were not at war. It made me uneasy that I had been at war with Iraq all this time without knowing it.

"Ah, here it is," said Benjamin, taking over from Father Jonas in order to find another newscast.

"Eight F-16 jets and six F-15 escorts left the Sinai at 4:40 yesterday afternoon on the fourteenth anniversary of the Six Day War, following a course that carried them across the Gulf of Aqaba and along the border between Saudi Arabia and Jordan. They varied their altitudes so as to avoid the Arab radar screens."

"You planned that, Benjamin, didn't you?" I hooked one arm around my son's neck and kissed his cheek. "Looks like you figured right."

"Not exactly," said a voice from the doorway. "We got picked up by the Jordanian radar in Malan. Where's Mother?" Joel tossed his flight jacket on the couch and was circled by all our arms, so that Carolyn could hardly fight her way through us when she ran out of the bedroom.

"You certainly know how to keep a secret," Carolyn cried, letting her tears and mascara run all over Joel's shirt. "Who does a mother have to call around here to find out if her son's in Baghdad or just down the block? Some country. Some son." She held Joel's square-jawed, handsome face, her hands running over the black bristles sprouting on his cheeks.

"We were in the air ten minutes after getting our orders. No time to call." Joel reached around his mother and managed to hold Maxi too. "Be a hawk, Dad. Just for today." His eyebrows lifted, as if he were asking a question. "Congratulate me. We don't think anyone was killed in the raid."

Joel had been raised almost entirely in the kibbutz, not by his parents, yet to him, Maxi's slightest frown had brought on tears when he was young and apologies in later years. Once he had received a little pocket knife for Hanukkah and had tried its sharpness at once by cutting a chunk out of his parents' new olivewood coffee table. Maxi did nothing but run his fingers over the raw place and shake his head. Joel at once gave the knife away to his sister, never wanting to touch it again.

"Congratulations, of course," Maxi said, not looking at Father Jonas, who knew what he really thought of the raid. "You're lucky to be alive."

"So is everybody!" Joel threw back his head with its heavy cap of dark, waving hair, and laughed, his teeth white against his tanned face. "I never knew before how lucky everybody is to be alive. Now I see why the rabbis say to give thanks always." He pulled Carolyn down on the couch beside him.

Benjamin was dialing the kibbutz and calling over his shoulder. "We've got to tell Yael he's all right. She must have heard about the raid by now. Hold the details, Joel, I'll be right along."

"It will take them years to make another Tammuz," Joel said when he had finished telling us about his part in the destruction of the Iraqi reactor. He held Carolyn's hand tightly, showing his tension in no other way.

"Time enough, maybe," Father Jonas said, "to make peace instead. Borrowed time."

"All time is borrowed, after all." Benjamin stood at the window, watching the sunrise. "Look, we even borrow the sun. Think how men would scheme and fight if they thought they could own the sun and keep it from shining on anyone who didn't pay them first. It's good, isn't it, that the big things like time and sunshine are only borrowed?"

On the way home to Kiryat Anavim, Benjamin talked to me about his group of young people, who meditated together for the peace of the world. They lived communally, making me feel as if he were no longer mine, but borrowed too.

Yael felt he was hers though, and when we got home gave him such a hug that Dan Dworansky frowned and rubbed his scruffy chin. We had found the two outside by the *tel*, ready to start work on finding a well.

"You've been away too much." Yael let Benjamin go and turned back to the instruments she had set up next to the foot of the *tel*. "Isn't this your home anymore?"

"As much as any place is." Benjamin sat cross-legged beside her on the ground, his hands folded on his lap, his eyes so bright the sunlight seemed to be reflected from their depths. "I don't think of home as here or there. Home is just wherever I happen to be. But yes, in a manner of speaking, if I have a home, it's here."

"Well there's no other home for me," Yael said, writing figures in her notebook, and then pausing to squint through the lens of her instrument. "A still point on the turning world, that's what Kiryat Anavim is. Sometimes I think that if I dug my bare feet into the ground, they'd take root. And that would be all right with me."

"Yael's going to go back and forth between here and the university," Dan put in, extending his tall shadow so that it fell across her in the light of the morning sun. "We've planned it already."

Benjamin said nothing, only drew in the sand with the pointed end of a stick and looked at the two of them as if he knew how little good planning did in the long run.

Suddenly Yael paused, her pencil over her notebook. "If the formulas are right," she said, jumping up, "we've got something to go on. Three points in a row. Dan, get Sol and tell him we'll be digging today."

Benjamin and all the other men of the kibbutz went to work, their bare backs wet and heaving as they dug up the pale reddish earth. Dancing around them on her toes, Yael called out impatiently and pointed where they had gone slightly off course. By that evening the piles of dirt were higher than a tall man's head and still growing. Yet no sign of the well had been uncovered.

"In Exodus, all anyone had to do for water was pray or hit a rock with a stick," Yael fumed, chewing on her pencil. "Too bad that doesn't work anymore."

After a few minutes, one of the men shouted. "Maxi should be here! We've found some kind of rock circle down at the bottom of the hole. Rough, but cut with tools."

"And some steps," another cried. "Go easy. We might hit some clay pots. Looks like we've got an oven." Like everyone who lived in the Israeli countryside, he had become an amateur archeologist.

"Got one. It's broken, though." Dan brought the base of an ancient vase over to Yael and laid it in her hands. "A jug, I think."

"Not exactly a work of art." Yael examined the rough, lumpy surface. "Just an ordinary jug. The sort women must have used every day." She looked in the jug again.

"There's no stain in the bottom," she cried. "Oil or food would leave a stain. It's a water jug!" She tossed it aside and ran to the edge of the hole. "Keep going," she cried. "This is the well my father said would be here!"

She kept them digging until the moon came up and their damp bodies shivered in the evening chill. Fragments of broken water jugs lay everywhere, like the potsherds in Maxi's workroom at the university museum.

"I'm sinking," Dan yelled suddenly. "Pull me up." He was at the bottom of the hole, which was now at least twenty-five feet deep. When we leaned over the edge, between workmen who hauled away bucketfuls of earth drawn by ropes from the bottom, we saw Dan buried to the waist in mud. He caught onto one of the ropes, and we all stood around the circle, watching the water bubble up, darkening the sand, rising from the bottom, reflecting the moon that looked in, too. Yael waved her arms slowly, like some ancient priestess and sang, her upturned face blue-white like the moon.

"*Sh'ma Israel, Adonai elohainu, Adonai echad*." The others picked up her song. "Hear O Israel, the Lord your God is One."

Benjamin sang too, his hands open in front of him, full of moonlight and his voice soft as if he were meditating. When the others began to dance the hora as they sang, he seemed not to hear them at first, but stood smiling at the edge of the new well that had nourished this spot of land perhaps eight thousand years ago, if Maxi were right. Then Benjamin laughed, grabbed me around the waist and pulled me into the circle of dancers.

Closing my eyes, I thought of Joel's bombs dropping deep into Tammuz 1, buying a little time for Israel, just as this well would buy some time for Kiryat Anavim. When time and the well would run out, no one could know. So in each moment, I thought, letting Sol whirl me out of my son's arms into his, we would dance, mindless and glad as atoms. I felt blessed to be alive and dancing, but then I had always been blessed. Only now, since Yeshua had come into my life, I knew it.

The next day was Carolyn's birthday, and Joel wanted me to go with him into the Arab markets in Jerusalem to buy her a present. "Your life is gift enough," Carolyn said, her arm around her tall son's waist, her head against his shoulder. "Stay here with me."

But Joel had it in his mind that today he would find the hand-woven, embroidered Bedouin tapestry his mother said she had always wanted for the empty wall over her bed. Because it was a fine, sunny day, we walked all the way across the Allenby Bridge to the market. Joel strode along beside me in his uniform, his Uzi rifle slung over his back. He was so tall, like Maxi, that he had to bend his head down to pass under the striped canopies hung by the vendors over their stalls, which crowded the sides of the narrow streets of the Arab Quarter.

Sometimes when I walked beside Joel, he seemed to be Maxi at eighteen, and I was the young Dora again, with no marriage, no job, no history. We were in a new country, with all things possible, the future spread out in front of me as far as I could see. At such times I wondered if Benjamin were right that the past no longer existed, for the time that Maxi and I were last together, with no husband, wife, children or distance to separate us was always with me, always real. Now, with Joel walking next to me and wearing an Israeli army uniform like the one Maxi had once worn, the old moment came to life and twenty-five years dropped away so suddenly that I gasped from the vertigo and lightness.

When I took his hand and held it tightly, Joel looked down and smiled. "My mother does that too. It makes me feel like a little kid again, crossing the street for the first time."

"Do you mind?" I thought he must mind, since he was so tough and independent, more like me than like Maxi. As a baby, he had always wriggled out of my arms after being held only a moment, eager to be on his way, while Benjamin had been glad of all the cuddling he could get, and so had Yael. Now Yael had Dan to cuddle her, and Benjamin apparently had no one, perhaps because he had gotten all he needed from me long ago. And of course no one ever cuddled me anymore, except Maxi, when he had energy left over from Carolyn's demands, which wasn't often.

"I used to be embarrassed," Joel was saying, "about having my hand held, I mean. But not now. It feels good. Guess I'm still thinking I'm lucky to be alive. Somebody touching me is a reminder. Dad says no one should need a reminder that he's still alive."

"We could stop by at the museum and visit him afterwards," I said. "You haven't seen the reconstruction he's done on that little statue he found at Jericho. The one that was blown up by the Arabs when you were little. It should be finished just about the same time his book comes out. A whole book on one little statue. Who would read it?"

I found it hard to believe what Father Jonas said about Maxi's book, that the origin of monotheism would now be seen by scholars as a union of male and female, positive and negative, power and love, just because of Maxi's find. My brother had always said that behind complexity was original simplicity, and for him, this statue was a symbol of that primal oneness. "*Sh'ma Israel,*" I said out loud. "The Lord our God is One. That's basically all Maxi's book is about."

"Dad sent out review copies to other scholars," Joel said, stopping to examine some squares of embroidered cloth that an old Arab woman held out. "So somebody must have read the book already. He's just had an offer from some big university in New York to take their chair of Biblical Archeology. Mother wants him to accept. Didn't he tell you?"

My stomach suddenly lurched, and for a moment I was so dizzy I had to hang onto Joel for support. Never had I expected that Maxi would go away. I couldn't even imagine it. He loved me too much to leave me.

"Don't flip out, Aunt Dora." Joel held me up with both hands under my elbows. "Dad's not going anywhere. Last night he told me that he'll decline the offer. He's waiting for the right minute to tell Mother. Don't say anything to her. Just now, nobody's supposed to mention New York because it sets her off. We all told her that New York was more dangerous than the Golan Heights, but she still wants to go home."

Picking up one bright red cloth, I held it out, trying to keep my voice steady as I spoke. "She would never go without you, Joel."

"And I'll never leave this place," he said. "It's part of me. Yael feels the same. This red and gold piece of embroidery is good, isn't it? Shall we settle?"

When I nodded, he began haggling with the woman in Arabic, as was the custom when buying anything in the Arab market. Perhaps it was his uniform that turned her voice shrill, for the woman wrapped her veil more tightly over her face and pointed at the walkway, ordering him to leave. Joel was determined to have the cloth and advanced a step closer. Two young Arabs, their stained white keffiyahs hanging raggedly around their shoulders, their shirts outside their pants, came between two curtains at the back of the shop, one carrying a length of iron pipe.

"You want to buy, soldier boy?" said one in halting Hebrew. "Talk price with me."

Before Joel could turn around, one of the Arabs had swung the pipe against the side of his head, knocking his cap into the pile of Bedouin cloth, leaving a bloody gash in his temple. Almost as Joel hit the floor, the other Arab had torn my nephew's Uzi from his shoulder and the two of them had run back through the curtains, out of sight.

By the time the police arrived a few minutes later, pushing past the shouting crowd who stared at us over each others' shoulders, the two Arabs had vanished in the back alleys of the market, one gun the richer, leaving the Ben-Aris one life the poorer.

My eyes were dry and my face still as I bent over Joel's body, which had fallen curled up on his side, the way I remembered him sleeping when he was a child, not so long ago. These curious, cold people would not see Joel's blood, I said to myself. Would not see me cry. I sat down and took Joel's head in my lap, feeling for a pulse in the unbloodied temple and not finding one.

A policeman squatted down beside me, checking Joel over. "Looks like it was instantaneous. The death, I mean," the officer said. "He didn't suffer. Your son, ma'am?"

"Mine, yes. Nephew, not son." The words came out choked, more like coughing than speech. Joel seemed very much mine, as Yael did, as all the children on the kibbutz did. We cared for them while they were with us and mourned them when they were gone, whoever the parents were. "Ours," I corrected myself.

"The policeman was going through Joel's wallet, taking down his home address and his army identification number. "We get a lot of these attacks on soldiers," he said. "You never know when they'll hit, but it's more likely after some big Arab defeat. That Iraqi raid must have fired them up." He rose and shook my hand over Joel's body, which was about to be put in an ambulance. "Want a ride home, ma'am?" he asked.

"No, I'll walk, thanks." My voice was still not mine, sounding low and gruff as a man's. I was in no hurry to get back to the Jerusalem apartment.

Mechanically, I handed the Arab woman some money, far more than the cloth was worth, and put the red embroidered square into my shopping bag. Carolyn would not need to know her son had died for it, only that it was his last gift to her.

The police had already left the apartment when I arrived. They had stayed with Carolyn until Maxi could be brought from the museum, but now the three of us were alone, waiting for Yael to come from her university laboratory. Carolyn half-lay across Maxi's chest as they sat together on the couch, her face hidden against him.

"I don't believe it," she kept saying between sobs. "I won't believe it."

Maxi said nothing, only ran his hands through her hair and stroked her back. Neither of us wanted to argue the fact of Joel's death with her, knowing she needed time to take it in.

"It didn't happen. It didn't," Carolyn cried, and I remembered Maxi saying the same words, not wanting to believe how bad things were when the bombs fell. If there were a faith that could move mountains, I thought, here it was. Yet the mountains didn't move, and Joel was still dead. I laid the red cloth over Carolyn's hand.

"Joel bought this for your birthday," I said. "He wanted you to hang it over your bed."

Carolyn sat up and studied the embroidery, running her fingertips over the golden flowers sewn thickly over the red field. Suddenly she looked up at me, very still. "He's really dead, isn't he? If he were alive, he'd have brought it himself. That's how I know he's dead." She laid her face against the cloth. "My son, my son," she called out in a hollow voice, that seemed to echo as if she spoke in some large and empty room.

Yael, who had come in without a sound, knelt down at her mother's feet and laid her head on Carolyn's lap. "We'll help you bear it, Mama. Let us help you." She stroked her mother's hands, which were still holding tightly onto the red cloth.

"I want to go home," Carolyn rocked back and forth in Maxi's arms. "I just want to go home."

"Let's go right now," Yael said. "I'll call ahead to Kiryat Anavim, so they'll know what happened."

"No, I mean I want to go home to America." Carolyn stopped rocking and looked up at my brother. "Maxi, will you take me home? I can't live here anymore."

I stood rigid, my hands clenched behind my back, my mouth dry and hanging open, stupid as a fish's, waiting for him to answer. Carolyn was lucky to have her weakness working for her, I thought. If I were nervous like Carolyn, people might give me what I wanted. But no one ever asked me, and I wouldn't know what to say if they did. It would feel so queer to be asked.

Maxi closed his eyes and put his head back against the couch. "We should decide this later," he said finally. "It isn't the time to think clearly."

"I want you to say yes or no right now." Carolyn rubbed her eyes with her knuckles, and then stared up at him like a crazy woman, her hair sticking out every which way. "It's not something I can wait for." She turned to her daughter. "Will you come with us, Yael, and finish university in New York? You're all I have now."

Yael's face was white except for two bright spots on her high cheekbones, and her wide-spaced, slanted brown eyes filled with tears. At first her mouth opened with no words coming out. Then she swallowed and started again. "If you need me, yes. I'll come."

She bowed her head and sat looking at her hands, which lay outstretched on her lap as if she were asking for something to be given or giving something away. Maybe both, I thought, remembering Dan and his body sheltering her from the sharp sunlight.

"Maxi?" Carolyn reached up and touched his face. "Please, yes. Please."

"All right, Carolyn, we'll go to New York." Maxi didn't look at me, and I walked out the door quietly, so they wouldn't notice I was gone.

15

New York..............................1981

When Claire accompanied her daughter up to Buffalo, nobody said much. Paul had stayed behind to work, and Tim was driving, with Julie beside him in the front seat. Annie sat with her grandmother in back. The little girl kept turning her head to one side like a bird whenever Claire spoke to her, for she had not yet learned to see gracefully out of one eye. Every time Claire saw her granddaughter cock her head, she felt a sharp contraction in her chest, as if the impact of the blow were still reverberating through the bodies of them both.

She remembered that at the divorce hearing, Charles affirmed that he loved his daughter and had not meant to hurt her. Tim had pointed out dryly to the judge that it was clear whom Charles had meant to hurt. Charles had sat slumped in his chair beside his lawyer, glowering at Julie, who never once looked at him throughout the hearing. For Julie, Charles no longer existed. She had blocked him out, and where he had been, the edges of her life were coming together, knitting whole.

Only once had Julie broken down and cried, and that was with her father, just after the hearing. Paul had reported to Claire that their daughter felt she was a failure. The only important decision she had made in her short life had been a wrong one, and now she was afraid to decide anything except to join Tim in Buffalo, for Annie's sake. The one thing Julie had been sure of, throughout the divorce, was that Annie should never see her father again. She had been so firm on the subject that even a notoriously hard-nosed judge agreed to interview Anne separately, away from the courtroom in which both parents sat insulated from each other by their lawyers and seven years of history. The seven lean years, Tim called them, promising Julie that the next seven would be fat and happy. After talking to the child, the judge had agreed with Julie that Annie should not see her father until she was eighteen, and then only if she chose to.

As they drove north, Julie said nothing about the trial. It was hard for Claire, as always, to imagine what Julie was thinking. She hoped her daughter was contemplating the promised seven fat years to come, but doubted it. Julie's red-gold hair, parted in the middle, was gently folded back like wings framing her pale face, and tied neatly at the nape of her neck. She was wearing a black turtleneck sweater dress and high black heels. *Julie looks like she's come straight from a funeral,* Claire thought with a sigh. *I wish she'd wear those fluttery pastel dresses I've bought her over the years. They just hang in her closet like ghosts of the woman she could have been. If the girl doesn't put herself together better than this, the next seven years will be lean too.* She hoped Annie would tell her mother to stop wearing black, as she had insisted that Julie cut her hair to shoulder length. She wanted Julie to look more like other mothers, Annie told Claire, as they bounced uncomfortably in the back seat of Tim's little Japanese car.

Certainly the battered women's shelter in Buffalo was not the sort of place to begin the seven fat years. Tim had offered Julie a room in his own apartment, but she was afraid Charles might find her there. So it was the heavily guarded women's shelter that they pulled up to after a nine hour drive from New Jersey. A local Catholic church had closed off the rear part of its under-populated convent. Half a dozen women occupied the small cells and their average of four children apiece slept in an attic dormitory. Tim introduced his family to the minister who had begun the program, a shy little man with thick glasses and a slight, apologetic stammer.

Reverend Jerry had not been successful as a preacher, Tim had explained beforehand, but he had been eloquent enough to persuade a flinty Catholic bishop to let a group of Protestant churches use his convent as a sanctuary for abused women and children. The minister took Julie into his office for a private interview. When the two came out, Reverend Jerry was no longer stammering and Julie was smiling as she talked, her cheeks pink as when she had been a girl.

"I asked him what I could do for the Center," Julie explained as Claire walked back to the car with her. "It turns out they have twenty women on their waiting list. Tim only got me in because Jerry owes him a favor." She pressed her full lips together tightly for a moment. "Some of those women may not live long enough to make it here. I told Pastor Jerry that tomorrow I would start visiting the presidents of every corporation in the city, begging for money. That's what we'll need to build a real sanctuary for these women." As an afterthought she added, "For people like Annie and me."

Her voice was strong and low, not uncertain as it had always been in the past. Claire felt suddenly that she hardly knew this slender young woman whose wide blue eyes always seemed to be focused somewhere far away. *I can't imagine Julie volunteering for anything. What magic did this Pastor Jerry work on her, I wonder.* "Did the minister ask you to give this kind of help?"

"Not exactly. He did say no one will listen to him when he asks for money." Julie pulled two suitcases out of the trunk and began carrying them into the convent before Tim or Claire could help her. "I think he's very shy. Maybe it's time somebody asked *for* him."

"You feel strong enough to do that?" Claire tried without success to take one of the suitcases away from her daughter. *After all she's been through, rest is what she needs,* Claire thought, *not work.*

Julie put down a suitcase and opened the heavy carved wooden door of the convent. She braced herself against it so Claire and Annie could go in first. Then she insisted on picking up the suitcase again.

"No, I'm not strong enough," she said, "but there's no one else to do it. The strength will come from God. These women will be helped." She turned to her mother. "You can't guess how they're suffering. And how lost their children are. What happened to me was nothing compared to what Pastor Jerry told me about the women who come to this sanctuary."

As he drove his mother across town to his apartment, where they would stay for a week, Tim explained to Claire and Paul that Julie was right about the needs of the shelter.

He knew a great deal about it, since he had given *pro bono* legal services to many of the shelter women. *Ah,* Claire said to herself, *that was the favor Pastor Jerry owed him for.* Nowadays she felt like an intelligence agent, piecing together hard-won information, so little did anyone tell her directly.

"Julie used to have a way of sealing people off," Tim said. "Like she knew it would hurt too much to know how they felt. Now she knows, and she can handle how bad it feels. I told Jerry to get her doing something, and he did. Now we'll just stand back and let her do it."

He carried Claire's bag into the apartment, then handed it to her. "Mom? Try not to ask her what she's doing and don't give her any advice about how it should be done, okay? Just watch and let her do her thing."

Not sure Tim was right, Claire stayed on for three weeks longer than she had planned, so that she could watch Julie help Pastor Jerry with St. Monica's shelter. The first thing Julie did was to photograph the women when they arrived at the shelter. After a few weeks she showed the photos to Claire, who went through them silently, feeling sick. One after another the faces stared out at her, some with smashed noses and broken teeth, others with dislocated jaws and eyes swollen shut. *Those men who beat poor Belinda outside the Pentagon,* Claire thought as she studied the faces, *they must have been as sick as the husbands of these women. Family men, all of them, but cruel to their dependents as Nazis were to their prisoners.* She gave the pictures back to Julie, who sealed them in a manila envelope, then wrote a name on the outside.

"Are these men crazy, do you think?" Claire asked. "They can't all have been hit with Agent Orange like your Charles. Is it something built into them that they enjoy hurting people who can't defend themselves?"

"My doctor told me that men can't think and feel at the same time. Something about the two sides of their brain not connecting the way women's do," Julie said. "Empathy is hard for most men. If no one teaches it to them by loving them when they're young, maybe hurting is the only way they know how to interact."

"And anger is the only emotion men are allowed to feel," Claire said. "If they're scared or vulnerable, other men make fun of them." *So they hurt someone else before they can be hurt themselves.* Claire thought of Charles and shuddered.

"That must be the appeal the Nazis had for men," Julie nodded. "Charles liked the Nazis," Julie folded her arms in front of her tightly, as if for protection. "He hated Jews. I think he despised women too, for being weak." She changed the sheets on the extra cot that was meant for Annie, in case the child didn't like dormitory life. "What Charles really hated was anything weak in himself. He'd rather hit me than deal with his own weakness. Christ was a great offense to him, as you can imagine. He said the Crucifixion made him sick, and not from pity."

Claire looked up at Julie, standing sun-drenched, slim, and graceful in front of the single window in the little room. *How could a man want to break this fragile, glowing vessel of life, when he should be filling it with love and children?* Claire rose and put her arms around her daughter, feeling a rush of tenderness for this soft female form that she had brought to life with blood and pain and then guarded against the small dangers of her small world. In the old days, a daughter was given to a larger world that protected her too, just because she was a bearer of life, a chalice of love. *Maybe because we have too many people now, too much life, women are despised and raped and called dirty names.* Claire sighed and let her daughter go.

"You see what men did to Jesus," Julie said, pointing up at the crucifix that still hung on the convent wall, "They seem to be in love with machines and guns that smash life. Didn't Jesus come to teach us better than that?"

Claire's hands felt cold as her daughter spoke, and she rubbed them together, trying to think of what she could say to defend men against Julie's cool, critical observations. *What if Charles has soured her on men forever? She says she'll never marry again. What if she means it?* Thinking how many years it had been taking Tim to purge his emotional toxins, Claire worried about what she might expect from Julie over the next decade.

Tim came in and Julie turned to him. "Did you get me that appointment with the mayor and city council? And the police chief? I want to ask him why his men don't arrest a man for assault and battery when he's broken his wife's arm."

"Yes and yes. The Mayor will see you right after lunch. And I've arranged for you to speak to some women's groups." Tim picked Annie up and hugged her.

"You're in politics now?" Claire could imagine the Countess rolling her eyes, complaining that men protected women from nothing anymore. *Better that the old aristocrat hadn't lived to see Julie making political speeches or arguing with the chief of police. This is my daughter, and I hardly know what these terrible times have made of her.* Claire chewed on a broken thumbnail, willing herself not to criticize.

"Everyone's in politics," Julie said, swinging her black velvet jacket over her shoulder by one finger, "whether they know it or not. Want to go with Annie and me to see the Mayor of Buffalo?"

Claire, feeling like a vestigial organ, followed Julie downtown to City Hall, not knowing what advice she could give her daughter. *What kind of world is it,* she wondered, *where a mother can offer her daughter no better advice than not to get involved with the police?*

"Remember Belinda," she said to Julie as they went into the council chamber. "Once a woman steps out of line, she's going to get punished worse than a man."

"I remember Belinda very well," Julie said, slipping her jacket on. "So does Tim. That's why he's running for Congress. Didn't he tell you Larry Keim has the nomination sewed up?"

Claire felt her eyes burn, and she blinked. *Tim talks to Julie but not to me. No one seems to talk to me anymore, except Paul.* "Has he a chance, do you think?"

"Keim says so. He wants me to speak for Tim at some women's groups. But I'm not sure I want to." Julie pushed open the door to the council chamber and walked to the middle of the room, where she put her briefcase on the table.

Claire sat beside Annie in the second row of chairs, behind the half-dozen portly, middle-aged councilmen who chewed on cigars and nudged each other as they looked Julie over.

"Miss de Montfort?" The Mayor said, standing up and thrusting a hand at her. "Am I saying it right?"

"Pretty close," Julie said, and sat down behind the table. "Nobody gets it exactly right except a Frenchman, and you don't look like a Frenchman to me." She smiled and let her long lashes drop.

The man knew he was being paid a compliment, and he chuckled.

"That's right, young lady, nobody ever thought I was that. Just a meat-hacking Polack, is all." He pushed up his sleeves over thick, hairy arms and smiled, glad to be what he was. "Now, what about this women's shelter you got in mind? Understand, the city has no money to put up women who can't get along with their husbands. I hate to be the one to tell you."

"I've got a promise of matching funds from the presidents of three local corporations." Julie laid out some papers on the desk. "If I can find housing and you can arrange for welfare checks to go directly into a support fund, we're in business."

"Housing's a big problem. We can't afford to build anything," the Mayor said, scratching his belly where his shirt opened. "Recession, you know, and we just strapped ourselves to put up this new City Hall. The citizens wouldn't stand for any more spending, especially to keep families apart."

"I've brought some pictures I'd like you to look at." Julie got up and passed around glossy color eight-by-tens of the women who were waiting to get into St. Monica's. "It's men like you that these women look to for protection. They haven't got anyone else."

She held one picture up. "Ellen was hospitalized last month with a broken jaw and internal injuries. She applied to the shelter, but we had no room. She had to go home, and her husband attacked her again. Three days ago I took this picture of her while she was in a coma. The doctors don't know if Ellen will live. Multiple stab wounds to the face and chest, plus a skull fracture. It wouldn't have happened if she'd had a place to go."

The men passed the picture along, glancing at each other. One waved the picture in the air. "She must have given him some hard time to get this."

"Ellen complained because her husband drank up all the grocery money," Julie answered, her voice even. "They have three children under the age of five. The children were probably giving her a hard time too, because they were hungry."

She smiled at the man and shook her finger at him playfully, as Claire had seen her do at Paul. "You look like the kind of guy who'd take care of a wife-beater fast. Too bad you weren't there."

The man looked down at his fists, then after a pause nodded at Julie. "Sam," he said to the mayor, "What say we offer the little lady funds to match what those corporations give, if she can find a place? Can't have this sort of thing going on. Someone's got to take charge."

"You think you've found a place these women can live?" The Mayor looked through the pile of pictures, holding each one at a distance. *Either because he wanted to see more clearly,* Claire thought, *or because he wants to keep the whole evil business at arm's length.*

"I'm seeing the Bishop this afternoon," Julie said, gathering up her pictures and laying them in the briefcase. "He has a convent outside town that he may decide not to sell. It would be a good place for the children. The kind of place men like you would want to see children raised."

"Do we need a vote?" The Mayor nodded to his secretary. "Just note down that we'll match any corporate funds raised, and we'll put the welfare payments into a shelter account. Keep me posted, Miss de Montfort." He shook Julie's hand. "You keep up the good work, and we'll back you all the way."

Outside, Julie tied up her hair in a bun and wrapped a black silk scarf over it, tying the ends at the nape of her neck. "They're not bad men. You just have to remind them now and then that their only reason for being alive, biologically speaking, is to protect females and their young. Want to go with me to see the bishop? He's the main one we have to convince. And he doesn't care about his biological duty. He's celibate."

Claire meekly followed her daughter and Annie into the bus that delivered them to the diocesan office building. It stood next to a sprawling gothic church that looked like a wedding cake. "I've heard he isn't much for charities," Claire said as the tall carved door closed behind them. "Just wants to keep the Catholic schools going."

"We'll see about that." Julie gave her name to the secretary and whispered to her mother. "To him, I'm Julie Frazier. Tim's tangled with him a couple of times. The de Montfort name wouldn't do me any good."

"Why would Tim fight with a bishop?" Claire tried to imagine herself as a young person fighting with the Bishop of Rheims and gave up.

"Tim asked the bishop for support against Vanderzell's effort to smear him as a jailbird. But the Bishop needs funding for his schools, and Vanderzell's rich friends pay the bills. He and Tim didn't part friends."

"Won't the bishop want to sell the convent for more money?" Claire knew that bishops were not known for giving away million-dollar properties.

Before Julie could answer, a priest opened the door and ushered them into the bishop's huge, mahogany-paneled office. Without rising, the bishop gestured them to chairs. He was very old, with a hard brown face wrinkled as a walnut. Julie sat on the edge of her chair, her white-gloved hands folded in her lap.

"First of all, Your Grace, I'd like to thank you for letting us use the convent at St. Monica's," she said. "The women and children at the shelter asked me to thank you. If you hadn't helped us, we would have been in the street. You've been very kind."

"Not kind enough, apparently," the old bishop said, rubbing his amethyst episcopal ring and turning down the corners of his thin mouth. "I gather you women want the convent all to yourselves now."

"Not St. Monica's. We're asking for the big empty convent at the edge of town, St. Mary's of Mercy. We need space."

"St. Mary's is on the market." The bishop's mouth tightened. "It's not up for a giveaway to homeless women."

"It's not just the women who need a home, it's the children." Julie leaned forward and held out a photograph. "There's no more room for them at St. Monica's. Look, here's a picture of the Donnelly kids. Four of them in one room with their mother. And here's a picture of her, just after her release from the hospital. We've had to turn away families like this. Twenty of them, just this month."

The bishop looked over Julie's pictures, his face not changing, and handed them back. "Tragic, of course. But the Church is here to save souls, mind you, not support unfortunates like the Donnellys. Have you asked the Mayor for money?"

"He's agreed to pay support for operations, if you contribute the building, Father. Do you mind if I call you Father instead of Your Grace?" Julie tipped her head to one side and smiled, then looked down modestly.

The bishop cleared his throat. "It's been a long time since anyone called me Father. No, I don't think I would mind in the least. But understand, young lady, the parishioners of this diocese wouldn't want me laying any more financial burdens on them. This idea of yours sounds to me like a very big burden indeed."

"The president of Mod Computers didn't think so," Julie replied. "He offered $50,000, and said I should come to you."

"Chuck Murphy said he'd give $50,000?" The bishop rocked back in his chair. "He never gave me more than five. How'd you manage to squeeze that much out of him?"

"I just asked. Maybe it was God who talked him into it." Julie wrapped her gloved hands tightly around one of her crossed knees, telling Claire how tense she was under her appearance of calm. "By the way, Mr. Murphy says to tell you that hotel chain isn't going to buy St. Mary's convent after all. They're going out of business. In fact, Mr. Murphy thinks you'd be better off to wait on the sale and let us lease the building for five years, until the recession's over and prices go up."

"Well, that's a thought," said the bishop, frowning. "I'd counted on the motel, damn it. Haven't had another bidder since I put the convent up for sale."

"If we could use the building for five years," Julie kept her voice soft and her eyes cast down chastely as a nun's, "we could approach the state about buying it as a permanent women's and children's shelter. It could be a model for the whole country, and the diocese would get good press. We've planned a big media promotion of the idea, Father, and it could help your drive to make Buffalo an archdiocese, don't you think? And that's a cause close to all our hearts."

She raised her blue eyes to his and tipped her head charmingly to one side, reminding Claire of Annie. "And besides, as you've always said, the Church must step forward as a protector of children, born as well as unborn."

"I did say that." The bishop rubbed his furrowed chin. "And it wouldn't hurt our image to have some corporal works of mercy in the pipeline. Not at all." He swung his chair around and looked at the wall for a few moments, thinking. Then he turned back to Julie.

"Well, young lady, you've got your convent. A lease for $100 a month. But only for five years, mind. Then a sale will be necessary, to the state if you can manage it. Otherwise the diocese will sell it to whoever has the cash."

He scribbled out an authorization and stamped it with the episcopal seal. "Here, this will allow you to take over St. Mary's. Mind you now, not a cent from the diocese for expenses."

Julie knelt to kiss his ring with a great show of filial gratitude, and he patted her on the head. "Perhaps I'll give the diocesan Christmas party at the new shelter," he said. "Could you arrange press coverage for the event?"

"Certainly, Father," Julie answered, bowing her way out of the room as if he were the pope. "I'll arrange everything."

When they were outside the building, she pulled off her scarf and shook out her hair in the sunlight. "Well," she said. "We have a place now."

"But you had to scrape and fawn for it," Claire objected. *How did Julie come by this ability to manipulate? It was never a strong point of mine. I always just blurted out what I had to say, and then got angry when I was turned down. Maybe that's why I never felt as close to Julie as I did to Dora Lebenthal. Dora and I were the same.* Claire had to admit to herself that she often resented how Julie could get from Paul what she herself could not, and now she understood why.

"Your father must have taught you how to do that. You never learned it from me."

Julie flushed and began walking fast toward the bus stop, Annie's hand in hers. "I can tell how I must look to you. But I know what works in my world. In yours, everything goes the way you want it to, but I'm not used to that."

So Paul is right. Julie feels inferior to me, Claire thought in a rush. *She couldn't act like me, so she wouldn't act at all. And now I may have pounded her right back into the ground again, just as she's climbing out of the hole she's lived in for so long.*

She hurried forward and hugged her daughter. "I do my work alone," Claire said. "To satisfy myself. You work for the good of other people. There's no comparison here, Julie. A lot of women's lives will be better because of what you've done today. That's all that counts."

Julie brushed tears out of her eyes and didn't answer. But she held her mother's hand until the bus came, and Claire could not remember such a moment since her daughter had been a little girl.

Until she had helped Julie move out of St. Monica's, Claire stayed in Buffalo. For three weeks, she, Julie, and Pastor Jerry had worked together to move thirty-five women and fifty children into their new home. Julie decided to put all the school-age children into the enormous third-floor dormitory. She and Pastor Jerry built partitions so that the children could be placed four to a roomlet, as she called it, with members of their own age group. She had read that this plan had been successful on Israeli kibbutzim, and wanted to try it at St. Mary's. Mothers rotated the night supervision duty among themselves, but the real tending was done by the older children, whom Julie herself took charge of. Even the lazy adolescent boys and sulky teen age girls, Claire noticed, would act grown-up when Julie spoke seriously to them in her soft voice, treating them as co-workers, not children, as their mothers did.

When Claire looked into the dormitory to say good-by to Annie, she found her grand-daughter training a six-year-old boy to change his little brother's diapers.

"Watch out for the pinpoint, Harry," Annie said, her voice as quiet and sure as her mother's. "See, you have to put your own finger just barely against the sharp part, so you won't risk sticking the baby."

Harry worked slowly, his brown eyes wide and his plump cheeks tense, his concentration reminding Claire suddenly of Maxi's when Dora had taught him to peel potatoes.

"I can't get him to hold still," Harry said finally, trying to hold the flopping diaper together as the baby kicked.

"Try giving him something to hold," Annie advised, folding her arms, letting Harry cope.

"How about I give him my Rubik Cube?" Harry said after a moment's thought, and pulled the toy out of his pocket. "Hey, look at that. He likes it! He's holding still!"

"Don't stop to look," Annie urged. "Work fast or he'll get bored again."

"When he's bigger, I'll teach him to play with it right, the way I do," Harry said, pinning the diaper awkwardly, so that one side flapped out like a wing. "Am I done now? Can I go out and play?"

"Put him in the play pen and go on out." Annie said. "I'm on duty for another hour." She snatched up the toy and ran after him to the door. "Here, you forgot your cube."

"Oh yeah." Harry took it from her, and then paused to look back at the baby. "If he cries, call me. I can always get him to stop."

"Harry's very proud that he can get the baby to stop crying," Annie said to her grandmother. They watched the boy run down the long hall, its walls broken by niches for statues and votive candles. "He'll be a good daddy when he grows up." Her face turned away for a moment, and Claire wondered if the child were thinking of her own father.

She reached out and smoothed Annie's thick, coarse brown hair "And you'll be a good mother. You're learning to be one now."

Annie shook her head. "I don't want to get married and be a mother," she burst out, her hands over her face. "Not ever! I'll be a nun like Sister Mary Rose, or a teacher, but I'll never get married."

Sighing, Claire held the girl close to her, saying good-by and wishing Tim was there to remind Annie that not all men were like her father. Tim came every weekend to take Annie wherever she wanted to go. She had even begun to accompany him on political trips since he had begun to seek nomination for a congressional seat. Whenever Tim came in the door, Annie's face lit up, and she ran to him, raising her arms. Her uncle would then grab Annie and dangle her high above the floor, although she was getting much too tall for this old game. *Tim needs a child, Claire said to herself as she watched the two, and Annie needs a man to father her. It's just as well they're all staying in Buffalo together.*

As she said good-by to the little family, Claire felt her work with them was done. Even though she wanted to hang around on the margins and advise them for a while longer, it was time to let them go. *Too bad it had to happen,* Claire thought, *just as I'm becoming wise enough to tell them something useful. Once grandmothers were necessary to a family's survival, but now, they're just supposed to get on an ice flow and drift away like superfluous old Eskimos.* Paul's mother, after all, had been forced to learn the same lesson, and Claire had been the one to drive her off. It seemed to Claire as if times were changing so fast that the old had no relevant wisdom to give the young. Or perhaps the young did not trust any advice from the past. Paul had told Claire as much, but like the young, she had to learn the truth for herself. There would be a brief reprieve, since Tim was driving her back to New Jersey, but after that he would be gone again. Her soul felt like a tree stripped of its leaves by a winter wind.

When she got home to Pine Lake, Claire said to Paul as they sat down for dinner, "I don't know whether Annie got this hatred of marriage from Julie or Tim. He's brushed off the idea, you know, ever since Belinda was killed."

They had been waiting for Tim to arrive after his conference with Larry Keim in New York, but the food was growing cold.

"Nobody wants to get married anymore," Paul said, touching his napkin to his mouth after sipping a little wine. "Tim's not the only one. Besides, he's only twenty-eight. Hardly a confirmed bachelor like your Mr. O'Hara."

Claire blushed and looked down at her plate. Even after fifteen years and a confession to Paul, she was still ashamed of the time she had briefly lusted after Brian O'Hara in the choir stall of St. Michael's church.

"Anybody home?" Tim's big voice called at the door and echoed down the hall. "I'm on television in five minutes. Just made it here in time."

He took a pork chop from the plate and began to eat and talk at the same time, waving his fork for punctuation. "My opposition's a company man, Barry Gordon. Worked for defense industries, on the board of two major chemical corporations, one of them owned by Vanderzell. I don't know who's bought him to run against me, but it's going to be expensive for them. Got any salad left?"

Tim's thick dark hair was standing on end the way Paul's did when he scratched his head and forgot to smooth his hair down again. A small piece of pork clung to his thick mustache, and Claire picked it off.

"I was saving it for later." Tim grinned at their old joke. "Can we make an exception to your rule, Dad, and turn the TV on during dinner?"

Paul, who had allowed a television set back in the house only when Julie was married and gone, pushed back his chair and led the way to the living room.

"This debate with Gordon," Paul said, "it's about his links to Vanderzell Chemical interests, isn't it? I thought Gordon wouldn't dare run, after that conviction for taking kickbacks from industry. Everyone knows that he let toxic wastes to be dumped in his district."

"You've been reading up on all this, haven't you?" Claire was surprised at how much her husband knew. "I hope you're impressed, Tim."

"I only hope other people know as much," Tim said, peeling his apple carefully. He believed pesticides made the eating of contaminated skin a suicidal act. "It was Gordon's boss that was convicted, not him. Gordon was just a sidekick. Got off clean and easy. Now he makes like he never heard of Vanderzell and the Canal scandal. I got him dead to rights, though. Watch!"

Claire hitched her chair up close to the screen, not wanting to miss anything of this debate. General Gordon, as he liked to be called, although he had been a civilian since the Korean War, was a bulbous sixty-year-old, his soldiering days obviously behind him. Because of his military status, the general was allowed to speak first and came down forcefully at the end of each sentence, as if firing a weapon at his young opponent. His voice was strong and certain, but the substance of what he said was so vague, Claire couldn't get hold of it.

"Is he really saying that a war protester can't be trusted? That you don't have a family to protect as he had?" She turned to Tim and put her hand on his arm, reassuring him that he had a family as real as the general's. "It's going to hurt you in the election that you're not married, Tim."

"Maybe among the older voters, yes. I'm counting on Annie to help me out there, and Julie too."

On the television screen, Tim was calm and deliberate as he answered Gordon. "It seems to me you can trust a man who goes to jail for his beliefs more than you can trust a man who gets paid to believe what he's told to. Letting chemical companies manufacture poisons for the U.S. government is the real issue between us, General. How about we discuss Vanderzell's contract with the government for a delivery system to spread lethal viruses all through the eastern hemisphere?"

"I don't know what you're getting at, young man" the general replied coolly, looking from side to side as if to secure support among saner, older onlookers who would smile away Tim's words.

"Then we'll get down to cases." Tim held up a letter and read from it. 'If you are elected, General Gordon, you can expect to be given a place on the Defense Committee. We will welcome your expertise, as a man who for so long served the private sector as a member of the Vanderzell Chemical Board.'" Tim held up the paper and the camera zoomed close in, showing the signature of the House Minority leader. "Isn't it true, Mr. Gordon, sorry —General—that your company, Vanderzell Oil, stands to gain billions for its part in arming America with weapons that go against international agreements? Isn't it true that if we use bacteriological warfare, we can't prevent viruses from sweeping across the whole planet, the U.S. included?"

"My corporation was working for national defense before you were born, young man," General Gordon muttered, no longer smiling. "Since I've resigned from the Board to run for this sacred office, it would be inappropriate for me to speak here about Vanderzell Oil."

"I understand that Vanderzell has promised you your old job once you've finished serving in this sacred office. The show must go on. As you say, your company has been around for a long time." Tim stepped toward the man, as if he were in physical pursuit. "Wasn't it around in 1942, when Vanderzell signed an agreement with Hitler to protect the interests of the German chemical cartel? Didn't Hitler agree to do the same for Vanderzell, if the Nazis won."

"That's ancient history." The general gripped his lectern tightly. "I was only a lieutenant then, serving in the Normandy invasion." He looked around, proud to have scored.

"My point is that those who don't learn from history will likely repeat it." Tim paced back and forth behind his lectern, hands folded as if in prayer, seeming to have forgotten about the cameras.

"Yes, I had forgotten," he said when Claire asked. "I just wanted to nail Gordon. Pass the cookies, please."

The screen-Tim went on. "If the same men who produce munitions and biological weapons serve in government offices that buy those very weapons, what chance do we have for an arms control agreement, would you say, General? Or don't you want one?"Tim turned to the unseen audience as to a jury, his deep set eyes fierce. "Do you think he does?"

When the other man reddened and did not reply, Tim hammered on. "Don't your backers have a vested interest in war, General? The thing is, the rest of us, especially the young ones like me, have a vested interest in staying alive, not in lining the pockets of the nation's corporate bosses."

"Or of Vanderzell," added Paul, who was sitting on the couch, his cookie untasted in his hand. "Isn't that what you're really saying?"

"It's as far as I could go without getting slapped with a slander charge. No proof yet, but I'm working on it."

General Gordon's jowls shook as he spoke, and his voice trembled. "I don't know anything about that letter. And I'm not responsible for what a company I no longer work for may have done while I served my country in the war."

"Then I assume that if you're re-elected," Tim said softly, "you won't accept any position on a defense-related committee? And that you won't return to Vanderzell Chemical's board, now that you know of the company's genocidal research?"

The general's mouth opened and closed a few times. "I won't make any promises until I talk to my advisors," he finally choked out. "Promises are sacred to me young man, though you may not understand that, being a draft dodger."

"I understand very well, General," Tim finished, closing his notebook and folding his hands over it. "The only ones I'd consult about my promises are my constituents and my conscience, which was what wouldn't let me fight in Vietnam."

The debate was over and Tim switched off the TV. "My goal was to get him to admit that he'd been bought by corporate interests. Think I did it?"

Claire clapped her hands. "You did. I hope Vanderzell saw it."

"If not, he'll hear about it soon enough." Tim looked soberly at her and put his hand on her shoulder. "How'd you like to come stumping with me? Could I borrow her for a few weeks, Dad?"

"Would I have to make speeches?" Claire put one hand to her heart. "I've never made a speech in my life."

"Only if you want to. Just giving interviews would take a load off me. And you could back up Julie at women's clubs."

Paul lit his pipe and stared into the glowing bowl. "Could this campaign be dangerous, do you think? Vanderzell must know you're gunning for him, not just Gordon."

"Now that I've got their whole scheme out in the open, they wouldn't dare." Tim smiled, tossing his jacket over one arm and hugging Claire with the other. "Gotta run now. Press conferences in Manhattan tonight. Now that I've got Gordon on the run, I have to keep pushing."

Tim pushed so hard that by November 1, Claire was too exhausted to give the last speech, scheduled for the University Women's Club in Albany. *Julie tends to develop a sore throat at critical moments, on purpose,* Claire was sure, *just to push me into public speaking.* But this time, Julie decided to speak herself. Tim was to make a brief appearance afterwards, when husbands were invited for a coffee hour, so he could speak to the men.

As she watched Julie stand easily at the lectern, her black knit dress looped at the waist by a gold chain, Claire wondered where the dreamy-eyed, uncertain girl of a year before had gone. Now her daughter spoke in a strong voice, charming the audience as she had charmed the Mayor of Buffalo, carrying them with her. At the end, she had a questioner who was distinctly not charmed.

"Isn't it true that your brother was imprisoned for rioting in a war protest?" a man called out from the back of the room. He had just entered the hall and was lounging against the door jamb, his hand in his pocket.

"Yes, like a lot of people who worked together to stop the war," Julie cut him off crisply and disengaged the microphone from around her neck.

"No more questions, please. I see my brother's coming in. Can some of you ladies bring more chairs and make room for the men? Please leave some room in the middle for him to pass."

Tim was working his way through a forest of waving hands, shaking two at once as he went. His long, lean body was encased in a conservative dark blue suit. *He looks more like a bank executive than like my son,* Claire thought.

Tim smiled and blinked while flash bulbs went off and photographers stood up on chairs to get better shots. Men were now mixing with women in the big hall, finding their wives and trying to shake the candidate's hand. Claire could hardly see Tim as he moved up the middle aisle toward the platform on which Julie stood.

Suddenly Claire leaned forward, her hand at her mouth, for she saw the man who had challenged Julie press through the crowd circling Tim, holding what Claire thought at first was a camera. As the man lifted his arm, Claire saw a gun and screamed, "Tim, get down!"

The shot echoed in the hall, and Tim dropped to the floor. The circle of people started to close around him, but the men who had come in with Tim broke through and stood next to him.

"Everybody back," Larry Keim was shouting. "Call an ambulance."

"I'm a doctor," said one of the men in the crowd. "Let me through."

Claire stood silently in her place, looking where her son lay on the floor. She hardly noticed Julie's arm around her. Police had closed the doors and rushed in to drag the struggling gunman from the hands of the men who held him. The gunman shouted as he was pulled through the crowd and out the door, but Claire couldn't hear what he said.

All she heard was the voice of the doctor, who knelt beside Tim and turned him over on his back. The crowd quieted, waiting, while the doctor opened Tim's jacket and shirt. Claire gasped as she saw the blood running down his body, matting the hair on his chest, and she sagged against Julie.

Oh God, God, she prayed, *remember what a beautiful man we've made together, you and I. Don't let him die.* She remembered holding Tim when he was just born, when he fell off his first bike, when he lost Belinda, all in a flash before her eyes as if she herself were dying.

"High chest wound," the doctor called out. "A good thing he started to drop when he did, or he'd be dead. Somebody tell his family they can ride with us in the ambulance."

Claire didn't need to be told, but was down the steps and waiting at the door when the paramedics came in with the stretcher. All the way to the hospital and throughout the operation to remove the bullet, she sat silent, her mind focused on Tim's heart, willing it to beat strongly, willing the bullet away from it. *God help him,* she kept repeating silently. *Christ have mercy, Kyrie eleison.* Sometimes she was asking and sometimes demanding, but the words were the same, echoing in her ears like sirens, deafening her to the sounds in the hospital hall. She longed to see again the momentary vision that had once convinced her Tim was safe, but this time she saw nothing except the gleaming tiles in front of her, and the occasional nurse who stopped to tell her that the bullet was lower than had been initially thought, and too near the heart for the operation to be finished quickly.

Only when the surgeon stepped out into the hall, slipping off his mask, did Claire close her eyes and lean back, a wave of resignation sweeping through her as she stopped praying and surrendered. *He's yours, God, your will be done. Just help me bear it, whatever it is.* For a moment she stood suspended in a breathless peace, feeling light and warm, sheltered as if she were in her mother's arms.

The surgeon spoke to Julie, who had leaped up to meet him, and Claire overheard as if from a great distance. "We got the bullet from just above the left ventricle," the doctor said. "A near thing, but he'll be fine. And we fixed a leaky valve in his heart as well. You can see him in a few hours, as soon as he starts coming around."

Claire sank down, folded her hands on her lap, and took deep breaths. She wanted to thank God, but had no words left. All she could do was feel the warmth that had settled around her, while deep in her ears a waterfall of music washed her mind clear of any thoughts at all.

A week later, at home with Paul, she tried to explain how she had felt at the hospital. "Like a stone had rolled away from a hole in my heart and light had come pouring out of it," she said, marveling at the memory. "When I saw Tim, I could hardly talk. It was as if I'd had a stroke. The mouth would open, but no words came."

"We have much to be grateful for. I have never thanked God for what we have, but I should." Paul sat down hard on his chair. Claire's news had apparently made him feel too weak to stand up any longer.

"You have no idea what God has done for us. The surgeon told me that Tim had a defect in his left ventricle that could have killed him at any time. It was repaired during the operation to remove the bullet. So in its way, the bullet was a gift."

"And Tim?" Paul clasped his hands together waiting to hear. "Did he say how he felt?"

Claire poured some tea for them both. "Only that the doctors had told him he would be better than new in a month," she laughed, blowing on her tea to cool it, then looking around her guiltily as she still did whenever she behaved like a peasant. *Though the Countess has been dead so many years,* Claire thought, *her presence is still in the room, at least for me*. "He said he'd wanted a rest after the campaign, and now he can take one with a clean conscience."

"He won by 250,000 votes," Paul said. "The last returns came in just an hour ago. It was no contest."

Claire put her cup down. "I wish he'd lost," she cried out. "Because now there'll be another election and another. And whoever it was that tried this time will try again."

"The newsmen say the assassin was some Vietnamese war veteran, a mental case." Paul took both her hands. "He acted alone. Believe that and your mind will be more at ease."

"You believe it?" Claire clung to him. "I can't."

"He'll be protected, now that he's in office," Paul said, "as protected as anyone ever is. The world is no gentler, Claire, than it was forty years ago. Mr. Marcus told me so the other day, and he remembers Bergen-Belsen. He sent you a note, by the way. It seems your music made quite a hit in Jerusalem."

Paul handed her the letter, and she read Mr. Marcus's awkward English aloud.

Dear Lady,

You will be winning an award for your kindness to our people during the war, as I have been told by the Israeli Government. We would wish you to visit Jerusalem this coming March, with your family, so that we can bestow on you our thanks in first person. Father Jonas Grey, who has arranged a performance of your Easter Liturgy at St. Elizabeth's Church, begs the honor that you should stay with him at the Anglican rectory. A joyful occasion this will be for us all.

Your friend,
Yehuda Marcus

"Only four months from now." The note fell from her hands and she looked up into Paul's face. "Next year in Jerusalem," she said.

16

Dora's Journal

Israel..............................1982

Because Maxi had to finish his year at Hebrew University, he and Carolyn couldn't leave Jerusalem until after Passover. For once I was glad Maxi was a professor and was bound by the academic calendar. Yet it was the world of the university and his discovery of that ancient monotheistic god figure which had brought him the offer of the job in New York. Sometimes I hated the autographed copy of Maxi's book, *The Primal God*, though I kept it on my dresser beside my menorah. Maxi had autographed the fat volume under the dedication, which was to me and not to Carolyn. Waiting for Maxi to stop by and pick me up so I could accompany them to the airport, I opened the book and leafed through it, trying to understand what my brother really believed God is.

The picture of the statue smiled blandly at me from the frontispiece. It looked like some of the statues Maxi had brought back from a dig in Ethiopia. Only the first half of Maxi's book was about the find at Jericho. The rest was about his theory that worship of a female creator began in Africa and spread from their over Asia and Europe, where eventually the male aspect had been joined to the female.

I had tried to explain to Maxi that the Ha-Shem of the Jews was as wise and loving as both father and mother, and that the God I knew had no gender. I wanted to tell him about the motherly love of Yeshua. Yet I could not begin to explain to him how I had come to love an embodiment of God who appeared not in dead, ancient soil but in the living human heart.

Looking out the window, I kept my finger in the book to hold my place. I was waiting for my brother's car, which would take him on the first leg of his journey away from me to America. Like Lev and Benjamin, Maxi had turned his back on the kibbutz. Lev and Joel had ended as warriors, not farmers, while Maxi had from the start been a scholar, living in his head or in books. Benjamin, it was true, still loved the land, but paid it no more than lip service while he pursued his scientific studies and New Age meditation in Jerusalem. No woman, including myself, seemed able to draw him into love. His path was solitary, like that of my beloved Rabbi Noah, and I grieved the loss that both of them had suffered by not taking a woman into their lives.

Since Yael was accompanying her parents to New York, only I of all my family would be left to tend the gardens of Kiryat Anavim. Men like Sol and Dan stayed, because they were simple, had no ambition for themselves, had no curiosity about the outside world. But all my men had left. I looked at the picture of the statue again, the god-goddess who had been buried and alone for so long, feeling that I too bore the heaviness of the earth on top of me. I felt like a seed must feel as it waits underground through the long winter, not knowing if it will ever be set free into air and light.

Dan knocked at the door and the two of us stood near the window, he trying to turn his head away so I wouldn't see how red his eyes were.

"Will they come back, do you think?" The sturdy young giant held his arms around himself as if he were shivering. "Maybe New York will be too cold. Yael hates the cold."

"New Yorkers live inside all the time," I said, speaking strongly, although I wasn't sure. "So they don't notice the weather."

"Inside? All the time?" Dan shook his head and pushed back the dark waves that fell across his face. "Yael could never stand that." His voice rose hopefully. "She won't like New York."

"Yael will be at the university studying science," I said, trying to let him down fast, before he was out of sight like a kite with a snapped string. "She'll have no time to be unhappy. Look, there they are."

Under one arm Dan settled a package wrapped in flower printed paper and followed me down the stairs into the driveway. "Doesn't it seem wrong to you that such a female woman as Yael should study chemistry and physics like a man? It seems all wrong to me. What does she want to do that for?"

"To be complete, I suppose. To be as much as she can be. As much man, as much woman. We live in odd times, Dan. A woman fears to be feminine, for she doesn't want to be some kind of slave."

When we got in the car, I asked Father Jonas what he thought about the gender of God.

"Dora, remember Paul wrote that there is no slave or free, male or female in Christ?"

"You can't be sure," Yael objected. "What if there's no divinity at all? What if man himself is all the god there is?" She clutched Dan's gift, a white shawl of Bedouin wool, close around her in the air-conditioned car.

"We've tried making man into God," Maxi answered, steering around a herd of sheep and an Arab shepherd who waved his stick over their backs to hurry them out of our way. "All we got were gods like Hitler and Stalin and hells like Bergen-Belsen. When you kill off God, it seems to me, you kill off the divine in man too. Then there's no reason to treat your neighbor as if he were any more than a combination of chemicals. I have no experience of God, but I understand the need for God, if that makes any sense."

"Then why didn't you put those feelings in your book, Maxi?" Father Jonas spoke gently, not arguing, just wanting to know. "Because it isn't scholarly to go beyond the evidence?"

"Maybe by the end of our century, we'll have a clue as to the reality of a spiritual force wrapped invisibly around the material world, like the numinous envelope of mind wrapped around our physical bodies. If the human race is still around." Maxi said, slowing down as the traffic near the airport grew heavier. "Until then, my little statue is just a beautiful dream of original oneness, and we are merely dreamers."

"Maybe it's the world of the concentration camps and bombs that's the dream," Benjamin said, leaning his head back against the seat. "Maybe it's a nightmare we're waking up from, one by one and moving into a heaven that's been right here around us all the time."

"Well this world seems to me all there is." Yael sat up straight, away from Dan's encircling arm. "While the Nazis were building ovens to destroy the Jews, rabbis sat around talking about just such stuff as you're talking about now. And what good did all that talk of God do anyway?" She jerked her new shawl tightly around her and stared out at the red, barren hills rolling like ocean waves as far into the distance as we could see. Joel's death had hit Yael hard. She no longer wanted to talk with Maxi and Benjamin about scientific or metaphysical theories. Now only the here and now seemed real to her.

"Well, for one thing," Benjamin said, "the Nazis are gone and we Jews are still here, talking about God."

"Not me," Yael retorted. "All I care about now is finding out what it was my grandparents knew that scared the Nazis at Farben, and when I do, letting everybody know it. It's all I have left."

There was something of the warrior in Yael, despite her delicate face and pale gold halo of hair. I recognized that spirit because I had seen it in Lev. Yael had cried only once since leaving childhood behind, and that was because as a girl she would not be allowed to carry a gun during her army service.

Dan ran a large, clumsy hand over her hair and stared into her face, moistening his red lips in preparation for speech. "You could learn all you need to know here at Hebrew University or at the Rehovoth Institute," he said. "You don't have to go away."

"I promised and I'm going." Yael's voice began harshly and ended high-pitched and uncertain when she looked up at Dan. "My father says that in the States I can learn more than I can in Israel. Maybe you'll come too."

Dan withdrew his arm and kept his eyes on a plane dropping to the runway. "No. I belong here. Just like you used to say you do."

As the car pulled into the parking lot, Carolyn jumped out, holding open the door. She had not spoken much to me since Joel's death, but then she hadn't spoken much to anyone, since that day. "People belong wherever they choose to be," she said crossly, pulling out her suitcase from the trunk. "No use getting mystical about where you hang your hat."

I followed her and Maxi into the terminal building, watching my brother walk slower and slower, as if he were being blown backward by the wind that stung our faces with the little grains of sand it carried. Suddenly he turned and took my hand in his.

"I told the airline to hold an extra ticket, Dora," he said, bending his head down toward mine. "Will you come too? At least for a little while?"

I was glad there were no tears in my eyes, only the throat lump which they couldn't know was there. For a moment I swallowed hard, unable to answer him, wanting to say yes, I would go with him, yes that nowhere would be home without him, yes, we would always be together.

Hanging onto Maxi's hand, I stood looking around at the low, concrete buildings and the flat, windswept stretch of rocky desert to the east. High above were the reconnaissance planes keeping watch day and night against the constant Hezbollah incursions over the Lebanese border. All around us were young soldiers, carrying their rifles on their backs and laughing as if they bore no burden at all. For a little while, I imagined myself back in the vegetable garden of the kibbutz, my shovel over my shoulder like a weapon, my feet so deep in earth they seemed to sprout roots and hold me like a tree planted by the waters.

Gently I disengaged my hand. "We'll be together in a way," I said, pulling his head down so I could kiss his cheek. "We always will."

Maxi buried his face in my neck, not answering, and held me so long that Carolyn had to pull him away, saying they would miss the plane if he didn't hurry.

Only when the big jet had lifted off the ground and drawn its wheels out of sight like a bird tucking its legs up behind as it begins to fly, did I let Father Jonas hold me while I cried. Later, on the way back to Jerusalem, I would have done the same thing for Dan, since he seemed in need of it, but he just ground his teeth, stared out the window, and answered me in monosyllables. Without Yael, he seemed harder and less communicative, for she had been the voice and heart of the couple, he the strong arms and hands. Like Maxi and me, those two had grown up twinned, and when separated, they lost their other half. Yael did not know that yet, but in time, I was sure she would.

Dan pointed out the window and upward at the war planes streaking north toward the border. Israel had been attacked once again just the night before by invaders from Lebanon, who had burned a kibbutz and killed three women on duty at the infant house.

"Leaving now is a sort of betrayal," Dan said, his voice tight in his throat. "Like running away in battle. I can't forgive her for leaving just when she's needed most."

"When we're all needed," Father Jonas added, and I remembered that he had given public support to Israel's retaliatory raids against PLO bases in Lebanon. "There are so few of us in this little country. So many of them."He stopped the car in front of the kibbutz residence hall. "We can't afford to lose even one. God keeps count of us like sparrows. That's why the Lebanese Christians are fighting alongside the Israelis. Whether Christians or Jews, we know we are both sparrows fighting winter hawks."

As he spoke, I felt my heart contract as if it had dried up in the instant of recognition that my brother was gone from me for good. Until that moment, I had not felt his going as a betrayal, but suddenly I was angry, not so much at his abandonment of me, but of Israel at such a time. Maxi had always been a private person, cautious about committing himself, except to those he loved. For him, Israel and even Judaism were abstractions, mere words in the book of life, as he put it. The life itself was going on somewhere else, in the dirt of a dig or around the family table.

Lev's displays of public passion for causes had been incomprehensible to Maxi, who believed nations should conduct their affairs as sensibly as he ran his household on Ha'Maravim Street. If we stopped fighting the Arabs, he reasoned, they would stop fighting us. I think he left when he did rather than admit to himself that the Arabs would never recognize Israel or stop fighting us, however much land we gave back to them. It was not only Carolyn's strategically timed nervous fit about staying in a "war zone," as she put it, that made Maxi leave. Everybody's life in this messy century is being lived in some war zone or other. Ever since the assassination of the president of Egypt, Israel's only ally in the Arab world, we had all felt a sense of heaviness, the kind I remember in London as a child, when the sirens blew before the air raids. Maxi said that for him, the feeling began when Israeli planes destroyed the atomic reactor in Iraq, though he hadn't hurt Joel's pride by telling him so.

"They will do the same to us," Maxi said to me at the time. "One day a nuclear bomb will drop on Tel Aviv or Dimona without any warning, and you can be sure the Arabs won't be gentlemanly like Menachem Begin and schedule the attack when no one is at ground zero."

Of course Maxi had approved of the decision to give the Sinai back to Egypt, but he had no idea what that sacrifice cost. If he had been with Benjamin at Yamit, the Israeli settlement that was destroyed by our own people, he might have been less cheerful about giving away our only secure base between Israel and Cairo. It was the first time in the history of our people, maybe even the history of civilization, that a nation, after being attacked, had given up territory won in battle and settled by its own citizens. Most of us didn't feel as good about the destruction of Yamit as my noble Maxi did. In fact, we felt terrible. Even Benjamin, who was pretty much a dove, hated being told to go down there and clean our people out of the Sinai. He wrote me this letter the day the Egyptians took the Sinai back:

Dear Mother,

How strange that any government calls theirs this stretch of desert, these wrinkles on the earth's face made of valleys between moon-mountains. Last night I went walking and wound up on top of a hill that gave me miles of view. The sunset turned the sea red and for a few minutes the sun hung in the sky as if it were afraid to get wet, just growing fatter and redder until it filled up my eyes.

The noises down in Yamit brought me back to my senses again. Our captain was standing before the new white concrete town and nervously twisting the buttons on his shirt.

"The reason I asked you to come down here, Ben," he said, looking like he had been punched in the head, he was so tired, "is that somebody's got to talk to these people. They've gone crazy, like the Masada Zealots. So go down and tell them it's no good making a stand. They've got to leave."

I went from house to house, hearing these people who had for a decade built their homes in the Sinai and who looked at me as if I was the angel of death and should have passed over them.

"It's where we live," cried a plump woman with a child on one hip and one growing under her loose, flapping army shirt. "We've put everything into it. See, the pictures of my family. They're all dead from the old times in Poland. See, I'm growing flowers under my windows where the morning sun comes. Don't let them take away all we've made here. There was nothing but sand. No one else wanted to be here. Only us."

All I could do was tell them how much we cared about the gardens they had grown and the pictures on their walls and that we would save what we could for them. What else could I say?"

"Give me the pictures," I said to the woman. "Just in case. You'll want them back later, and I'll keep them safe."

She piled her family treasures in my arms and the small daughter gave me her favorite toys. The woman's husband wouldn't part with any of his things. He just stood at the window looking out at the sand hills beyond the tanks.

The next day the soldiers closed in, calling to the people through bullhorns to leave, saying another home would be found for them. But the trouble is, once you've found your home, you don't want another. I know the Palestinian Arabs feel the same way as the Palestinian Jews. Even if most of the Arabs haven't been in the Holy Land any longer than the Jews have, they still want their homes back. Who wouldn't?

So there they were, the people of Yamit, throwing rocks down on us and crying, while we began to destroy their community, bulldozing it block by block, crushing it into the sand as though it had never been. No one like Uncle Maxi will ever dig up this town because we've left it dust. Some of the soldiers cried as we toppled walls and smashed windows. I keep telling myself that our act was intended to show the Egyptians and the world our good faith, to let them know we would do anything for peace. Will they reach out to us in return? I pray they will, but history does not offer much hope.

I hope you're not still mourning for Uncle Maxi, rending your garments and all that. He'll be back every year to visit, you know he will. And, for whatever it's worth, you still have me. I'm not planning to go anywhere, only home to Jerusalem.

Your Benjamin

The press made all sorts of noble remarks about Israel's sacrifice of the Sinai, but after Benjamin's letter, all I could see was the woman who had raised her child on a piece of earth and then was driven off it. The diplomats probably kissed each others' cheeks ceremoniously and went back to their mansions, while this woman's home was pushed into the sand like garbage.

The next day, I was still angry, still sad, imagining myself in front of Kiryat Anavim, nose-to-nose with a bulldozer. That was when Father Jonas called and said Benjamin and I must meet him at the Kiryat Anavim guesthouse in half an hour to help him welcome his visitors from America. Because he was so excited, he rang off before I could ask why. The only guests from America who could excite me were Maxi and his family, but they had just left.

I hurried off to find Benjamin who had just stopped in on his way back from Yamit. I found him in the kitchen helping to put away the breakfast dishes. He was still wearing his army uniform, and looked more dressed up than I did, for I had been called out of the vegetable garden and wore my blue denim blouse and a long, dirty denim skirt. My hair was tucked under a kerchief in my usual Orthodox fashion. All the way from the garden, I had tried to peel the dirt out from under my fingernails and had given up just before arriving at the door of the guesthouse. Benjamin curled my fingers under his, so no one could see the dirt, and brought me into the parlor. There Father Jonas sat with a slim, aristocratic looking couple and a young woman with reddish gold hair who looked like a movie star. She sat watching us from across the room.

"Dora," Father Jonas called out to me, bringing the elegantly dressed woman toward the doorway where I stood. "This is Claire. Claire, Dora Ben-Ari."

At the sound of that name, I dropped Benjamin's arm and stood apart from him, my flesh prickling, my mouth hanging open, ready to talk, but with no words. That this was my Claire, from long ago, I had no doubt, but would she know me? Was I still her child, her sister? Was she mine? I felt like a statue, hopelessly cold and hard, not able to show any feeling for this half-known woman.

She stood looking at me, her hands opening like fans, her face widening until the dimples I remembered showed on either side of her smile. At first she didn't speak, just stood looking at me with her eyes on mine and her arms out.

In a small, choked voice she said, "Where are the bears? Do you still have the Ben-Ari bears?"

Before she could finish, I had her in my arms, her face against mine, her mouth on my cheek so that her words were gone as if blown away in a high wind. I had forgotten or never noticed that Claire was so thin and insubstantial. My arms seemed to meet through her and touch each other.

"Have you been well?" I stammered, trying to be polite, the rough years at Kiryat Anavim having trained me the other way. "Are you the same as ever?"

"I still play music," Claire whispered into my ear, the air going hard into my head. "Do you still sing and make speeches?"

"Not the same songs," I said, my lips feeling stiff, like they weren't mine. "But yes, I sing."

"This is your son?" Claire drew back and looked at Benjamin, who was halfway between us and the blond girl, not turning his head.

"Benjamin," I called, trying to wake him up, for he seemed to have traveled somewhere else. "Come and meet Claire, my friend."

He only half turned in our direction, and then back toward the girl. She stood up and put out her hand.

"I'm Claire's daughter, Julie," she said. "Don't I know you from somewhere? I feel I do."

"Yes." Benjamin took her hand and held it up, like a prizefighter having just won a match. "I feel the same."

The two of them were the same height, Benjamin stocky and strong as a rock, and Claire's daughter thin and fragile as a beam of light, like Claire herself. My son and Julie did not look as though they were natives of the same planet.

"Let me get you all some tea," Father Jonas said, busying himself around us. "Sit down and let me take care of you."

I sat on the sofa close to Claire, my arm outstretched along the back of the couch, aching because Maxi wasn't between Claire and me where he belonged.

"Maxi's gone to New York," I said, still feeling rubber-lipped, my words gummed like an old woman's. "When you go back to America, you can see him whenever you like. I wish I could."

Claire touched my cheek with one hand, and then held me off so she could see most of me at once. "I didn't expect to see you ever again, and here you are between my hands." She spread her arms and laid them again on my shoulders. Then she gathered me up in a hug, as if she couldn't get close enough with mere talk. The bulb in my throat rose and swelled, then, as she held me, it dissolved, and I cried on her elegant silk blouse until the sleeve was all wet. I didn't care who saw. For me, she was Mutti and Aunt Rachel and all my lost past. In her arms I felt mothered as I had not since I was a little girl.

After I had got myself together, Father Jonas introduced me to Claire's husband, holding him tightly by the hand as if he might get away and insisted that I know him too. Although I remembered dimly that this slender, quiet man had once fallen on top of Maxi and me, saving our lives, I couldn't think of much to say to him. I left him to Father Jonas, as I left Julie to Benjamin, while I went outside with Claire.

I showed her the olive grove and the greenhouse where I spent my days, and the garden where Lev and I had talked late at night when the rest of the kibbutz was asleep. All my life came flooding up, past the dissolved hysterical bulb into my mouth and into words that wouldn't stop coming. We visited my room so Claire could see the Ben-Ari bears, once again sitting on my dresser, since Lev's death. I lent her my journals so she would know how it had been with me over all these years. Even to Benjamin I could not say as much as I wanted to say to Claire, who seemed to know what I would say before I spoke.

When Claire heard of Joel's death, she told me about her son's near-assassination. "They should be with families," she said, "raising children. Why can't there be grandchildren anymore? Are our sons too busy? Too scared? What?"

Her words stopped me dead, because I'd given up on Benjamin marrying and having children, on ever having new Ben-Ari lives growing around my table like olive plants.

"This is a terrible time," I murmured in Claire's ear. "Without the children of our children, we just wither like dead branches."

Claire and I sat together on a bench by the gorge watching Benjamin and Julie standing where Lev and I once stood, talking gravely, hand in hand.

The next day, alarmed in some way I couldn't get a handle on, I asked Benjamin what he had said to Julie and she to him. Benjamin threw up his hands and was unsure.

"She wants to take care of the poor," he said, "to put people back together again. She thinks you can't just take off and be a spirit, the way I do. I'm thinking she's right."

"Well, yes," I replied, trying to imagine what Noah would say to Benjamin's mad ideas about separating soul from body and floating off in a meditative cloud. "I've always thought that way. Look how a tomato grows. You start with dirt and water and light. What do we need to grow a person?"

"Love, Julie says, and you can't love at a distance." Benjamin seemed to be thinking out loud, his forehead wrinkled. "Loving is done up close or not at all. I'm beginning to see that."

Benjamin spent the next week trying to find out what else there was to know about Julie and came home more and more often with her words in his mouth, as Claire told me his words had become her Julie's. He finally got her to talk about her life in America, but it took some time, for the girl apparently didn't like to talk much about herself. Only because Claire told me, did I know before Benjamin did that Julie had been one of the beaten women at the shelter she ran back in New York.

"We got state funding for the home and bought it from the church," Julie explained, sitting cross-legged beside Benjamin on the grass, near the bench where Claire and I sat watching the two of them, overhearing what we could. "The bishop was so surprised when we brought him the check that he chipped in for a bus to take the children to school. We called it the Bishop Cochran Memorial Bus and had him stand beside it for the TV cameras.

Now he feels like we're family, like he's the man in our lives, and I guess he is." Julie bent her head and a lock of her red-gold hair fell over her cheek like a veil.

Benjamin had picked a buttercup and now he tucked it behind Julie's ear with great concentration, arranging her hair around the stem. "So the work there is finished," he said, taking his hands away from her very slowly, as if he were having second thoughts about moving anywhere but closer. "You've done what you felt you had to?"

"I think so." Julie looked around for a moment until she saw her daughter playing tag with the kibbutz children, then turned her eyes back to meet Benjamin's. "Now I feel very free, very empty and good. No more agendas."

They sat together for a while, being silent. As I watched them, my breath was held much of the time, for I was afraid to guess what Benjamin would say next to this beautiful, strange girl.

"I have an agenda for you, if you like," Benjamin said in his clipped British English."Come stay with our community in Jerusalem. You and Annie both. We need you to help us. It's time for us to serve as much as we pray. You're right about that."

"How can I help?" Julie light blue eyes stared into his, and for a moment he leaned forward until his face and hers were close enough for kissing. "What service?"

"So far, we have only meditated together," Benjamin said, sitting back on his heels, weaving a circlet of buttercups and clover as he spoke. "You saw that when you visited last evening. And you said something I now believe is true. Love is not love until it's in the flesh. Made incarnate. Father Jonas uses that word because he's a Christian, and I use it because it's true."

Julie smoothed the grass under her palms as if she were massaging the earth. She smiled and tossed him a clover blossom. "I'm glad it's Easter. Time for Resurrection."

She jumped up and ran off to join Annie. Benjamin followed Julie at a quickening pace until he was beside her. After placing the flower crown on Annie's head, Benjamin took her hand and Julie's. The three of them stood so close together in the distance that I couldn't see where one left off and the others began.

"What's going on with those two?" I burst out to Claire, my hands cupped around my eyes, the light too much for me. "Something's going on, I can feel it."

"From what Julie has told me, they're finding out that they love each other," Claire said slowly. "And they don't know what to do about it."

I guess I should have seen it coming, this love Claire was setting in front of me like an unwanted meal. Stupidly, my mouth saying secondhand things because my mind had stopped, I said, "Benjamin's a Jewish man, an Israeli, a kibbutznik. Lev is gone, and when I'm gone Benjamin will be all that's left of us, all that's left to make the next Jewish generation. He can't marry outside. He can't. It would be the end of everything when Jews no long marry Jews. You've read my journal, Claire. You know how hard I've tried to make Benjamin understand what it is to be a Jew."

"I feel the same way about Julie's faith in Christ." Claire put her hand over mine and curled our fingers together. "It's made her whole again. Without it, who would she be? No, I don't want her to marry someone who would not share her religion." Claire shook her head. "Not even Benjamin, not even your son, and he's a good man. The best. It's not suitable for either of them" Her face arranged itself in sadness again. "My mother's word, remember? When something was what she thought unsuitable, we had to give it up, not questioning her rules and reasons."

The pursed mouth of Madame Leclerq and the vertical lines between her brows were suddenly before me in the flesh, and I leaped back as if to avoid a blow. How like her we had become, I thought. We were clucking like old hens that could no longer lay, full of ancient, useless lore, which was intended for the good of the tribe and for our own peace of mind. Just as the old men made young men fight wars, we, the old women, made the young ones obey the rules of the past, so times could be kept from changing, sweeping away us and what we had made.

"You should let them alone." Paul's voice was strong, and he leaned on the back of the bench, his head suddenly between ours. "What do they care about preserving your past or your notions of what the future should look like? Let them be."

I stiffened and pulled away from him. "For three thousand years there's been a Jewish people," I said, angry at them for not knowing what it was to carry that long a history in such frail vessels, across deserts, into concentration camps and most recently into kibbutzim in this tiny country now being shelled by Lebanese missiles. "In two generations of intermarriage, our people could be wiped out, as Maxi says most of them were, in Biblical days when they married Canaanites. You have history and numbers on your side. We have only the Covenant. That's all and that's everything."

"You'll have to talk to Julie," Claire said to Paul, after we had all sat for a while in silence, looking anywhere but at each other. "She won't listen to me. This marriage, if that's what's in the wind, won't do. Someone has to tell her, Paul."

"Let Father Jonas talk to Benjamin," Paul said, moving from the bench to the grass at our feet. "And Julie too. He knows what's happening to them better than we do. Maybe better than they do."

"You've spoken to him?" I looked into Paul's face, now freckled so much by the Israeli sun that his wrinkles had faded away behind the spots. He had disappeared often while Claire and I had our long talks, and until now, I had not wondered where he had been. "You and Father Jonas have been together, these last days?" I said, knowing the answer.

"He's a wise man," Paul said. "I keep wanting to spend more time with him. But I can't talk about what he's said to me. I feel too new yet, like one of those moths with wet wings, waving them dry before taking off. Talking is the last thing I want to do."

Claire shook him lightly. "What is it, Paul? If something's going on, you should tell me. No more secrets, remember?"

"You'll know any secrets I have, but not by talk." He smiled as he got up, stretched, and then leaned over to kiss her on the neck, ruffling her hair with one hand. as Lev used to do to mine. "Only by loving, and I'm too new at that to speak it in words. But I'm able to say I'm happy, Claire. That much I can tell you."

He was relaxed anyway, not tense and silent as he had been when he first came. Looking at him, I saw his whole body unstrung like a bow hung up after an ancient war. I remember the night Father Jonas came into his hotel room saying how happy he was, and wondered if Paul had caught religious mania from my old friend. I had grown used to the joy that swept through Father Jonas and through Noah, suddenly and from nowhere, like sunlight falling out of holes in the clouds.

"You can face leaving Julie here?" Claire's voice was high and surprised. "That's what it may mean, you know. Not seeing Julie and Annie anymore."

"Nothing can separate us," Paul said before walking on, his step so light it hardly seemed to bend the grass. "That's the way it seems to me now," he called back over his shoulder as he went toward Julie.

"He's talking like Benjamin," I said to Claire. "We can't depend on him to tell the children anything sensible. Father Jonas will have to speak to Julie and Benjamin. They'll listen to him."

So I went to St. Elizabeth's rectory the next day, while Claire got ready for her concert that afternoon. Leaving her to rehearse the St. Elizabeth's choir, I went up the spiral iron staircase, past damp white walls with their niches glowing red from votive lights under plaster saints. Father Jonas was working at a little table which he had moved out onto a balcony overlooking Nablus Road, where Arab shepherds and their flocks alternated with cars and trucks. His room was so situated that wherever he looked, a balance of old and new was struck. He cleared aside his papers, leaving the little table almost bare, as if to show me that nothing was on his mind but me and what I had to say. Father Jonas's face was paler than I've ever seen it, and the lines were deeper around his mouth, where the skin seemed to be sinking right to the skull.

"Have you been eating enough?" I asked him, looking over his long, bony frame. "You don't look all that healthy."

"Time is eating me up," he laughed, hitching his chair closer to mine. "Eating me like a starved thing. Nothing left but ashes, pretty soon. As it should be. I'll be eighty this month, Dora. Old bones."

'No, not old." I reached out to shake his arm. It seemed to me that if I didn't hang onto him, he too would go away, like all the others, before I was ready to give him up. "Not yet. I can't lose you too. First Maxi. Now maybe Benjamin. No, it's too soon." My face started crumpling up like a baby's, and waves of self-pity rocked my body back and forth as my arms closed around my belly, which ached as if from hunger.

Father Jonas stood up and looked down at me from his full height, lifting his hand over my head as if he were giving me a blessing. "No loss, Dora," he said. You have us all. Benjamin too. You think that because he loves Julie, you've lost him?"

"Yes I do," I cried, mourning as though my son's dead body were stretched out in front of me. "If he loves this girl, she'll take him away with her. He'll be lost. How can you stand there and say he won't be lost? He and his children and their children after them? Lost to me, lost to the Jewish people. Will you tell him how I feel, Father? Tell him he's all that's left. If he marries that girl, it will be the end of me. Tell him."

My words were ground between my teeth, barely audible, and it was hard to know how much poor Father Jonas heard of them. But he knew to put his arms around me and be close.

"Dora, Dora," he whispered, rocking me as he had in the old days back at St. Hilary's. "It's only because you cling so hard that you feel yourself alone. Let go, dear one, let go, and you won't suffer this way. Remember, you have me and you have Noah. His heart is entirely yours, I know."

"Well, I don't know that." I was taken aback, since I could not imagine that Noah would not just drift at the periphery of my life until we both turned up our toes and died. No, my son was the only one I could count on.

"Trust me," Father Jonas said. "Trust the providence of God, Dora. Just trust, that's all. Give up what makes you suffer so, and yes, die to it. Leave it buried where it fell. Only you and God know what gives you pain. Only you can let it go. Now, Dora, now. Just let Benjamin melt out of your hands into the air you breathe, so that he will live in you and you in him."

"I can't give him up. I can't. He was born out of all my blood and bones and he's mine, mine, mine." The words came out thick and loud, as words do in a bad dream, when you wake up hearing yourself croak and groan. I wanted to wake up from this nightmare of demanding what was mine, but I couldn't. I cried out to Yeshua, who had been silent lately, probably because I had been too busy to consult him.

"I'm sick of losing and I can't lose any more. Don't ask me to."

"I won't," Father Jonas said. "I'm just going to ask you to bring Benjamin and Julie to the Shabbat service tomorrow at Beth Shalom. Noah wants to meet them."

"Benjamin doesn't know about Yeshua and Noah and Beth Shalom," I said, feeling suddenly shy, as I did whenever it came to sharing Yeshua with anyone. "And Julie's an evangelical Christian, Claire tells me. They wouldn't know what to do, what to think."

"You'll see how broad your son's sympathies are," Father Jonas said. "His soul is big enough to include all there is, but don't fear. He's still a Jew, whatever else he is. Bring the young ones with you and let Yeshua touch them. By yourself, you can't do anything. You know that."

I did know, but couldn't help trying to do something anyway, being my own stubborn self. All the way to Beth Shalom, I tried to explain to Benjamin that my messianic Judaism did not make me any less a Jew. Meanwhile, Father Jonas sat in the driver's seat, trying to explain to Julie that the first Christians worshiped in much the same way as what she would see at Beth Shalom. Julie looked polite but reserved, while Benjamin was astonished that I had never told him of my belief in Yeshua and that there was a messianic congregation in Jerusalem. In all his years of meditation with Muslims, Jews, and Christians, he had never heard of Yeshua.

We had grown very quiet and distant from each other as we entered the Beth Shalom loft, with its high metal ceiling and track lights over the bimah, the Torah, and the flickering candle in its red sanctuary lamp. We sat in the front row, since I wanted to be as near Noah as possible.

Julie and Benjamin sat together on my right side and Father Jonas on my left. The two young people gave a start as Rabbi Noah entered, his tall form imposing, but the forward tilt of his leonine head quite humble. He looked like a patriarch straight out of Exodus, his full-length talus slightly ragged, clutched around him by long, thin fingers. As always, his eyes shone and a smile played around his gentle, sensuous mouth. Out of the corner of my eye, I saw Benjamin sit up straight to stare, for once, not at Julie.

"Mother," he whispered to me, "This man is like no rabbi I've ever seen."

Rabbi Noah read the Torah portion aloud in his deep, husky voice, pausing at certain words, caressing them with silence. He read first in Hebrew, then in English, since he knew that there were foreigners in the congregation. Then he spoke, and it seemed as if he looked at Benjamin and Julie with a father's love, perhaps because he knew they were with me.

As often happened when Noah spoke, I fell into a reverie and forgot my surroundings, even my dear Benjamin. The words came from Noah's heart, for he knew no other way to speak. Yeshua, the Mosiach, he explained, embodied Ha-Shem, the otherwise unknowable Spirit. This same Holy Spirit, the Breath of God lives in us as Ruach. It inspired the prophets that led the Israelites into the Holy Land and blessed them with his presence in the temple.

"After Yeshua was killed, the stone Temple was destroyed," Noah went on, "and a temple was built in the human heart. Not blood sacrifice on an outward altar, but the practice of mercy was the mark of a believer. Not the dry, study of a book, however holy, can save a soul from despair. Only loving Yeshua, calling him by whatever name you know him, and being loved by him, only sharing of this love with all humanity, all beings seen and unseen—that love is our salvation, our Yeshua."

I glanced at Benjamin to see how he was taking Rabbi Noah's words. Benjamin's eyes were closed, and his face was as peaceful and still as if he were sleeping. Only his alert posture told me he was not. Julie leaned forward, eyes fixed on Noah. She breathed irregularly, sighs torn out of her, it seemed, as if she were suffering pain. When the service was over, she and Benjamin sat still for a while, not moving until Noah came over and spoke to them.

"I think you must be Dora's son, Benjamin," Noah said. "She has shown me your picture. I would guess she has not shown you mine." He smiled at me, and then turned to Julie, looking at her in frank admiration, forgetting his Orthodox duty to keep his eyes downcast in the presence of a woman.

"You look so much like an angel," he said to her, "that I am sure you are very close to Ha-Shem, the name we call the Holy One. Am I right?"

"Never as close as I would like to be," Julie murmured. "But here, with your congregation, Rabbi, I feel as close to God as I ever have."

"Then you must come back and join us often," Noah said, nodding with a smile at me. "And bring your mother, Benjamin. I have missed her lately."

I wanted to say that I had missed him as in England I had missed the sun, and that my heart was starved for his words, my hands longing to touch him. But I just said something silly, not wanting to let Benjamin know I loved this man. Despite my efforts, Benjamin turned and looked hard at me with a knowing little smile. On the way home, he was mostly quiet.

Just before he and Julie got off the bus, my son put his arm around me and whispered in my ear. "You can't fool me, Mother. This Rabbi Noah and you are more than friends. And a better more-than-friend I could not have asked for you."

Perhaps he was trying to get me married off, I thought, so his poor widowed mother would not be on his back. Or perhaps he was just wanting me to be happy. I could never tell what Benjamin was thinking and couldn't this time. As Benjamin walked away with Julie's hand in his, heading for his communal residence, I did not, for some reason, feel as bereft as the sight of their closeness usually made me feel.

The next day, when we met over lunch, I talked with Father Jonas again about my worries over Benjamin and Julie. He was reassuring, but I was not reassured.

"Benjamin and Julie will do nothing to hurt you, Dora. That I can promise, knowing their hearts as I do. What you ask of them, you'll get, because they love you. If you don't want them to marry, they won't, however much they want to. Paul understands. Maybe he can tell you."

"Claire wonders what's gone on with you and Paul," I said, balling my napkin up tightly in both hands. "I suppose Paul is going to get mystical and strange like Benjamin?"

"No stranger than I am," laughed Father Jonas. "Tell Claire not to worry about Paul. No loss there either, only change, which is all there ever is on this earthly plane, Dora. Now dry your eyes. We'll be late for the service, and Claire will be anxious."

Claire was waiting for us when we came in the side door of the church, her face tense, but her eyes wide and bright like Benjamin's when he's just come from his prayers or whatever he does with that community of his.

"The organist sounded like he was playing an altogether different liturgy from the one the choir was singing," she said, one hand over her heart, as if it were working too hard and she were trying to settle it down.

"But I think we've finally got ourselves together. Father, all you have to do is wait for the organist to give you your note before you sing your part in the liturgy. They're holding seats for us down in front, Dora. I do hope Paul will have a handkerchief. Mine's all used up from hearing the Sanctus six times in rehearsal. The Sanctus always wipes me out."

She took my hand and pulled me off to my seat between her and Benjamin, who sat beside Julie, of course. The two of them were sitting with their heads and hands close, like one body, reminding me of how Yael had been with Dan. I didn't say anything to them, since they seemed too engaged to include me. Claire and I leaned forward when Father Jonas came out, dressed in a white, shining cloak with a lamb embroidered on the back. He bowed to the altar first, very low, and then turned, his arms out like the cruciform shape above the altar, inviting us all to feel held and loved.

"Christ our Passover is sacrificed for us," Father Jonas said," and he is risen, Alleluia, alleluia."

The words were familiar to me, and I couldn't think why until I remembered that Father Jonas had said something like them to me when he wanted me to bury the old grief, to let go of it. Sacrifice Benjamin, I guess he meant. Be buried as your sacrifice and rise again when the sacrifice is over. Change is at the heart of life. Accept it. Don't drag your feet. The choir was singing Holy, Holy, Holy, as if to tell me where change was taking me, whether or not I wanted to go.

Paul was kneeling now, and tears were in his eyes. I could hear him whispering "Sanctus, Sanctus," many times. I wondered if he had discovered what was holy for him.

"I told you it was a good Sanctus," Claire said into my ear. "It's supposed to sound like angels and saints singing to God. Just listen!"

I took her hand, which she hardly noticed, because her eyes were on Paul's face. Benjamin followed Julie up to the altar, and Paul went after them, with a glance back to see where Claire was. I clutched Claire's fingers hard. Later I learned from Father Jonas that I should have let her go with Paul to take Holy Communion. But she stayed behind with me, giving up the bread and wine to keep our fingers entangled. I felt Claire was where she wanted to be and that she and I had our own communion going on between us.

While Julie knelt to receive the bread from Father Jonas, Benjamin stood behind her, his hands on her shoulders. For a moment, Father Jonas paused, then handed her a second wafer, which she swallowed with the first. As he gave it to her, he looked over her head to Benjamin, and their eyes met. I think the second communion wafer was meant for my son, his yarmulkh pinned at the back of his head, his square brown hands covering Julie's small shoulders. But Benjamin would not say so when I asked afterwards, only smiled and said, "It was meant for all of us."

He and Julie stood close together at the airport, where we went after the Easter Service. It was just before her parents got on the plane that Julie told me she and her daughter were planning to stay with Father Jonas at St. Elizabeth's.

"I will be living in Jerusalem," she said, glancing at Benjamin and avoiding my eyes. "I don't know what direction the wind is blowing me in but I'm going with it."

Claire and Paul held her and Annie for a long time, not saying what I knew they felt, that this was not the place to stay, not Julie's country, not the right man for her. But they knew better than to compete with Benjamin, who stood within arm's reach of Julie, ready to pull her back if she should break and run. Or so his intention seemed to me.

"You'll come to see Maxi and us?" Claire's arms were around me now. "We want you to, often. Please, Dora."

"I'll come." My hands met around her back and didn't seem to want to come loose. "Not for long, though. My home is here."

Claire looked into my eyes. "And we'll come to you and Julie. Dora, the two of us have always been together in the same place, don't you think?"

I thought so too, but couldn't say anything, with my voice so shaky and unreliable at this time of losses. Only after she and Paul got on the plane did I think to say out loud, "You mean that we've always been saying hello and good-by as a formality, a nod to what Benjamin calls material considerations. We've always loved each other and have lived on the point of the same pin, like angels dancing."

The plane began to move down the runway, and I could no longer see Claire's face, except in the eye of my mind.

"Good-by, Mother, Father," Julie cried out suddenly, breaking from under Benjamin's arm and running a few steps toward the plane as it gathered speed. "Good-by, I do love you!" Then she laid her face against Benjamin's shoulder, and Annie closed their circle.

17

New York................................1983

After returning from Jerusalem Claire felt bleak and lonely. Her daughter was far away just at the time she and Claire had found each other again. There would be new grandchildren in Israel, but Annie was gone *She will hardly remember our times together,* Claire mourned. *I will just be a figment of her imagination as she grows up.* She wished she could share what she felt with Paul, but he was too happy to burden with her grief.

Ever since he had spent those hours with Father Jonas and shed tears during the Sanctus, Paul had been light-hearted in a way Claire had never seen him. "It was a very good Sanctus," was all Paul would say when she asked why he had changed during that time in Jerusalem. "I think it opened my heart."

"You seem always to be either praying or painting now," she complained, following him to the study door. "It's boring for me, you know, having a saint for a husband."

After that remark, he had suggested having Marcus to dinner, and even helped Claire prepare the moussaka, chopping and peeling vegetables with an artist's concentration. Marcus had been the first to notice that Paul had become a different painter. He had gone with Paul to the study, where Claire had been ordered not to enter until the painting was finished, and she could hear their words in snatches.

"So much life," she heard Marcus say, "and power too, such power these colors have, where the blue separates into violet and white. Like this it must have been when the Big Bang broke one white point of light into the whole rainbow universe, *nicht what?*"

To Claire over dessert he exclaimed, "I am happy to say it, your Paul is making a masterpiece. You see what Jerusalem does for an artist?" He sat back in his chair and rubbed his stomach, round with Claire's Greek dinner. "And you? What music did you bring back?"

Claire at first felt ashamed that she had done no work, while Paul had been so fruitful, and then caught herself, realizing that she did not inevitably diminish if he grew. For so long it had seemed that only one of them at a time could create, while the other sat brooding in darkness, like a dragon on his hoard, spending nothing. *Sometimes I find this absorption in painting as tiresome as his obsession with Julie used to be,* Claire admitted to herself. *What do I want? The same kind of romantic attention a woman gets during courtship? That time is over with, and I have another kind of love.* What she had was this strange, reborn Paul, who was not withdrawn and angry anymore, and who helped her in the kitchen and with the gardening, work he had never before noticed needed doing.

"Don't you miss Julie and Annie?" Claire finally asked him, as they were clearing away dead leaves from around the rhododendrons. She didn't mean her tone to sound accusing, but sensed that the words came out that way. "I miss them terribly. And Dora. Just when I found her again, I had to say good-by."

Paul stopped shoveling leaves and turned his face to the summer sunshine. "We'll have visits," he said. "And the months between them will be full of memories. Have you felt, Claire, that the time goes quickly now? They say that happens as you get old, but I don't feel old at all."

Once he would have remarked coldly to me that I must learn not to pity myself, Claire thought, *but now, since the trip to Jerusalem, he just turns my words around until they make me smile.*

"I'd have thought you'd be the one to miss Julie, not me," Claire said, stretching out on the grass to catch the sun's warmth. "What did Father Jonas say to you anyway?"

Paul lay down beside her on his stomach, propping up his chin in his hands. "Father Jonas reminded me that I'm no more in charge of events than I am of the blowing wind. That I never have been." He took deep breaths as he spoke and closed his eyes. "I was only stuck in the web of time, like a poor, trapped bug."

"You mean you've let go of those men of yours who died in the war?" Claire spoke cautiously, afraid to stir the memories at the bottom of Paul's mind where they had lain so long, decomposing into ugly gases and coming up at all the wrong times.

"Of all the mistakes I've made," Paul answered mildly, "but yes, mostly of those men. I'd like to tell you how it was, if you'd like to hear. It's not a pretty story."

Claire turned over on her side, facing him, and nodded. She wanted to stroke his face, bristling with a day's worth of beard, but he had already turned too deeply inward for her to reach him.

"We were told to drive into Nazi territory," he said, laying his hands flat on the grass, so that it came up between his fingers as if they were bare earth. "The orders were sent from the General himself, and he promised that the American planes would cover us all the way. Maybe he thought so. All I know is, they didn't come. I had to choose whether to disobey orders and stay where we were, or blindly go ahead as I was ordered to do."

Paul tore up some grass and scattered it over a bare spot in the lawn. "It was night when we got to Courtrai, and some of my men wanted to bivouac outside the town until dawn, until we could see what was happening. General's orders, I insisted, and in we went, right through the old gates built by the Romans. They had built the wall and gates to keep the barbarians out. We were fighting our way through, to get at the barbarians in the town. Everybody thought he had history on his side, of course, and God."

He wiped one hand across his forehead and sighed. "All I knew was obedience," he said, "since I'd never had any experience at war. Young men like I was then shouldn't have been given command, and that's the truth of it."

"Maybe no one else would have done any better than you," Claire murmured, rolling close to him so that his breath cooled her cheek. "Maybe no one could have won at Courtrai."

Paul went on as if he had not heard her. "So I did what I was told, not thinking for myself, not listening to the old non-commissioned officer who warned me, and I led all of them straight into the town. The Nazis knew we were there, but let us string out, into houses and alleys. Then, when they had us where they wanted us, they came out shooting. From everywhere, they came out."

He put his hands over his eyes, not wanting to see what they still saw. "You could see their white faces under those square helmets. You could see them behind their flame-throwers. The first men to go in were dropping all over the streets, their hair on fire, their clothes burning. Hardly more than boys, these young men were, and I knew them all by name."

Twisting her fingers together, knowing she could help very little with her words, Claire bent her head. "Horrible," she said in a low voice."

"One boy not out of his teens ran up to me, his face melting, the skin pulled away from his bones so you could see the rounds of his eyeballs. He was screaming, wanting me to shoot him, and I couldn't. All the time I kept looking up, hoping and praying to see the American planes, but the skies were empty of everything but stars. I remember thinking that I hated the stars for being so cold, so far off and safe, watching us burn like ants on a log, I and my men. There seemed no difference between my men and me. Their flesh was my flesh, their bones my bones."

"You didn't retreat?" Claire felt her tongue being wooden and unsure. "That was very brave, surely."

"No, very stupid. My father said so, and he was right. I was too cowardly to retreat, not too brave. Some of the men with me begged me to go back. Later, one of them told my father what happened." Paul let his hands drop to the ground again. "But I was going to link up with the General's troops on the other side of town, as I had been told to do. Nothing was going to stop me from carrying out my orders, and nothing did. I and ten of my five hundred men finally joined the General's troops, for whatever that was worth. Not much, in the long run. Not all those lives, for sure. But I was in charge, as I wanted to be, as I thought was expected of me."

"And Father Jonas? What did he say to you, besides that it's not so good to be in charge all the time?" Claire felt she ought to shout, her husband seemed so far away.

"He said to tell you, because I had always been afraid to. You might say what my father said, that I was a fool, useless, no sort of man he could recognize."

Claire pushed closer to him and pressed her lips to his cheek. "You're man enough, for me," she said. "I've always thought so."

He said nothing, only wrapped his arms around her, burying his face against her neck, and she rocked him as she had rocked her children when they were small.

"Why did you cry when you heard the Sanctus," she asked suddenly, thinking *I'm not sure why I want to know, but maybe it will help Paul to tell me.*

"For so long I couldn't see the holiness of God," Paul said, his words hard to hear, they were so soft. "A lot was in the way. After talking with Father Jonas, I could. That's all. As he talked to me, I began to feel nothing was ugly or burned, nothing was there anymore except the Sanctus, the Holy, and letting go of what stood between me and God."

"Even Julie? She stood between too?" Claire felt her chest tighten. *I wonder if that old obsession is still there? I know Julie stood between Paul and me.*

"What I loved was not Julie," Paul said, "but myself. Always myself."

"Not now, though," Claire pulled him to his feet and tucked her arm under his. "Not anymore?"

He kicked a pile of leaves and watched them fly in the wind. "I hope not anymore. Father Jonas said not. What a healing it was, Claire. If a man could die of a healing, I think I died of mine."

"And came back" Claire said as they walked. "It was Easter, after all."

"Yes, it was. Alleluia." Paul threw back his head and sang a snatch of her liturgy. "Smell the night air," he said. "How sweet it is." He glanced at his watch, and then broke into a run. "We'll be late for Maxi's dinner," he called over his shoulder. "Tim will get there ahead of us and wonder where we are."

Tim had not met Maxi's family before, since he had been busy in Washington until the Labor Day celebration Carolyn had planned. For some time, she and Claire had wanted their children to meet, but Yael had been as busy in her university laboratory as Tim had been in his congressional committee. *To humor their mothers,* Claire supposed, *the children had agreed to come this time, if only for the dinner itself.* Both had set up escapes afterward, before the older people began the after-dinner reminiscence in which Tim and Yael could not be expected to share. Carolyn had already warned Claire that her daughter had an experiment she had to tend at Columbia University, and Claire knew Tim was expected in a last minute caucus before a major toxic waste hearing on Tuesday.

The young people seemed preoccupied when they were introduced, and not until Tim learned Yael had majored in organic chemistry did he notice her, pulling his chair closer to hers at the dinner table.

"Had any experience with vinyl chloride?" He asked Yael over their asparagus soup. "We're looking for some way to breed a bug that'll eat whatever VC it finds in the waste."

"That's more in the biochemical line than mine," Yael answered, brushing her wispy blond hair back behind her ears. "What I'm trying to learn is which toxic wastes are by-products of Agent Orange and acid rain. Then I'd like to find out what government agency is covering up for that corporation you talked about. The one Vanderzell owns."

"You think the government's covering for the dioxin leaks? That's the real problem at the Vanderzell dump, you know." Timothy dabbed at some soup he had spilled on his tie, then impatiently pulled the tie off and stuffed it in his pocket. "We think so too, but we have no proof. God, I'd love to nail Vanderzell Chemical for that. Their little herbicide operation has killed a lot more than foliage. And that's just one of his subsidiaries.

Claire looked from one of them to the other. *I shouldn't be surprised that Timothy never married, if he can find nothing more intimate to discuss with a pretty girl than the dumping of dioxin. And she seems as obsessed as Timothy. When Paul courted me, I'm sure he never talked about the military-industrial complex. The young are so impersonal these days. No wonder so few of them get married anymore and so many that do marry get divorced.* She looked at Carolyn and shrugged.

"Maybe," she whispered in the other woman's ear, "the only way the young have of being intimate nowadays is to share the same obsession."

"They don't think in words, you know," Carolyn whispered back. "Just in mathematical formulas."

Yael rested her small, triangular chin on one palm, her slanted brown eyes bright as she looked at Tim. "I can prove it," she said. "I've got samples of their trichlophenol that match the dioxin by-products from that dump you're going after."

How romantic, Claire groaned to herself. She rolled her eyes at Paul, who smiled and concentrated on his soup.

"Tests you can replicate? You're sure?" Tim rested his arm on the back of her chair and put his face close to hers, his voice low. "How about coming down to Washington with me next week and talking to my congressional subcommittee about those tests? We're trying to get the Environmental Protection Agency to admit they're dragging their feet in the Vanderzell case. Proving the link between the dioxin from the dump and their plant would be a start. Would you testify, Yael?"

"I have an experiment going that needs me to be there," Yael said, folding her long, slender fingers together one by one in the same quick way her mother did. "Sorry."

"Let me talk to your Department Head," Tim said. "You wouldn't believe the little perks congressmen get. He'll find someone competent to substitute for you. I'll promise him an energy grant for Columbia. Actually, they'll be getting the grant anyhow, but he doesn't know that. Say you'll come, Yael."

"She can't go to Washington with you," Carolyn objected carving the lamb and passing it around. "It sounds archaic to you hip American kids, I know, but some people still believe in chaperones."

"You do, of course," Yael retorted, half-turning her head toward her mother. "Nobody else thinks the whole waking life of young males is spent sniffing the air for female pheromones."

Carolyn turned her palms up and shrugged. "Well, that's what they've been doing for the past million years. Unless the human species has undergone some great evolutionary leap forward in this generation, which I doubt, pheromones are still where it's at. Though maybe dioxin's withered everyone's gonads by now."

"No, only our brains," Tim laughed. "At least in Washington. Mother," he turned to Claire, "would you come too? You've been saying you want to watch me do my thing. This is as good a time as you're likely to get."

"Yes. I'd like to know how deeply you're into this business," Claire said, setting down her fork and looking hard at her son. "And why Vanderzell's office keeps phoning the house trying to get hold of you. Maybe herbicides aren't all they're worried about."

Tim stirred his coffee, lifted the cup to his mouth, and then put it down untasted. "You're right," he said soberly. "They're worried about disarmament, since it would cut into their profits. The real issue is that they fear an end to their role in policy-making. The militarists can't afford any bad press just now. Naturally Vanderzell would like to talk to me. That's not all he'd like to do."

"The warriors don't want their swords beaten into plowshares," Maxi said. "Warriors never have. To them, disarmament is poison. I hope you decide to testify, Yael. Your grandparents tried, you know, but never made it to the courts."

"I know. And yes, I'll testify." She put out her small hand solemnly to Tim, and he took it for a long while, until Carolyn dropped the chocolate mousse with a scream.

They all had to eat around the shards of earthenware that she served up. Maxi made a joke about how sooner or later in life, everyone had to do some archeology. They all laughed, all but Tim, who kept his eyes on Yael's tanned, glowing face and seemed not to hear what anyone else said.

Carolyn had made Claire promise to keep a close eye on Yael in Washington, but since the girl spent most of her free time going over reports in the EPA library, Claire had little to do. Sometimes Tim took them both out to dinner and pointed at senators and representatives who passed by their tables. He spoke with many of them as if they were friends. Once they were gone, he told Claire and Yael the scandals they were linked to.

Yael sat staring at the parade of important men, a line between her straight dark brows, her blue, man-tailored blouse open at the throat, sleeves rolled up as if for work, her navy blue slacks tight around her slim hips. Even for nights out, she wore the same thing, only adding exotic Middle Eastern earrings to her working outfit. Tim was used to cocktail dresses, thick make-up, and the conversation of dizzy young secretaries hunting for husbands. *He keeps staring at Yael,* Claire noticed. *The girl's eyes seem always to be looking somewhere else, as if she's in two places at once.* From time to time, Claire saw Yael lift her gaze to Tim's face, study him briefly, and then look away again, perhaps not having found what she was looking for.

"Are you going to see Vanderzell before the hearing?" Yael asked him one night in their favorite seafood café. "Maybe you could get something out of him. His secretary phoned me last night, but I couldn't figure out what she wanted."

"He had you called?" Tim's spoon stayed halfway to his mouth for a moment. Then he put it down. "How did he know you're involved? I haven't told anyone."

Claire remembered how frightened she had been to know Tim was in trouble with the likes of Vanderzell. *Now Yael too is mixed up in this ugly business. I wish she'd go back to Israel. She'd be safer with Arab terrorists than here with Vanderzell's thugs.* She said nothing, but looked from one young person to the other, knowing they wouldn't listen to any advice from her.

"For whatever reason, I was called," Yael said, calmly spooning gravy over her sliced roast beef. "Somebody knows the Columbia dioxin experiments are proving what Vanderzell doesn't want them to prove. That's what I think."

Tim's face was pale, and he rubbed his napkin across his forehead. "I'd rather they didn't know," he said. "It's not safe for you." He paused, thinking. "Look, I'm going to call a columnist friend of mine. If we're out in the open about what we're doing, they won't dare hit us. And I'm going to move you and Mother into hiding. A friend of mine has a cottage at Virginia Beach where you can stay."

That night, when Tim returned Claire and Yael to their hotel room, they found all the drawers pulled out and dumped, furniture ripped open and overturned, and closets emptied. Yael surveyed the mess, clutching her big briefcase in her arms, saying only how glad she was that she never left important papers anywhere that she couldn't keep an eye on them.

At the hearing, she opened the briefcase and laid her reports neatly in front of her, waiting for the time that the subcommittee chairman would call her to the stand. Witnesses came and went all day, most of them for the Vanderzell interests, men who spoke out in ringing tones about the coming globalization, the need for a fleet of tankers subsidized by the government, and for protection of their cartels. Only when one witness defended the Vanderzell Corporation for its deals with I.G. Farben during World War II did Claire see Yael stiffen and clutch her pen in her fist.

"Why didn't they talk to me?" Yael complained to Tim as she sat between him and Claire in the front seat, on the way back to the beachside cottage. "I had my testimony ready. They could see that. They certainly didn't mind hearing the Vanderzell people defend his links to Farben, did they?"

"My mother tells me that your grandparents worked for Farben before the war." Tim said, glancing down at her as he kept the sporty little Datsun carefully on the side of the narrow road.

"And were murdered by the Nazis when they tried to tell the Red Cross about Farben's poison gas." Yael held her briefcase against her chest and rested her chin on it. "In the end, of course, no one will do anything about these killers.

Claire rubbed her eyes. "Why is that car keeping its lights so bright, Timothy?"

"Is it an American custom to blind the driver in front of you?"Yael asked closing her eyes.

Tim jammed down the accelerator and took the next curve around an outcropping of rock so fast the tires shrieked.

"He's too close and too big. You always told me not to drive this little Japanese puppy, Mom, and you were right. Hang on, I'm going to try a side road."

The three of them lurched together as Tim steered the little car almost straight up a hillside overlooking the ocean.

"I don't see him now," Tim said glancing over his shoulder. "Maybe it was just some teenagers messing around. Mom, can you get the map and the flashlight out of the glove compartment? I know a lot of back roads, but not this one.

Claire's hands were damp and shaking as she unfolded the map and focused the beam on it. Before she could find the junction they had just passed, their car again filled with light, and she could hear the roar of the same big car behind them.

"Damnation," Tim muttered. "They're on us again, like they're going up our tail and down the other side. Ever hear of Karen Silkwood? She got pushed off a road this way before she could testify."

Tim pushed the accelerator to the floorboard and moved from one side of the road to the other as the other car lunged at them, trying to force them over the rocks to the beach below. Claire prayed and closed her eyes. *Lord, please don't let them die when they're just beginning to live.* Her heart pounded and she gripped the strap hanging over the door.

Yael pulled a fat manila envelope out of her briefcase and handed it to Claire. "This is what they're looking for. Hang onto it. We'll give them stuff that doesn't matter." She shoved some loose papers into the briefcase, snapped it closed, and laid it in Timothy's lap. "When you can," she said, "slow down and throw this behind us. Maybe they'll take the bait. Claire, can you shine that flashlight behind us when Tim opens the door?"

The other car screeched to the side of theirs, then followed Tim around the next bend, where he skidded sideways, not letting them get ahead.

Rolling down the window, he shouted at their pursuers, "You want it that bad, you can have it."

Before the briefcase had hit the road, lit by the beam from Claire's flashlight, Tim had pulled away, heading down another side road away from the shore and toward town, where they lost themselves in traffic.

"You're sure you still have what we need?" Tim asked as he drove up later that night behind their beachside bungalow.

"I have enough," Yael said. "I never throw anything useful away. You learn that on a kibbutz. I even have in my purse a disk with all my data on Agent Orange."

"I never asked you about that," Tim said, unlocking the side door and letting Yael and his mother into the cottage, which smelled of mildew and fish. "You think Vanderzell's got an exclusive with the U.S. government on biochemical warfare?"

Yael took the papers out of the manila envelope and laid them on the dining room table. "No evidence there's any other corporation involved. Look here, at the investments they've made in the dumping sites. Every time we tried to get samples from their sites, we ran into the same blank wall. They wouldn't give us passes to go in. Naturally we went in anyhow and stole our samples at night."

"Way to go." Tim grinned and took her hand. "Wish I had half a dozen Israelis on my staff. I'd be president next time around."

Yael looked at him seriously. "You'd certainly have my support." She smiled, but took her hand away from his.

Claire watched Tim light some logs in the fireplace and sat dozing in an armchair. *I guess they'll just talk,* she thought sleepily. *That's all they ever do. Carolyn has nothing to worry about.* She finally staggered off to bed, hearing their voices behind her. Claire's muscles were tight and sore from clutching the strap as they had swerved to avoid the other car. She tried not to fall asleep but the voices from the other room were growing softer as she drifted. Her body kept shaking awake, remembering the long pursuit beside the cliff. Whenever she awoke, the lights in the living room were still on and she could still hear voices. *I have to stay up,* Claire told herself. *I promised Carolyn.* Then she felt herself slip off helplessly into another nightmare

The next day Yael sat in the witness chair at the congressional hearing, without her exotic earrings, her papers neatly piled in front of her. She reviewed them in her soft, brisk British-accented voice. One by one she ran over the proofs that the Vanderzell dump had taken in toxic chemicals which were by-products of chemical devices proscribed by the Geneva convention. The Vanderzell lawyers repeated that they had delivered their refuse to the usual carting companies and been assured the refuse would be legally disposed of. No one could prove which carters had taken which refuse to which dump. Vanderzell had made sure of that.

"Then please explain why the same contaminants found in Agent Orange and the forbidden biochemical devices have been found in your plants by those of us who were able to gain access," Yael said finally, holding up a sheet of figures. "We followed the carters and know what plants they came from. And you haven't explained why the government hired Vanderzell Corporation to be the exclusive producer of these chemical weapons."

Before Yael had finished, many congressmen were on their feet, demanding to know why Vanderzell was allowed to control government policy without the knowledge of Congress.

Are they angry at the inhuman nature of the Vanderzell chemical project? Claire wondered, having learned a certain amount of cynicism from her son. *Or because their own favored corporations were shut out from such a profitable business?* As she watched, Yael and Timothy posed together for photographs, and television cameramen called out to them to stand where they were, so the microphones waving in front of them could pick up their voices.

"It's no wonder Vanderzell sent someone out to get us the other night," Tim said, as they drove back to Virginia Beach. "Yael, you were fine, really fine." He kissed her hand on the palm and wove his fingers around hers as if her hand belonged to him. Yael bent her head and said very little, but her eyes strayed to Timothy off and on through the evening, often finding his on her.

"Vanderzell came out against Israel today, you know," Tim said before they all went to bed. "It was just a matter of time and Arab pressure. Nothing to do with your testimony, trust me."

"I hope not." Yael's blond head drooped. "God knows I don't speak for anyone, anything, but the facts." She turned her face up to Timothy's as they stood in the doorway to her room, and he put his lips gently on hers.

Claire watched them anxiously, wondering what Dora and Maxi would think of this unlikely union of minds. Somehow, it did not feel to her like a union of hearts, and she worried that Tim would suffer because of this cool, remote young woman. *Please God,* she prayed. *Let Yael love Tim as much as I love Paul.* Remembering the flimsy, romantic sort of love with which she had begun her own marriage, she blushed at her judgment of Yael.

The media made much of Tim's hearing and Yael's testimony. Their pictures appeared on magazine covers and on the front pages of newspapers across the country. Editorials called for Vanderzell to be fined and for a full investigation of its chemical links to be launched. Tim had held back Yael's most damning information, the sheet of figures from the Vanderzell biochemical operation, knowing that another clash with Vanderzell would surely come, as it did, two months later. At that point, he told Claire that he would use what Yael had learned. He also told her Yael was pregnant.

"I want to marry her," Tim said, looking young and pompous and unsure of himself, all at the same time. "I don't want her to have an abortion. I'd want to marry her even if she wasn't pregnant."

Yael shook her head, tears flying, her thin hands working together. "My mother will be sick over this," she said. "An abortion is the only way. Mother thinks illegitimate pregnancy is the worst thing that can happen to a girl. I can't tell her. My mother isn't any too stable, you know."

Claire laid her hand on Yael's forehead. "Don't upset yourself, she said softly. "Your mother will welcome this grandchild, as I will. You are our family now." *She will have a fine baby in her arms soon,* Claire told herself. *Nothing makes a woman forget her worries more than a new baby. But Yael is so very odd, not like any girl I ever saw. I guess that's why Tim loves her. I must try to love her too. She's Maxi's child, after all.* But Yael seemed to want no love, not from her, not from Tim. She only sat out on the deck by herself and looked at the lake. Then she would close her eyes as if willing herself to be somewhere else. It took her two days of this solitude until she announced her decision.

Because Tim and Yael were married before Carolyn could hear about the pregnancy, the predicted hysteria was averted. Carolyn was pleased that Yael was marrying an American congressman, sure that now her daughter would forget about returning to Kiryat Anavim. Yael never talked about Israel with her mother, but tried to explain to Claire that no other place felt like home. It was necessary, Yael insisted, that Claire understand, so that later, she could make Tim understand too. *What is she getting at?* Claire wondered. *I'm afraid to know. Maybe once the baby's born, Yael will settle down and bring that alarming mental focus of hers to bear on the task of motherhood.*

Toward the end of her pregnancy, Yael stayed at Amberfields while Tim was away campaigning for his next congressional term. When she went into labor, the uncomfortable conversation about Israel continued.

In the hospital labor room, Claire tried to tell her daughter-in-law that women invariably fall in love with their first baby.

"I know it's strange to you," Yael whispered in short bursts, stopping when the pains came, "but I never think about the baby, only about home and how far away it feels. The baby doesn't seem real at all. Right now, Tim doesn't either."

Claire remembered that Paul had felt just as distant from her when Tim was being born and thought she understood. "That's only because you're in such pain," she said, sponging the sweat off Yael's face. "Later, nothing will be real except the baby. Believe me, that's how it always is."

Gripping her mother-in-law's hand, Yael propped up on one elbow. "Not for me. You have to understand," she said, panting. "I'm not like you. For me, there's only my work, and my home. Only Kiryat Anavim. Tim's a good man, and I'm fond of him. But I can't seem to feel romantic as other women do. I can't seem to love that way." She took a sudden deep breath, held her belly, and cried out, "Dan, help me!"

Claire ran to the door calling for the nurse and stayed beside Yael all the way to the delivery room, holding her hand. Yael rolled her damp head back and forth on the pillow, wisps of hair plastered darkly to her forehead. "Dan," she kept murmuring. "I need Dan."

Trying to forget that Yael had said she could not love Tim, Claire squeezed the girl's cold hand, her own body contracting each time Yael's swollen form jerked under the sheet. "Not much longer," she whispered, "have courage."

The Countess's words, Claire thought. *Now here I am saying them.* She stood outside the delivery room door, clasping her hands together. *Why doesn't this strange girl love my Tim as he should be loved? No one is more lovable than Tim.* A momentary anger flooded through her, pounding like the blood in her veins. *The girl is crazier than her mother.* Yael suddenly seemed alien to her, a wrong note on a page of music. *God, why couldn't you have given Tim a woman like Julie who would love him as I do?*

Claire realized that she was doing what she always had with Tim, assuming he belonged to her and that only she knew what was good for him. And poor, struggling Yael was only trying to live the life she had planned for herself. *At least Yael admits that she doesn't know how to love, which is more than I ever could. She is honest about wanting to be in charge of her life. That's a truth I could never admit about myself.* Claire heard Yael cry out, a loud scream, wrenched from somewhere too deep inside her to have an anatomical name. *Christ, help her, have mercy.* Claire suddenly felt that she herself was giving birth again, that she and Yael were the same person.

With Yael's next cry, she heard the baby's also, and bowed her head, her arms bending suddenly as if she already held the child. Remembering the Countess's eagerness to hold Timothy, Claire was ashamed, and then smiled. *I was angry with her for loving Paul and Tim so much, for seeing me as nothing but a hollow tube down which babies dropped, nothing in myself. All the while she knew she too was only a reed in the wind, as are we all.* Her eyes blurred with tears, and she could not see who it was that jogged her elbow.

"I was caught in rush hour traffic," Paul said, trying to catch his breath after running. "Just got here. Was that the baby's voice?"

Claire looked at him blankly. *I forgot again,* she said to herself. *Once I'd phoned him about Yael's labor starting, I forgot. Poor Paul.* Here he was, a quarter of this new child's protoplasm, and he had been forgotten. Claire touched his lined, pale, freckled face, running her finger down the deep seam beside his mouth.

"I think we have another grandchild," she said.

Dr. Fairfax came to the door, a white-swaddled form in his arms. "Have a look," he said from behind his green protective mask. "A boy. Eight-six. Quite a big fellow for a seven-monther, eh Paul?" He nudged Paul with his shoulder and winked.

"Let me have him." Paul's arms were around the baby, before Claire could reach out, and his face lay against the small, red damp cheek. "How beautiful," he said, rocking the child against him."How beautiful. Has anyone told Yael how beautiful he is?"

Claire couldn't answer, for she was watching Paul's face, so close to the baby's that they seemed one flesh. *This is a father,* she said to herself, staggered into silence. *This is how a father loves. I had no idea.* All the fathers, her own and even God, suddenly came into focus for her, and she was ashamed because she had not believed they could love as she did.

"He's sure crazy about the little son of a gun," Dr. Fairfax chuckled, rubbing his chin, perhaps thinking about his own four grandsons.

"Yes." Claire said, her arm reaching around Paul's shoulders. "He surely does love. How is Yael? Can we see her?"

Dr. Fairfax looked uncertain. "She's pretty much out of it," he said. "I don't know why. Hardly any anesthesia, after all. For a first birth, this one was a piece of cake." He scratched the white stubble on his chin, apparently mystified as to why Yael wasn't sitting up in bed, demanding dinner and her baby.

Claire and Paul sat beside Yael for a long while, not knowing if she were asleep. Claire was holding the baby, because Dr. Fairfax said Yael should see him as soon as she opened her eyes. After half an hour, Yael's lips began to move, and she called Dan's name again.

"We're here. So is your baby," Claire said, leaning over her daughter-in-law.

Yael's eyes opened and she took the child, resting him uneasily on her chest. "Should I nurse him now? No, I guess it's too soon." Sighing she gestured at the bundle on her body. "Here, you take him, Claire. He weighs too much for me."

Her heart as heavy as Yael felt the child to be, Claire took the baby up. "What's his name? He should be baptized with a name."

Yael's body pulled together stiffly and she clutched her arms over her heart. "He must be circumcised by a rabbi," she said. "My parents are away. Will you see to it?"

For a moment Claire had a flash of memory and saw little Dora's face long ago in Rheims, asking where she could find a rabbi who would give her Hebrew lessons. She imagined Dora as Dora was now, her square, stern face set on what was right, and felt her to be as close as breathed air. *If God ever sent anyone to me to show me who he is, he sent me Dora, not because Dora is so holy but because she is so human.* It came to her suddenly that being holy and being truly human were the same, but she could not stop to savor the sameness because Yael was waiting for an answer, her breath hardly lifting her chest.

"We'll find a rabbi," Claire said. "He'll tell us what to do for the baby."

"My son's name is David," Yael said slowly and clearly. "Nobody needs to baptize him. His mother has given him his name." She turned her head on the pillow and closed her eyes, hands folded against her flat body.

The next day Tim arrived, back from the finale of his senatorial campaign, which he had won in a close race. He found David and Yael at Amberfields, where Yael was asleep in an upstairs room. His parents greeted him at the door, the baby in Paul's arms.

"Is the baby nursing yet?" Tim said, reaching out to take his son from Claire's arms. "Where's Yael?"

"Asleep," Claire said. "She does nothing but sleep. Dr. Fairfax says Yael has no milk. That happens sometimes. We've put David on Similac and he's fine. Gained three ounces just today."

"I guess Yael shouldn't be waked," Tim said, his face buried against the warm damp place between the baby's neck and shoulder. "I wanted to tell her that I won the election."

"And what does it mean to you to be a congressman?" Paul asked. "Here, sit down in my chair. It's the best place for holding David, I've found."

Tim sat in his father's chair and laid the baby down on his lap. He leaned over him, studying the slightly slanted smoky blue eyes, the pumping arms. "Only that now I can deal with Vanderzell from a position of strength," he said. "Only that there might finally be disarmament, so this little David can grow up in peace."

He looked at his parents and laid his hand over the child's stomach. "He's not going off to fight some old fart's war," Tim said. "I won't let that happen. No more wars started by old farts. That's one slogan of my independent party."

"Independent party?" Paul took Claire's hand, clearly expecting one of Tim's political tirades.

"We need to break with the old parties, before they get us blown up," Tim said, checking the baby's diaper to see if it needed changing. "Our base is just ordinary people, no special interests. I believe in quaint notions like peace and justice. Like a fair deal for the poor. Josh, my bodyguard, calls it the Jesus platform. I hope he's right."

It had been Josh who had resurrected her son from jail and from the pit of adolescent rage he had fallen into so long ago. *A soul guard,* Claire thought with a smile. *That's what Josh is to my son.*

Tim gently massaged David's bare stomach, and then bent over to kiss the soft flesh. "You're going to be raised to save life, not take it. As I was." He looked at Paul and held out one hand. "As I was, by you."

Paul took Tim's hand and held it, reaching out with his other hand to take Claire's. "Thank you for remembering," he said.

Little David's *bris* ceremony had to be held off for a week until Maxi and Carolyn returned from Israel. Yael insisted that Maxi be the one to hold the baby for the rabbi. The baby's cries of pain made Maxi turn pale, and his wife had to take his place so he could sit down. Carolyn was so excited she could hardly stop talking when the rabbi finished his work.

"Think of all we can do together," Carolyn bubbled, hugging the baby. "I'll take him to art museums when he's older, and Maxi will take him to the Natural History Museum, won't you, Maxi? David will have four grandparents to love him while you and Tim work, Yael. Won't that be splendid? What a family we'll be."

She didn't notice the look on Yael's face, but Claire did, and felt cold inside. Maxi and Carolyn left for New York after a celebratory dinner. They would have taken Yael and David with them, but over Carolyn's objections, Maxi insisted that their daughter needed more time to rest at Amberfields with the baby and Tim.

When they had gone Tim sat his family down over coffee and told them what he and Yael had done to the biggest corporation in America.

"I had an interview with Vanderzell yesterday," Tim said, holding little David on his thighs. The baby tried to pull his head up, all red-faced and grunting while his father held his hands. "It was quite a scene. I could tell the guy would have liked to kill me."

He shifted David into the plastic rocker seat on the coffee table. "How'd you like to be the son of the man who ruined Vanderzell?" He asked David seriously. "I told the old thief we had photocopies of all our information on the history of his connection with the oil and chemical cartels. They've been the running the world for too long."

"Does the U.S. government know Vanderzell and Hitler were friends?" Yael closed her notebook and set it on the table beside the baby's rocker. "Does the American congress know that Farben's cronies contributed to presidential election campaigns?"

"When I tell them, they don't hear me." Tim said, letting his hands fall in his lap. "It'll take time. Even Vanderzell hardly heard me, and we were practically cheek to cheek. He actually offered me a job and thought I'd give up the Senate for his paycheck."

Claire put her knitting aside and kept her eyes on Tim. "You didn't, of course?"

"No. Wasn't even tempted." Tim jiggled the baby's rocker until David stopped fussing. "He acted like a sick man, and I have to say, I hope he gets a lot sicker. We sat together looking out over New York City for a long time, and he kept choking on his cigar. God forgive me, I wished him dead. I couldn't help thinking this guy should be put down like a hydrophobic dog."

"Did he listen to anything you said?" Paul asked. "Did you explain the new disarmament plan? He must know the plan is all that can save us from another holocaust."

"I told him the disarmament plan would end the Cold War. The Russians will throw away the weapons they want least, and we'll do the same. One for one. At worst, there'll be a freeze. At best, down the line a few years, the atomic weapon stockpiles will start melting and Vanderzell's corporations might start making windmills and solar cells. He didn't like the idea, since his heart pumps oil instead of blood."

"Let's hope someone better takes over when he dies," Claire said.

"He can't fight the historical process. Or nature." Paul reached out to run a hand over the baby's soft, silky head. "I heard he has cancer of the throat. And the Russians have agreed just today to the One-for-One plan. You've done good work, Tim. Yael."

"It's just beginning." Tim looked up at his wife, who stood beside him. "Yael, will you be part of what I'm trying to do?"

"You can do it fine without me," Yael said, looking down at her child and studying him coolly, as if she had never seen him before. Claire's heart contracted as it had when the girl had said she didn't know if she could love her baby.

"David belongs here," Yael said finally. "With all of you. With my parents. I couldn't give him the kind of life he would have here." She reached down and awkwardly touched the baby's cheek. "We kibbutzniks aren't raised to have the old family loyalties," Yael said, putting her hand on Tim's shoulder, then letting it drop to her side. "Not like you and your family, Tim. The only family I have is the people I was raised with. It's taken me a while to get that, but now I do."

"Are you in love with Dan?" Claire took her son's hand.

"Dan and my other age-mates, yes." Yael stepped away from Tim and the baby. ""It's the sort of love I can't explain, except to say it's like being one person with the others. You forget yourself."

The baby fretted and held out his fat arms to Claire. She picked him up and held him. *It's like holding Tim so long ago,* she said to herself, *except that I'm wiser now and won't try to take him over. He will be whoever he wants to be. God's, I hope.*

"He's never smiled," Yael said sadly. "Did you know that? And it's time for smiles, I think." She turned to Claire. "You'll do well with him. So will my mother. This way she may not have me, but she'll have her grandson."

Tim had no words, for once, and stared at her as if trying to memorize her face.

"I'm glad, Tim, that I could help put you where you are and to win what you've won." She started walking to the stairs, then continued, not looking back at them. "I did it not just for you, but for my grandparents and all the ones who died with them. My things are packed, Tim. Will you bring my luggage down? And I'll need a ride to the airport. I would have asked my parents, but I couldn't face my mother just now. I'll call them when I get back to Israel."

David held tightly in her arms, Claire watched out the window as her son and his wife went out to Tim's car, its bumpers covered with campaign stickers. Her eyes blurred as she tried to read them. Paul came close and put one arm around her, one hand under the baby's head.

"Carolyn and Maxi will help us," he said. "This baby will have all of us to mother him."

"Do I have the strength for it, Paul?" Claire felt tired deep into her bones. "Do I have enough left to give David what he needs? I may be all used up. After all, there's been no music for a long time."

"There'll be music again." Paul took the baby from her and led her into his study. "I want you to see how much music you've given me. Are giving. Come."

Claire stood in front of the easel under the window and saw the shine of the setting sun on the huge, luminous canvas that seemed to burn from inside by its own light. *If stars of different magnitudes filled the sky so full there was no darkness left between them, the heavens would look like this,* Claire thought. *No room for anything but light*. Toward the center of the painting, the dabs of brightness turned violet-white, and almost hurt Claire's eyes. "What is it?" she whispered. "What's this wonderful thing called?"

"Marcus named it 'Jerusalem Night.'" Paul said, holding the baby up so he could see too. "That feels right. But when I painted it, your Easter Sanctus was in my ears. For a little while, as I worked, I saw Christ rising like the sun."

Claire reached out and touched the canvas with one finger, ready to be cooled or burned, she was not sure which. The baby extended an open hand toward the painting and a smile spread across his face.

"I see him too," Claire said as they both leaned over the baby like trees bent by the same wind.

18

Dora's Journal

Israel..............................1983

It had been so long since I had seen Benjamin that I'd begun to wonder if he too had fled to America. I understood how mothers feel when their sons are missing in action, too much sorrow to hope and too much hope to mourn. I was like that while Benjamin was introducing Julie to life in the Jerusalem community, and Julie was gathering Arab children from the streets, teaching them how to keep clean and not to steal. It was as if the two of them had forgotten they had any family, or as if they thought their family was the whole world. That's how taken up they were.

"The Israeli government's afraid to step in and help these children," Benjamin explained in one of his short phone calls. "The Arabs don't like interference with their own. Remember what happened when the Jewish authorities tried to force Arab children to go to school? The parents wanted their children free to roam the streets so they could bring home money from begging and stealing"

"I remember. The Arab protests nearly shut down the city."

"Although he can't say so openly, the Prime Minister approves of what Julie is doing. I hope you do too."

"What I think doesn't matter. Are you happy, Benjamin? Is this community of outcasts your family now?"

"No outcasts here at Sinai House," Benjamin laughed. "Father Jonas says we're being gathered up into one fold with one shepherd. Rabbi Noah thinks so too."

His words were Noah's own. One world united into one family is Noah's dream, and now it seems to be Benjamin's too. For me, on the other hand, my own family is enough. Noah has said that this possessiveness of mine, this "poverty of vision" as he calls it, is the reason I suffer. Until I give it up, God cannot work freely in my life.

My plan is to ask forgiveness for this sin later, when everything is being taken away anyhow, along with my life. Until then, I hope that the world as it is will continue. It's good that my son has no trace of this selfishness, but I fear he will waste his life taking care of people who would as soon kill him as not. Because of Joel's murder, my feelings toward the Arabs are anything but charitable, Noah says. He tells me I must forgive if I expect to be forgiven. I'm afraid that such forgiveness isn't in me. So, over the phone that day, I was rather harsh with my son about his generosity to our enemies.

"Benjamin, I want to know what you think you're doing with this community of yours," I said crossly, forgetting that my grown son was no longer mine to command. "I hope you're still earning some kind of living."

"My government job pays for the community and its work," Benjamin said. "Between that and tending the children who come to us, I'm too busy to think about anything else." Benjamin seemed to be smiling around his words, and I could imagine him bending over the Arab children as he did over Annie, his face full of love.

"Mothering takes all my time, and it was from you I learned it. Have to go now. Julie's calling me." He rang off and was suddenly, totally, gone. I hate that about telephones. They don't give you a chance to touch the person you're talking to or to say good-by. The connection is somehow bogus, not to be trusted.

My hand was hardly off the phone when it rang again. This time it was a nurse from Hadassah Hospital, telling me Father Jonas had suffered a coronary embolism and was asking for me. My own heart pounding and hurting, I went directly to him.

Father Jonas was wrapped in a white blanket, lying in the light of an open window when I came into his hospital room. He looked, as I told him, like a swaddled, newborn baby. He had told the medical staff to take away the oxygen tent he had had around him, so we could talk together with nothing to separate us.

"Though I don't have anything to say, really, Dora. Just that I hope you will come to understand how much Benjamin loves you." Father Jonas moved slightly, and a shadow passed over his face. "And how much I do. Just now, I need your closeness."

"You have it, Father," I said, laying my hands on his forehead, then his cheeks. "And all my love."

He smiled, turning his head so his lips touched my fingers. "That's what I tell God," he said, "when I tell him anything. You and I are not separate, Dora. God sent you to teach me how to love. Dear little girl." He lifted his hand as if to bless me, but it fell back on the sheet, the palm open and empty.

"Father, you can't die yet," I cried out, suddenly aware how barren this loss would leave me. "Stay, stay, I need you to love me. Who will love me when you're gone?" Rocking to and fro like the praying men at the Orthodox synagogue, I was sure he was my last person. The very last one who would love me. My well would be dry, and unlike Kiryat Anavim, no new source of life could be found.

"Dora, Dora." Father Jonas's breath made a little puff, just enough to stir the hair at my temples when I leaned over him. "God loves you as you need to be loved. No one else can." With an effort he breathed on my cheek. "There. What God has given me, I give to you." His voice was suddenly full and strong. "The Lord bless you and keep you and give you peace, Dora, child of God."

My eyes were closed during this blessing, so I didn't see when he died. But after I looked at him, it seemed as if his whole body had dissolved like fog in sunlight at the foot of the desert hills, and I felt no end of his love.

I needed to mourn, and what better place for that was there than Yad Vashem, the plain white memorial in the hills of Jerusalem, built to honor all the lost ones of the Shoah, the Holocaust. I had never spent time there, not wanting to find my mother's name on the walls inscribed with the names of the dead. Before he died, my father sang songs, left a name. But my mother was just gone. If I didn't see her name, somehow she would seem to me to be still alive. Now that Father Jonas was one of my many lost ones, I wanted to say his name aloud in that sacred place, along with hers. Around the building were gardens, full of spring life, protesting memorials. Inside was a long dim hall with a railing. The walls held plaques full of interminable lists of names. A few lamps sat flickering on the stone floor.

I stood in front of a lamp that had almost gone out, remembering my lost Father Jonas, my own father who had sung songs and pushed me on a swing, and the mother who had given me up in order to save my life. Then I thought of Maxi. And Joel, And faraway Yael. And Benjamin, who was now Julie's. "Where is there an end to losing?" I hissed the words between my teeth."I think that now I have nothing left to lose."

Next to me a breath was deeply drawn, like Father Jonas's as he had lain dying in my arms. An old woman with a black shawl over her head, her face lined like ploughed dirt, rocked beside me, her rutted cheeks dry, as if there were no tears left in her.

"What has she seen?" I wondered, imagining that she might be my own mother, unrecognized, grown old. For some time, we bowed our heads, sighing as if we were on our last breath. Then I reached over to her and held her as if she were all anyone had, the last mother in the world.

"Maybe this woman is my mother," I said to myself. "Maybe she escaped from Bergen-Belsen and came to Israel. Well, she's somebody's mother. Let's say she is mine. Why not?"

The woman leaned her head over my shoulder, patted my cheek, and went away, not saying anything. I was glad that she who was everyone's mother had consented for a moment to be mine.

Benjamin and Julie stood beside me during Father Jonas's funeral, which was conducted in the messianic Jewish way by my Noah. He made little of death, saying it had no sting and no victory, because Father Jonas, my tired old friend, was not just himself anymore, but Yeshua's own. At least that's what I made of Noah's words. To me, death was death. In my experience, death always won in the end, leaving me by myself, still alive, but barely.

After the burial at Kiryat Anavim, Benjamin took me by the hand and led me away to some rocks that rimmed the cemetery, marking it off from the road.

"To me, he doesn't seem gone," Benjamin said. "But how is it for you, Mother?"

"He's gone, all right." I tried to keep my voice low, and held his hand tightly, willing him not to let go. "For me, it's terrible, if you want to know. All the father I had is gone."

Benjamin rubbed his square, dark-shadowed chin with one hand looking as if he were testing to see if he needed a shave. "Loss is terrible, yes," he said finally. "That's one side of it. The other side is that you're not alone. Let me tell you how I feel about it."

I nodded, knowing he would tell me mysteries I could not understand, but wanting to hear them because they were my son's truths.

"You aren't alone, Mother. You're the whole universe, in one package of temporary skin and bone. You're Father Jonas, and me, and my grandparents. In the womb of God, we are all one, never separate. We are ourselves, but we are everyone else too. It's a paradox. A mystery."

I tried to remember what it was Benjamin had once said about each person being more than just himself alone. "When I scattered seed in my spring garden, I was thinking that something of me was buried with my seeds and would take root, grow, live. Is that what you mean?"

Benjamin took my hands and danced me around in a hora, our feet making a scuff of dust in the earth. "'My' has no meaning when you stand at the center of the great spreading sphere that is our universe. Father Jonas, you, me—we're altogether in God. What is it Father Jonas said? One vine, many branches."

"In heaven, yes, but we are here on earth. In this place, trying to survive as a nation, as a people. Are you not a Jew anymore, Benjamin? That would break my heart."

Benjamin held his arms wide, as if to take the measure of all he included in himself. "I'm still a Jew, Mother. I always will be. If I have children, they will be Jews also, and while they are in my house, they will keep Shabbat and learn Torah. Julie wants that as I do. One side of the human coin is the body and place we were born into, and we must not forget it. The other side…"

He folded his hands and pressed the palms together. "The other side is what we see when time and space drop away and we simply *are*, with no conditions, no laws, no names, just naked before God like Yeshua on his cross." He looked at both his hands as if he had never seen them before. "What coin has only one side? he asked. "What man is only himself."

"Are you telling me you're going to marry Julie?" I cried, moving one step closer to him, getting down to cases, away from all this talk of mystery and spheres. "How can you remain a Ben-Ari if you marry a gentile? How can you possibly still be Jewish? The mother of your children must be a Jew if your children are to be Jews. You know that."

His hands cupped around my shoulders, Benjamin looked so intently into my eyes that I had to close them. "Because of you, I know who I am," he said. "A Jew, a Ben-Ari, your son. You've made me, brought me into life, given me a name and a faith. Nothing will ever take away from me what I am, what is your part in me. Understand, Mother, how much yours I am."

"I don't understand anything." My body seemed to be melting in the hot sun that had risen over the hills to the east. "You're gone, like everyone else. You're Julie's now, not mine."

Benjamin took me in his arms, as I'd held him long ago in the vegetable garden. "Little mother," he said. "Listen to me. Rabbi Noah is going to marry us, Julie and me, in the name of Yeshua. Julie wants to convert to Judaism. Messianic Judaism, of course, because she would never give up Jesus. You have nothing to worry about. We and any children we may have will be Jews and will belong to Yeshua. Ask Rabbi Noah. He will tell you that Julie and I are going to be part of his congregation. Of yours."

How simply Yeshua had taken care of the matter, I thought, as the air rushed out of my body in one giant sigh of relief. All my rages and demands had accomplished nothing. Maybe I was losing Benjamin to Julie, but I was getting him back in Yeshua. Wordlessly, I embraced my son, and when Julie came to join us, I gathered her into our family, our sphere, of which, as

Benjamin says, God is both circumference and center. When they left me to go back to the kibbutz dining hall, I did not feel abandoned, as I usually did at seeing them go off together.

The Lord, gives, the Lord takes away, I whispered, repeating the words Father Jonas had so often said. *Blessed be the name of the Lord*. My cup was running over, and I finally dared to open my heart so blessings could pour into its dry places. *Surely goodness and mercy will follow me all the days of my life, and I will dwell in the house of the Lord forever.* The words of David the Psalmist came to me, for I did not any longer need words that were merely my own. I was grateful, and I went on my way rejoicing, praising Ha-Shem, thanking Yeshua for watering that poor, parched seed, my soul, until it came to life. I sang as I walked around Kiryat Anavim, wanting Father Jonas to hear, to know that all was well with me.

Dan met me on the bridge over the gorge. He was holding a paper in his hand and leaping and capering about as if he had just learned to walk on air.

"Yael's coming home," he cried. "And she wants us to send a Ben-Ari bear for her baby." He stopped jumping around and looked at me in confusion. "I don't understand. If she's coming back, why can't she give it to the baby when she gets here?"

I touched Dan's cheek, remembering how Maxi felt under my fingers when he said he would come back. Poor Dan, I thought. He's seizing at straws as I always did. "Well, maybe for a little while she'll come back. But Dan, she's married now, with a child. Don't get your hopes up."

Seeing how downcast he was at my words, I tried to make him feel better. "She'll always love you, Dan. In a way, she'll always be here with us. It's where we know she wants to be."

Benjamin's way of thinking seemed to have become mine, I reflected, as I walked across the bridge and looked down the long steep slopes to what was deeper than I could see.

No separation, just the mystery of being ourselves and not just ourselves. I leaned over the railing and looked below at the olive trees that waved new young branches in the wind, affirming that they were there, nameless and reborn. That's what Benjamin meant, I think. It was a matter of being there, saluting with all the branches you had, with no notions about which way the wind should blow them.

It was time to separate the Ben-Ari bears, I said to myself. One would belong to little David in America, and the other would belong to the children of Benjamin and Julie. For the first time, I allowed the thought of their children to give me pleasure.

"Where have you been all this time, Dora?" Sol's voice interrupted me. "You're hard to find."

"Well, it seems you've tracked me down," I said, looking at the rocks at the bottom of the gorge, then at Sol's stained feet, clasped in sandals. "Here I am."

"You're alone so much, Dora," he said, his voice anxious, as if he were the one who was alone. "I've wanted to tell you that you needn't be alone anymore. You could be my wife."

Sol's face was sad and old-looking. His hands were on my face, smoothing my lines away. The hands felt like my own, and for a moment I saw what Benjamin meant, that the skin between our bodies is only a thin veil that a breath could blow away. In his hands, I felt Benjamin, Claire, Father Jonas, Noah, and all my large family swelling within me as if I were a seed heavy with new life. To let them live in the will of God, not mine, I would have to drop by myself into the earth and die. I took Sol's hands in mine, laid them on his heart, and shook my head. My life belonged to Yeshua and Noah. I could say yes to no one else.

"I'll wait," he said after a while, putting his hands behind his back as Lev used to do. "I don't mind waiting."

There was no one to wait for, I felt like telling him. I have died to what I was and what I used to need. I was with the seedlings in the ground, busy with the rituals of grave, resurrection, and the shedding of old skin.

Sol walked away, the sunlight enveloping his body as he walked away and finally blotting him entirely out. He would have been a sort of answer, I said to myself, digging my toes into the damp earth. He would at least have been mine. But Noah was the only husband I wanted, and he wouldn't be my husband unless I left Kiryat Anavim for Jerusalem. So it was good-by to him, too. Noah's face receded in my imagination, as I reminded myself that he was now one more of the many I had loved who had gone away.

In my mind, all the lost faces shifted in front of my eyes. For a moment I could not think where I left off and the others began, so much one body we were. Well, let it go, I thought. Let it fall to the ground. Being buried like a seed is all right, after all. It's being born again into another life. I felt my body relax and the perpetual frown between my brows smooth out. I walked to the vegetable garden and looked at the tomato plants coming up reliably as ever after all these years growing in the same familiar soil.

My feet barely touched the red earth as I danced like a spirit over its own grave. "Come, Breath of life," I said to myself. "Come Holy Spirit. What's happening is not so bad. There's no loss." When I looked out over the garden and beyond it to the soil of Kiryat Anavim, it was as if I saw my own skin, saw the spread of it as far as the eye could reach, felt my bones stretch on the rack of the land and painlessly break, resolving themselves into dust, and at last, into new, green shoots. I lay down on the ground, my arms out, listening for Yeshua's voice, for I had no one left but him who contained the earth and all that was in it, including me. "Yes" would be my new favorite word. It tasted good on my tongue. Instead of Yeshua's voice, I heard someone else's.

"I've come back." The words soared over the field, along with the rainstorm just blowing up from the west, carrying clouds and longed-for water. "I'm home for good."

My hands dug into the ground and came up full of earth. Someone was home to be welcomed, but for the life of me, I couldn't think who it was. Something was being given back, just when I needed nothing at all and was asking for nothing.

Yael was coming home, and another person was with her, a tall figure in a black coat who ran ahead, just as the first rain drops fell. Noah was here, materializing out of my dreams.

"Dora," he said, taking my hand. "Everybody seems to be coming to you at once."

So it was. Yael's blond hair flew in the strong, rain-filled breeze. "I'm actually here," she cried. Can you believe?" Dan was right behind her, close as always.

I held out one hand, open and empty, for I had let go of the dirt I had held and dropped it without caring where. "So you are, my dear." The words came out cool and still, like the last sigh before sleep, carrying nothing of the day's heat. I lifted my face to the sky, feeling as light as air. "What a wind there is," I said to her. "We need the rain it brings, just the way we need you."

Noah gripped my hand, reminding me that he was there. What he wanted, I could not be sure, but like Yeshua, he was part of me, as present and needed as air. I turned to face him, seeing him in a new light. Not as rabbi, friend, or husband. He was simply my beloved, who had shown me in himself who Yeshua was and what it felt like to drink living water.

Standing close to me, he whispered in my ear. "I see now how we can marry, dear one," he said. "It only just came to me. Half the year, the winter half, we can live in Jerusalem, at Beth Shalom, and the rest of the year, the growing season, here at Kiryat Anavim. Jerusalem is close enough for me to get into the city for services. Why could I not have thought of this before?"

"Waiting is not always the worst idea," I said. "God's time is not ours, I'm learning."

"What do you think about this idea of mine, Dora? Come, say nothing but yes." Noah let go of my hand, as if to let me know he was reluctant to leave me with a choice, but must do it anyway.

"Yes, darling Noah," I said, using my new word. My arms were around him as I spoke. The wind was blowing rain straight into my face, but I hardly noticed. "Yes," I said. "Yes to everything."

Epilogue
by Julie de Montfort Harkavy

Israel...............................2013

Thirty years have passed since my mother-in-law married Rabbi Noah Halpern. At that point, she stopped writing in her journal, since, as she put it, nothing of general interest happened to her after the day she and Noah came together. I think what she meant was that she was too happy to bother with writing anymore. On the day our oldest son, Lev, was married, just last year, Dora gave her journal to Benjamin and me, saying she had gathered up the past for her descendants, and here it was.

Dora has lately been in the mood to give everything away, even Father Jonas's old menorah and the last Ben-Ari bear, ragged and eyeless. The bear was the friend of our four children, now grown up. One son, Avi, is in the army, and the other, Lev, is in medical school. Our twin daughters, Mimi and Rachel, are both studying neurobiology in New York, at the university where Maxi teaches when he isn't visiting us in Israel.

My daughter Annie became a nurse and a sister. Her religious order works among the women of the Palestinian poor and their children. She lives at the community house Benjamin created in the Arab Quarter. If Annie remembers the violence of her childhood, she never speaks of it. But the lifework she has chosen tells me she has transmuted her fear and pain into acts of love, and I no longer grieve for her suffering or my part in it.

Because Maxi and Carolyn fear another war is imminent in the Middle East, they urge us to come live with them in America. But our place is here. We spend much of our time at a kibbutz called Givat Haviva, where Jews, Christians, and Muslims work and learn together. Once you have prayed, cooked, and gardened with people of a different faith, it is impossible to hate or fear them. We call it an "experiment in peace," and hope it will grow beyond our small group to include everyone in this Holy Land.

Yael and Dan have three grown sons, all of them living at Kiryat Anavim with their parents. Though they come to Jerusalem to celebrate the High Holidays with us at Beth Shalom, their religion is the land. Dora understands them better than I can, for the land is part of her religion too.

My parents come to see us for a few months out of every year, along with Senator Tim and his son David, who has become a minister. Yael finds her first son's passion for Christ very odd, but attributes it to some whimsical twist of the double helix that runs in both our families. The "faith gene" she calls it in her clinical way, though sometimes she wishes she had it too. I think this passion we have is part of that current carrying all humanity God-ward. The old atheism that used to make men so proud and independent is crumbling, and in its place a faith is rising that will in time unite the world in love and service. At least Benjamin says so, and he's just about always right.

At this time, all of Israel holds its collective breath because of a threatened nuclear bomb from Iran. Dora warns darkly that another Holocaust may be at hand, but she goes right on doing Davidic dances with her beloved Noah, and raises her tomatoes as she always has. On some level, tragedy cannot touch Dora, I think, because she knows death is not the enemy. She has seen enough of death to know. Benjamin and Rabbi Noah remind me that the body will die from one thing or another, but the soul lives and moves and has its being in God. Every death is a sort of Apocalypse, an End of Days, and every touch of the Holy Spirit is a Second Coming of Christ. One soul at a time, the kingdom of God is being born.

We hear from various traditions that the world is coming to an end. Benjamin and I believe that is true. The world as we have known it, stuck in its ancient consciousness— 'me against you,' 'my nation against your nation,' —is ending. A single hydrogen bomb dropped on Israel or anywhere else can destroy civilization on our little planet. Nuclear winter would mean the end of us all. From a world of divided, selfish, crazy individuals waving flags for their particular religious points of view, their corporate profits, their strutting little nations, we must unite as citizens of earth, our God-given mother planet. We must care for those who suffer from war, famine, and pestilence as if they are our own family, for they are. We must change our hearts so that such care is possible.

Benjamin reminds me that we in the twenty-first century are privileged to know that the earth, the solar system, our local galaxy, are like a pinpoint compared to the inconceivable number of swirling, web-like galaxies that exist in our universe. That universe itself may be only one, Benjamin tells me, of a number of universes. Each is surrounded by spiritual dimensions, shining with a light to which the sun is shade. We are not merely physical beings, nor is our universe only a physical thing. It swims in light and energy out of which our sun, planet, and bodies are material precipitates. For too long we have mistaken them for the only reality there is. *Selah*, as Benjamin loves to say. Pay attention to what is, all of what is, not just to what our senses tell us.

My daughters tell me that the DNA in our bodies is almost the same as that of all animals, and not much different from that of plants. For me, this means that all creation is a family, to be cherished as God's own. Our bodies, say Rachel and Mimi, are composed of elements exactly in proportion to the elements of the universe itself. We are made of star-stuff, but we are more than that. We are the growing consciousness of the universe itself, of all the universes there may be, reaching toward the Being who brought us into being, who blows life and light through us. Jesus taught us that the Kingdom of God is within us and that we are temples of the Holy Spirit. Can we accept that we are embodiments of divinity as he knew we were? That he knew he was?

The Second Coming of Christ, Benjamin and I believe, is the Holy Spirit's transformation of each human soul into pure Love. The energy of God spreads like a light-storm into the consciousness of humanity. Benjamin and I, we choose to join what is infinite, what is true, what is love. We are ready to make light of the world, and of ourselves, and to shift into the Being of God when our time comes for eternal flowering. We are ready. It is time. God is making all things new.

And so we are at peace, Benjamin and I, even while hearing rumors of wars. God's will be done on earth as in heaven, we repeat aloud during our evening prayers on the roof of our house in old Jerusalem. The setting sun turns the stones of the Kotel, the Cross of the Holy Sepulchre, and the Dome of the Rock into one seamless garment of shimmering gold worn by the Holy City like a wedding robe. For a little while, we exist outside time, in motherly arms that contain the sun and other stars. "*Maranatha*" we say instead of Amen. "Come Lord" even as we know that he is already here.

The End

CPSIA information can be obtained at www.ICGtesting.com
Printed in the USA
LVOW131937200213

321039LV00001B/27/P